Copyright (c) 2012. Mike Effa.
Published by Phantom House Books, Nigeria
House L, National Assembly Estate,
Dape District, Life Camp, Abuja Nigeria 999999
in conjunction with Amazon Createspace PoD,
7290 B. Investment Drive, Charleston, SC 29418, Copyright ©
2000 - 2011, CreateSpace, a DBA of On-Demand Publishing
ISBN-10: 978-51078-9-2
ISBN-13: 978-978-51078-9-0
www.phantomhouseafrica.co.nr
[international dialing code:] 23481 3954 0895

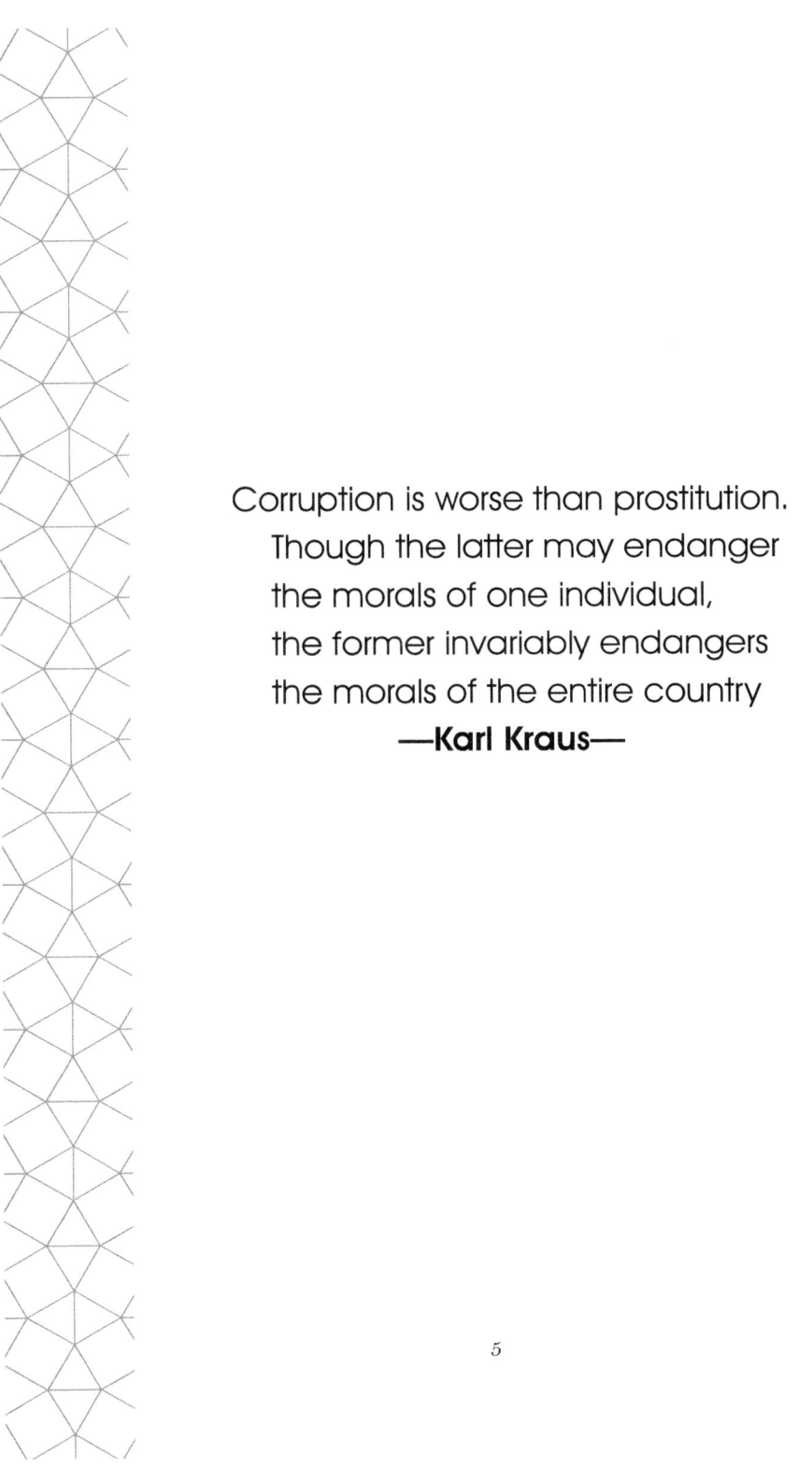

Corruption is worse than prostitution.
Though the latter may endanger
the morals of one individual,
the former invariably endangers
the morals of the entire country
—**Karl Kraus**—

The

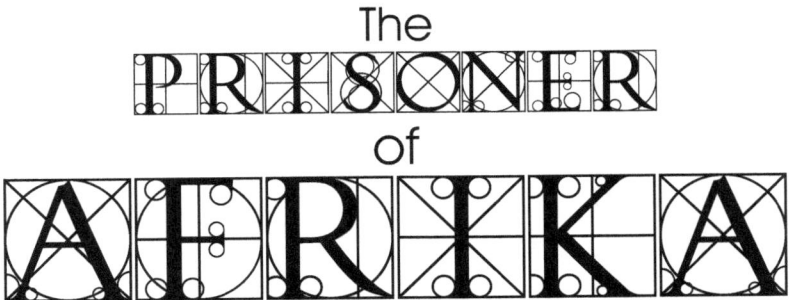

Political Fiction By Mike Effa

To God Almighty for a dream fulfilled.

To all Nigerians who have been at the receiving end of corrupt governments who have remained insensitive to the cry of the masses.

To all my colleagues in the agency who have been impoverished, robbed and deprived of their very source of livelihood by different and greedy chief executives and their management teams.

Do not lose hope, for the wicked will not go unpunished.

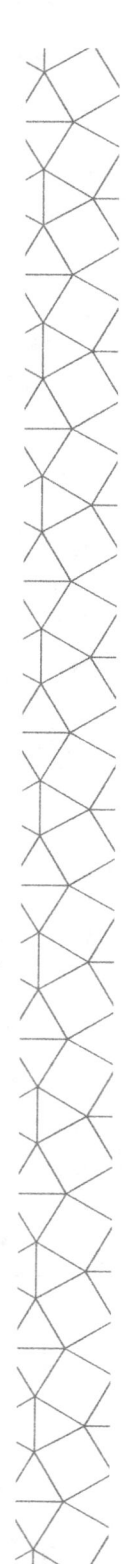

10

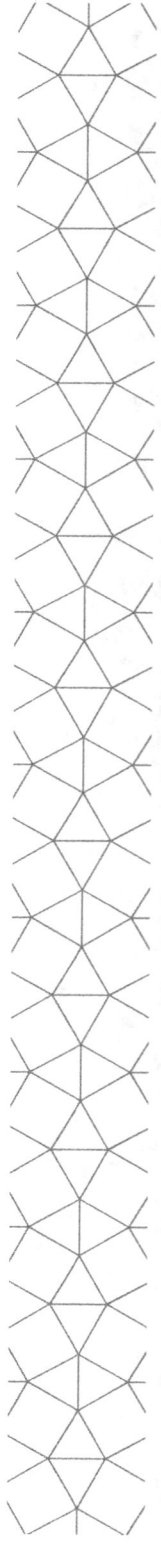

Chapter One

The wind of change had been blowing across the continent since the end of the Second World War. Many nationalist and political activist had been sent on exile. Many had lost their lives all in the quest for self rule and to put an end to almost fifty years of exploitation, rape, and discrimination.

Afrika being a heterogeneous nation, the colonialists in agreement with the nationalist had modelled a confederal system of government. With the conclusion of the First general election before independence, the Afrika Nationalist Party had won an absolute majority and was going to form the first government after independence. At the regional levels they were premiers who were more like governors. The constitution also allowed for the existence of office of a president. But the post was mostly ceremonial as the real power resided with the Prime Minister. This was the political setting agreed upon and entrenched in the constitution, when independence was finally granted on that twenty-ninth day of November.

Mike Effa

This particular day was going to remain indelible in the minds of Afrikans. Proud and gaily dressed Afrikans had begun arriving at the parade ground as early as seven O'clock in the morning. The parade ground was filling up gradually; it was going to be a great day. The previous day, the Prime Minister's lodge had been a beehive of activities as eminent personalities had been treated to a cocktail party. Today was going to be a confirmation of it all. It all started with the lowering of the Union Jack, with this completed, the green, white, red flag of the newly independent nation was gradually hoisted to replace the Union Jack. Many Afrikans could not contain their emotions and tears of joy flowed freely as the flag was finally hoisted and the new anthem played. Afrikans gave a big shout of joy and waved their flags happily, in celebration of their independence and the exit of the colonialists.

The whole parade ground went wild with the shouts of joy as the new Prime Minister mounted the dais to be sworn-in. The Prime Minister of the newly independent nation of Afrika beamed a long distance smile at the crowd and waved his flag out of excitement. "Congratulations", the outgoing governor-general said. "Thank you", the prime minister replied as he mounted the Podium to shake hands with the Queen of England. Then the British Monarch made the final declaration, "with these documents I finally hand over the control of this geographical entity called Afrika to you. The destiny of the people of this nation is in the hands of your government. Afrika henceforth ceases to be a British Administered territory. "Congratulations on your election".

"Thank you your majesty". The prime minister replied and proceeded to read his first independence speech.

The ceremony continued with schoolchildren, the armed forces, marching past the dais with the Prime Minister taking the salute. Guests were treated to traditional dances, which displayed the rich cultural heritage of Afrika.

While Afrikans celebrated their independence from Britain, it was a double celebration in the Shakkassalli's Family. Their second son Dike, shared the same birthday with his country, the house was filled with "congratulations and happy birthday!" He merely smiled without knowing what to say, "this boy will be a great man" his father said fondly, "yes very true" his mother concurred with a glint in her eyes. The Shakkassali's returned from the parade ground at half past three in the afternoon. Immediately Dike's birthday party began. Everybody was proud and happy to associate with the young boy who was marking his birthday, on the same day with his country, which had just become independent.

Mr. Shakkassalli was a civil servant with the Ministry of Works in Ekko City, which of course was the seat of government of the newly independent nation of Afrika. Mrs. Shakkassalli was a teacher at St. Bernard's Primary School Obalende. Dike was born here at a time when the quest for independence had gathered momentum. Altogether, the Shakkassalli family consisted of three girls and three boys.

Dike was the second among the boys. Mrs. Shakkassalli treasured her sons immensely, the cruelty, mockery and pains she had suffered at the hands of in-laws were still too fresh to be forgotten, and neither was she going to forget how she had been nicknamed "Manager" on account that she'll soon be operating a brothel because of her first three daughters. But God being merciful had smiled on her and the boys started to come one after another, her joy knew no bounds more so as God had silenced her critics. Being a devout Christian, Mrs. Shakkassalli knew she owed God the duty of training her children the way they should go so that they would not depart from it when they come of age.

Despite her travails, she never indulged her sons anyhow; she disciplined them accordingly and encouraged or praised them whenever the need arose. Dike's mother also ensured that her boys were not bullied or harassed in any way by their sisters. Whenever she mediated in a dispute involving brother and sister, after settling the dispute she would tell the girls, "these are the owners of the house, one day you would go away with your husbands; but they will remain". Of course her daughters were never pleased with such a comment they would retreat murmuring inaudibly leaving the boys who were always winning to indulge in their fantasies.

II

ith the exit of the British and the union Jack, the time had finally arrived for the politicians who had succeeded at the General Elections to prove their mettle.

Mike Effa

As the nation continued to adjust to self – rule, the years were also moving. At this time many other countries had just achieved independence. So like Afrika, they were also taking shaky steps like an eight -month-old baby towards attaining a perfect and lasting democracy. But perfect democracy was not going to come so soon, it took the Western world many years of errors to finally shape out their democratic structure, while we in the African continent were trying to attain within a short space of time.

Three years later, Afrika adopted a Republic status and became a member of the Commonwealth of Nations with the Queen as the Head. As the various nations continued their democratic journey, there was a false sense of security, underneath cracks had occurred. In some countries, little disagreements soon blossomed to full-scale civil war. Afrika had gradually been moving towards becoming the next crisis point. The government had seen the signs but somehow they refused to take steps to diffuse the tension. In the East, the National party still held sway with the premier enjoying the support of his people, with the mergers which had come to ensure the Afrika Nationalist party enjoys an absolute majority in parliament, the people's unity party had opposed the merger and had opted to be the opposition party. But as the next General elections came, it was clear most people had since lost faith in Prime Minister Ibrahim's Government. The premier of the western region had changed camp and the leader of the people's unity party had been arrested, tried and jailed on charges of felony.

As the elections came closer so did the west experience an escalation in violence, the premier was no longer enjoying the support of majority of the people since he was no longer a member of their party. They wanted him out of office but the party in power did not think so. Then the west started burning and the government in Ekko City merely said there was no cause for alarm.

Meanwhile a young army lieutenant – Colonel was secretly teaching the premier how to shoot. When the news broke out about the looting and rioting in the western region, everybody was badly shaken and prayed fervently that it would be controlled and much damage to property and loss of lives be minimized. Initially it appeared the government in Ekko city was confused. Even when government decided to act, its actions were clearly against the opposition group. Chief Koko, the leader of the opposition group was serving a life sentence in the

Mike Effa

Port city of Kalabar, unknown to him his supporters were being persecuted seriously. So many of them had been arrested and many were languishing in the newly constructed prison in the western part of the country. While all this wrangling was going on, the Afrikan army with an officer corp of highly trained young men tried their best not to take any interest in the events in the west.

Prior to this point the Afrikan army was experiencing inputs in many forms; first a young graduate of history from Cambridge University joined the army as a recruit. But later the officers found who he really was and the stuff he was made of. He was subsequently sent abroad for training and later returned as a commissioned officer and thanks to his sense of discipline and hard work he rose to the rank of colonel and was put in command of the 5th Army Battalion in Dogawa state in the Northern part of country. Another Officer who was to later play a significant role in the politics of his county was major Eze. One of the officers trained at the Royal Military Academy Sandhurst. He was very unassuming, a revolutionary to the core and a man of vision.

Major Eze was posted to Zaria state as the physical training officer. The young officer being a man of vision had great plans for his country but the politicians were going to destroy this great nation. It did not take long for other officers in his Military cantonment to notice his impatience with the politicians and the Military hierarchy in general. As the days progressed he became more vocal in his utterances. One morning he openly told his men, "Do not mind these officers, one day you will look at them from the sight of your rifles ". Another major nearby rebuked him for making such utterances but Major Eze was not perturbed he had just said what was on his mind and that was it. Later a formal complaint was lodged against major Eze by his colleague but the Military authorities it seemed were too pre-occupied with other things to bother about the utterances of a frustrated army major. And the refusal to act by the army authorities turned out to be the army's greatest undoing. One officer did remark that "Major Eze was an officer in haste and if he was not checked early enough could start serious problem for the nation". This warning was also not heeded–as the New Year drew closer; the election fever heightened so did the bloodshed and chaos. It was now a common sight for party stalwarts to slash themselves with all sorts of weapons. The various political parties continued with their campaign. While the East, mid–West, North etc remained relatively calm; the west was burning seriously with clear indications that if the situation was not checked it could spread. A state of emergency was declared but with little effect, on the other hand, the party in power had reached a decision and was planning to eliminate all those opposing their man in the west and these were mostly Chief Koko's staunch supporters. A date was going to be fixed but it had to be after the general election because government could not afford an escalation of the violence that had engulfed the western part for so long. Lt. Col. Yelwa who had been teaching the premier and some of his supporters how to shoot was mandated to do this job but he was yet to be officially summoned and briefed on this task . The violence continued with whole families being roasted alive because of the political view of the head of the family. People now used flimsy excuses to settle old scores. The carnage continued as the nation approached the 1964 elections. As the government in power watched while the west burned claiming there was no cause for alarm, a group of concerned officers watched the political chaos with interest, unlike the politicians, to these officers there was cause for alarm and the time to act was now or their beloved country would disintegrate.

III

On returning, Major Eze was first deployed to Brigade headquarters as an aide–de camp to the commanding officer where he was promoted three years later to a full Lieutenant and remained Aide–de camp to the Brigade – Commander, a very fine officer who was to die in the coup attempt that was to come a few years later. With his subsequent promotion to the rank of captain he was moved to Zaria state, where he was later promoted major and put in charge of physical training of the enlisted men in the Brigade.

When major Eze was a senior at the Military Academy, there had been a group of young officers who admired his way of doing things. Really Patrick Eze had charisma, charm and was a handsome young man. Though he was commissioned ahead of these young men, fate was to bring them together again. Frank Emeka then a student of the University of Afrika had excelled at the Commonwealth Games in Auckland where he had won a gold medal in the High jump event. His name had already become a household name before he joined the army. But one flaw with Frank Emeka now a major was his inability to stand the heat for long. He was a coward. While in the University he had taken part in a student's demonstration, he was one of the ringleaders, when things got too hot he turned round to betray his friends.

Many people did not know the other majors prior to the coup across the country like majors Eze and Emeka. Upon reporting for duties as a commissioned officer, officers were posted to any Military base or unit across the country. Therefore on returning to the country while major Eze was already in the Northern part of the country majors Emeka, Olu and Onyeka were all staff officers in the Chief of Army Staff's Office a development that was to be to their advantage later. Only major Ezi was in the west. As the year drew to an end the campaigns continued and the Western part of the country continued to burn. While the politicians continued to play hide and seek with the nation at large. Major Eze continued shuttling between Zaria State and the Federal Capital Ekko State. Unknown to Military High Command, the five majors and two captains were holding clandestine meeting which lasted till the early hours of the morning when they will adjourn with a resolve to meet on a future date to review the situation in the country.

On the face of the looming crisis life in Ekko State gradually began slowing down. There was uncertainty in the air, everybody was worried and on full alert because if the carnage in the west was not contained early enough they was the possibility of it spreading. The capital and seat of the confederal Government was in Ekko. Ekko State itself was in the same axis and only a few kilometres from the zone of confusion.

One day Mr. Shakkassalli returned from work with anxiety clearly written on his face. This was Dike's first time of seeing his dad look worried as if he had just seen a ghost.

"Welcome daddy", he greeted and stepped aside to make way.

"You look pale", his wife said as she also greeted him.

"Is there anything wrong?" She asked in a bid to engage her husband in a conversation, which she succeeded in doing.

"The situation is getting out of hand", he said. "But not in the capital", his wife countered.

Mike Effa

"I don't have to wait for it to reach here before I leave Ekko for home, "Mr. Shakkassalli said. "In fact, before the end of the year we might have to go home".

Dike was not happy with his father's decision because if carried out it meant he would not have the joy of spending Christmas in a city as big as Ekko. Dike had marked his next birthday very quietly because the bloodshed was too much for any celebration. The carnage was too much. People in other parts of the country were now afraid of expressing their views.

While reflecting on issues Mr. Shakkassalli reasoned within himself elections are a normal experience in the life of any nation that is at peace with itself, but this was not the case with Afrika. The ruling party of Sir Ado Ibrahim and his Coalition Forces had terribly disappointed the people who gave them the tickets to the seat of power; everybody was tired of the government which was spending money on white elephant projects with reckless abandon without any thoughts about the welfare of the masses. "This administration probably has a policy on how to mismanage Public Funds or else how could one explain a situation where the finance minister will dress in very expensive materials". Mr. Shakkassalli said one day. The Finance Minister's dressing in most cases constituted of the Dutch Wax popularly known as Hollandaise which was always dragging on the ground like a wedding gown and a boy following to prevent the Ministers wrapper from dragging on the ground. This was opulence of the worst order; it clearly showed that the politicians had lost touch with reality and accountability. While some of the citizens were experiencing one hardship or the other, the government was busy clothing itself at the expense of the public and with the taxpayer's money. Certainly time had run out on this group of bandits who were using their position to fuel the crisis that was gradually displacing innocent citizens. "One day all this confusion and squandermania will end", Dike heard his father say while listening to the news.

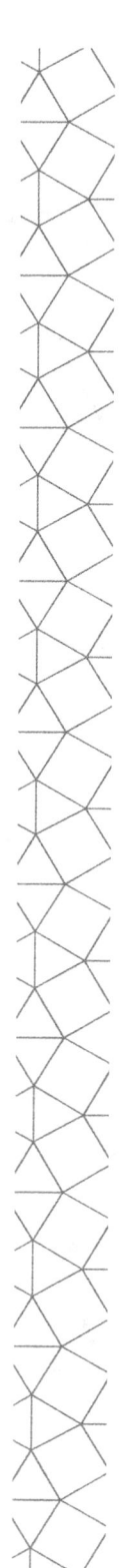

26

Chapter Two

At last the day of reckoning finally came, election were going to hold in August and September. The Party that emerged victorious would assume office in October. As was anticipated voting went on smoothly in some areas, while in other areas there was allegations of rigging and electoral fraud. In the West violence reigned supreme as elements of the People's Unity Party clashed with opponents from the Afrika Nationalist Party Policemen drafted, to various polling centres were helpless as a result no election were held there. The elections were characterized by mass boycotts in some other parts of the country. At the end of the day the Afrika Nationalist party declared itself the winner and remained in office in readiness to perpetuate another four years of misrule and mismanagement.

Only four years after independence the nation was already experiencing so much bloodshed. There was outrage from many quarters, but the ruling party was adamant. As far as it was concerned the elections had taken place and everybody had been given the chance to discharge his civic duty.

Therefore the outrage by some local and international media organizations amounted to "giving a dog a bad name in order to hang it". The Afrika Nationalist candidate Alhaji Ado Ibrahim had been sworn in and had promised to rule accordingly as the constitution stipulated but would he? Only time would tell. While the Politicians played games with their countrymen and the Military watched with interest.

The ruling party was not making any bold attempt at arresting the break down in law and order. Why should they? After all the Prime Minister had declared in an interview with the BBC "there was no cause for alarm".

The sixth independent anniversary was marked under tight security, in areas that has boycotted the elections; 29th November was just another ordinary day. The Prime Minister's independence day speech was carried on the nation's radio and television stations nationwide..." The high incidence of anarchy was being examined with a way of controlling it being planned".

The Prisoner of Afrika

his is nonsense", Mr. Shakkassalli blurted out "which other means do these liars want to use in quelling the situation that is engulfing the country?" He asked in anger.

"Why this outburst?" his wife asked looking up from the novel she was reading, Dike could not help but adjust his position.

"It is because of events that I decided we should spend Xmas in the city", Dike's father said. "What has it got to do with us?" Mrs. Shakkassalli asked. Her husband explained his position and the matter were rested. Dike was happy that he would be spending Xmas in Ekko City.

"But that's not enough reason for you to explode in such a manner", Mrs. Shakkassalli said.

"What do you mean?" her husband fired back, "can't you see what's going on?"

What do you think of the P. M's speech? Mr. Shakkassalli asked.

"The speech is alright", their mother said. "At least the government has finally broken the ice on the crisis" she said, nobody said anything for a while then Dike shocked everybody with what seemed like a prophecy.

"At this rate", he had began" before the year ends

the army might do something", he was still young to express such views so it surprised everybody that he had said this. "That's true", his father agreed. "You see when elections were conducted initially, in other parts of the country, it had not held in the West due to the volatile situation there", he said "But the government was interested in following the due process of law" his wife countered. "Government had been following events closely and so it feels it is now safe to go ahead with the elections. "A big mistake it will turn out to be", Mr. Shakkassalli said like a prophet.

II

Campaign began once more under a false sense of security. Since it was a by-election, only two weeks was allowed for parties to briefly carry out a campaign to make their candidates known. Immediately after the campaigns election followed the next day. Polling began by 11. 00am after accreditation had been completed; those who did not find their names in the voters register were asked to leave the vicinity. While polling was going, the peace was shattered when gunshots were heard outside violence had started once again. Initially

The Prisoner of Afrika

many people did not know the cause of the whole thing. But when the dust settled, it was revealed a pregnant lady had arrived the polling station to vote, everybody believed she was pregnant but just as she was about to enter the polling booth her frock gave way and she was delivered of ballot papers. This was too much for the opposition who saw it as an attempt by government to impose an unpopular candidate on the people. Whereupon the lady was given the worst beating of her life, suffering serious injuries to the head and other parts of the body, she was eventually rescued by anti-riot Police but she had already lost consciousness and so the violence was contained and polling resumed amidst glaring electoral fraud perpetrated by government party agents. The next day, the different newspapers carried different versions of the elections. Many cases of irregularity were highlighted. One of the cases of election irregularities highlighted by the Pyramid under a bold headline of "Government Party rigs out opponents" on the front page further helped to heighten the tension that morning. Explaining further the paper alleged that the figures issued by the Electoral Commission were false. A breakdown of the figures was given and at the end showed that more people had voted. In their hurry to rig the election the government party and their stooges the electoral officers had not taken even the most elementary precaution to cover their dirty, hideous trail. The stage is set for a series of electoral petitions. This time they will not get away with this daylight robbery". The paper concluded.

Still suffering from a hangover of the previous day's event everybody was going about his duties without premonition of what was to come later. The last straw that broke the Carmel's back had started in Chief Oloko Street just before noon that day. A taxi driver who belonged to the opposition had hit one of the premier's cars at the roundabout near the entrance to the town. The taxi driver was thoroughly manhandled but a situation of this nature does not last, suddenly things took a different turn, as it became a free for all. The Premier's car was set ablaze with his thugs inside, from here one party office after the other went up in flames, the riot continued to spread without any attempts or efforts to suppress the riots being made. Meanwhile the rioters engaged themselves in looting, murder, arson and rape. For the West there would be no Christmas, meanwhile the government remained helpless.

The Prisoner of Afrika

While events continued to unfold, Mr. Shakkassalli made sure he kept abreast with events in his nation especially as he had a family to cater for. Christmas had come but again it was a low-key affair suddenly everybody had lost interest in Christmas, who would not? Given the spate of killings and violence that was rocking the Western part of the country. . The Government had become very helpless and clearly showed that it could no longer handle the crisis, but was reluctant to ask the Military to intervene in any way possible but was rather content to use a Police force that was more like a toothless bulldog or a barking dog that could not bite. Later on historians will discover that government was merely playing games with the situation in that part of the country by systematically allowing the people to kill themselves.

The New Year had come in amidst a lot of uncertainty over the future of their beloved country, political disagreements still continued in the West. The Prime Minister in his New Year and budget speech had talked on these problems but was not very concrete when it came to measures being taken to quell the problem.

Mike Effa

Unknown to the generality of Afrikans, the ruling party had after the budget speech fine tuned their plan of action which included a meeting in which a list of political opponents opposed to the Premier in the West will be made available to Lt. Col. Dauda Yelwa, an army officer serving in the only Military unit in that part of the country. His job here was to see to the systematic elimination of those who made up the top echelon of the People's Unity Party. Their conviction was based on the argument that with Chief Koko already in prison, subsequent elimination of the Party's top men will lead to the demise of the party and the opposition to the Premier and the Afrika Nationalist Party would then be easily brought to an end. The party in power was determined to rule for as long as possible, therefore every bit of opposition had to be removed early enough to make for an easy ride. While the politicians continued with their games, a group of young military officer continued with their plans to change history. Major Eze and his group met for the last time on the 13th of January, Major Eze in his residence hosted the meeting. "Gentlemen, the time is ripe to strike", Major Eze said, "Events in the country have shown that the politicians have a hidden agenda".

"The earlier we sack them, the better", said an

The Prisoner of Afrika

anxious Major Onyeka. This particular officer, rumours had it that he liked adventures very much and was always keeping his ears open for anything that will bring him excitement in one way or the other. "Gentlemen this is our plan of action, " he said pausing to circulate copies of what he wanted to read out to the group.

"I will take care of the Premier of the Northern region, Major Emeka will take care of the Prime Minister and two of his Ministers as well as the Chief of army staff and –

"What about the West?" Major Ezi interrupted. Major Eze did not like this but because they were here for an important meeting and a noble cause at that he took everything in his stride.

"Why major, everything is spelt out in that paper in front of you and of course Major Olu will handle the West he knows what to do". He explained patiently.

Gradually everybody got to know what role he was going to play in what was going to turn out to be the nation's first Military coup, that will bring the Military into politics as well as put Afrika in the league of African nations with a record on Military intervention. 15th January was agreed upon by all the officers involved as being ideal and suitable for actualizing their plans. In most cases, Military coups by their nature are always given code names, though this is also not a hard and fast rule as well. The issue of code name depends on the disposition of the officers involved with the planning and execution of the coup.

Major Eze drawing on his vast knowledge of the language of the area, in which he was born and bred, opted for "Operation Zaki. " translated it meant "operation lion. " The reason for choosing this name was very obvious the coup as they now knew was going to be bloody. Using the lion as a code name lent potency to the importance, weight and seriousness of the issue at stake and major Eze impressed this when he made what looked like his parting speech to his colleagues in arms.

"Our ability to put an end to political thuggery and deceit will restore peace and sanity in this country and "operation zaki" will now be a Military and historical precedent

III

The fourteenth day of January came and went without any event. In fact being a working day, Mr. Shakkassalli had gone to work as usual and returned looking very depressed. Everybody understood the cause of his depression who would not be especially if one had a family, as evening approached the family had taken their meal just like any other family. Mr. Shakkassalli had retired earlier than usual leaving his children in the parlour to watch television. "I'm going to bed, you children behave yourselves" he had said. They didn't know it but their father had a premonition that something very terrible was about to happen. That night while the nation went to bed, a group of "concerned officers" stayed awake waiting for the time they would strike the government of Alhaji Ado Ibrahim. An action which was going to change the history and destiny of the nation and affect the minds of the different ethnic groups which made up the Republic of Afrika, while Afrikans slept the clock ticked slowly towards zero hour. All was set for action. At exactly 03. 00 Hrs Afrikan time, Dike woke up from sleep and proceeded to the toilet to ease himself. On his way to the toilet he saw his father lying on the cushion chair in the sitting room with his eyes closed, it was hard to tell whether he was sleeping or not. By ten minutes past three, they heard gunshots from a distance. Dike had come back from the toilet and did not want to go back to sleep since everybody else was in the parlour. Their father had also sat up   The gun shots continued to echo from the distance, Dike was terribly afraid and could not enter the room and go back to sleep so he remained in the living room with his parents. "There is serious trouble somewhere", their mother broke the silence.

"Those are the sounds of army rifles, probably the riots are beginning in this part of the country too. We're becoming prisoners in our country, what is government doing about this crisis which is tearing us apart?" Their father asked with resignation. The sound seemed to increase with every passing moment as if more soldiers were joining in the action, he looked at the clock it was 5. 00 O'clock. They could see the clear signs of dawn of a new but bloody day. Their father not knowing what was really happening instructed his family to remain indoors.

At about 7. 00 O" clock Kris turned on the radio, there was nothing unusual but by 7. 30 in the morning, the news began to filter in. They were all talking excitedly when Ninkai their elder sister ordered everybody to keep quiet and listen.

"News time" she said drawing closer to the set. The newscaster read three other news items before dropping the bombshell. . . . "Soldiers of the Afrikan Army in the early hours of this morning attacked the

The Prisoner of Afrika

residence of the Prime minister. So far the whereabouts of the Prime Minister is unknown. Also reported missing are the Minister of Finance, and the Minister of Internal Affairs. The prime minister according to sources had returned from a meeting with the premier of the northern region. Stay tuned on what is turning out to be Africa's first Military coup. " They remained tuned to the station. At about 9. 00 O" clock, Mr. Shakkassalli had just sat down when they began to play the National Anthem on the radio. After a few moments, a voice said: "Fellow Afrikans, I bring you something special. This is Major Patrick Kadona Eze, Physical and Training Instructor of the 2nd Infantry Division of the Afrika Army. I speak to you this morning at a very unfortunate moment in the history of our beloved country Afrika.

You have all been witness to the tragic events of the last three years in which many properties have been destroyed, many people killed and many others injured or maimed. You have all watched the inability of the civilian government, charged with responsibility for the maintenance of law and order, to arrest the situation that had grown worse as the days went by. It is now obvious that law and order has broken down to prevent a further deterioration in this very bad situation the Army has decided to take over the administration of the country till further notice.

I have been chosen by my colleagues in the three armed forces to lead this military government. I have accepted to serve in this very high office deeply conscious of the very heavy responsibility it entails. We do not intend to perpetuate military rule in this country. Efforts shall be made to form an interim Government of National Unity to oversee the affairs of the nation with a view of putting the country back on the path to lasting democracy. I solemnly pledge to you my countrymen and women my determination to discharge this responsibility honestly and diligently, with the interest of the nation first and foremost in my mind. We should together ask for divine guidance in the common task of retrieving our fatherland from the depth of degradation to which it had been plunged by self-seeking politicians to the height of prosperity, happiness for everybody, and dignity in the world community nations.

Long live the peace loving people of Afrika, long live Afrika. The National Anthem played again. After the anthem, the radio station could not continue with its scheduled programmes. Throughout the whole day, the airwave was filled with martial music. As far as

The Prisoner of Afrika

everybody was concern the army had seized Power little did, they know that the coup did not have the blessing of the Military High command. The chief of Army Staff was already aware of the situation and they had conferred, and came out later with a statement calling on the coup plotters to surrender. On the first day of the coup, things had gone almost as planned. In the west, which had been the bone of contention, Major Olu and his boys had killed many politicians of less importance. Then they had marched on the premier's lodge to arrest him but the premier was not going to surrender without a fight, thus they had been an exchange of fire much to the surprise of the invaders. But this temporary setback was taken care of and the premier was instantly eliminated inside his lodge. In Ekko City, the seat of Government the revolutionaries had achieved 50% success. Major Emeka in the early hours of 15th January had gained access into the prime - minister, residence and had taken the prime Minister and two other Ministers away. The setback suffered by Major Ezi and captain Bassey had been their inability to arrest the chief of Army staff who had gone to a party organized for senior officers within the army. Many Brigade commanders had escaped death by a stroke of luck, one of them was col. James Aziza who was commanding the fifth Military Battalion in Dogawa state, he had gone to town that evening with his wife and their baby and they had spent the night out of the barracks. His assailants waited till morning and then made their move but unfortunately it was aborted and the two men arrested. Later the chief of Army staff called by telephone to brief him on issues and they agreed that all soldiers be disarmed and confined to their barracks. It was not easy disarming as the soldiers now were really itching to kill more politicians. Later another signal came from Major Eze ordering col. Aziza to hand over certain documents to him this was not granted, despite the threat of being invaded which was never carried out.

Reports filtering in on the first day of the coup had it that in the Northern axis, Major Eze had gained access into the premier's residence by blowing off the gates with a grenade. There was an agreement with his men that upon gaining access into the premier's residence proper, if after five minutes he did not show up they were free to level the house with grenades Major Eze had thought and planned to make it a quick job but circumstances unforeseen caused delays, though he decisively tackled the issue but the delay was dangerous,

The Prisoner of Afrika

because his men not knowing what was happening inside proceeded to attack the house with grenades of course he had had no choice other than to dive out through the window with shrapnel's embedded in his neck.

A brief summary of the day's activities revealed that the three premiers of the three regions were all dead. The prime Minister and his flamboyant Minister for Finance, Chief Festus Amachree were all dead. Lt. Col. Yelwa who was supposed to carry out the decisions reached in a meeting with the prime Minister and the premier on the elimination of opponents in the west never reached his destination. He was arrested and shot dead in Ekko city by forces under captain Bassey.

The Network co-ordinated by Major Ezi and captain Bassey had done their assignment partially, though unable to get the army boss, they had been able to kill quite a number of senior Military officers, which included Brigadier victor Ade who was shot dead as he was about leaving for the office, Brigadier Adeoye was killed in the early hours of the morning. He had gone out for a jogging exercise only to meet his assailants on his way back and they had wasted no time in dispatching the Brigadier. Brigadier Shobanjo's case was the most gruesome.

Mike Effa

He was blasted to eternity with a grenade and he died without a hint of was happening. His wife was seriously injured and was rushed to the hospital unconscious she never regained consciousness. The next day, it dawned on a numb nation the magnitude of destruction of lives that occurred on the first day of the coup. Eminent politicians had been eliminated in the North, west and Mid-west. Those not considered important enough were put in prison. The East had lost only three politicians. Unlike the other regions the East could still boast of formidable politicians.

With the army confined to their barracks, an investigation was conducted to know those who had left the barracks in the early hours of the morning of the 15th, many enlisted men were arrested and when tortured admitted to being part of the coup. The Army High command having disassociated itself from the events of the 15th, first and foremost labelled major Eze's action a mutiny and then proceeded to promise all those involved that they will not be court martialled thus it was important that they surrender.

At this stage, Major Eze was confused and worried. They had eliminated senior Military officers from other regions with the exception of the East. Though

The Prisoner of Afrika

not a deliberate attempt, but he knew unless officers from the East were eliminated there was going to be serious cracks within the Military very soon. If the offer of state pardon was anything to go by, then he might cash in on that opportunity and use it to do a mop up operation, still in that state of confusion, he sought the advice of Major Awwalu Yau. Majors Eze and Yau had attended the same course at the Royal Military Academy in Sandhurst, apart from being colleagues they were very good friends. If any of them had a problem, they confided in themselves and quietly they improvised means of solving their common problem. Given the position of the Army, major Eze and his group had no choice but to surrender since the chief of the Army Major General Dan Kio had promised a state pardon to those responsible for the mutiny, his friend had advised. Later major Yau was to be arrested and questioned on the part he played in the coup, the major explained that he got involved under duress and was allowed to go, but the high command had a hidden agenda on this issue

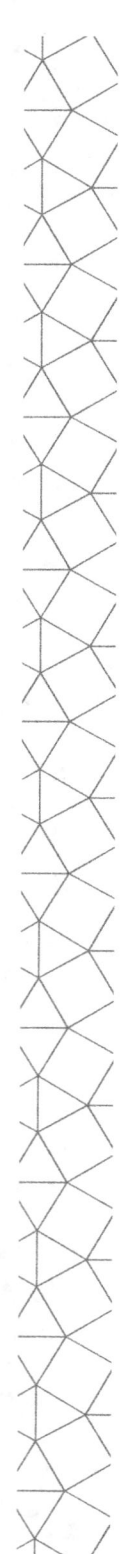

46

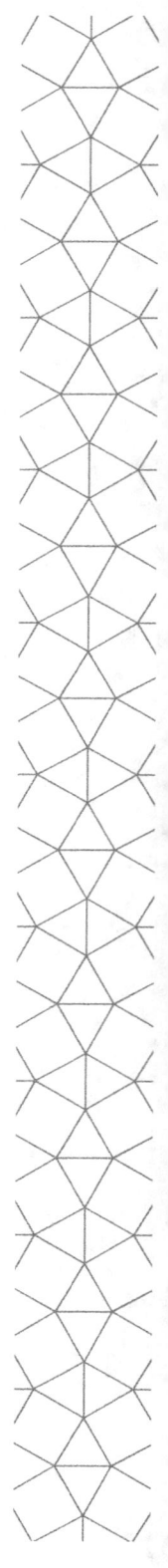

Chapter Three

Major Eze's decision to surrender was made known to Military authorities who immediately announced it on the radio as a way of telling other officers involved to do same. Immediately an aircraft was dispatched to the air force base in Zaria to convey major Eze to the capital. Accompanied by the base commander in whose house he had lodged for the past three days, major Eze boarded the aircraft. That was the last time he was to ever set foot on the state he loved so much.

At the international Airport, there was tension. The atmosphere was so tense you could slice through with a knife. A few metres before the runway began were an anti-aircraft gun manned by two mean looking air force men. At the end of the runway was another anti-aircraft gun manned by two army men in camouflaged gear. As the aircraft began entering the air space over Ekko city, it entered into dialogue with the control tower. Security at the airport was very tight. Soldiers were posted everywhere; Army authorities had sent a convoy of two ferret tanks, four land rovers and two Jeeps to the airport so as to provide maximum security for the prisoner while also ensuring that his chances of escaping were nigh null. In a short while the Military aircraft appeared on the horizon and was cleared for landing, it reduced its speed as it approached the runway and then it taxied to a halt at the section -reserved for the Air Force. Immediately Soldiers surrounded it, while waiting for the door of the aircraft to be opened the convoy took position with the land Rover that was to carry Major Eze parking very close to the aircraft. Major Eze walked calmly into the land Rover and was driven straight to the Gwamina maximum prisons.

With the coup leader in prison, Army authorities across the country intensified the hunt for the remaining officers. In the absence of a democratically elected Government, the Armed Forces reached a consensus that saw Major General Kio assuming office as the Head of State and Commander in Chief of the Armed Forces. Everybody was conscious of the fact that the new Head of State shared political and language affinity with the officers involved in the Mutiny. Lives of eminent persons had been wasted; many wives had become widows overnight and many children fatherless. The whole nation had been united initially, but after counting their losses the North and the Western regions discovered that they had been Short-Changed. The reaction to this discovery is better imagined than witnessed. It first started with demonstrations, followed by courtesy calls by Emirs and Oba's all calling for the heads of the coup plotters.

So far all the officers involved had been successfully rounded up and were being detained in Gwamina Maximum Prison. On impulse the Military authorities decided to scatter the officers by sending them to other prisons across the country. Major Eze, Onyeka and two Captains were sent to a prison in the East. Major Emeka remained in the Gwamina maximum prison in Ekko prison. Majors Olu and Eze were sent to two prisons in the West, the essence of this movement was to forestall a situation whereby any aggrieved group could easily reach these officers or persons seeking revenge. The army knew what was supposed to befall the officers inform of punishment but it was not yet decided. As a way of reassuring and soothing the aggrieved interest groups, the rank and file soldiers were made to face a Military tribunal headed by Major D. Farouk after one week of a lopsided hearing, Major Farouk read out the tribunal's verdict:" With the conclusion of hearing, the tribunal is satisfied beyond doubt of your involvement in the events of 15th January. In consonance with military laws, the punishment for any involvement in any treasonable offence is death. The tribunal therefore finds you guilty of aiding the overthrowing of a democratically elected government and the murder of top government officials. The tribunals hereby sentence you to death by firing squad. This is subject to approval by the Supreme Military Council. "

A couple of days later the Supreme Military council met and later ratified the death verdict, which was carried out three days later, with members of the public in attendance. Yet still, the various interest groups were not satisfied they wanted the ringleaders to be executed as well. Army officers from the two regions most affected also echoed their dissatisfaction and called for the execution of the coup plotters.

The army finding itself in power immediately began moves to consolidate its position. First, it abolished the confederal structure and adopted the Unitary system of Government, divided the country into four zones with Ekko city remaining the capital and the seat of Government. Under this arrangement, the four zones were to be administered by Military

The Prisoner of Afrika

Governors. Based on these arrangements Col Aziza was mandated to resume duties in the West While the remaining officers were posted to other parts of the country. . Seconds after postings was confirmed by the Supreme Commander, Col. Aziza protested, and proceeded to point out "given the situation in the country, it would be nice for each officer to serve in his area of origin. " It made sense to all of them. The Commander in Chief, gave in to this demand but not without a stern warning to Col. Aziza and so the postings were reversed to reflect area of origin. Under this new arrangement, LT. Col. Bayo was posted to the West, Col. Aziza to the East, and Col. Oniha to Mid-West while Yau, Major Eze's confidant and now a Colonel was posted to the North.

II

With the coup plotters rounded up and already in various prisons across the country, life it seemed had returned to normal. But not for long. It began with violent demonstration mostly in the Northern part of the country. The bone of contention was the refusal of the Unitary Government to put the officers involved in the coup on trial.

Then a promotion exercise was carried out in the army, eighteen officers were elevated to new ranks, while from the other regions very few officers were considered. To aggravate matters further the Head of State personally dropped his key advisers, and proceeded to appoint new advisers. The shortcomings in this appointment laid in the fact; it did not reflect what may be termed "federal character", in other words the geographical spread was terribly poor. Over 95% of his advisers came from the same area like him.

Unknown to the Commander-In-Chief, the other regions were pissed off with his new cabinet, coupled with the fact that he had not kept his promise on the trial of the ringleaders of the bloody coup. The regions most affected by the coup showed their displeasure, more so coupled with the recent appointments of certain officers as advisers because they came from the same area with the Commander-In-Chief. There were riots in most parts of the country. Arson and looting became the order of the day, most affected were citizens from the eastern part of the country soon events took a new dimension when easterners were being killed outright. Soldiers were called back into the streets, and initially it looked as if the government was

The Prisoner of Afrika

winning. Then without warning a major tragedy struck the nation and events took a new dimension. Following the spate of events that had befallen the nation and subsequent installation of a military regime to the country till such a time when power will be returned to the civilians again. The head of state of the federal republic of Afrika felt it was about time he carried out a tour of the four regions to meet the people and know their problems. His first port of call was the mid-west, then the east. In these areas he was warmly received, and his tour proceeded without a hitch, then he moved on to the west and things changed very fast. On the 31st of July seven months after the coup the head of state and commander in chief was kidnapped by junior officers in the Afrika army, the officers were from the rank of major down, the military governor of the west rather than allow his commander-in – chief be abducted like a chicken, did his best which included dialogue and when everything failed. He placed himself between the kidnappers and the head of state. Not to be deterred by this obstacle the officers took him along and a couple of days later his bullet riddle body was found and taken back for burial, while the body of the head of state was never found till date. In a space of six months two bloody military coups had taken place in a country that was just five and half years old. Where as many other countries that achieved independence as far back as 1847 were still enjoying relative peace and prosperity. With the mysterious disappearance of the head of state yet to be resolved, anarchy of the worst kind descended on the country, especially in the northern part of the country. Non-indigenes were being massacred like chicken an act that came to be known as the pogrom. Lives and property were lost to rampaging crowds of aggrieved individuals, military officers from the regions most affected by the first coup and who now had played major roles in the second coup knew that the head of state was dead. Immediately Lt. Col. Yakubu Muazu who was then chief of army staff was mandated to fill the vacuum created by the "sudden disappearance" of the head of state. Immediately after the kidnapping, soldiers attacked the two prisons in the west and in the process killed Major Zacky Ezi but Major Olu was lucky, knowing what the soldiers had done in the first prison, the warders in the second prison aided major Olu's escape into the bushes outside the prison walls. Thus when the soldiers came it was an empty prison cell that confronted them.

With northern elements mostly in control of the government, a systematic annihilation of officers from the east was embarked upon. In their bid to remove the monster of marginalisation, these group of officers threw caution to the winds and proceeded to appoint the chief of army staff as Head of State by passing the Chief of Staff Supreme Headquarters who was higher in rank than the army boss.

Brigadier Bola Bayo was more interested in saving his neck instead of contesting for the leadership of a nation that was now taking delight in shedding the blood of its leaders. Matters came to a head for Brig. Bayo when a few days after the abduction of the head state he had summoned a private in the army and given certain orders only for the private to cheekily inform him that he will have to consult his commanding officer. The private and his commanding officer were from the north and they had just taken over power, so he was not taking orders from anybody even if he was a brigadier in as much as they did not share language affinity. This development was too much for Brig. Bayo for fear of being killed he took refuge in a visiting Russian warship that had berthed off the coast of Badagry.

Mike Effa

He followed the ship back to the Soviet Union leaving his family in Ekko City. Meanwhile to forestall the death of another rebel, Lt. Col. Muazu gave instruction and major Emeka was flown to a prison in the East. Out of the four governors of the four regions, only col. James Osmond Aziza of the eastern region refused to recognize the new head of state Lt. Col Muazu. His reason being that Col. Muazu was third in the line of command, it was wrong to bypass Brig Bayo, this development gradually turned into a serious war of words. With the flagrant abuse, killing and looting of property belonging to non-indigenes resident in the north, the government wasn't acting fast enough check this trend so Col. Aziza thought, rather than allow his people to be killed he issued a directive calling on non-indigenes to return, even the military authorities in Ekko city supported his line of action but they did not know he had different plans entirely. "It is good for non-indigenes to return home for a while to let tempers cool down", Col. Muazu had responded to a question from a reporter, at Heathrow Airport while in London to brief the queen about events. As the refugees began to return, a new problem also arose that of settling the refugees one thing the regions did not have was financial autonomy, they relied on

The Prisoner of Afrika

the central government for money to implement their programmes, Col. Aziza informed the head of state of this problem.

But nobody listened to him, not because they were delighted in seeing other people suffer, rather because Col. Aziza had refused to recognize Col. Muazu as the new Head of State. There was no way they could do business together, even when asked to come to Ekko city personally. He took this invitation as an attempt to arrest and imprisoned him He rather decided to send his Commissioner for Finance to see the Head of State. As it was an issue of national importance the commissioner was sent back without even seeing the Principal Staff Officer to the Head of State. It was a disorganized commissioner who arrived to inform Col. Aziza about the development.

The refugee situation was getting out of hand as more easterners continued to return home, the attack on non indigenes had began to lose steam, but since a directive had been issued it was safer to go home than to remain in such a hostile environment and nobody could tell what problems the next day will bring with it. The only succour had come from the Red Cross and international aid agencies. The government of national unity still refused to act in any way to alleviate the sufferings of the refugees.

III

Mr. Shakkassalli continued to monitor events closely. One Tuesday evening while watching television, he said something, which disturbed everybody seriously. , "the actions of Col. Aziza will gradually lead to Civil war". Nobody said anything for awhile- then Mrs. Shakkassalli spoke.

"Why do you think so?" She asked. They all knew that a Civil war would be very devastating, especially to the Eastern part of the Country. They silently prayed that Col. Aziza will not plunged millions into hardship and grief out of a selfish desire to achieve his personal ambitions of seceding to form another Country wherein he will serve as its Head of State. Everybody know it well be it a foolish thing to do because the superior Afrikan armed forces will crush his secession attempt but with a huge loss of life to both sides.

"Look, at the statements he has been making", Mr. Shakkassalli, said pointing at the lead story in one of the National Dailies. "Since the death of the Head of State and the appointment of Col. Yakubu Muazu,

The Prisoner of Afrika

he is the only governor who has refuse to recognize the commander- in- Chief. , In the military that could be termed an act of mutiny and would be court martialled and either dismissed from the army or sent to prison or he could be shot, ". He said.

"Let him recognize Col Muazu, now?" Kris said joining the discussion.

"Only God will deliver us from what is about to happen, " Mr. Shakkassalli said.

The discussion went on and on, while Dike quietly watched the Television without making any noise or comments. He was grateful to God that in the midst of , the uncertainty, his father was convinced that it was safer to remain in Ekko City instead of moving East. After all, East was where the problem was. Following the second Coup, the sporadic shootings they use to hear since January had finally subsided; the Head of State had made a broadcast assuring people of their safety and calling on them to return to work. The Government had gone a step further in its bid to restore confidence by lifting the curfew.

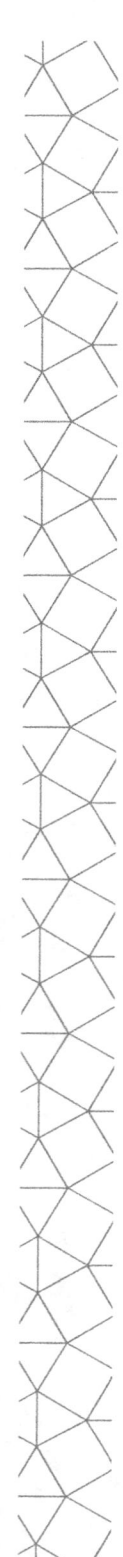

60

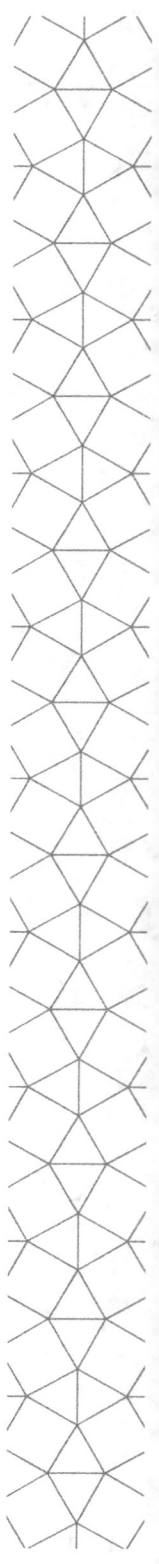

Chapter Four

The Commander–in–Chief, Col Muazu a young and handsome officer discovered that ruling a heterogeneous nation like Afrika was not easy. , Still he was determined to do just that. At first, he pardoned and ordered the immediate release of all political prisoners. Chief Koko of the defunct people's unity part was one of those who benefited from the act of clemency. Life was also returning to normal in the West, . With the release and subsequent appointment of Chief Koko to the Post of commissioner for Finance, the confidence of the people in the west was restored. But the Head of the State now faced fresh problems this time from army officers of Northern extraction; they wanted to pull the North out of the Country. Eventually, these officers were summoned to a meeting with the Commander–in Chief. It would have been easy for the Head of the State to order them eliminated, but Col. Muazu had had enough of the bloodshed. To him dialogue would be the first option and it worked with this group of officers. Especially when he told them what they would be losing if they pulled out.

Mike Effa

Muazu wondered why his brother Officers would settle for only a piece of the pie whereas it was all theirs for the taking. Before departing State House the officers agreed to settle down and savour the national cake that was now at their beck and call. But the question here was;, were Col. Muazu and his fellow officers really going to enjoy as they thought? Things moved very fast for the new government. The flagrant attack and abuse of non-indigenes was almost history. The new problem was that of settling the refugees, but because Col Aziza had refused to recognize the military regime in Ekko City there was no way aid was going to flow to the East. With the food shortage becoming severe, the victims were children who gradually began to suffer from starvation and, kwashiorkor. Col. Aziza once more sent an "SOS" to the government; still no aid was forth coming. A desperate man is a very dangerous man to contend with. Col Aziza summoned his cabinet and informed them that they had now become a war cabinet, sooner they will be a broadcast on the stand of the people of the East. For now they were to keep the information close to their hearts, as any leakage will result in nothing short of death for the offender and his entire family. The rag-tag cabinet of Col Aziza knew he was a man of

The Prisoner of Afrika

his words and would carry out what he had just said to the letter. Some of them even wished he had kept his war plans to himself longer. The deadlock continued between the National Government in Ekko City and Regional Government of the East. Many eminent persons within the continent and abroad began spirited moves to break the logjam. Both leaders were invited for talks in the beautiful city of Abidjan. With the talks successfully concluded the famous Abidjan, accord was signed and both leaders shook hands and promised to co-operate in its implementation. One of the concessions was a total withdrawal of military officers of Northern stock from the West. What this was supposed to signify nobody clearly understood but to a few it was to reduce tension in the west. It did not make sense after the entire West was already calm.

Ironically, the weapons that would be used to inflict defeat on Col. Aziza's rag-tag army of rebels are the very guns he had taken delivery of when he was Quarter-master General just before the Coup of 15th January. Then in May the Government of Brig. Muazu increased the tempo further when out of disregard for the Abidjan accord it abolished the regional system of Government. In its place the federal system of Government was adopted, the government also created twelve States to support the Federal System of Government. One of the conditions by Col. Aziza for keeping the peace was that the region be allowed to stay, given more powers with less power residing with the central government. Government had agreed and also put pen on paper, only, for them to backpedal at the last minute, Col. Aziza felt betrayed. However, the Commonwealth of Nations and the United Nations continued last minute efforts to see that the solution was resolved amicably. Other smaller countries looked on in consternation wondering, which other country within the continent will be able to play the peace-keeping role like Afrika did in the Congo crisis. The Military Junta of Brig. Muazu had two reasons for adopting the Federal structure. First, they hoped it would hasten the reconciliation of the various groups, next given the intransigent behaviour of Col. Aziza the exercise now left him without a solid base in terms of people and landmass. One thing the Government had overlooked was the fact that boundaries cannot and will never be an impediment for people with a will and cause they believe is noble. Easterners possessed this will.

The Prisoner of Afrika

II

Mr. Shakkassalli and his family continued to show signs of anxiety towards political developments in their country, most of their Uncles and Aunts as well as other family relatives were in the East.

"I hope Col. Aziza sees reason with the Federal Government", he said, barely able to contain the worries in him any longer.

"We hope he does", Mrs. Shakkassalli said joining in the discussion.

"Besides it is the East that has a lot to lose".

"The East is not strong enough to face the rest of the country", . her husband said, this time moving towards the window so as to get a commanding view of the main road in front of their house. But from his position it was not possible to see the gate. Unknown to them, one of Mr. Shakkassalli's sisters had just arrived, even when she entered the living room Mr. Shakkassalli and his wife were so wrapped in thoughts that they did not even hear her greetings until she moved closer to both of them near the window.

"Brother good evening, good evening madam", they turned at the same time.

"Good Heavens, look who is here!" Dike's father

exclaimed like a young lover. The relief on his face was so plain that even a blind man could see.

"How is everybody back home?" He fired the next question unconsciously preventing his wife from asking any questions.

"Hunger and disease will kill any family that decides too late to vacate the trouble zone", his sister replied.

"Be rest assured all members of our family including our in-laws foreseeing what might happen very soon have left the East for other parts of the country". , she concluded.

Mr. Shakkassalli and his wife heaved a sigh of relief.

"Ah thank God" Mrs Shakkassalli said. outwardly relieved.

III

Many International bodies had made last minute efforts to prevent a civil war from breaking out. But it was very clear that the parties involved wanted to settle their differences in a war front. For instance Col. Aziza had changed his so-called War–cabinet. It now included Military Officers too, he had even promoted himself to the rank of Brigadier, a very serious offence in the Military. On the part of the

The Prisoner of Afrika

Federal military Government, creating and adopting the Federal structure coupled with the outright refusal to allow aid to flow to the refugees in the East amounted to daring Col. Aziza to see if he will be bold enough to carry out his threat. So far, the beleaguered Colonel was playing into the hands of the Federal Military Government. At every peace Conference, Col. Aziza always insisted on the implementation of the Abidjan Accord, something the regime of Brig. Muazu did not want to implement at all.

Therefore on Saturday, the 19th of May, Col. Aziza made a startling speech that heralded other events. In his speech, Col. Aziza had this to say, "Following the events of 15th January, and the scheming on the part of a group of officers which saw Brig. Muazu taking control of the Armed Forces and the nation in general. I wish to state here that this is unconstitutional, coupled with the flagrant attack on non-indigenes residing in the North, the government bluntly refusing to act in any way that will provide succour for those who have been turned refugees in their own country. Government refusal to send aid to the refugees in the East and its refusal to abide by the Abidjan Accord signifies a grand design to marginalize a part of the nation from the scheme of things.

Therefore with the powers conferred on me by my war cabinet; I Brig Aziza wish to inform you all of the secession of the East to form its own Republic which will be known as the Republic of Malabor. Thank you and God bless you all".

Following the secession message of Col. Aziza, it was now clear that at last the much-dreaded Civil War was no longer avoidable. The new Republic was fast in acquiring many things, it floated its currency known as the Marks, the map of the new Republic was drawn, it covered all the minorities, who it seemed, were being colonized again. The Federal Government watched events keenly not willing to act immediately, the Government wanted to see Col. Aziza's next line of action -it came immediately. As Head of State, he appointed Ministers and Military Governors to govern the various states that made up his Republic.

If Col. Aziza thought he would get away with his acts of high treason he was in for a big surprise, in fact the Federal Government had a gift for his country. Every country or nation has a capital city; the new Republic was no exception. The Republic of Malabor consisted of ten states with Onitchar as the Capital City; the swearing in was to take place

The Prisoner of Afrika

there. So that morning while the new Head of State was preparing to swear-in his cabinet, the Military High Command in Ekko City had swung into action, the Air Force Commander had received his orders and passed them on to his men. Col. Aziza had exhausted the long rope given him to draw by the Federal Government. With that rope exhausted the government now felt it was time to bring him back to his senses. A war plan had been drawn, under this plan, the Afrikan Air Force with its array of sophisticated jet fighters which included the famous American F-23 and the British Jaguar jet and the notorious American B-42 bombers were to start by carrying out day and night bombing missions against the rebels for three months. At the expiration of three months the air raids will be reduced to allow the Afrikan army with its brilliant corp of infantry and armoured units to advance. These units would be adequately supported to make their advance successful. To add pep to the striking power of the infantry and armoured corps the third and fourth marine commandos were created, majors Olu Hakot and Benjamin Musa were put in charge of this outfit, their job was to cripple oil installation in the east. The swearing -in began without any premonition of it being disrupted. The head of state

Mike Effa

had arrived and the national anthem was played, then Col. Aziza gave his speech. The applause had hardly died down when the sound of aircraft was heard, everybody rushed out to see were heading, but when the dull sounds of explosion reached their ears, the citizens of malabor knew that the federal military government was not going to fold its arms and watch the country be divided by some clown in the name of preventing a particular group of people from being "marginalised". The war had began, every day the voice of Afrika, gave news bit on areas that had been hit. The international community refused to give up in its efforts to settle the problem amicably. The federal government refused to heed initially the calls to stop the air attacks, but later the raids were suspended temporally and then resumed when col. Aziza's delegation to the peace talks still insisted on the Abidjan accord and to worsen matters Col. Aziza still refused to recognize the regime of Brig. Muazu, the air raids continued and the refugee problem took a different dimension

The Prisoner of Afrika

The rebels as they were commonly called by government had thought they would defeat government troops, hands down because they had enlisted the support of mercenaries from Portugal, and North Korea etc. Col. Aziza and his war cabinet were disturbed by the air raid that they had no reply to. However, the few anti aircraft guns they had were being over stretched. After three months the ground forces rolled into action to "mop up" what had been overlooked by the air force. As ground war raged, Col. Aziza advanced to a four star general, a coup attempt by a group of officers led by major Emeka failed and they were summarily executed on a chilly Christmas morning. Gen. Aziza's mercenaries had swung into action on arriving but were soon frustrated by shortage of arms and ammunition.

The rebel government had been recognized by Zanzibar which had sent an aircraft loaded with arms but the pilot missed his way and landed in government held territory, the plane was impounded and the pilot arrested. The government of Upper Volta had also sent a ship load of arms and ammunitions but it was raided and boarded by members of the third marine commando when it entered Afrikan waters and was heading for the port city of Brass. The civil war raged as rebel and government forces battled for control of strategic cities. As the civil war raged on, Gen. Muazu was concluding plans to bid bachelorhood goodbye. In December he finally took his girlfriend of five years to the altar. Guests were conveyed to the wedding venue by helicopter, the drinks were also conveyed by air. This act drew a lot of criticism from many parts of the world., The war continued, . Cities continued to fall as government forces advanced steadily towards achieving their goals being to dislodge the rebels and arrest Gen. Aziza.

In his bid to spite the north and the west, the rebel leader had given orders for the release of Major Patrick the architect of the coup of 15th January. Being an educated and charismatic officer, Major Eze's vision for his country did not include secession. Therefore upon being released he made attempt to reach Gen. Muazu in order to discuss ways of ending the war. Unfortunately, this charming and intelligent officer was killed without being able to make contact with government forces. The head of state was informed and he ordered that major Eze be given a burial in the Burma Road cemetery reserved strictly for senior military officers. With Christmas and the New Year only weeks away, it was

The Prisoner of Afrika

now clear to those who could see that the war was won and lost. Before Christmas, Gen. Aziza and his family left the country for Upper Volta on self exile. Four years after the war began, Major Gen. Philip Ibanga officially surrendered to the third marine commando officer in change, Col. Olu Hakot in the port city of Brass, a couple of hours later a meeting was called to discuss a reintegration of all sides. A broadcast was made by the commander in chief; at last the civil war was finally over.

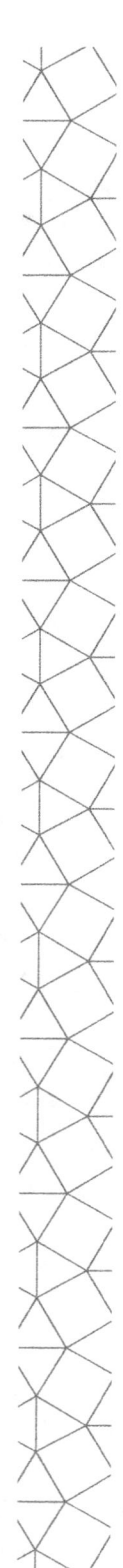

74

Chapter Five

The end of the civil war meant many things. To the nationalist government of Gen. Yakubu Muazu, it meant a total re-integration of all parts whether North or South, East or West to enable the nation move forward. Thus, in his speech to declare an end to the hostilities, the head of state and commander-in-chief had this to say.

"Today, the 18th of January, Gen. Phillip Ibanga second in command to General Aziza of the defunct Malabor Republic surrendered to col. Olu Hakot of the third Marine Commando thus ending a thirty-month attempt to secede. Today also brings to an end the events, which had caused a lot of bloodshed and led to the civil war. I call on everybody to forget the past and let`s face the future. All citizens of this country are free to reside anywhere that they desire to. The federal military government hereby grants a state pardon to all those who fought on the side of the rebels, moreover there is no victor and there is no vanquished. The task of rebuilding is quite enormous and therefore only the collective efforts of everybody will see us through. Thank you and God bless. Long live the federal Republic of Afrika".

The Government next unfolded its development plan made possible through the abundance of crude oil from the Delta and Riverine Areas of the country. The Eastern part of the country was given enough funds to rebuild all the areas devastated by bombing raids carried out by the Air force and the shelling by the Army, Coal which was a mainstay of this region till the Civil war broke out forcing the mines to close down was later to play a significant role in rebuilding these areas especially when the United states of America, and many European countries indicated their interest to buy Afrikan Coal because of its high quality. The opening of the mines saw many indigenes of the state going back to work. The federal government's development plan involved the building of more roads, bridges, hospitals, schools e t c. it was quite a bold and aggressive plan possible through the good prices that the crude oil attracted.

The Prisoner of Afrika

II

Following the implementation of Gen. Muazu's development plans, the bulk of the development cantered on Ekko city, the seat of government. Flyovers and very long bridges were being built in Ekko city because as the seat of government with three major seaports and an international Airport, the major problem foreseen was traffic congestion, hence the construction of flyovers to ease traffic problems. The major contractor had been Joncker Burger, a German construction firm that had been handling construction jobs in the continent for a very long time. On the political front, the Military Government was doing very well, Gen. Muazu was elected chairman of the organization of Unity for Africa a position he occupied two years. At this point, the nation had made so much money from the sales of crude oil and it seemed from the way things were moving that the upsurge in the nation's finances would last forever. This era initially was called the Oil Boom Era. Many factors accounted for this positive development, first the brand of crude found in Afrika was initially not available in other parts of the free world then with the existence of communism and the cold war between the

Mike Effa

Western world and the Eastern part of Europe, or preferably between NATO and WARSAW countries, it meant NATO countries could not buy anything from countries in the communist bloc because trade was forbidden. Thus the NATO countries had to come to Afrika to buy crude oil because it suited the heavy machines of industries in Western Europe. With the boom of oil sales, had come widespread corruption at the federal and state levels. It was now a common thing to see government officials openly looting government funds. When asked on this unhealthy trend, the commander-in-chief had naively replied, "Money is not our problem, but how to spend it". The government had lost control and was drifting like a ship without a rudder; the military governors had become very powerful overnight. Such was the level of decay in the system that the state Governors had the guts to challenge the head of state. Military governors were now governing their state as if they were different or independent regions. The Military government of Gen. Muazu had two years earlier made a promise to return the country to Civil Rule.

But with his subsequent appointment as the Chairman of the Organization for Unity of Africa, Gen. Muazu made it clear that the handover date earlier proposed was no longer feasible. , He went on to inform the nation that a more feasible date would be announced for the commencement of the transition programme. Within the Military, signs of disaffection over Gen. Muazu's regime were beginning to show but the amiable and peace loving commander-in-chief was not perturbed. The head of state himself knew he had been on the hot seat for quite some time and it was clear to him many of his colleagues in the armed forces were itching to take a short at ruling the country. On the whole his regime was characterized by massive fraud and plundering of government funds. Matters were not helped either when a journalist was incarcerated for struggling for the affections of a lady with the Head of State, a social critic, who later in the post war era criticized him for flying food to the venue of his wedding was arrested and detained for daring to challenge the Head of State.

Following the boom in the sales of oil, corruption and embezzlement reached an all time high the government it was very clear had lost control completely. It was clear to many officers in the SMC that Gen Muazu had become a lame duck. Coupled with his unwillingness to effect a change in the power structure, it was clear, in fact it had become necessary to overthrow him and they also agreed it will be a bloodless coup because the Head of State had done a lot for the country and he should not be rewarded for his services by being killed. The rebels were in a slight fix, in that they wanted to stage the coup when the C-in-C was out of the country, they continued calculating and hoping for the right time to strike.

Then came the new year everybody had high hopes for a higher level of prosperity, the Head of State had echoed this in his speech. But one thing he had not succeeded in doing was checking the level of corruption amongst government officials especially the State Governors. Other Military officers could no longer hide their disgust for the commander-in-chief. Then a break occurred, as Chairman of Organisation for Unity of Africa, Gen. Muazu was scheduled to address the next summit opening in the Gold Coast, and he certainly knew he would not return as Head of State. Before boarding the Presidential Jet he whispered to his townsman Lt Col. Garba of the Guards Brigade. "I hear you're plotting a coup. Make sure it's bloodless" With that he boarded the presidential jet, which immediately took off for the Gold Coast.

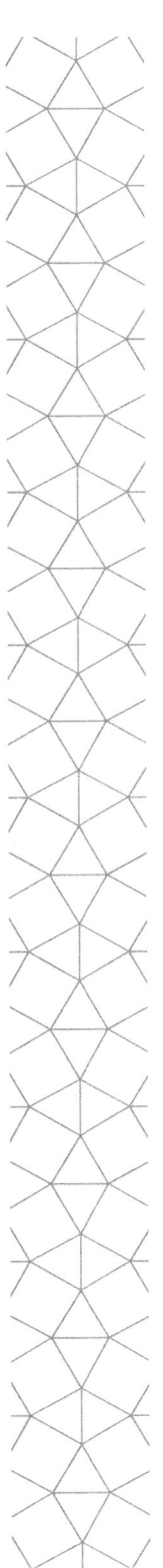

The Prisoner of Afrika

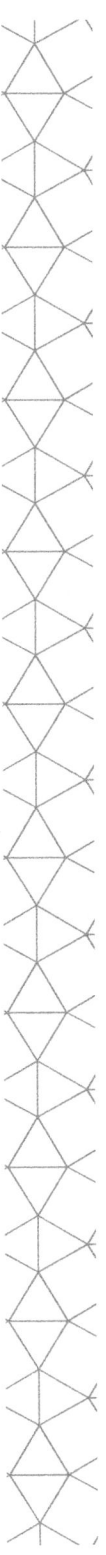

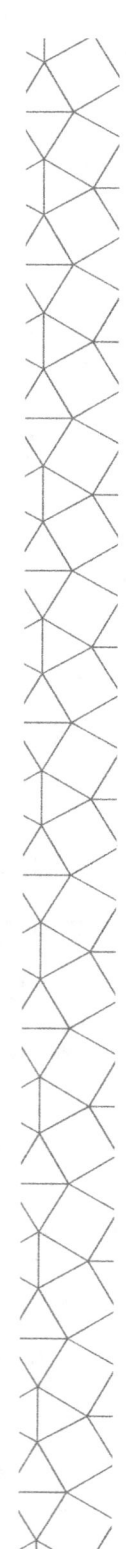

82

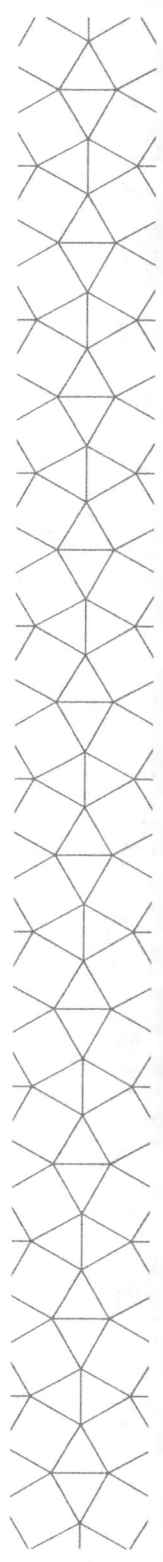

Chapter Six

With the Head of State away on an official assignment. Life went on smoothly. Everybody went about their business without the premonition of anything. Schools were in session. Everybody seemed certain the Military had learnt a lesson from the Civil War, but this was not so. Five years after the war, 29th July precisely the nation woke up to series of martial music played from the nation's main Radio station. If people were perturbed, they did not show it. Being a Saturday many people including Civil Servants, teachers and school children were all at home. Dike remembered that morning very well. His father and he were in the sitting room watching television and listening to the radio too. His father was not bothered with the martial music probably his intuition would have told him already.

Eventually the music was interrupted and a voice came on with the following.

"Fellow countrymen, I bring you good news"

"what good news?"Mr. Shakkassalli asked nobody in particular, eventually he kept quiet and they continued listening to the speech. , though they missed the name of the officer reading the speech. "Following, nine years of corruption and misruling by Gen. Muazu and his clique of officers in the Supreme Military Council, a period characterized by embezzlement, fraud, lack of direction and vision. We, of the armed forces, have come together and decided to put an end to this mess.

Therefore the regime of Gen. Muazu is hereby overthrown. Also affected is the chief of staff Supreme Headquarters and the three service Chiefs including the inspector-General of police, the comptroller- General of the Customs and Immigration. All Military Governors of the twelve States of the federation are advised to remain calm and be vigilant till further notice. All airports, Seaports and borders will remain closed till further notice. All law-abiding citizens of the Federal Republic of Afrika are advised to stay calm and go about their lawful businesses without any hindrances. All diplomats, non-nationals are advised to remain calm as their safety has already been taken into consideration. Fellow countrymen, today marks a turning point in the history of our great nation, as the forces of corruption have been displaced to pave the way for a leadership with foresight and purpose. Long live

The Prisoner of Afrika

the Federal Republic of Afrika. Thank you and God bless our nation". The National Anthem played again and the station continued playing more martial music.

"Fourteen years after independence, Afrika is experiencing yet another coup", Mr. Shakkassalli said.

"Three Military coups, one civilian Prime Minister and three Heads of State in the space of fourteen years ", Dike concluded.

They all laughed at this summary of their country's political development.

"I wonder what the new administration will have in store for the citizens of this country", Mrs. Shakkassalli said. "By the way, who is Gen. Bako?" she asked.

"Not much is known about this guy, but it is rumoured that he was the Brigade Commander of Mechanized infantry Div. in the middle Belt State of Goma". , Kolum said.

"To add to what you just said, " His father began, " following the counter coup he was supposed to have assumed leadership of the country but at the last minute he was beaten to it by Gen. Muazu whom he has finally toppled to fulfil a lifetime ambition of being the number one citizen of the Federal Republic of Afrika. A lover of animals, Gen.

Bako is a very highly disciplined officer. Do not be surprised to see that all the Military administrators will be sacked from the armed forces". He concluded

II

At exactly 7. 00-p. m Afrikan time, almost everybody in the house was in the parlour to listen to the new Head of State's speech. They were somehow excited, but they talked ensuring that they did not raise their voices. At about quarter past the hour, the national anthem was played, after a brief silence of about five seconds Gen. Bako, Head of state, Federal Republic of Afrika began reading his address to an audience of over 55 million Afrikans. "My government will pursue an open door policy, no acts of indiscipline would be tolerated, and corruption must die a natural death. Fellow citizens if we are to make any progress as a government and nation respectively, all vestiges of corruption must be eliminated completely. Therefore in this regard, all military administrators of the twelve states are hereby dismissed from the armed forces; all Federal civil service officers from Grade Level 14 and above are also sacked with immediate effect. The administrators should hand over to the Unit

The Prisoner of Afrika

Commanders in their areas, while all officers should over to their next in command. This measure is intended to sanitise our system and propel us to greater heights of economic maturity. Long live the Federal Republic of Afrika; thank you".

After the Head of State's speech, there was a spell of silence in the living room. , "What a Country, " Kris said.

"The new head of state is really a harsh man o, " Dike remarked.

"What do you make of the Commander-in-chief's speech?" Mrs. Shakkassalli asked her husband.

"Everything is clear", her husband began. The government is bent on eliminating corruption and fraud, ". He said.

"But the Head of state's decision to retire so many civil servants is biased," one of their daughters said.

"why?" their father asked looking at her sharply.

"You will notice that the top positions in the civil service are held by the Middle Belt mostly from the same area with Gen. Muazu", she concluded leaving the statement hanging of course, . It was very clear to everybody that Gen. Bako was trying to rid the civil service of the Middle Belt influence while at the same time preparing it for a grand take over and total domination by the core North whom it seemed had been denied a fair share of the National Cake by their brothers who constituted the Middle Belt axis. Everyone got tired of discussing politics and changed the topic to something else, thirty minutes later they gave in to one fundamental need, sleep.

Gen. Bako adjusted to the post of the nation's number one citizen faster than people expected and was always ahead in everything, therefore it was quite difficult to anticipate his next move, a development which made people guess he must be a good chess player. Having consolidated his position, the next thing was to fight corruption which he charged headlong like a bull. Afrika being a heterogeneous society, a development that the ousted regime of Gen. Muazu had not taken into consideration during the state creation exercise, so he had ended up bringing groups that did not share any cultural affinity together. The administration of the states had not been easy. It was not surprising therefore that after nine years the state structure was adopted, the clamour for more states had begun again. What most people did not know then was, the clamour for states and the willingness to accede

The Prisoner of Afrika

to such demand will become a common development in the future to be exploited by self seeking individuals and crafty Military regimes looking for an excuse to stay longer than necessary in power. The new Military regime was very sensitive to the needs of the various groups that wanted states of their own and the Head of State had promised something positive towards this area.

One pleasant August morning Mr. Shakkassalli was called into the office of the Director of Personnel and was courteously informed to proceed on transfer to Kalabar state to assume the position of Director of Field and support service in the Ministry of Works, Area Office. On returning home, he broke the news to the entire family. His children were sad because they were leaving Ekko City to an unknown area, but their father was able to assure them over their worries. He was very excited over the prospect of moving to another area for a change. "You children should not worry; you will all like the state" he said, "What is your problem?" their mother asked. "Don't you want to go home to your own land?"

"Oh o please help me ask them-o" their Father said.

"I will miss my friends," Dike said.

"I will miss all my friends too," Mr Shakkassalli said too, but not out of imitation. "As you leave the friends here, you make new friends in your new area of abode, so we will all make new friends okay--I hope we are all satisfied"

"So when are we leaving Ekko City?" Kolum asked.

"I'm expected to report on Monday-that means we shall be moving this weekend". "Oya-you children should go and pack immediately," their Mother ordered.

On Saturday morning the Shakkassallis bade goodbye to Ekko City as their lorry drove through the tollgates heading for Kalabar. Kalabar state, was one of the states created in May by Gen. Muazu shortly before the civil war, the state capital was rumoured to have seen serious fighting between government troops and rebel forces. The state is also unique or rather remarkable in many ways, before independence was granted by the colonialist Kalabar state then known as St. Christopher's town had served as the capital for the British Occupation forces. Even when the BOF was later moved to Ekko City, Kalabar state could not be forgotten in haste as it still possessed many other historical land marks amongst which were the seaport and the Canaan City Prisons. The trip down

The Prisoner of Afrika

south was quite an interesting one, as they saw many things of interest. Before , Dike had not known that they were large bodies of water and bridges which looked like houses down south. . . . His experience ended in Ekko City where he was familiar with the famous Bonny Beach. And talking about bridges, he would never forget the famous First and second Mainland bridges. And then, there also was the Ahmed Karter bridge which spanned almost fifty kilometres. How the German engineers manipulated such large quantity of massive steel and cement into existence remains a mystery to so many people. However Dike was astonished when they reached the mid western state and he discovered here again laid another German magic that is the famous mid western bridge which covered almost thirty kilometres; the bridge was rumoured to have been destroyed by rebel forces during their retreat from the federal troops superior fire power. It was repaired immediately the civil war ended so as to facilitate the movement of relief materials to the war-ravaged areas of the east.

"This country is truly blessed with everything that can make it a great power in the continent Mr. Shakkassalli said,

"But we need a leader with focus and vision to

move the nation" his wife added.

The journey continued without any hindrance, though they were slowed down a bit by police checkpoints at different parts of the road. With the policemen asking them the same question, "wetin you carry," the reason for the numerous police checkpoints was to combat the high wave of armed robbery especially in the western and mid western part of the country. But then, the various police post did not stop the robbers from depriving innocent Afrikans of their properties with some even losing their lives to callous armed robbers. By God's special Grace, the Shakkassalli family continued with the journey stopping in East central State for fuel and food. Their father rushed them, through and did not really allow them time to savour the pounded yam, bitter leaf soup and goat meat that was served them. A delicacy always associated with this part of the country. Dike remembered some of the stories he had read where such delicacies featured prominently in occasions. He also recalled how in "Things fall apart" by Achebe a cold bitter leaf soup and pounded cassava was a common feature in the lives of the umuofia people. "To say the least, the journey from Ekko city to Kalabar state was quite interesting. Their father guided the lorry drivers to

The Prisoner of Afrika

their new house situated at no. 5 pearl street in the historical city of Kalabar but here too a moment of discomfort was to follow. Being a newly built house, the lights had not yet been put in place. This meant probably a month or two of darkness and mosquito bites.

"Well, people we're here," their father said.

"Ahh this is not like the house in Ekko city", Kris remarked.

"Never mind. it's still new when the job is finished you'll like it" their father assured. "Come on join the rest of the family to off load. We must finish before night comes."

The Shakkassalli family settled down once again and Dike resumed his schooling while his father resigned from the federal service and joined the state civil service.

The New Year had started and the clamour for new states had reached a point of no return. Kalabar state being too big for easy administration, the sons and daughters were canvassing that the state be divided into two. Delegation after delegation had visited the head of state to drive home their point and they had been given a fair hearing, with a promise to look into their situation. Therefore at this point, everybody was now waiting for the head of state's broadcast scheduled for a date yet to be announced. The Shakkassalli were in this state of expectation when Mrs Shakassalli's youngest sister paid them a surprise visit. She was on her way back to Abijang division having gone to visit their eldest sister. While staying with them, one day their father returned from work with a copy of the Duketown "Herald". On the front page was a lead story captioned "pupil stabs teacher."

Dike's aunty asked him to read it out, and he read it aloud without any delay. She smiled a smile of satisfaction. "That's good Dike. I'm sure you are doing well in school she said.

"Ah my son is intelligent o. I'm sure he wants to be a lawyer. Is that not so? His mother asked.

"Yes when I finish my schooling I shall become a lawyer," Dike replied, he was grateful to God for the kind of stature and features he had. At seventeen he was dark in complexion, not very tall like most boys within his age bracket. While some already had moustaches in his case his face was still as smooth as a baby's buttocks.

"I suppose you know that you must study very hard", his aunty said "if not for all the disturbances too Dike would have really gone far," his mother said. "By the way, what class are you doing now? Aunty Sarah asked, "Next school term I will be going to primary four," he replied. "You are doing fine for your age, so don't let anybody disturb you" aunty Sarah said. "My son you are not lagging behind what happened in the country is not your fault so anybody that complains about your academics then must be suffering from intense bad belle", his mother said. "Anyway I'm sure one more year from now I shall be in secondary school, looking back Dike could not help but agree with his mother. Besides he was still within his age range and moreover he was intelligent and he would enter secondary school from primary five, he vowed.

The much awaited broadcast of the head of state finally came during February of that year, a total of seven states were created while the people of Kalabar state were told "to learn how to live together".

This particular development did not go down well within the military and the civilian population. The military High Command did not care about the feelings of any group of people either. Events moved very fast and the nation was almost pushed into a civil war following the assassination of the new

Mike Effa

Head of State. In his broadcast the leader of the dissidents, a lieutenant colonel in the army and an indigene of Goma state described the late head of state as a dictator; a man without direction and vision. He concluded his speech by imposing the all too familiar dusk to dawn curfew and the closure of the nation's borders, seaports, airports and so on. Summary execution awaited anybody caught looting or involved in any acts of lawlessness. Troops were put on red alert in case of anything; the nation spent an eventful Friday without really knowing who was in charge.

But on the 14th of March, which was a Saturday, calm began to return to Ekko city following the disarming and arrest of the leader of the group. His arrest was somehow very dramatic. A colonel who incidentally was the youngest officer ever to serve in the supreme military council did the arrest.

With the brutal assassination of the Head of State, his second-in-command Lt. Gen. Olu Hakot took over control of the affairs of the nation.

The New Military administration swung into action immediately by setting in motion a panel that was given the responsibility of rounding up every coup suspect. With the nation still numb with shock over the brutal manner in which Gen. Bako was killed,

The Prisoner of Afrika

many political watchers cited instances, which may have led to his being killed on that fateful day in March. One of the reasons was his refusal to create a state off Kalabar state, a move which would have seen Lt. Col. Bitus being made a Military Administrator. Another school of thought also added that the assassination was sponsored by the United States following Gen. Bako's hard-line position on the Angolan crisis; therefore Lt. Col. Bitus had been a willing instrument in the hands of the CIA and had been used in planning and effecting the assassination of the Late Head of State. The new Head of State, an Engineer by profession and Sandhurst trained, continued to receive condolence visits from members of the Diplomatic Mission. Many world leaders telephoned personally to register their shock and disapproval of the assassination of the Late Afrikan strongman.

With the rebels finally dispatched to their graves and their lackeys serving various jail terms, the government of Gen. Olu Hakot and the nation in general heaved a sigh of relief. But, nobody was going to forget in a hurry the hide and seek game that Lt. Col. Bitus had played with the nation. To the Art world, the country had just won the right to host festival of Arts and culture known as FESTAC. This grand occasion which finally took place in September featured countries from different parts of the continent. Before the eventual commencement of this great event a lot of things in terms of structure have been put in place, Government had released millions of pounds to ensure that no hitches were experienced. A large piece of land had been acquired and blocks of flats built, it was commissioned and named Festal Town and hotels were built by the government, commissioned and named "Festal Group of Hotels. The Festac Mascot was a mask acquired from the ancient Bini Kingdom. Everybody was excited about this great occasion even when it was over, the excitement remained for quite some time, what nobody could tell was the profit or the gain in financial terms made by the nation, but one thing was obvious there were a lot of corrupt practices in the awarding of contracts. Within government circles, it was a guarded secret.

III

s the New Year progressed, the Military Regime of General Hakot unveiled a transition timetable and lifted the ban of politics. With this positive

development, politicians once more were let loose after about fifteen years or thereabout in the cooler. With a solid constitution to guide the nation, five political parties were given the green light to participate in the transition programme to the second Republic. To make room for total representation, limitation was not placed as to how many political parties were to come from any of the different parts of the country. Thus from the whole Northern part of the country three parties emerged, while the eastern and western part of the country had one each.

With a timetable in place election were to commence in December first with the Local Government Election, which were going to be on party basis. To ensure that the programme did not experience any hitches, the five parties were screened again. Then came party conventions, in which the different positions existing in the parties would be occupied. With the different convention concluded all the various political aspirants were known. The different parties began touring the nation because each party had members across the country. Throughout that period the nation was caught by the transition fever as parties traversed the Length and Breadth of the nation presenting manifestos and outlining programmes they will execute if voted into office.

The Military Government watched the political activities from the sidelines. The different parties in their quest to win the forthcoming elections committed themselves with some biting more than they could swallow. For instance, the leader of the political party from the western part of the country had told his listeners, "I will probe the Military if I am voted in office." Quite a brave thing to do against the Military, considering the fact that they had guns and could topple any civilian government in a jiffy.

Many people were happy with this speech because the Military had embezzled a lot of money especially earlier in the year when over three billion pounds had mysteriously disappeared from the nation's coffers. They had been rumours that the money was on its way to Europe probably to Switzerland but had fallen into the hands of Gen. Idi Amin, the Ugandan dictator and the Afrikan government was at a loss on how to recover the money.

To many people this was a smoke screen by the government, according to insiders the money was safe in a British Bank and lodged in the name of a construction firm and was operated as a fixed deposit account.

Therefore in the view of many Afrikans, if the leader of the United People's party would fulfil this promise of probing the Military then he should be given this opportunity. Following past events in the country and in other parts of the continent, every right thinking individual dreaded the Military because they were too violent and could shed blood with impunity, therefore politicians wanted to be in their good books. But here was a brave politician who was very willing to attack the military. The transition programmed gathered momentum with the local Government or county elections. At every polling station, voters queued up and waited their turns to cast their vote while soldiers armed to the teeth kept watch. Gradually, the elections continued at the different stages and in August that year the Republic of Afrika was going to have another Civilian president again. When results of the presidential elections were finally announced four days later it was not the united people's party that won the elections. The Military knew what they were doing; Gen. Harkot was not going to hand over power to a government that will hound them for the rest of their lives. While people were generally surprised at the election result, political analyst were not surprised because anybody who committed himself that much will certainly not get what he was gunning for. Petitions challenging the presidential elections were received and studied and even then nothing came out of it, the military began preparation for handing over power. At long last, after thirteen years the military was once again going back to the barracks.

IV

Dike sat for the Common Entrance Examination while in primary five and was successful and he also did well at the interview, which was conducted in the premises of the college he had chosen as his first choice. The result was sent to his parents two weeks after. "Congratulations," his parents had , "so you're going to secondary school!"

Everybody was happy that at last he was entering secondary school. His parents did not waste time they saw to it that everything listed in the prospectus was acquired without delay. In September, he reported to the Vice-Principal Administration accompanied by his parents who after greeting them warmly confirmed his formal admission into Government Secondary School, Bokkos. His parents saw him off to the hostel he had chosen to live in during the interview.

"Dike, remember your God," his father cautioned, "also study hard".

"I will" Dike promised. At the door they said their goodbyes and his parents returned to Kalabar.

As soon as his parents departed, he was overwhelmed by loneliness and was always shedding tears anytime he thought of home. His situation got more complex by what prevailed in "Govisco" as the secondary school was fondly called. With time he fought off the loneliness by making friends, soon he began to enjoy his environment, and getting involved in one mischief or the other in the name of adventure. Even though he was slightly older than most of the boy in his class, Dike was not bothered by this. Rather, he focused on passing his exam and moving on to a new class.

Then the twenty-ninth of November came being the date that Africa achieved independence from the British. The day was always marked with pomp and pageantry and this was not going to be an exception. Govisco had rehearsed for the past two weeks and were now set for D-Day which was only hours away. This particular independence anniversary was going to be special because once again after thirteen to fifteen years of Military ruler power was being handed over to the Civilians again. This particular action had been hailed by the developed nations as a very positive development. Everybody was in high spirits, though the handing over itself was taking place in Ekko city, which served as the seat of government, and capital city of the Republic of Afrika. Other parts of the country did also share in this great occasion by taking part in the March pass. Government secondary school being the oldest in Bokkos county was popular and because of that every father wanted his son to attend this great school which was almost like a "Spartan Training Camp".

Besides, the school was notorious for its high level of brutality which the school authorities felt was good for every boy therefore so no effort was made to check this hopeless situation. Govisco was also noted for its ability to cause trouble especially at football matches. The school overlooked the 103 Infantry Battalion and there had been reports of serious clashes between students and soldiers. However, on this particular day, a sense of friendliness ensued in the playground used for the parade.

Dike had wondered why his parents opted for this

The Prisoner of Afrika

school whereas there are good schools in Kalabar notably the Hope Waddell secondary school and St. Francis secondary school located at Harbour Estate; both schools were noted for exemplary standards. Their reasons were not farfetched. His parents wanted independence. And besides, Bokkos County was their place of origin. Some controversial uncles and aunts both ways were residing here. Mr. Shakkassalli in particular felt it would be good for his son to school here so that he could appreciate so many things about his place of origin as well as its rich culture. Moreover, this would afford Dike the opportunity of getting to know his cousins too, hence their decision to send him here.

The first term examination came earlier than scheduled and due to the nature of the examination timetable they finished their first term exams ahead of other schools, but the principal refused to close for the Christmas break. Students were angry, but the man knew what he was doing because any contrary actions will incur the wrath of the education authorities. Mr. Athenassius did not want to lose his job, so the students had to wait till the fifteenth of December when all Secondary schools were to officially close down for the Christmas break.

Mike Effa

An idle mind is a devil 's workshop as, the saying goes. In the midst of the idleness Dike sneaked out of school and went to town with one of his older cousins as they went to the river which was just behind the house . The very same river that his parents had warned against.

"In the least, I'm not swimming," he said to himself. Dike sat on a big rock and watched while others had a nice time swimming. His cousins made jest of him.

"Mr. Stone", they had shouted. He looked away and pretended not to hear,

"Come in and swim. You will not drown ". They all laughed and swam deeper, when they were tired of swimming they came out and they left for home.

"Did you swim?" one of his aunties inquired.

"No, he does not know how to swim," a cousin replied

"He's as heavy as a stone ", another cousin added.

When he could not stomach the mockery anymore Dike lashed out. "Will you leave me alone; is it everybody that must swim?"

He asked nobody in particular. On Sunday, he and his cousin returned to school. On the way, they had met a friend of their family. He questioned why Dike was not in school. Dike could not give him a

The Prisoner of Afrika

favourable answer. Two days after returning to school, he took ill and was vomiting seriously. He was disturbed by this negative development and started wondering if he had not eaten something funny. One Friday afternoon, a week before closing, his eldest brother came and was permitted to take him home. Meanwhile his guardian in school had explained what happened and Dike's brother was fuming with rage.

"Papa will hear this", his brother said, " Please don't tell him now", he pleaded.

"I didn't swim, I only sat and watched".

They left Bokkos that same day arriving in the City shortly before 6.30 p.m. almost a three-hour journey. Their parents and other members of the family were happy to see them. But things went sour when his parents were informed of his adventure to town after the first term exams. His parents were angry but he was not punished, eventually the first term results came and he placed third out of fifty. A result that saved him from the wrath of his parents. He vowed to himself never to go near the town; even less of going to the river with any of his cousins again .

Chapter Seven

With the transition Programme successfully implemented and the soldiers safely tucked in their barracks, the stage was set for a new administration and one without arms. Afrikans had a cause to be happy. Then the New Year rolled in and the nation watched eagerly for the change that the politicians had promised to set in motion, programmes that were supposed to change the life of the masses. The average man on the street was willing to give the new government in the least a year to settle down and then use the remaining three years to change many things.. The Afrikan congress was one of the parties that reflected mass followership across the country; everybody was willing to bury deep-seated hatred and suspicions in their quest for a United and prosperous nation. This was one of the factors, and coupled with the enticing programmes billed for implementation if voted into office that eventually saw Alhaji Shehu Badamasi and his colleagues get the mandate to rule the most populous nation in the continent for the next four years. If experience was anything to go by, the politicians it appeared had learnt a lot from the mistakes made by their colleagues in the first Republic mistakes that had led to an orgy of rape, and wanton bloodletting, it was imperative that the new government imbibe the spirit of fair play. The current year rolled out with hope, for a better and prosperous new year. The budget for the year was read by President Badamasi. The future looked very promising.

Dike had returned to school a few days after the New Year to start his second term. At this time of the year the harmattan was its peak, and in Govisco the morning bell was usually sounded at 5:30 a. m in the morning. Woe betide any junior student who did not jump down from his bed to prepare for the day's activities. Normally, when the bell goes early in the morning, they all assemble under a tall casuarina tree complete with their buckets and cutlasses still feeling groggy. After the morning prayers, they are divided into two groups and marched off like prisoners in a war camp. Out of the two groups, one group supplies water to the school tank while the other group weeds the pavement. Immediately after the early morning bell, the Labour

The Prisoner of Afrika

Prefect armed with a very long cane would conduct a thorough search of the five hostels to fish out those students who refuse to come out. Pity any student he found in bed. He would be mercilessly thrashed, which turned out a bad way to begin a new day. In Govisco it was a must that respect is accorded to students based on their class, with such an arrangement it is only the Class One students that are losers because they must respect every other person with no persons to respect them. Some Class One boys decided to ignore this. One Wednesday evening, they had gone to the stream to cool down, Dike had just finished stripping when two boys average in height appeared from the path that led to the school premises. They thought they were all colleagues; they even invited them to join in the fun when one of them replied harshly.

"Did you hear what these foxes with smelling tails just said?" he asked the other.

His friend did not answer but rather contorted his face in a manner that made everybody burst into laughter.

"You are laughing at me?" The other boy charged. "All of you kneel down", he screamed. The class one boys just stood where they were and watched him rage, when it seemed they were not going to obey, his friend in a fit of rage slapped the boy standing next to Dike, they were dumbfounded.

"Idiot", the boy said slapping him back.

Dike moved in immediately and pushed his classmate away not knowing what else to do.

"You dare to slap a class two boy" his friend said. "Come on let's go", his friend who had just been slapped said pulling him along, both boys disappeared along the path; they were not quite sure of what the boys were going to do.

"So they are in class two?" Dike asked, quite oblivious of this.

"No wonder they are so proud", one of the boys replied. They changed their minds got dressed and made for the school.

"Being in class two does not give anybody the right to slap a class one student", the boy who had just been slapped said still rubbing his left jaw to ease the pain. They had thought everything was over with the conflict. When they reached their dormitories, it was almost half past six, Dike took his cutleries and headed for the refectory to have his dinner and then leave for evening prep. There were no signs to warn them of any trouble. The doors were opened and they went in class by class and took their seats. The prayer before meal was said by a Class Four student who mistakenly missed a line. The act earned him an "Ogadi". Dike had initially wondered what this meant; it was during his second term that he came to know it meant a painful slap on the back. They had hardly touched their food when a Class Five student charged towards the class one section.

"Drop your cutleries and put your hands on your head", he ordered. They dropped them and surrendered accordingly. His order was just like what you normally see in war films, when an enemy soldier is captured he puts his two hands on his head as a way of telling his captors that it's over for him. Their hands remained up for almost five minutes; Dike could not exactly focus on what could have happened to earn them this "War film" punishment. When his hands began to ache, he looked around their captor was of outsight he seized the opportunity and dropped his hands for some seconds, then he put them up again. Immediately he put up his hands, their captor appeared and came directly towards him and stopped a few yards from Dike, gave him a "Hitler like" look, then just before he turned to go he said. "If I perch on you, you will contract". Dike was not surprised as he suspected that he might have been watching from one of the refectory windows. The Class one Boys spent some extra minutes in the refectory while other classes finished their meal and left the refectory. Eventually their captor decided to let them finish their meal and leave the refectory but only after flogging the class one boy who had committed the offence. He left the dormitory for the classroom as soon as he dropped his cutleries. For the rest of the evening, they were all subdued, Dike was reading or rather pretending to read, his mind was miles away he was wondering why that Class Five student would above other things decide to perch on him as though he was a tree. The point here was Dike was still too fresh to comprehend so many things; it would take another two to three years for him to really understand the ways of the so-called Senior students. The 9: 30 pm bell indicating the end of the day's activities for the junior students eventually sounded and they left the class for the dormitory to sleep.

II

"Uneasy lies the head that wears the crown", the saying goes. The Civilian Administration was beginning to see the intricacies involved in governance.

The Prisoner of Afrika

Problems began to rear its ugly head at both the House of Senate and the House of Reps respectively. Being a multi-party system, the ruling party, the Afrikan Congress Party had to put up with a lot of opposition from other parties. Appointment of Ministers and other key government positions benefited members of the ruling party. When the opposition got to a point that the ruling party could no longer tolerate, the minister of Internal Affairs ordered the deportation of the minority leader of the House of Reps on the grounds that he was not an Afrikan National, but a citizen of Chad Republic. The controversy dragged on for some time before it was finally resolved. The ACP now resorted to arresting opponents on the ground that they were not citizens, because of this arm bending tactics; opponents of the Afrikan Congress Party simmered down a bit, and the ruling party now had its way but this was only in Ekko city. The ruling experienced frustration at its worst in the Western and Mid-Western States. In politics, especially in this part of the world, the ability of a party in office to get a return ticket in the next elections will depend to a large extent on its achievements while in office. Therefore while the Afrikan Congress fought and worked hard to ensure a return ticket the other parties ensured that the ACP programmes never made any progress. Money released by the Federal Government to the different states was properly used where Afrikan Congress Party candidates were governors while in the other states where the ruling party did not have a strong hold the money was either delayed in the banks or diverted for personal interest. Cases of fraud and embezzlement began to rock the nation. Yet, the Federal Government was too weak to act, a weakness, which its opponents capitalized on to, enrich their foul smelling pockets. Suddenly the politicians who were initially very docile became uncontrollable overnight. Contracts were awarded to friends and family members who were encouraged to do only five percent of the job then abandon the contract entirely. Close watchers of the civilian administration knew exactly what would follow if the politicians did not behave.

"Don't be surprised, that the Military will return to power very soon", Dike had overheard his father remark to a friend.

"Really I won't be, because the ruling party has become a toothless bulldog". The friend replied, he couldn't wait to listen anymore he sauntered off to do something else. Then in 1981 they were forced to go home when teachers in the whole state went on strike following inability of the state government to pay salaries. While the teachers were angry with the state government, they in turn blamed the Federal Government. The irony of it all is that Kalabar State being a stronghold of the ruling party could never be deprived of funds. The State Governor had diverted over two million Afripounds meant for teacher's salary into constructing a road to his village to ensure a smooth ride for his late father's corpse. While the governor was busy with the burial of his father, teachers in the state had stopped work due to non-payment of salaries for almost eight months. Strikes were not a new thing to Dike in particular, the teachers could not be bullied or coerced into returning to school so the strike persisted. The only solution came from the same person who caused it. How he did it, nobody knew. Neither did anybody care to know. All that interested the people was the fact that their wards were going back to school.

III

he Civilian Administration it was now clear had lost direction and was drifting like a ship without a rudder. The Western and Mid-Western States were enjoying

free education while other parts weren't. Although this was quite understandable because the UPP leader had promised free education besides probing the Military, those states controlled by his party had to enjoy free education, things went from bad to worse. The masses became visibly hopeless., Salaries were no longer paid regularly, . It got to a stage civil servants could not get their salaries for almost six months. They could not go on strike because their leaders having been bribed were not willing to disappoint the government. Things became very bad for the masses; it was even difficult to afford a decent meal daily there was despair everywhere.

"All this nonsense will end very soon", Mr. Shakkassalli said to his second son one afternoon. Then he was in Class Four in Govisco. "I thought the politicians had learnt something from the past "

"The government has lost control," Dike said.

"The only remedy lies in the return of the Military," his father said, apparently annoyed at everything. It was clear the politicians were baiting the Military, and it was clear, they would launch a strike action soon but nobody knew when. The constitution allows a democratically elected government to spend four years in office, after which it was to seek re-election.

Towards the end of their first tenure, the nation was again gripped with election fever. It was time again for the ruling party to test its popularity. To get people to vote for them, the ruling party had to entice the masses especially in areas that requested for additional states. Meanwhile, more counties had been carved out of the existing ones. Kalabar State, which had seventeen counties now, fathered forty-seven. The exercise had been bastardized to the extent that the county the speaker of the State House of Assembly came from was divided into two With father's village becoming a county while his mother's village was also made a county, the masses were tempted to believe it all during a campaign trip, the Senate President, Dr. Boco Waires an indigene of Kalabar State had told his gullible audience more lies.

"You want a state? " He had asked.

"Yes-s----s-s, they chorused excitedly.

"Vote for the ACP and you will get a state in fact the state is right now in my pocket, I can give it to you here". He said. The crowd mostly motor park touts, market women and school children who did not know their left from their right and who were not there because they understood all the jargons and big grammar, but because of their desire to see the beautiful cars the politicians rode in. The campaign train traversed the length and breadth of the country, other political parties were not left out, the two most vocal political parties; The Patriotic Trust Front (PTF) and the United Peoples Party spent most of their campaign time deriding the ruling party and telling its audience why the Afrikan Congress Party should not be voted for. While the campaigns lasted, many people especially those in the working class watched the politicians and their gullible audience with contempt. They would not be swayed by the lies that the ruling party was telling its audience nor would they be moved by the campaign of calumny the other parties were waging. The elections came and the Afrikan Congress Party emerged winner., Other parties challenged the results and dragged the ACP to the election tribunal where the results were upheld and the other parties asked to pay a fine to the winners. This victory, on its part, proved true the saying that "you can't beat an incumbent". Especially, in the black continent of Africa. The election was marred with mass rigging and violence; civil servants were forced to vote against their choice. You had to vote in favour of the ruling party or lose your job. At this point in time, life had become terribly difficult for the masses especially, as the nation's treasury had been looted completely. Salaries were no longer being paid. The politicians in their timidity and foolishness still had the temerity to beat their chests and tell the whole world, that they had done very well in their first four years in office. The media were not left out in the lambasting of the politicians. Various dailies carried articles calling on the government to resign in that they had failed. The voice newspaper reflecting on the last four years that the politicians had held power highlighted the calamities that had followed the government; earlier in the year the imposing telecommunication building had been gulfed by fire. Fortunately, no lives were lost. Then in the third quarter of the year, an Airbus 310 belonging to the Afrikan Airways had crashed and burst into flames while attempting to land with thirty souls sent to eternity., Several diseases were ravaging the people while the hospitals had become mere consulting rooms. The politicians and their families and friends on the sign of even a slight headache were flown abroad for treatment. Many cities had become very dirty. Refuse was being dumped everywhere and politicians did not care. No one could blame them because most of them like the Senate President and many state governors lagged academically, in fact they were semi-illiterates. But what confounded people was the manner in which the Senate President was addressed which in turn raised questions as to where he got his doctorate degree. While the Senate President was okay in terms of spoken English and ability to engage in any topic of discussion raised., This was not the case with most governors. For instance, the governor of Dogawa State when asked about the mineral potentials of the state had quickly replied;

Dogowa State is rich in minerals such as siprite, panta, cwoke etc. The reporters not able to hold themselves had burst into laughter so one could not really blame them for their inability to tackle certain issues. But squandering the wealth of a whole country was unpardonable and this was one of the grievous crimes the politicians had committed against the masses.

"At the rate things are moving another period of anarchy is not too far," the voice newspaper warned. "I hope the politicians are not indirectly inviting the khaki boys to seize power again "it concluded.

nless the Military intervenes only then can we be spared the agony of another orgy of bloodshed and arson," Mrs Shakkassalli said.

"I hope school will resume soon," Dike prayed and indeed the schools had resumed once more, with him reporting like other students, but two weeks later he was sent back due to inability to pay school fees. It was not his fault, neither was it his father's fault after all their salaries for the last six months hadn't been paid yet. To say the least, the victory of the Afrikan Congress party had shaken every true citizen of this great nation because this negative development signalled another four years of depravity, mismanagement, embezzlement, and fraud in high places. Despite promises of better things to come, the people's anxiety could not be lessened. Government had given the green light for parboiled rice from Thailand to counter the activities of rice hoarders and bring relief to the suffering masses, instead the minister of transport who was the Chairman of the task force on importation of Rice had made a mess of the project and over twenty million Afripounds lost to fraudulent practices. Importation of goods had suffered a setback due to a lot of irregularities in the issuing of import licences. There was despair clearly written on the faces of everybody and there seemed to be no solution in sight. The question on everybody's lips was," when will the suffering end"

Here stood a nation that was once prosperous, but behold it had been laid waste by politicians who were still wet behind the ears and as such could not rule over fifty million people who made things easier for them by voting and giving them the mandate to rule. The politicians had abused this mandate and definitely will pay for their crimes either in the present or in the future, only time would tell.

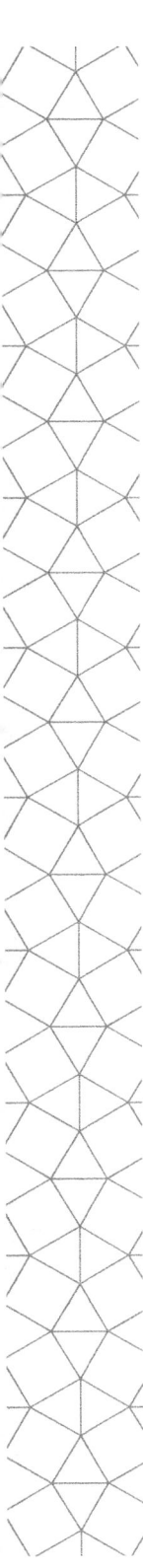

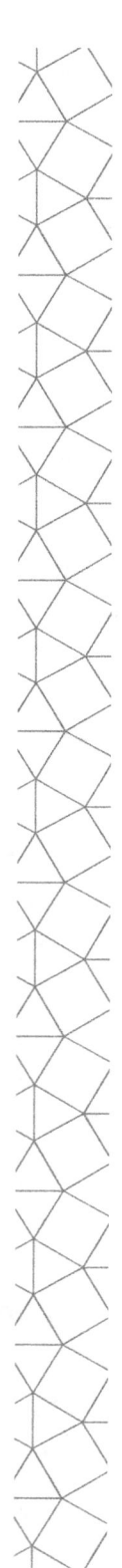

126

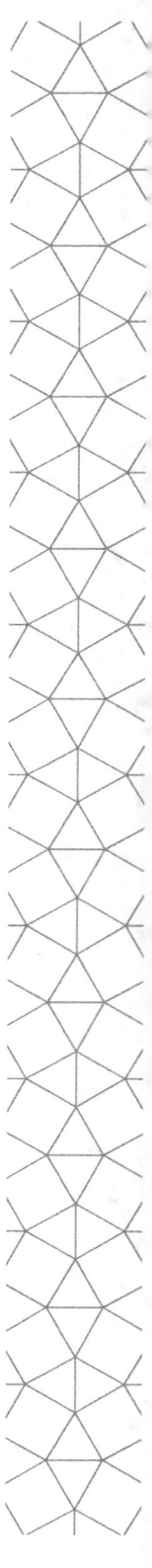

Chapter Eight

Following the victory of the Afrika congress party at the polls, the defeated parties had headed for the tribunal with the hope of getting a redress. When the verdict was made known the press, especially when the nation's number one newspaper, the carrier had made it a headline story. "Fraud of the decade" the headline screamed. The voice, a newspaper based in Ekko city, had been more vocal. In its editorial, the voice had called on the judiciary. to stop abetting corruption by defending a party, as well as a government, that had betrayed the sacred trust of the people.

The condemnation of the verdict had not gone down well with the government that had reacted by arresting the editor and deputy editor of both newspapers. While they could understand the position of the voice, that of the carrier was unpardonable for being a government newspaper it had been expected it defend the government every time.

"This government is stupid arresting journalists is a negative trend in democratic societies,". Dike heard a man remark on reading the latest development in the country.

"Truth is bitter" his friend said.

"The government cannot stand the truth" a man said. "Arresting journalist is a very bad thing to do" he concluded as they continued strolling along the way.

"But what does the government hope to gain from this dastard act?" his friend asked again.

"Last year, a journalist was killed, this is an attempt to silence the press and keep the nation in darkness while they continue their misrule".

Unfortunately, the arrest and subsequent detention of the journalists had not gone down well with the people as a result of which the following morning had seen demonstrators blocking certain part of the capital in protest. The demonstrators had blocked Pearl Avenue with placards that read, Release them now" "Arrest of journalist undemocratic and et cetera. Many other places like coca-cola square, Bata Avenue and many streets were blocked. Traffic was brought to a standstill. The demonstration was going on peacefully till at about half past one in the afternoon when the police arrive and began tear gassing demonstrators. A Peaceful demonstration turned violent as demonstrators" in-turn attacked the

The Prisoner of Afrika

police and hell was let loose, in the process scores of people were killed. The police and the government had failed, though more people were arrested for disturbing public peace. The news was full of the demonstration; the evening newspapers carried headlines of the day's event. At about half past one the next day the demonstrators converged and again there was confusion. Soon, the confusion spread to other parts of the country. The day after, the various dailies carried stories of arson, rape and plunder. In an interview the government spokesman had allayed fears that there was no cause for alarm, meanwhile lives had been lost and many more were being decimated at a terrible pace.

His mother summoned him for the morning prayers which was brief. With the last amen said, Dike was about rushing out when his dad walked into the parlour and turned on his powerful transistor radio to the voice of Afrika which was beginning transmission at 6. 00 0"clock in the morning.

The programme announcer had hardly started when she was cut off, then the national anthem followed. After a few seconds a strange baritone voice followed, "My fellow country men and

Mike Effa

women, this is Brigadier Sani Ahmed General Officer commanding 2 mechanized division of the Afrikan army. I speak to you this morning at a very sad moment in the history of our nation. You have all been witness to the tragic events of the last three days in which many properties belonging to government, individuals have been destroyed, and many people injured with many lives lost. It is now obvious that law and order has broken down and it is also clear that this administration has become inefficient, corrupt and too weak to contain the situation. To prevent a further deterioration in this very ugly situation the progressive and peace loving Army of the Federal Republic of Afrika has decided to take over the administration of the country till such a time as it considers fit to return power to a more purposeful civilian government. When the time comes such a government will be elected by the people freely exercising their vote without the gross abuse to which elections have been subjected within the short space of time since we started our existence as an independent nation.

Fellow countrymen and women the entry of the armed forces into politics has been necessitated in order to salvage the economy of this country from total collapse. You will agree with me that our great

The Prisoner of Afrika

and beloved country has become a beggar in the International Community. . It is common sight to see the civilian administration cap in hand going up and down on various begging missions. The Army had intervened solely to check this disgraceful and demeaning act by the politicians who no longer knew what to do besides begging money from European countries.

I urge you all to remain law abiding and to go about your businesses without any hindrance with the interest of the nation first and foremost in our minds.

We should together ask for divine guidance in the common task of retrieving our great nation from the depth of poverty and degradation to which it had been plunged by self-seeking politicians to the height of prosperity, peace and happiness for all our peoples, and dignity among nations of the world.

All borders and airports are hereby closed till further notice. Long live the Armed Forces of Afrika Republic. Long Live Afrika Thank you all.".

After the Anthem there was a spell of silence in the parlour everybody was reflecting on what had just happened.

"I had always felt it in my bones, " their father said breaking the silence.

"What a terrible way to start the New Year, " his wife said joining the discussion which was beginning to gather momentum.

"That is the repercussion for fraud and corruption. " Dike said just as Brig. Ahmed's voice came back on the airwaves with a more definite announcement. "Politicians are advised in their own interest to safeguard government property under them and also to appear in the nearest police station. Failure to comply with this directive meant that such culprits would be summarily dealt with". The Army spokesman once more reminded the entire citizens of Afrika to remain peaceful and law abiding as the Armed Forces had done everything to ensure safety of lives and property. At this point Brigadier Ahmed signed off again while the voice of Afrika continued to play martial music.

"This is the price the politicians must pay for mismanagement and fraud", Dike added "The new year starts a few hours from now", one of his sisters said.

"What a new year for the politicians", their mother said.

"A gloomy one at that", Kris said looking outside the window. Throughout the day, transmission by voice of Afrika was dominated by martial music and occasional announcements by Brig. Ahmed. Towards midday, a clearer picture of the officers who planned and executed the coup began to emerge. The next announcement, informed bewildered Afrikans as to who was going to be the Head of state and also the service chiefs. People were not surprised when the name of the Head of State was mentioned. General Attah disliked politicians with a passion; he was one officer who had never hid his dislike for the political class. Things came to a point, when as a Brigade Commander in 1981, he used excessive force in driving a band of refugees from the neighbouring Chad Republic. The politicians had not been happy with this, but the General had remained adamant justifying his actions based on the conviction that such groups were responsible for the high wave of armed robbery in that part of the country. This development had made him distance himself from the politicians. Being a disciplined officer, everybody was convinced he was the right choice for the position of Commander-in-chief. The Chief of Staff Supreme Headquarters was another no-nonsense officer. The two a formidable force supported by their colleagues, the nation's economy would be on the course of revival once again. With their assumption of office on 1st January 1985, the new regime suspended the constitution, retired all Senior Military Officers including the then Inspector-General of Police who had announced to the press before the coup that "thirty million Afripounds meant for Police welfare had disappeared into thin air". The politicians being the corrupt people that they were had not bothered to order an investigation. Even then the Police boss got away with it because the new government didn't want to probe their colleagues. Then the government ordered all politicians be arrested and detained while investigations went on to ascertain those who had embezzled public funds. Before the coup took place, certain ministers had gotten wind of the situation and had fled the country notably amongst the asylum seekers was the Minister for Transport and Chairman Task Force on importation of Rice. Many party officials had fled abroad too. With this new directive, the nation was divided into four zones, each zone had a tribunal where suspected embezzlers were to undergo trial and if found guilty be sentenced to various jail terms. Afrikans were happy at the turn of event especially Kalabarians because under the current dispensation the former governor of Kalabar State who was being held in

The Prisoner of Afrika

Goma State prison would soon be asked to give account of his stewardship. But unknown to many, it was not going to be. As soon as Military Governors were appointed, the military governor of Kalabar State destroyed the files that would have sent Chief Jameston to prison. Eventually, when it was his turn he was discharged due to lack of evidence. But later on, Commander Archieson was removed as governor and dismissed from the Navy for acts of indiscipline that ranged from drinking to sleeping in the office during working hours. A lot began to happen in the country. The Government House was moved from Marina Road to Reje Crescent, which was a very neat area and well planned. Unlike the Marina Road that smelt of weeds and rotting herbs. Many people had judged the coup as one of the most peaceful in the continent unlike the coup in Togo, the first coup in Nigeria and the coup in Liberia respectively. These countries had experience very violent Military interventions, all the civilian leaders in each of these countries had been brutally murdered by the so-called Revolutionaries. Thus, to many people what had just happened in Afrika was child's play compared to these countries.

Mike Effa

Dike returned to school once more to start the second term, unlike the good old days when he used to return to school loaded with provisions and pocket money. This time things had taken a different dimension. Following non-payment of salaries, his father barely managed to gather just his school fees so that he will not be sent home.

"Dike" his father had called that morning.

"Yes dad", he answered expecting something not really pleasant, because he could see his face was not cheerful.

"You've got to manage for the time being till salaries are paid which could be sooner or later no one knows," he said. "Yes Sir", Dike answered totally drained of the will to protest. He collected his fees and the little pocket money made available, bade them farewell and left for the Motor Park. Their driver gave him a ride to the park, which was about thirty minutes from their house. Fortunately, he found a Taxi with just one chance left he took the seat the driver wished him a safe journey and left for the house. Dike was lost in thoughts, all the while the man in charge of loading had been talking to him but his voice seemed to come from a distance. It was only when he nudged him that he came out of his reverie; He looked at him and demanded what he wanted. "Oga, abeg gie me your moni", he said in Pidgin English.

"How much is it?" He asked

"Oga from here to bokkos Na twenty-five Afripounds, "he said Dike dipped his hand into his pocket brought out some money and paid him and he issued a ticket and walked off.

Throughout the journey, which lasted over three hours, Dike was completely lost in thoughts he was totally unaware of his immediate environment. On reaching Bokkos, he took a bus from the park to the school compound. The school premises looked very dry, half of the students had returned, January being the peak for the Harmattan period meant there would be no grass to cut but they had the morning cold to contend with. Their only solace laid in the fact that shortly the government will be handed over to them to enable the Class Five students prepare for the school certificate Exams, which was in May and June of every year. He headed to the Accounts Department and paid his fees for the term. He was surprised to see the office open on Saturday, which was not a working day. On inquiring, he was informed the measure was taken to avoid cases of school fees being stolen from returning students. It was a very nice measure because in the past many boys had lost princely sums of money to "dormitory rats". The school authorities wanted to put an end to this negative and ugly development hence the measure. After setting down he began to search for his friends and other classmates whom they related on certain levels. A week after academic activities picked up, in the morning they went for lectures, and after the day's activities they went for evening prep. One Saturday evening, Dike went to read with a close friend Henry. While opening his book, a letter he had written to his sister who was working in Ekko city fell out. Henry picked it up and started reading it.

"So you like military regimes?" Henry asked without taking his eyes off the letter.

Dike laughed at his question, he remembered starting the letter by asking Ninkai his eldest sister her opinion on the coup that had just occurred. He did not answer Henry's question, he gave back the letter.

"I like Military regimes too, Henry said. " when I finish my school certificate, I intend to proceed to the Defence Academy where I will qualify as an Army doctor then I will come and marry your sister " he said. They all laughed, "So what are your plans for the future?" Henry asked.

"Not as ambitious and daring as yours" he said smiling. "After here I intend to study law and become a SAA and put corrupt politicians behind bars just like the military are doing.

"You think khaki boys are saints?" Henry asked. "Remember the past years; I can assure you that Afrikans will not see any difference between the military and the politicians".

Dike kept quiet for a while.

"Well there's not much we can do except trust God to take us to the promise land by giving us good leaders with the fear of God in their hearts". "Let's just keep praying, " Henry said.

Henry's anger at the Military could be understood. His father was a politician in the administration that had just been toppled and was still being held for questioning and likely go to jail for embezzlement

II

The tribunals set up to investigate politicians were doing their jobs very well as reported by most dailies, Governor jailed for two hundred years, that was a caption on the front page of the African

Herald.

Dike had not seen it initially. It was Henry who first saw it and decided to attract attention to the story.

"What? Two hundred years", Dike asked in serious doubt Henry decided to read it all.

"The civilian Governor of Bida state, Dr. Rafiu Aboki yesterday afternoon was sentenced to a jail term of two hundred years. Handing down the verdict, the chairman of the tribunal Navy Commodore kilo Suleiman said the governor had been found guilty of all the four count charges levelled against him hence the sentence".

"What about his assets?" Dike asked shaking his head.

"The government has seized all of it there is a decree to that too", Henry, said.

"So if you are found guilty and convicted you lose your assets?" he asked again.

"Yes that is what it implies", Henry replied.

The Armed Forces it was very clear was really serious with cleaning the country and purging it of corruption both economically and health wise a move, which had led to the declaration of every Saturday for environmental sanitation and the launching of a crusade against indiscipline and disorderliness in public places. These was a good and very positive catalyst for moral development, which had been thrown to the dogs during the political era.

If there was any country that needed a sanitation edict, it was his beloved country. Right from Ekko city, the capital seat of government to the last local county, all reeked with filth. It was a common sight during the ill-fated second Republic to see people openly dumping refuse in public places the whole country smelled terribly, the after effects of refuse dumping without control. Thus, the essence of the environmental sanitation was to rid the country's public places of unsightly refuse and reduce the outbreak of epidemics and other preventable diseases. To give impetus to this exercise a decree was enacted and signed by Maj. Gen. Tunde Akoka, Chief of Staff Supreme Headquarters. To build up the spirits of the people, awards of huge sums of money was introduced for the cleanest state capital, local county etc. Dumping refuse illegally or loitering during sanitation hours if caught carried a jail sentence of three years, or an option of fine of up to five thousand Afripounds. The odds were against everybody especially the masses; therefore it was necessary for Afrikans to be careful. While the new regime was trying to come to grips with the situation, Brig Ahmed the officer who announced the coup stormed Ekko city to protest the fact that he was not adequately compensated for his role in the coup which toppled the civilian Administration, he was unfortunately arrested and detained for twenty days after which he was released and sent to Mokola state the Headquarters of 2 mechanized Division. The signs of discord had been sown, thus. A few months thereafter Brig. Ahmed was promoted to the rank of Major–General, but his posting did not change.

Before the coup, many Afrikans had become heavily involved in drugs. Overnight Afrika had become the Columbia of the African continent as drug barons used the various airports as transit routes. The situation took a dangerous dimension when Afrika became a consumer or user nation. Top politicians were involved in this illegal business, so were top officers in the armed forces and it cut across both serving and retired officers.

Thus, when the army seized power and a decree was promulgated making drug trafficking a treasonable offence punishable either through death or by hanging or firing squad, nobody heeded this decree till three young men were arrested at the Dogawa International Airport with over ten grams of pure heroin. Their passports were seized following their arrest. They were arraigned before a tribunal, which found them guilty on a two, count charge of importing drugs into the country. With little or no chance for defence, sentence was passed on them,: "death by firing squad subject to confirmation by the supreme military council".

Appeals began to flood Ekko city and Reje crescent, the seat of government for clemency and a committal of the death sentences to life. The controversy dragged on

For some time nothing was heard of the drug saga. But the next day was one Afrikans were never to forget. It was a holiday. Dike Shakkassalli got up as usual completed the morning chores and decided to visit the news stand after the sanitation exercise. Together with Kris and Rhoda their younger sister headed for the newsstand, the headline "DRUG SUSPECTS EXECUTED", which formed the lead story on the front page of the Kalabar Chronicle, was boldly displayed. Dike nudged his brother Kris whom together they had come to buy newspapers for their dad that morning.

"Look at this", he said pointing at the front page, of

the Kalabar Chronicle, his brother looked at it and was quiet. "Yesterday, I had a serious argument about this in the bus with other passengers because of this" Dike said.

"Let's pay for one copy and get out of here, we will get the whole gist at home", Kris said, paying the vendor in the process. When their father saw it he was flabbergasted.

"Wha-a-a-t," he exclaimed. Mrs. Shakkassalli was the first to appear.

"What is wrong?" she asked her husband.

"Look at this", he pointed at the front page of the newspaper. "Listen while I read; "Drug suspects executed", he began. "Three young men who were arrested at Dogawa International Airport with ten grams of pure heroin were executed in the early hours of Saturday. " He paused then he continued. "According to our correspondents the three young men were tried by a Military tribunal which found them guilty on a two count charge of importing hard drugs into the country and endangering the lives of people through their illicit trade . The sentences were ratified by the Supreme Military Council which met yesterday. After the meeting, while fielding questions from reporters the Minister for justice and Attorney- General of the Federation had reiterated Government's position on drug trafficking by saying and we quote, "This government is committed to restoring sanity in our nation, because this is the only country we have. Therefore, this get-rich-quick mania must be drastically curtailed. Gentlemen, death for convicted drug traffickers have come to stay thank you". The minister had concluded. Reactions of different shades poured in, the nation was numbed except for the Military of course.

"A female journalist sent to cover the event had fainted" Dike said looking at his dad with a frown.

"Who told you that?" He countered. Dike pointed at the back of the newspaper. While his father was reading it, his mother was surprised to hear this new development.

"Why should they send a lady to cover such a terrifying event" She asked.

"What a man can do a woman-", shut up his dad ordered,

After this incident no other execution took place, but arrest of traffickers continued. The government continued to jail politicians who embezzled money. Then in June the government asked the British authorities to extradite the former Minister of Aviation back to Afrika to stand trial. While the British authorities were considering the proposal, rather than keep quiet the former Minister began his attack on the Military by mounting campaigns and abusing the head of state and other members of the Supreme Military Council. Nobody responded to his tirade of abuses, the government rather decided to keep silent in the face this attack against it. Then three weeks later the whole world was stunned with the strange event that took place in London. There had been attempts to kidnap Dr. Usman to an unknown destination; everybody was surprised at this. More so, it had occurred in broad daylight. Information was scanty at first, but towards evening it became clear who had organized the kidnap attempts, which if it had succeeded would have made Delta Force commander Lee Marvin Green with envy. Angered by Dr. Usman's attack against it, the government had wanted to teach him a lesson by bringing him back to stand trial thus a kidnap team comprising of an Israeli, a major in the Afrikan army and also an ex-SAS Captain had all been quietly assembled in London. They had gained access to Dr. Usman's residence drugged him after which they drive to Gatwick Airport where an Afrika Boeing 737 waited on the tarmac to receive a "diplomatic baggage". Unfortunately for the assault team, the former Minister's steward on discovering his Master had disappeared immediately alerted the police who acting on tip-off drove straight to the Airport where they identified the Blue Dodge that other inhabitants of Park lane had seen drive away from Dr. Usman's house at break neck speed. On searching, the police found a crate labelled "Diplomatic baggage, property of the Afrikan Embassy". Suspecting something funny, the British authorities breached protocol and proceeded to examine the crate only for them to find a grown man whom they identified as Dr. Usman, drugged, gagged, and stowed in a crate to be airlifted back to his country. The three occupants of the Dodge Van were arrested and the Boeing 737 parked at Gatwick Airport was impounded. The Military in Afrika responded by impounding a Boeing 747 Jumbo jet belonging to British Caledonia, as well as an airbus belonging to Danish airlines. Both countries recalled their High commissioners; the Military Authorities went a step further by calling on other countries especially members of the UNO to place sanctions on Britain. Throughout its stay in office, there was no diplomatic activity between Afrika and these countries. With the kidnap saga watered down by actions and reactions, the Military Junta continued its trial and sentencing of guilty politicians. One morning going through the voice of a national daily, Dike saw a story "Woman arrested for drug possession",

"aha", he said loudly and a bit excited.

"What's happening again?" Kris asked.

"A woman has been arrested for carrying drugs", he replied pointing to the page.

"Drugs?" one of his sisters Roda asked very surprised.

"People will never learn in this world", Dike said.

"Can I go through the story?" she requested.

"I will read it for everybody", he replied "woman arrested for drug possession", he began, "Narcotics agents at Dogawa International Airport yesterday afternoon arrested a woman with ten grams of substance suspected to be heroine. The substance was contained in the battery compartment of a Radio set. The lady who was identified as Modestus Adebo said the radio was given to her in Brussels by a male friend of hers to deliver to his parents in the village. The lady's passport was impounded and—"He was cut short by another question.

"Are they going to shoot her too?" Rhoda asked.

"No one knows yet for now she is under arrest"

Dike answered attempting to satisfy her curiosity.

Following her arrest, Modestus was arraigned before

The Prisoner of Afrika

a Military tribunal, which jailed her for life; on her way to prison she vowed to mention all the big wigs involved in the deal. But she never had the chance, three weeks later according to a newspaper report Modestus was dead. But then, she had to talk to one or two persons already and the names involved would send a cold shiver down anybody's spine. Nobody gave much thought to this any longer, but the issue remained on the minds of those involved.

Gen. Attah's crusade against drug trafficking, indiscipline and corruption, as well as the weekly cleaning up of gutters as well as major streets was yielding fruits. For once, Afrika became a sane and disciplined society. People were now conducting themselves in market places and at bus stops. The regime apart from its crusade on the ills plaguing the society, which was very much in order, the Head of State and his colleagues, carried their war on sanitizing the society too far by enacting the infamous Decree No. 2 this decree forbidden the press from criticizing Military officers as well as the Civilians holding political officers. The military Junta did not have patience for University students, a position which the Chief of Staff Supreme Headquarters did not hesitate in elaborating when he addressed a press conference. He had reiterated government position on student unrest and had concluded by stating that any act of student unrest would be violently suppressed. Furthermore, all University students were to pay the sum of one thousand Afripounds every session and he meal ticket system under which student were fed at subsidised rates was abolished forthwith. Gen. Attah and his colleagues, it now appeared were turning their anger on the same people they had come to save from the clutches of the politicians. Despite the criticisms and calls from prominent individuals and bodies on the government to soften its iron grip on issues, the government still went on and later that year two journalists were sentenced to various jail term for criticizing the Military Governor of Bida State over the brutal manner he had suppressed a recent student's unrest. Even within Military circles all was not well, there were rumours of a faceoff between the Chief of Staff Supreme Headquarters and the Chief of Army staff, unconfirmed report had it that both men had exchanged words after a Supreme Council Meeting. They had been unconfirmed rumours of plans to retire the COAS from the Army following his involvement in many shady deals and some other public misconduct.

The Prisoner of Afrika

III

With the announcement of a resumption date for all Secondary schools by the State Ministry of Education. Dike began preparing to return to school. As usual he submitted a list of the things he would need for the third term. Moreover, he was returning to school as a senior student as they were now in-charge, having relieved the Class Five student of power to enable them prepare for the Certificate Examination which was very close. His parents provided what they could to make his stay in school comfortable.

" make sure you study hard" his father advised.

"yes dad" he replied. That weekend he returned to school, throughout the journey, he reflected on the way he had to disturb his father before he could get what he needed for the third term. With the "Government" in their hands one had to gather all the "gatherable" to make life comfortable. He tried to sleep for a while but sleep eluded him with his mind roving to and fro eventually memories of his days as a junior student began coming back and he remembered something that happened during his third term in class two it was so funny he laughed out which in-turn caused those inside the car to look at him with funny expressions on their faces.

"Sorry", he said and closed his eyes again.

When he was a junior student, they was so much brutality against the other classes by the senior students. No evening passed without the junior classes being flogged. The best time to get everybody was during lunch and dinner, this was the time every assignment like supplying water to the school tank was checked with every amount of strictness. Woe betides any junior student who erred. You could escape if you were a prefect's pet. But if you were not, then you were in trouble because you will be flogged and in most cases starved. This act was a tradition. The school authorities were not perturbed it was part of the training they were supposed to receive. One sad thing with it was that there was always a tendency for people to abuse everything whether good or bad. Therefore, it did not surprise anybody when some other students seized this opportunity and used it to terrorize many junior students into missing their afternoon or evening meals.

Every Monday their evening meals consisted of rice, stew and fried fish with banana or in cases something that looked like banana but to the students it was more like unripe plantain. Then there was one particular student, he was a native of Bokkos and was then in Class Four while Dike was in class two. Besides, they were cousins. So when power or control of the junior classes was handed over to Class Four to enable the outgoing form five students prepare for their school Certificate Examination, Papa T as he was fondly called was one of the happiest person in school that day. He was one of the prefects after all, with government in their hands, his cousin felt it was time to let the Govisco community know that he existed. So that Monday evening during dinner while waiting to be admitted into the refectory, his cousin had come in from the football field to collect his food on discovering the door was yet to be opened he decided to bully the junior students.

"Foxes", he had shouted at the top of his voice.

"Yes senior", some of the junior students answered while some did not.

"Yes refuse to answer me?" he screamed.

"No", they all chorused. "For that all of you lie down", another Class Four student commanded and they all proceeded to lashing them with their belt, some even used their bathroom slippers while some decided to slap their faces.

"Next time when a senior calls you will answer",

another Class Four student said.

"Foxe-e-e-s", his cousin bellowed like an army officer during morning parade.

"Yes senior ", they all answered still on the ground.

"Alright stand up", he commanded. They obeyed and stood up like army recruits.

Every Monday evening is my birthday ", he began while everybody listened, "therefore when I say today is my day you will all reply papa T". He concluded and went on to test them.

"Today is my day ", he barked in his commander's voice.

"Papa T", they all replied. The refectorian arrived and the junior students were spared the terror and brutality. It was easy to understand why they behaved this way, power was in their hands, and no more morning bells for them they were now so free they could do anything they liked. One other thing, Dike had observed about Afrikans was the tendency to abuse everything they have. . . Thus, the freedom so intoxicated the new rulers to such an extent that many of them neglected their books the main reason why their parents had sacrificed so much time and money to ensure they acquire education, an opportunity which they were unconsciously abusing. The third term or promotion

The Prisoner of Afrika

exams came and with confidence every student had written it before the school closed for the long holidays., They all departed in high spirits. Throughout the holidays Dike was reading books meant for Class Three students, his mother was happy because it was a sign that he was convinced sure of moving on to the next class.

"Is it in Class Three that you'll choose subjects?" she had asked.

"Yes, "He had replied "but mostly during third term".

"What areas will you chose, Arts?" His mother asked.

"Arts- I want to be a lawyer" "That's it hold on to your dream and make sure. Yes, see it through," she said and walked away.

The holidays ended and the junior students returned to school to discover two things; first the grass was taller than most of them and had plenty of rabbits and snakes. Secondly, many of the Senior students were not going to return after all, having failed the promotion exams. Many had been driven away thus being denied the opportunity to repeat while those who were given the chance to repeat could not come back out of shame, because they would have to seat in the same class with boys they had flogged four months ago. Papa T as he was called was among the failures. The food prefect also failed

Mike Effa

(too much food you might say), but was not driven away. Even then, he refused to return.

Dike smiled to himself again and opened his eyes just as the taxi entered the motor park. Having reached Bokkos by midday he went to town to do one or two things, before returning to the school compound. So many times, while reflecting on the years he had spent in govisco leaves him rocking with laughter because right from the different principals to the staff right down to the students every person is funny in one way or the other. For instance, when they came to Class Four newly their Mathematics teacher, an indigene of Kalabar State and a native of one the surrounding villages under Bokkos county had come to class one morning. He had taught and left. Being a Science class with very intelligent Students, this group of students had lodged a complaint with the principal which eventually got to the Mathematics teacher. During the next maths class he appeared tense, unknown to the class this was going to be his last contact with them.

"Good morning Sir", the students greeted.

"Good morning ", he'd grunted back.

Which one of you reported me to the principal?" He asked there was stone silence, and when no answer was forth coming he had continued with a fierce glint in his eyes

"Look", he thundered, "let me tell you boys all of you are beneath me ", he said almost losing his balance.

"In case you've not heard of Mr. Duke Thuram, go out and ask", he dared the class while, advancing menacingly towards them.

"I was jobless for over three months because many schools wanted me to come and teach them Mathematics. You are all very stupid. I will see the grades you will make in your May/June exams idiots". With that he stormed out almost knocking down the Economics teacher. They were sober and frightened,

The third term had kicked off brightly, and two weeks later the school Certificate Exams had started with the practical subjects being given priority. The third term was always the shortest of all the terms. After a fee drive saw debtors being sent home, the promotion exam Time Table was released. All the students began to prepare for the promotion exam which later came up and was finished quite early to enable the teachers compile the results and hand over same on closing day. With the -promotion exam concluded, the students were denied permission to even go out to the town. A few days to closing date a send-off party was organised for the outgoing Class Five students and many of them received prizes . Closing date finally came. When given his results, and to his utter discomfort, Dike discovered he had failed mathematics again. In overall, he was promoted to class five based on the other art subjects passed . Dike was sad and it showed on his face even though he had done well.

"Hey what is the problem?" Henry asked when they met on their way to the dormitory to clear their belongings

"Nothing" he replied feigning a smile.

"Nothing?" Henry asked.

"Look Dikey you cannot fool me with that fake smile, so what is the problem?" He asked again. Knowing there was no other way out. He brought out his result and showed it to Henry hoping he will understand why he was looking worried and visibly disturbed.

"But you passed now?"

"But what about this red pen. How do I explain its presence to my parents?" He asked.

"Look" Henry began with his right hand on his shoulder

"Take heart worry less at least you are going to the

next class we will make amends in Class Five," he said.

"Thank you for your concern and have a nice holiday". They parted on that note.

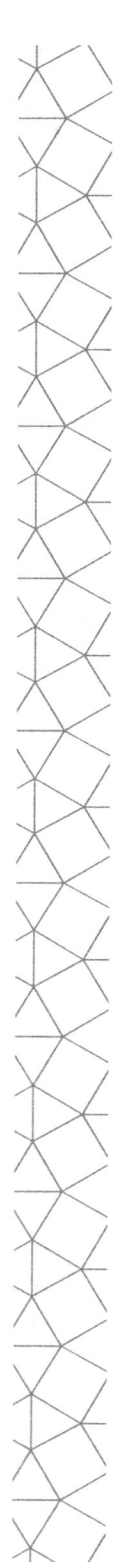

160

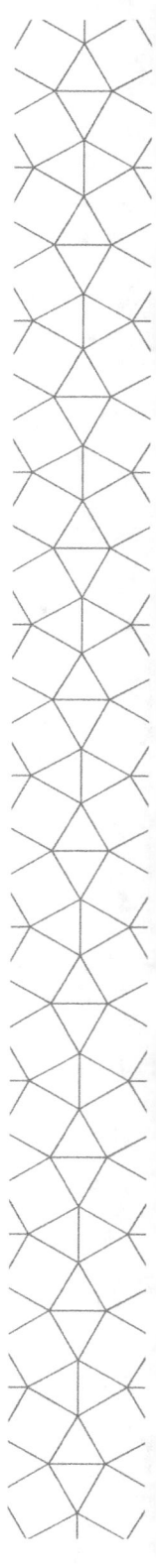

Chapter Nine

The Military Junta of Gen. Attah, despite entreaties from eminent personalities, continued to perpetuate their fascist rule with disregards to fundamental human rights. With the coming of the military, Afrikans had thought strikes would be a thing of the past, but it was not so. First pilots from the national carrier went on strike over poor conditions of service. The government reacted by sacking all the pilots and asking them to reapply. The same fate had befallen Medical Doctors who dared the Junta by going on strike, their leaders having been forewarned had fled to Britain and other European countries while their colleagues had been sacked and asked to reapply. The situation was becoming critical, citizens were being sent to jail for very minor offences. Everybody was being very careful.

In Bokkos County, there were many secondary schools but three were most prominent. They were the Government College, otherwise known as Govisco for boys, and two other secondary schools. One was a commercial and mixed school while the other was entirely for girls, so it became a common affair for Govisco boys to make the girls school their hunting grounds. They were always very excited to attend any important event hosted by the girls whom they regarded as their wives. Though Dike did not have a girlfriend, even while in Class Five, this was due to his religious background and he was also very shy. You could call him a coward because he could not muster the courage to chat up a girl. He favoured the traditional way of getting a girl which was through letter writing, but alas. Things were changing, the society was becoming more and more sophisticated and it seemed he was going to be left behind. One Saturday morning, Dike had come out without checking the shorts he was wearing; there was a stain on the shorts to the naked eye. It looked like dried semen so when a classmate pointed at it he was angry.

"Don`t go and find yourself a girlfriend you hear. Be there and continue having wet dreams", he had said . Dike was livid with rage and reacted accordingly too.

"Idiot. who told you this is the result of wet dream", he replied pointing at the stain on his shorts. "Then what is responsible for the stain?" he asked.

"You must be a clown", Dike replied, advancing

towards him even though the child was bigger. Still, Dike advanced forward even pushing him before the other boys moved in to ensure that they did not fight. While reminiscing on Govisco a place with funny memories, he remembered one Tuesday morning, they were having breakfast when the new principal Mr. Pen as he was fondly called walked in. Mr. Pen despite his status as principal still struggled for the attention of the girls with his students. Thus, anyone could understand why he was mad that morning with the outgoing students. "Class Five, you boys went and told your female counterparts that I am a booboo", he barked. When none of the Class Five boys responded he suddenly lashed out at the boy nearest him. Quickly, Dike left the refectory. He was not going to be starved by one egomaniac called principal. His class mates followed en suite as they abandoned the dining hall, finished their food outside, and rushed to class. As Dike and his colleagues began preparing for the school certificate exams, the harsh words of Mr. Thuram continued to echo.

Two weeks to exam proper, two Class Five students were caught trying to steal ceramic while washing sinks and toilet shanks, they were suspended and had to write the school certificate exams as day

Mike Effa

students. At last, the D-day came and the exams started with the practicals, the exam dragged on till June the fourth with students offering agricultural science declaring the cease fire. It was a day of jubilation for all, one student on coming out from the hall was so happy to have finished Class Five, he pulled out his white shirt and trousers threw them on the road and ran naked without any pants to the dormitory. It was quite funny. After the send-off party organized by the school authority, Dike packed his boxes and went to town. His aunty was happy to see him.

"How was your exam?" She asked, surveying him seriously.

"It was fine", he responded with a smile.

"You`ve lost weight tremendously", she said while helping him stow away his boxes in a safe place till when he will be ready to go.

"By the way when are you travelling to Kalabar?" She'd asked.

"Weekend, " Dike replied without taking his eyes off the TV set. For fear of being misunderstood, she quickly added, "my reason for asking is to enable me make arrangements for your journey", she said. Dike continued watching television.

"Wait-o, do you have enough money for your trip?"

The Prisoner of Afrika

She asked.

"Ehm, " he began, "well just enough," Dike said taking his eyes off the set briefly.

"Aha", you see the reason why I was asking,", she said. "You need to carry sufficient money because you never know what might happen on the road". She said looking at him directly in the eyes. He returned her look. Dike was dumbfounded over his aunt's sudden concern. He could recall on one occasion how he had been on the receiving end of Aunty Sarah's anger and mockery, and all because he had approached her for money and even after she had refused him she had made uncomplimentary remarks about Dike's mother, being her elder sister. Angered by her remarks, he had written to his mother and father jointly using his father's address and knowing his father will receive the letter and read it first before passing it over to his wife. He had forgotten about the letter when three weeks later, on a Sunday morning he was about going to take his bath and his cousin who'd been in the same class with him came to inform him that their aunty was around.

"Did she say why she wants to see me specially?" he had asked.

"Yes," his cousin replied, "she even asked me to call

you", he'd been told.

At this point, not knowing the nature of the message and not wanting to keep her waiting, Dike went into his room dropped his towel and put on a pair of shorts and went out to greet their aunty. They exchanged greetings on a cordial note then she proceeded.

"Dike, " she paused for a second or two, "it's you I came to see", she said. Dike was excited and even adjusted his position to receive the good news he was anticipating.

"Why did you write that letter to your parents?" she asked;. On mentioning the word "write" the smile on his face disappeared and he immediately became tense knowing what was coming. "Ehm, why did you write that kind of letter filled with such lies?"

"They are not lies that is −"

"Shut up," she barked, cutting him off.

Dike looked around to ensure nobody else was watching. His cousin was confused and began trying to calm her down.

"Make sure you do not come to my house again".

With that she stormed off leaving them staring bewilderedly at her retreating form. Dike was dumbfounded and confused.

Quietly, he returned to his room, looking subdued.

The Prisoner of Afrika

"But Dike you should not have done that", his cousin chided

"Never mind you don't understand what happened", he replied. Quietly he went to the bathroom had his bath and left for church. Despite the sanction Dike didn't stop going to her house, though each time he visited, she was always cold towards him. He couldn't help being surprised at this sudden change. On Saturday, morning he left for Kalabar his aunty was a bit sober from the house till they reach the motor park.

"Greetings to everybody", she said as soon as he had taken his seat in the taxi cab she waved goodbye and Dike responded without wasting time. A couple of minutes later the taxi left the motor park and the trip to Kalabar was on. One problem with an examination like the school certificate he thought lied in the fact that the marking of scripts could span a period of over three months and unless you are lucky to engage yourself with something worthwhile idleness and anxiety will be your bed fellows throughout the period you spend at home waiting for results. This was going to be his fate and you could tell he wasn't too eager to return.

He snapped out of his thought when the taxi came

to a halt in the motor park. Everybody at home was very happy to see him and they showed it, "Welcome, they greeted. How was school?" Roda asked. "How was your exam?" His father was able to ask. "The exams were Okay," he replied

II

hile waiting for his result, his parents got him the Defence Academy form and at the end of the month he wrote the Defence academy exams.

At this time, the military just like professional football was becoming the toast of parents. Every father saw his son as a potential Commander –In-Chief. Three weeks later the results were released, Dike scored two hundred points out of a total of three hundred. He was invited for interview where he did well more so being very good in current affairs. After the interview, the Adjutant congratulated him for performing so well. The Academy wanted only fifty boys and so far after all the elimination sixty boys were left. That morning Dike appeared before the panel again, "so who do you know among the panel?" the chairman asked. "Nobody," Dike said. " Who's your godfather or who is sponsoring you?" the Chairman asked again. "Nobody Sir" he replied.

The Prisoner of Afrika

"No further questions, you will be hearing from us," Dike returned to Kalabar and waited for a long time but no letter came.

"So I lost out because I have no godfather" he said quietly. "Only God will deliver us from this injustice".

His father was mad, "this people are mad. So, everything is based on who you know?" He'd asked.

" Well life must go on" Dike said.

"That's the spirit" Kris said.

And so Dike lost the opportunity to become a military officer.

The military junta continued its rule on the nation with real iron hands but within the military they a lot of cracks. The chief of army staff it was obvious was itching to become the commander-in–chief, but this was not going to be possible because the Chief of Staff Supreme Headquarters was still very much around. Moreover Gen Attah was not due for retirement either so only a coup will give the Army boss the coveted position. Then an opportunity presented itself, they had been a lot of meeting by the rebels and the sallah period was chosen in the hope that the head of state and his second–in command will travel out of the city for the sallah festivities. Presto everything moved accordingly, Gen. Attah travelled down to Zaria state and the

Mike Effa

Chief of Staff Supreme Headquarters was made chairman of the task force on hajj. Therefore he jetted out to Mecca to perform the hajj and Ekko city was left in the hands of Maj. Gen. Idi Bello. There was no sign that anything was in the offing and even when the coup took place on the 27th of August many people like, the Shakkassalli didn't know even though radio sets littered their house. Mr. Shakkassalli was standing outside discussing with his wife when a neighbour whom they were friendly with crossing over to say hello asked, "How are you enjoying your new government?" He asked Mr. Shakkassalli

"What government? You can't be serious" Mr. Shakkassalli replied.

"Of course I am", he said. "oh good morning Madam" he'd greeted Mrs. Shakkassalli. "There's just been another coup in Ekko City this morning, it looks peaceful and only the Head of State and his second-in-command it seems were the most affected," he stated.

"Dike," his father called, "turn on the radio," he'd ordered. Dike went in as their neighbour left And his father came into the parlour. Mrs. Shakkassalli proceeded to the kitchen. Then a few minutes letter the national anthem was played, followed by a husky voice, "Dear Afrikans, I major – Gen. Sani

The Prisoner of Afrika

Ahmed after due consultation with my colleagues in the armed forces wish to inform you that the government of Gen. Attah has been overthrown. This had become necessary due to their vice–like grip on the nation, the government irrespective of whether it is democratically elected or a Military regime is for the people. No sensible government will distance itself from its citizens. This coup is necessitated by the fact that Gen. Attah has lost direction and vision; we cannot fold our hands while watching our beloved nation drift like a ship with a broken rudder.

Fellow countrymen after thorough consultation we in the Military have decided to retire the following officers with full benefits. Gen Attah and Maj Gen Tunde Akoka, former chief of staff of the Defunct Supreme Headquarters, the Supreme Military council is scrapped forthwith. All service Chiefs of the Air force, Navy and the Inspector –Gen . of police will remain where they are till further notice. The affairs of the country will from hence forth be directed by Gen Idi Bello," President, commander-in Chief and Chairman Armed Forces Ruling Council Federal Republic of Afrika. You are advised to stay calm and wait for the broadcast of the president. All borders, seaports and Airports will remain closed till further notice; a dusk to dawn curfew is hereby imposed with immediate effect till further notice. Long Live Afrika Thank you". The National Anthem played again.

"So a new government is in-charge" Mr. Shakkassalli said.

"I've always felt something like this will happen", his wife concurred.

"People like Gen. Bello are never satisfied with what they have, always they are eyeing the top", his father said.

"And they'll only stop when they've reached the top", kolum concluded.

"of course that's obvious" His mother said

". Did you notice something in that speech? His father asked.

"No", they replied.

"I know" Dike blurted out.

"Then, tell us" his father challenged.

"The position of head of state has been dropped."

"So what are they going to call him?" His mother asked.

"Just let him finish", her husband chided at her impatience.

"He is to be addressed as president", Dike said,

"Well we'll see how their tenure will be," his father

The Prisoner of Afrika

said as he left for the bedroom. Being a Saturday, Dike was contented spending the whole day indoors. The radio continued to play martial music till later in the evening when Gen Bello addressed the nation. His speech seemed a bit incoherent uninteresting. The next day, the major headlines had a different version of the coup.

"New government assumes office", wrote the Kalabar Chronicle, "Gen. Bello seizes power in a bloodless coup", this caption was carried by a national daily "the carrier". The most sensational headlines was the one carried by the Afrikan Concord; title "All hail the saviour. The story went, the military dictator of Afrika and his unsmiling chief of staff yesterday were toppled in a palace coup. The coup itself was timely because the nation was being held to ransom while the citizens of this great nation were being oppressed in their fatherland. We heartily welcome the government of Gen. Bello and his decision to reinstall all newspaper, which has made it possible for us to appear once again on the newsstands. We also salute his decision to respect human rights, a fundamental issue in the charter of the U. N," Dike dropped the newspaper like hot coal and walked away. The Concord was merely praise singing which in his opinion was too early, but given the fact that they were back on the news stand thanks to the palace coup left them with no choice. Gen. Bello, the president federal republic of Afrika settled down faster than everybody had expected. Ministers and military governors were appointed of course major Gen Ahmed was rewarded with the plum job of army boss. Even then everybody knew this officer will only rest after he assumes the number one position but nobody knew when. Many decrees, especially those which infringed on speech, were repealed. Many political prisoners were released including a journalist jailed a year before. The new regime was welcomed at home and abroad, especially as they had promised to return power soon to civilians . The British and Danish governments were the first to recognize the new government, and followed it up with the return of their high commissioners to Ekko city. While the new government had reciprocated by sending back the Afrikan high commissioners to Britain and Denmark. Almost every person was happy at this particular coup except for certain senior military officers who did not hide their disgust for the incessant palace coup. Within the military the first officer to throw in the towel was Maj. Gen. Aboi an indigene of Zaria state, before now Gen Aboi was Afrika's

The Prisoner of Afrika

ambassador at the large covering the Gambia, Senegal and sierra Leone with the announcement of another coup. He had quickly returned to Ekko city and turned in his resignation letter. On hearing this Gen Bello had tried to prevail on him not to resign, they had promised him even better positions with the new government. All these entreaties had fallen on deaf ears as the courageous officer had maintained his stand and dropped his uniform for good; the president was annoyed at the effrontery of the retiring major –general. Those who had jubilated when Gen. Attah and Maj. Gen. Akoka were removed soon began to look at the new government with suspicions. The first blow had been student unrest. in which seventeen students were shot dead by the police. " The worst is yet to come" Dike had commented to a friend on reading the story.

"The devil you know is better than the angel you know not," his friend had replied and they had laughed over the adage. Then came the issue of taking a loan from the international monetary fund (IMF). The government in keeping to its promise to respect the aspiration of the citizenry threw open the issue for public discussion, Afrikans just like fishes that swallow baits very easily without examining it quickly took the gauntlet. After making a fool of the academicians, professionals and economic advisers, Gen . Bello unilaterally signed and took the IMF loan. After the coup, Gen. Attah was placed under house arrest while the fate of his second In-command still in Saudi Arabia remained uncertain for the time being. But Maj Gen Tunde Akoka, being the bold and fearless officer that he was, signalled his desire to return to his father's land. It was granted and he returned. On arrival, he was arrested at the airport and placed under house arrest. The genesis of the coup had been the decision of the top two leaders to retire the former chief of army staff on the twenty-ninth of November from the army for his part in certain drug deals. This decision was taken in the presence of the chief of air staff who in turn had betrayed the trust by leaking the news to the army boss.

Gen Bello had however reacted faster while general Attah and Akoka had been caught napping and thus had paid the supreme price. Instead of retiring Gen Bello it was now the reverse both men along with forty-seven other officers had been retired from the army.

III

he months of July and August were gone and September was almost two weeks old and results were yet to be released.

"Forget about the past. Just keep reading for the university entrance examination", his mother had encouraged.

Dike smiled, "okay", he said, "but I just pray WAEC will release this result before the end of this month". But anxiety is a very difficult thing to overcome as he was gradually finding out. Most time out of idleness, Dike would find himself thinking about his secondary school days. Govisco was a secondary school with plenty of vices, they always fought at football matches win or lose. There was a time they had fought the army after a match which the soldiers won by 3-2 . The match play was on Friday evening. In the course of the fight a soldier was killed. This only enraged the soldiers who had wanted to burn down the school but were prevented when a strong message was sent from the 13th Infantry brigade which served as Headquarters to the unit in Bokkos. The soldiers were given twenty-four hours in which to return to their barracks and register their presence before the unit commander. Govisco was a tough school and every boy's delight. Parents also liked the reputation the school had earned for itself and they wanted their wards" names to be etched in the annals of this great school. Dike made it a habit of reading newspapers and also listening to the radio for any information about their results. The waiting finally ended later in October, his father was first to hear and didn't waste time letting him know, "your results have been released"

That evening, Dike discovered his father would be travelling to Bokkos to buy foodstuff for the household and thus was using that opportunity to offer him a ride. They left on Sunday afternoon, Bokkos from Kalabar is normally three hours, but his father was in a very good mood and was really firing his Peugeot car like a race driver and capped it all by whistling a favourite tune. It sounded funny.

They drove into a petrol station along the road to buy fuel and the journey continued. They reached Bokkos by five in the evening having left home by half past two in the afternoon.

"Good old Bokkos," his father said and they laughed again as he directed the car to the family house. The next day being Monday, Dike left for his former school while his father went to the market with one of their cousins. During the brief journey to the

The Prisoner of Afrika

school premises Dike was restless. His heart was beating so rapidly, he was afraid other occupants in the bus might hear. He cautiously surveyed the bus. Everybody appeared lost in thought, so he relaxed and tried everything possible to control his fear but to no avail and continued wondering.

"What if my result is bad?" He dismissed the thought immediately.

"Or supposing some subject is not released?", He refused to even consider that line of thought as they had all behaved properly throughout the exams. He reached the school compound then proceeded to the principal's office. He showed his receipts to prove that he was registered and did the May/June exams and that he didn't owe any fees. Satisfied with his evidence, the principal directed him to his secretary who after making him pay twenty Afripounds brought out the result from an envelope. "Here's your result. "

"Thank you sir," Dike said stretching out his hand to receive it. He was excited at what confronted him.

Out of eight subjects, he made seven credits and a pass in biology. He stared at what were his result and the piece of paper in his hand "stared" back at him in return.

Mike Effa

Dike left the school compound and rushed to the market to meet his father. But his father and their cousin had already gone home.

When his father saw the result he was happy, "Congratulations"

"Thank you papa". The result was passed around amongst uncles and aunts literate enough to understand what was happening. Dike was very happy and just like he had been advised the university was his next part of call. Two days later, armed with his result, Dike and his father left Bokkos on Wednesday morning for the return journey to the city. The atmosphere inside the car was very lively and jovial. His father was in a good mood and they discussed and played music, After which Dike closed his eyes and allowed his thought to roam about plans for the future. A few kilometres to Kalabar they stopped to buy fuel , while the station attendant was doing his job his father gave him a funny look and Dike could not resist the urge to smile and even though he tried not to eventually they were ended up laughing.

"What a beautiful day it is," his father said, as a way of starting a conversion.

"yes it is a beautiful day" he responded looking at his father with their tank filled up. They hit the road

The Prisoner of Afrika

again. His father kept his eyes on the road to avert disaster of any sort, "you know something?" he asked

"No", came the reply, "it's good to conquer fear and have self confidence that is the only way you can move forward, "his father advised. "You must've read the story of Abraham Lincoln"

"Yes," Dike answered.

"Therefore never be afraid of taking tough decisions in life, you need guts as a lawyer. Life has just begun for you so prepare hard for the university exam, " he warned gently.

"Yes sir" Dike said.

"And," he paused for a moment, "always remember that the down fall of a man is not the end of his life. A man's downfall only becomes his end when he decides to give up on himself completely," his father said, keeping his eyes on the road.

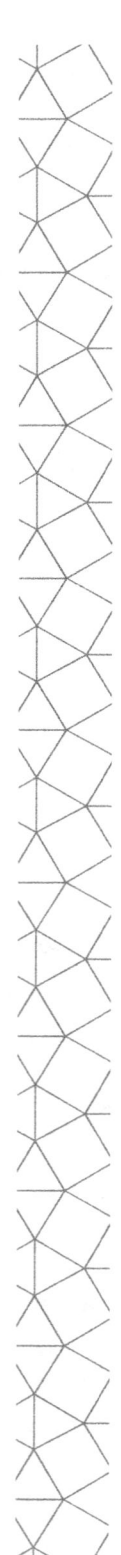

182

Chapter Ten

The new military regime of Gen. Bello had been in office for only three months when an attempt to oust it was uncovered, the news at the initial stage remained a guided secret, so the nation had to make do with rumours, but speculation ended when newspapers like the Concord reported the commencement of trial of the coup plotters in a headline story captioned, TRIAL OF SUSPECTS BEGINS,

The paper had this to say. "The trial of Maj. Gen Alidjoo and twelve other officers opened yesterday in Ekko city. The suspects were brought to the venue of the tribunal at about 10. 00 am in the morning in a police Black Maria and were herded into the hall amidst tight security from stern looking and heavily armed soldiers. Chairman of the tribunal Maj. Gen. C. B. Pam read out the charges to the accused officers who maintained they were not guilty of the charges. The tribunal adjourned thirty minutes later while hearing continues in a forth night while the suspects will be remanded in prison custody.

" What a mess,", Dike said to nobody in particular,

shook his head, and walked on. Dike was deep in thoughts and didn't hear his friends who had been walking behind him for the past five minutes called, it was only when he touched him that Dike snapped out of his reverie. "what?" He had turned

His friends laughed.

"What is wrong with you?" Koko asked. "Nothing really", Dike said with a smile, "I was just lost in thoughts", and he replied, "what about?" Koko asked. "oh everything,", Dike said. "The country, I, my family and our future especially in this country where we are treated like prisoners," he concluded.

"Yea prisoners of afrika,", Koko began, "By the way have you seen today's headlines?" He asked, "yes I saw just one the Concord", Dike replied

"so they was a coup attempt?" he asked again.

"Are you surprised," koko asked in return.

"yes, I am. Don't be," koko said. "This is Afrika, the giant of coups and we are in a big cesspool. We're now a nation with a bleak future-"

"Don't conclude so soon," Dike said, cutting him off.

"Why?" Can't you see that within the military it's now survival of the fittest?" Koko asked, looking at Dike's face.

"It's not,", Dike said, "then how can you explain this type of negative development attempting to topple a three month old regime?" koko asked, sort of challenging him to answer.

"Greed and misguided ambition" he said.

"Dike" he called drawing his attention to what he had to say, "believe it or not this nation is doomed and don't forget the bible portion-"which portion Dike asked, he scratched his head for a second "yes I remember it now, " he said excitedly, "those who go by the gun die by the gun" he quoted.

"not by the gun," Dike pointed out,

"it doesn't make any difference those days it was the sword but nowadays it's the gun", Koko said and they both laughed at the way he twisted everything.

They got home only to discover that the trial of the coup plotters was no more news to everybody, "But why did this group of officers think they would be able to topple a government that was still very much alert?" Kris asked.

"moreover one headed by the Chief of coups himself" Dike said.

"What do you mean by that? His friend asked.

"what I mean by that?" Dike asked "yes", he responded while others listened "it's simple, " he began, "apart from the first coup, every other coup that has occurred in this country always has Gen Bello's signature on it." Dike replied.

"So the planner of coups is now on the hot seat at last, " Koko said with a smile on his face. "And other officers are itching for a taste of power too. "

"Yes", Kris concurred every officer in the army sees himself as a potential Head of State", Kris said.

"Even when many could not pass their officers exams suddenly they feel the time has come for them to rule", Dike said, they all laughed again at the joke.

"The officers of our armed forces are too ambitious to rule, that's why throughout their stay at the academy they are all day dreaming on how to come and seize power, " Koko said.

"there are two generals, one of them is the minister of Zuma Rock territory, the other is a brigade-commander. The remaining fifteen are officers drawn from the three forces", "what are their reasons for the coup? Their father asked,

"Gen. Alidjoo is very loyal this to the former head of state, then with their removal from office. This officer was not happy and hence his attempt to bring back the overthrown commander-in-chief back to the helm of affairs after all. Maj. Gen. Tunde Akoka even though under house arrest still insists he is an officer in the army Secondly Maj. Gen Bolaji Warawa is annoyed that he was not given command of the

The Prisoner of Afrika

Third Armoured coup in Goma state."

"So these are their reason?" Mr. Shakkassalli asked. "But they cannot be killed. After all, the coup did not take place," Kris said. "You are mistaken, Mr. Kris". Koko began if you had listened to what the army boss said, sometime last week you won't say this"

"What did he say?" their father asked adjusting himself on his chair.

"Plotting a coup carries the same punishment as executing the coup," Koko replied.

"Very unfortunate," Dike said, "they are finished".

Throughout the remaining part of the year nothing was heard of the rebels, even the trial was blacked out. Reporters of various media houses were denied access to the tribunal venue. While the other officers were kept in the prison custody generals, Alidjoo and warawa were under house arrest still they lost the opportunity when Gen. Alidjoo tried to escape through the space his air conditioner occupied. Both men were then moved to the prison and their trial was hastened up. On the last day, the tribunal made its verdict known; out of the fifteen officers, Gen. Alidjoo and twelve others received death sentences with the right to appeal while Gen. Warawa was dismissed from the army and sentenced to five years for concealing the news.

Mike Effa

The thirteen officers sentenced to death by firing squad knew it was futile to appeal because their appealing would be ignored, since Gen. Bello was bent on eliminating them. They accepted the sentences as final. They were subsequently executed two weeks later. Pressmen were not allowed. The Chief of Defence staff informed the nation that evening. Truly, another era of terror had begun.

As a result of his brilliant performance at the last school certificate exam which was still being talked about in the house, having already put behind him the disappointment of the defence academy. Dike was warming up to write the university exam popularly known as JAMB.

"At last you're about to achieve your dreams", his mother said.

"Yes, I'm very excited and I intend to give my very best to come out tops". Dike vowed.

"Yes you've got to put in your best so that entering the university won't be problematic" Kris said.

"Besides I don't have a godfather to fight for me so I must put in my best".

The Prisoner of Afrika

Dike worked hard for the JAMB exams that came up three months later. He had chosen Ogoja County as his centre because the entire family resided there. He did most of his studies and revision out home. Then the exams came and went and Dike could once again relax. After the JAMB exams, he began another period of waiting.

But he did not wait for long, as JAMB results were released a month later. Dike did not make the cut off mark.

After failing to secure the pass mark to read law in the university, he had spent almost one and half years at home still battling to achieve his dream. He lost out in the second try, to the issue of not having a godfather to push him through. Finally, money was made available and he did the necessary things which landed him an admission into Federal school of Arts and Science. He was going back to school once again to freshen his brain for better performance.

II

he Military Junta of Gen Bello was now doing exactly what the last regime did. Decrees to check everything under the sun were being promulgated.

Mike Effa

Corruption was elevated and the government had no place for critics. To show seriousness, the editor of the weekend magazine was killed by what was believed to be a parcel bomb. The National Dailies carried different stories on the police began investigation. Every sensible person was touched. All prayed that the culprits will be fished out. While investigations were going on, certain disturbing facts began to emerge. Rumours had it that the female drug courier who was arrested then reported dead, did not die after all. Rather, she had been smuggled out to the U. S. The editor had met Modestus in the United States and had interviewed her. So, he had returned armed with this fact using it in blackmailing the president who ended up dolling out large sums of money to the Journalist. Suspicions were further fuelled when his deputy editor regained consciousness a few days later. When asked what happened he had recounted how he heard a knock on the door and how when the door was opened by his boss a parcel was handed over to him. His boss certainly knew where it came from. According to the deputy, he had smiled and said "from the President". With his back to his deputy, he had proceeded to open it and those were the last words he'd heard before losing consciousness. He was shocked to hear the editor was lying in the morgue as a corpse. People continued to express their disbelief and shock over the dastard act.

"Things we usually see in films are now happening amongst us .... . " a newspaper wrote. Most people were not surprised because Afrika and Nigeria shared a lot. They knew sooner or later the angel of death would move on. Thus, when a journalist was also killed by a parcel bomb in Nigeria, event watchers knew it won't be long before other dictators adopted this ruthless method of silencing critics. While the Police were pretending to be investigating the assassination., a very deadly robbery gang broke loose. The gang operated in a typical Robin Hood style robbing the rich and giving it to the poor. The genesis of it all had began when a friend of Judas Ukpabi had been arrested for armed robbery. Judas was told by the police that if he could pay one hundred thousand Afripounds, his friend will be set free. Judas had paid fifty thousand pounds with a promise to pay the balance later, but things had gotten out of hand and his friend had been executed for armed robbery. Judas was bitter. The police had betrayed him and so they will pay. A police commissioner was shot in the nose and subsequently was flown abroad for treatment. The nation was held hostage for almost six months before the gang was crushed by police commissioner Patrick O. Dole. The gang members were put on trial. It was a big drama, as three policemen were implicated.. The nation finally heaved a sigh of relief when these notorious groups were eventually executed along with the police officers who had been their source of information.

Dike reached his school on Wednesday afternoon and stopped at the gates with other students waiting to be admitted into the school premises. Having spent almost two and half years at home, he resolved to make the next JAMB examination. I must study law, he said to himself. If you fall once, you must rise and continue. He had failed on his First attempt., the entire centre's result was cancelled. The second time he had not made the cut-off point but lost out because he had no one to put his name on the v. c's list. His mother had suggested that Dike should read another course, but Dike was adamant.

"I must read law", he insisted. "Next time it will be different".

The Prisoner of Afrika

"Okay, I wish you the best", his mother said. They had left the discussion at that point, while hoping that going back to school again will place him in a better position. FSAS is among the twenty unity schools built in the country admission reflected the different ethnic groups and admission was open to everybody. There was no gender discrimination. The social life was something else. The school had very young and handsome male teachers who were at liberty to pick from the bevy of girls. Those teachers who didn't fancy the female students had the option of getting matured ladies in the town. One evening Dike saw his maths teacher stroll pass with a huge lady. Such ladies are commonly described as "heavy duty". They greeted and passed as his mind went back to an incident that had occurred while in Govisco. Their Biology teacher was a fat chubby man from Ghana had come back to campus that night with a woman of easy virtue. After using her for the night, it was time to pay. Rather their biology teacher began to act in a funny way. The prostitute got annoyed and followed Mr. Amega out of the house. The students were attracted to the scene because of the noise. They arrived to find the lady holding their teacher by the loin cloth he'd tied, "lady what do you want again?" Amega was asking to their hearing.

"you want to do me hanky-panky", the whore screamed.

"Look the students are watching us", Mr. Amega said.

"Dat one na your concern-o. I want my money", she said adjusting her hold on the loin cloth.

Just then one of the teachers who was passing saw the commotion and stopped, "serameg what is it?" he asked

"This lady says I'm indebted to her" he replied.

."why not pay her?" his colleague advised.

"I don't have the money", Amega said.

"today we go die here de time wey you dey do the thing you no know say you go pay?" the woman asked. It was so funny the students laughed at the lady's rhetoric.

"madam come make we do. I go pay you", a student said mockingly.

"go do with your mama", was the rancid reply that came forth. They were angered and began advancing to teach her a lesson, but the principal came to the rescue and they were all driven away.

Dike laughed at everything as if it had just happened, "well I hope we don't wake up to another no want pay situation", he chuckled as he turned to catch a glimpse of the fading form of his maths teacher and his catch for the night. Dike settled down quickly and faced his studies. He was determined to be in the University the following year.

III

irst term at federal school of arts and science ended on a good note. The students on collecting their transport allowance departed for their various destinations. Dike had only two friends Augustin and Mikel, and together they formed the "three Musketeers".. The second term started on a promising note, Dike and other students had returned to school too. Lectures commenced immediately. Afrika was no longer quiet following University students demonstration over the introduction and implementation of drastic economic measures. All Federal Government Institutions had been instructed to close down at the slightest signs of trouble; many Universities had been closed down already. At FSAS, conditions were very poor but the students continued to manage though underneath they were tensed up, but lacked the chance to air their grievances. The opportunity came sooner than they even thought.

Mike Effa

It all began on a Sunday morning. During breakfast, two girls were fetching water when a boy came out from the dining hall and approached the tap and the girls. "Excuse me please can I get some water in my tea cup?" the boy requested. Other students were on a queue waiting to be admitted into the hall though they weren't paying any attention but the exchange was loud and clear, "no don't put your cup" the girl had said. The boy was baffled. Rather than go away, he proceeded to tease her. Meanwhile a Miss campus had been organized the previous Saturday in which Martina was crowned Miss Campus. Everybody was aware though Dike had not attended as he was watching football in somebody's house.

"Is it because you were voted Miss Campus that you will not allow other people to drink water? He asked. This question drew a round of laughter from the boys standing nearby. Martina didn't answer and as the boy proceeded to get the water by force, Martina simply snatched another bucket and brought it down on the boy's head with all the force she could muster. Hell was let loose as the boy proceeded to give Martina the beating of her life. They fought on with Martina fighting back in every way possible while at the same time shouting "you

The Prisoner of Afrika

will kill me today. " The male students intervened and the drama ended.

"Old boy you want kill Miss Campus?" A male student teased. Martina's assailant merely ignored him.

On Monday morning the school principal handed down a two week suspension to the male student. Other male students rose in defence of their colleague and hell broke loose.

"We no go gree" the boys chanted while the girls looked on perplexedly. The school authority tried their best to restore sanity, but all to no avail. When calm could not be restored, the students were sent home and the school closed down which turned out the bigger mistake. If the school authorities had been willing to punish both parties, the riot would not have occurred. But due to the unfairness, the boys capitalized on the opportunity to express their accumulated frustrations which ranged from poor feeding to unhygienic living conditions. What actually took place was mild or could be termed as child's play. If the notorious students amongst the pack had had their way it would have been a very gory tale to tell. The students had acquired petrol which they intended to use in razing down two lecturers" houses. When it was time to act the group failed because they remained undecided on which house to burn first, thus losing out to sectional interest. When they eventually returned, all students signed an undertaking to be of good behaviour for the rest of the school period. Going for another round of food which was one of the demands by students was ratified but on conditional grounds you had a valid ticket.

FSAS could not be compared to Govisco, but the school also had its share of things to remember and very funny ones too. One particular event which will continue to make Dike rock with laughter had occurred during the final term, it was on Saturday evening they had all converged for dinner. Standing in front of Dike was another boy and he was very hungry as his actions were soon to show. The queue had been moving. Eventually it was his turn, he dropped his plate and a big piece of hot yam was put on his plate. Just then, the cook took his eyes away. This guy reached out took the piece of hot yam and without bothering to see if he was being watched dropped the hot yam into his pocket. The yam began to cause him some discomfort and he began to fidget while sweat covered his face then the cook looked at the plate then at the boy, "wey de yam wey I put here?" he asked in pidgin English

The Prisoner of Afrika

"Don't ask me," the boy replied.

"Please finish with me let me go I have other things to do", the boy said deciding to take an aggressive position to bluff his way out. The cook was not going to give in without a fight.

"Wey de yam", he said coming out to take a closer at the boy then he saw the bulge in one of his pockets.

"wetin be dis?" asked the cook. The commotion alerted members of the food committee who immediately surrounded the boy and a brief scuffle ensued. But the boy was subdued and the piece of yam was recovered from his pocket and put back on his plate. Terribly humiliated he carried his plate and left the dining hall. The news spread like wild fire and the boy became like an outcast, the price of greed.

With the school Certificate exams completed Dike returned home immediately, but there wasn't going to be any rest for him. He was immediately enrolled for an extra coaching towards the forth coming University Entrance Examinations. At this point , most of his younger ones like Rhoda were either in their first or second year in the university. Dike therefore resolved that he must enter the university that year.

Chapter Eleven

"This regime will not stay in office longer than necessary; neither does it intend to succeed itself". With these words, Gen. Bello President of the Republic of Afrika had released the timetable for the Transition Programme for the Third Republic. It had all commenced with the ban on politics being lifted. "Individuals have been given the right to form political Associations which will metamorphose into parties".

However, none of the thirteen Associations had made the mark in terms of finance and geographical spread. At the end of it all, the government did three things in an attempt to sustain interest in the Transition programme. First, the government banned all those who had participated in politics in the first and second republics; the ban also affected serving and retired Military Officers including the President himself.

The Afrikan leader was a very crafty and cunning fellow; many preferred to call him "Maradona" after the famous Argentine football star Diego Maradona. President Bello was a politician in Military uniform and could dribble critics and opponents on the political arena with ease and with no stress at all. Thus, banning everybody including himself was a ploy to lend credence to the transition programme while keeping his hidden agenda in the cooler till the right time.

With old politicians out of the way, a new slogan was injected to Afrikan politics. "The transition programmes was solely for "New breed Politicians", the President had said and this time the difference is clear and I can promise you a lasting democracy will be entrenched in our nation". A constitutional conference had been held at Zuma rock city. At the end, a new constitution advocating a two party system was adopted. Following the inability of the associations to meet government guidelines, the military regime- government of pres. Bello came out with two political parties; the National Republican Council and the Social Democratic Party. Government's decision was based on the need to prevent the hijacking of these parties by any individual or group of individuals. The transition program was open to all whether poor or rich, man or woman, government decided to sponsor the parties so that every citizen could participate fully without hindrance". The government spokesman

The Prisoner of Afrika

had disclosed in a press conference. The journey to the third republic will commence with elections into the three hundred and four counties in the country.

II

Dike finally gained admission to read law at the University of Kalabar. It was an ecstatic moment for the family and Dike. His father was all smiles, " the Afrikan boy" his father said smiling.

" I love your fighting spirit", his mother added. His brothers and sisters were not left out of the back slapping. Dike started school, giving his studies all the attention it deserved. The euphoria of his achievement evaporated like a smoke when Dike was driven out of Law faculty for exam malpractice. After five years of waiting, Dike had made it only to lose it in a twinkling of an eye. It had all started during the first semester examination one of their classmates had entered the hall with foreign material and was using it all the while. Suddenly the lecturer in charge of the course entered the class and began searching all the students. Knowing that he would be in trouble, Okonta quickly discarded his foreign material by crushing it into a ball and flicking it, away. In the process it landed at Dike's feet. Dike did not see this but other students did.

"What's this?" Mr. Dako asked picking the paper from the floor.

" I don't know, I did not put it there", Dike said. Mr. Dako would not budge despite entreaties from the students that it was not Dike who dropped the paper.

"That's your business", he said.

"Sir this is the boy who dropped the paper", a student said pointing at Okonta.

"Will you shut – up:, Mr. Dako bellowed. The exams continued but without Dike. Eventually he faced a panel consisting of five deans including Education. No one believed his story except the dean from Education who fought hard for Dike. At the end, he was driven away from the Law faculty but the dean from Education made a special case and Dike was transferred to faculty of Education to study community Development. He later found out that Okonta's father was a rich senator so Okonta was an untouchable. Well only God will judge. Dike said quietly.

At this time, Dike had just been re-admitted to read community development in the university of Kalabar . His admission had not been an easy one having come from law faculty where he was studying law before losing out to the frame up during the first semester examination for an offence he did not commit. He had been transferred to the faculty of education through the dean, but when the first supplementary list came his name was not in the list. He hadn't known this, so based on information from his contacts Dike went on and paid the school fees. When it was time to get the university's fee clearance card he was referred to the faculty officer who in turn demanded for his Admission letter. When he went to the dean's office, he was given a list to go to through. Alas, his name was not in the list.

"What's this?" Dike asked.

"Ehen what's the problem?" the dean's secretary asked.

"my name's not the list".

"My friend it means JAMB rejected you," the secretary replied sarcastically.

"On what grounds" Dike fired back like a lawyer.

"Okay be there and ask me foolish questions".

"Nonsense," Dike said walking away. "and I've just paid three hundred pounds to the university's account", he said sighing. The dean was informed and he promised to look into it and he did later, when a new list was prepared and sent to Ekko city, headquarters of the university commission. This time, the list returned with his name occupying the number one spot. , He finished the registration and joined his colleagues. He was late. It was very obvious. Thus, when he went to submit his class admit card at the political science department, the coordinator Mr. Udokang only had words of discouragements for all late comers, like Dike.

"Many of you will fail this course," he said. It appeared this was his way of welcoming students to the university. Dike submitted and left without giving the statement a second thought. He was in the university and nothing else mattered

III

Pres Bello. The Afrikan dictator had seized power to satisfy his selfish goals but claimed the government of Gen. Attah was distancing itself from the people. Those who are familiar with the military will always agree they are the same; they come in different shades but always do the same thing. Gen Bello was not different from those he had overthrown. No sooner had he seized power, decrees began to come. They affected every aspect of life. Already, he had a very poor human rights record. Corruption

The Prisoner of Afrika

was given a top seat in Afrika and then he turned on his constituency, the armed forces, which he polarized on ethnic and religious ground. Promotion and political appointments in the military became a privilege and only "favoured" officers benefited from it.

Despite the situation and position of things, not every officer from the north enjoyed this privilege because many had fallen out with him due to the way he was managing the country. His chief of army staff wasn't doing any better. Money disbursed for welfare of enlisted men and officers was diverted and stashed in foreign accounts while the men suffered. The president and his cronies were wallowing in the belief that everything was alright. This false belief was shattered when in the early hours of April 22. Many Afrikans woke up to the voice of major Gideon Ndjamena's speech "fellow Afrikans, men and women I major Gideon Okute Ndjamena bring you glad tidings, the dictatorial regime of Gen Idi Bala Bello has been overthrown, we all have been witness to six years of misrule, mismanagement, brutality which includes the parcel bombing of a seasoned journalist and execution of thirteen military officers on the false excuse that they were planning a coup. Fellow

Mike Effa

Afrikans we of the armed forces have resolved that no longer shall we be led by a homosexual, a man who believes in bottom power as the only way of getting to the top for serving military officers irrespective of gender. Fellow Afrikans, we the young revolutionaries propelled by the need to save our country have today taken this great step at this point in time. Do not be deceived by the transition program it's a farce, the military has no blue print of handing over power to the civilians. All boarders and airports will remain closed till further notice a dusk to dawn curfew is hereby imposed till further notice, fellow citizens I call on you to be law abiding and go about your business peacefully. Long live Afrika and long live the revolutionaries." The national anthem played.

"Another coup again" said Mr. Shakkassalli.

"I wonder where we are going in this country?" Maggie asked.

Presently a car drove into their compound, they could not identify the car so they thought probably they were looking for their neighbours downstairs. Then they heard a knock on the door, on opening the door, their sister Ada, a friend and her husband walked in and they all exchanged greetings. They all talked about the present situation in Afrika.

The Prisoner of Afrika

"From all I have heard so far it seems the president has been killed," their father said.

"It is good for him and that peacock wife of his", another of his sister who had joined them said.

"shh," their father cautioned her.

"lower your voice this are dangerous times", he advised.

For over seven hours or so the mutineers held sway, the first signs of trouble appeared when the four GOC's on finding out that the president was alive immediately disassociated themselves from the coup and went on to pledge their unalloyed and unadulterated support and loyalty to the president immediately after this announcement. Heavy fighting broke out in Ekko City, the Brigade of guards, the Amphibious Headquarters, the Ekko Military cantonment all experienced bitter fighting in their bid to rout the coup plotters who had taken over control since morning. Fighting did not end well till after half past four in the evening. With the all clear sounded the president and his group emerged from hiding flanked by the chief of general staff and chief of Army staff president Bello, thanked Afrikans for being law abiding and for their unflinching support, he also praised the Army in particular for crushing the coup. "However, it is with heavy heart and a deep sense of loss that I announce the death of my Aide-de-camp, " the President said.

Immediately the coup was crushed, all military Governors were summoned to Ekko City for a very crucial meeting with the Commander-in-Chief. When the meeting ended newsmen approached the governor of Bida state for his opinion and the meeting in General.

"Sir, how was the meeting?" a Reporter asked.

"Fine", he responded. "What about today's event?" Another reporter asked.

"oh, that! In fact, we thought that was major Ndjamena's version of April fool's day", he said as he got into a black Peugeot 504 SR salon car and zoomed off. On Monday, news began to flow on the coup. The ADC was dead and koboko barracks home of many military leaders was badly damaged by the fighting. Prominent citizens including the traditional leaders paid the Afrikan leader solidarity visits. Meanwhile most of the officers involved had been arrested and were been held in the gwamina maximum security prisons more than half of the key actors fled abroad. This group of officers were the ones the head of state would have loved to deal with because they were his advisers on the setting up of the dreaded national guard . The search for coup plotters still in hiding went on for a long time, people were warned not to harbour any rebels as they will all be shot together if apprehended. When pictures of the president's residence were shown on television, everybody was surprised while many marvelled at the lucky escape.

"Truly it was a lucky escape", Dike said while watching TV.

"Of course no amount of begging will save the mutineers", Rhoda remarked.

"What about major Ndjamena?" Their father asked.

"Nobody knows yet but if he is not dead, he is hiding,", Dike replied.

"One thing is certain, he cannot hide for long," Kris added.

"Yes he cannot!"

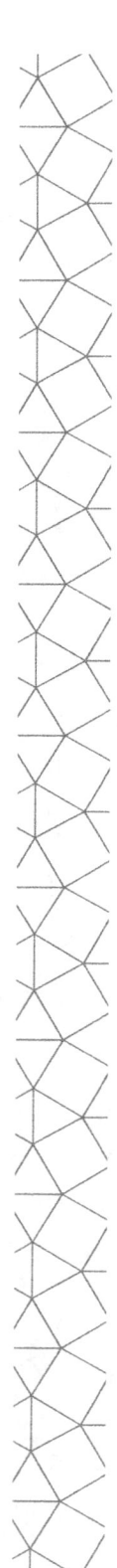

212

Chapter Twelve

Major Ndjamena was not dead neither was he hiding. He was arrested at exactly half past four on Sunday evening his arrest was very dramatic, having run out of ammunition and knowing that he was surrounded like the proud and brave officer that he was., He came out and surrendered to loyal troops and was immediately hand cuffed. The coup had failed. Definitely, the plotters already arrested were sure of one thing "death". It did not matter which form it took. Death is death. The weeks that followed major Ndjamena's coup were weeks of terror as Afrikans were subjected to military road blocks and searches of individuals and their vehicles and in the process many people were mistakenly shot by gun toting soldiers. Most of the officers involved in the coup but lucky enough to have escaped abroad were declared wanted and over half a million Afripounds promised for anybody who could volunteer information that would lead to their apprehension. The whole country three weeks after was still experiencing the after effect of major Ndjamena's coup attempt. Their trial commenced at the end of the month and lasted only five days after which tribunal chairman and General Officer commanding one mechanized Division; Maj Gen Okiti Omar read out the verdict "Having satisfactorily exhausted all the evidence of your participation in the botched coup of April 22, you are hereby sentenced to death by firing squad; subject to the approval of the Ruling council and you are entitled to appeal against the sentences so passed, thank you. " None of the convicted men or officers bothered to appeal they were convinced it will be an exercise in futility. After all, they were involved in the coup. Even when three days later the coup plotters numbering forty-two in all consisting of ten officers and thirty-two serving and retired men were executed at the Gwamina shooting ground, . One question people kept asking was the connection of a fishing magnate with the coup and availability of arms and ammunition. It was not a surprising question. The fishing magnate was a friend to most of the officers involved in the coup. He hated the Afrikan dictator and was ready to sponsor any group willing to take a shot at the "Presido", so when the opportunity presented itself he had grabbed it with both hands and had bankrolled the coup by providing money and vehicles mostly J5 buses

The Prisoner of Afrika

which in turn had made many people to call it the "J5 coup" because the plotters had used mostly J5 buses. Unfortunately, the coup had failed and he was lucky enough to escape through a private jet which had taken off without clearance at the Ekko City International Airport. Out of frustration, the army had arrested his brother who aided his escape and had given him a stiff jail sentence. As to the availability of the arms, Pres. Bello being a dictator with a hidden agenda had wanted to quietly set up a National Guard like the United States and Zaire. While the Americans use theirs to maintain peace, Pres. Mobutu uses his own to harass and intimidate political opponents and critics; the Zairean model was more appealing to the Afrikan leader. Arms had been readily procured, but there was no secret place to store the arms due to the advice of Lt. Col. Philip Archi and Major Victor Friday, who were later accused and declared wanted for their role in the botched coup of April 22. The arms were taken to Chief Lucky's fishing warehouse and stored there. These two officers in sympathy to Major Ndjamena's cause had made these arms available to the plotters. The President was dazed at the whole situation especially with the involvement of these two officers. These were men he thought he could trust but he had been betrayed. The transition program however remained on course, Pres. Gen Bello deserved whatever would've befallen him because those who go by the sword die by the sword. That he survived this attempt didn't mean he was free from those who might want to harm him. One other thing that baffled most people with his administration was their delight in putting "square pegs in round holes". It was not an uncommon sight to see individuals being made ministers over a ministry they knew nothing about.

This negative development didn't stop at the federal level. It cut across the states for instance in Dogawa State a school principal with no knowledge on health matters was appointed commissioner for Health while in Kalabar State a Barrister was appointed Commissioner for Agriculture and Natural Resources. It didn't matter to many dubious appointment seekers. After all, you don't need to be a professional to head a particular area. But, it still was necessary for the failures recorded by government was because of their putting the wrong people in the right places.

The Prisoner of Afrika

II

You must have heard my parents calling me the Afrikan boy!" Dike said one day to a friend who had wondered at this type of nickname. He had gone on to tell him why. , he had grown to cherished the name and on entering the University it had been boldly inscribed on his notebooks. He was so proud of the name that even the resit he bagged in the first year could not discourage him. Of course he had passed the resit. His second year in University of Kalabar was remarkable and a period he will never forget too.

"What was it that made the second year so remarkable?" people might ask.

Yes. He made better grades during the Semester exams. His colleagues always marvelled anytime they saw "the Afrikan Boy" on his notebook.

"What is the meaning of this?" they will ask and patiently he will explain to them. To some it made sense to others it didn't whatever their position on the issue. Dike didn't give a damn. For elective courses, one of the courses was "Africa in world politics". The lecturer in charge was Dr. Zedekiah Aboe who didn't even look like a lecturer. Dr. Aboe was a big disappointment and a disgrace to himself. Apart from his clothes which smelled like skunk, the Doc was a disappointed, disillusioned, and bitter man. Dike always wondered why he would come to class and the only thing you hear from his mouth is "Jesus is a White Man. Hence, his decision in allowing apartheid to continue in South Africa". The students saw it as part of the lecture, so they didn't bother challenging him. Apart from this, he was also very bitter against the Catholic Church. Dike never stopped wondering what his problem was with religion till the day he remarked to his sister, Maggie, who at this time was doing a postgraduate programme in the Political Science Department. They were all seated in the parlour.

"You know," he began. "there is one of our lecturers who is very bitter with anything that smells of religion", he said. Nobody laughed.

"Which department is he?", his sister asked.

"Pol. Science", he replied. "Is it Dr. Aboe?" she asked.

"Yes, " Dike replied and they all laughed. "Look", she began.

"This guy was ordained a Father but was driven away by the Bishop because he abused a class two student sexually".

"Was it a he or a she?" Dike asked and everybody

laughed at the wordings of his last question.

"It was a female student", his sister replied.

"Oho, now I understand why he behaves like this!"

"Please anytime his madness starts make sure you don't laugh or reply to anything he says", his mother warned.

"God will deal with him accordingly!" She concluded.

Dike finished the second year peacefully and without any resit. This gave him a clean bill of health to move on to the third year.

The Shakkassallis were in a festive mood as two of their daughters were going to convocate the following Saturday. "Truly man they say proposes but it is God that disposes". If not how could one explain the fate that befell Dike in the early hours of Saturday. The problem had started like stomach ache. Meanwhile he had attended a birthday party organized for Kris on Thursday evening. The situation got to a point whereby he threw up everything in his stomach.

"Ah oh. Dike what is wrong with you now? " Maggie asked.

" I'm just having stomach upset," he replied. " You

will go to hospital in the morning". When it was morning it was clear that he would miss the convocation, because he was feeling weak.

By evening, he found himself in the hospital victim of acute appendicitis. Surgery was billed for early Sunday morning, but before the operation his private part had to be shaved. It didn't occur to Dike till a female nurse approached his bed he did not see her because his eyes were closed.

"I have to shave you", she said. Her voice sounded distinct she then repeated the same statement again. Dike opened his eyes and realized somebody was talking to him. On noticing his eyes were open, she said it a third time.

"I want to shave you", "me?" Dike asked as if they had been two on the bed.

"yes you", she answered. He began wondering how this lady or nurse was going to shave his private part. "Please can't I do the shaving myself?" He asked.

"no you won't do it well", she replied. All his entreaties fell on deaf ears.

"Mr. , please hurry I don't have much time. By the way what are you hiding that I've never seen before?" the nurse asked rudely.

"What the hell. I guess you're right," Dike said and pulled down everything, closing his eyes while she carried on with the shaving. Fortunately, his mind was not on sexual issues so despite the way she touched his genitals he was not aroused. When she was through he pulled on his shorts and opened his eyes to catch her retreating form. He shook his head and muttered "thank God" while vowing never to "love a nurse talk less of marrying one". She returned again,

"What will it be this time?" Dike asked.

"I have to shave you properly" she said, without delay he pulled down his shorts after that she did not appear again.

Dike was successfully divorced of his appendix on Sunday morning and wheeled back into the ward for the recovery process. His parents visited him regularly including his sisters and brothers. Before the operation, his brothers had rushed in that Saturday evening thinking he will require blood. But the doctor, with a smile of affection, had said to them, "sorry he won't need extra blood his blood level is okay for the operation".

The financial aspect of the operation was handled by Ada and Maggie. Six days later he was well enough to go home. The doctor discharged him. He was happy to go because at this time the cup of nations had begun and he didn't want to miss the action.

Mike Effa

III

Dike was grateful to God for many things. At last come January he will be in his final year.

"So you're now a finalist, his father said.

"Yes-o and I thank God for his mercies too", Dike said.

"I knew it, we didn't make a mistake when we called you the Afrikan boy". They laughed again, "so congratulation and make sure it's second class upper," his father added.

" Why limit him?" his mother said from the dining room.

" Dike it won't be too much if you make a first class".

"I will do my best", Dike replied smiling.

Everybody was hopeful that the economy, , which had almost come to a stand, will show positive signs of growth. The transition programme was gathering momentum, the National Assembly would be inaugurated in the year and then by August. Gen Bello will hand over to the winner of the presidential elections thus bringing to an end ten years of Military rule. The politicians had no cause to doubt, everything was moving according to plan. University students were not left out in the great expectations for the New Year and Afrika in general. Students had returned to school excitedly, at least if lecturers did not go on strike many will finish and leave the university early enough

Gen. Idi Bello, the Maradona of Afrika and a man with a hidden agenda was what you will like to call a "pagan". Pagan here does not refer to somebody who does not know God. After all, the honourable president is a devout believer of his religion. But "PAGAN" in the context of a movie Dike had watched some year's back simply meant "people against good and neighbourliness". The Afrikan leader loved to disrupt the peace of his country when it mattered most. Lecturers had been on strike over poor payment of salaries; an agreement had been reached before the strike was called off. In the course of time there had been a cabinet reshuffle and Professor Benedictor Nwabuluke had been appointed Minister for Education. When the time came for the implementation of the agreement, with the backing of the President, Prof. Ben had told the lecturers union, " the agreement is not binding on government. In fact it is a gentleman's agreement," he had said. Angered by this the Afrikan Academic

Staff Union of Universities had proceeded again on a very long strike. Students were sad because unless government implemented the agreement of course many won't graduate on the scheduled date. Most students began to leave campus while some didn't with the hope that the strike will be called off, but to no avail. Despite threats which included government decision to eject lecturers out of their quarters as well as stopping their salaries, the strike continued eventually the University authority asked the students to vacate the hostels. However, with academics at a standstill, the transition train had gathered momentum and was a few miles away from the promise land. Meanwhile the first and second batch of presidential aspirants had been disqualified. With nobody willing to run the gauntlet, Gen Bello had convinced two of his best friends to vie for the Presidential elections. While the NRC aspirant was not known, the SDP candidate was a very popular man, known worldwide for his contributions to sports especially in the African continent. In order not to raise doubts on his promise to hand over power to Civilians, Gen. Bello had allowed the primaries to hold knowing full well where and when to botch everything, as was his character. Saturday, June the twelfth, would have been like any other day but it was not because on this day Afrikans turned out in large numbers irrespective of tribe, religion, et cetera, to vote for the man of their choice in the presidential election. Accreditation began by 8. 00 a. m. in the morning while polling took off by 11. 00 a. m. and continued up to 3. 00 p. m. In the afternoon, Dike's parent had voted so did most of his sisters including Ada whom he was once more staying with.

"This is the freest election this country has ever seen", she said on returning from the exercise. She was not alone in her opinion; the foreign observers who monitored the election said the same thing, most people interviewed on network news shared the same view. But the signs were there all right, two days before the election there had been a court injunction from a Federal High Court in Zuma Rock City. The new capital of the Republic of Afrika ordering the national Election Commission not to hold elections that Saturday, but thanks to a presidential order laced with "unseen intrigues" the election had held as planned. With voting concluded by 3. 00p. m, Collation of result began, "the NRC will win", Ada said.

"Maybe, but I think the SDP will win, its candidate is more popular and has done a lot for this country",

Maggie countered. The argument raged for quiet sometime before they started discussing something else. Dike was amused by everything but it was to be expected. A family of about twenty members would never see things the same way they must be divergent views. Moreover, Ada's support for NRC could be understood her husband was a staunch party man. In fact, the new job he got recently in Zuma Rock City was as a result of his faithfulness to the party. The national electoral Commission had begun announcing results when another court order asking the commission to stop was issued. Meanwhile, results from sixteen states had been announced already and Chief Dr. K. M. O. Bolaji-Sowoolu was leading with a clear majority, then the bomb shell fell on Friday when in a televised speech. The President officially cancelled the June 12th elections. The whole world was dazed, shocked and numbed by the dishonesty of Pres. Bello and his trigger-happy colleagues in the armed forces. One party was happy at the cancellation while the other mourned their loss. It was all right in view of the Republicans that the election had been cancelled after all in the sixteen states announced already they had done very badly; it was the Democrats that had actually lost out. Pres. Bello in his stupidity

The Prisoner of Afrika

fixed another election for the month of August and without a definite date for voting. Of course, it was clear the SDP was not going to be part of it. Riots broke out in many states and soldiers were called in and ordered to shoot at sight.

Demonstrators carried placards which read, Enough of the misrule, IBB must go , Down with the Maradona of the sub-region, were shown on television.

"Do you know the Afrikan leader and the Nigerian President have two things in common", Dike observed.

"What is that?" Ada asked without interest,

"Both have the same initials" He said.

"And both leaders have destroyed their countries", Ada said.

"No wonder the minister for education refused to negotiate with Universities lecturers they—"

He was cut off by Ada, "so you didn't know they wanted all universities closed down because of the Presidential elections"

Dike nodded his head in realization of fact.

"President Bello has disturbed and deprived the nation of peace of course he will also not know peace or in the words of Shakespeare, Pres Bello has murdered sleep therefore Afrikans should sleep no more.".

"The problem has just started," Ada added.

"But why do we have such terrible leaders in the continent?" Dike wondered.

"If it is not military dictators, it will be sit tight leaders who turn their countries into one party state so as to rule forever. Oh God deliver us from power crazy leaders".

The outrage that greeted the cancellation of the June 12 election was great, world leaders reacted to this act of daylight robbery and the sanctions began to come but stopped short at imposing an oil embargo. The riots continued despite the presence of armed soldiers on the streets. When politicians and academicians began criticizing the government, the Afrikans dictator turned his "hit squad" loose on them. In the end many including the winner of the June 12 elections fled abroad to save their lives. In a television interview, the Afrikan leader appealed to world leaders "to mind their business and let Afrika settle its internal problems as a family."

People were more enraged by the statement. president Bello's action had taken another dimension when he secretly liaised with his dogs of war and denounced chief Bolaji-Sowoolu as being an extremist, a fundamentalist that should be eliminated in his place of asylum. People continued to issue statements in reaction to the elections; amongst them was a fiery no nonsense lawyer and Human Rights Activists Chief Gbogboade Jackson. In a press release, he had said, "The cancellation of June 12 amounts to dishonesty and stealing on the part of government. It is an orchestrated attempt by the armed forces to deny the people of their rights. It is an act of betrayal, a neo – colonist plan while at the same time denying the winner his God given mandate and a flagrant disregard and violation of individual fundamental human rights. The military Junta should release the results of the election as no further election can be held in this country till the impasse is resolved".

The political Saga continued through the month of July with no clear cut solution. July rolled past and the month of August rolled by. To prevent the situation from deteriorating into a war, colleagues of Gen. Bello convinced him that the whole nation was not tired of the armed forces but at the same time they did not want to see the president's face anymore. Therefore, the only way out was to step aside and let the political mess be resolved. The president had no choice because if he refused the next coup will leave him a dead man. Once again, in a televised speech, Gen. Bello announced he was stepping aside for an interim government to take over. However, Gen. Sani Ahmed who was minister for Defence will stay on so as to provide covering for the interim government". While the nation was rejoicing, only one person, the first lady and wife of the president was sad. She had once said, "I will rather be the wife of the late Afrikan leader than to be addressed wife of a former president". However, the president had stepped aside hale and hearty how his wife was going to handle this was her own look out. The "stepping-aside" ceremony was held on the parade grounds in Zuma Rock City. The first lady watched sorrowfully as her husband stepped aside for others to continue. One could understand her position having basked in the razzmatazz of first lady ship for eight years in which the nation was ripped apart economically, the spectre of life like any other citizen was too frightening to imagine. Unfortunately, the honey moon was not going to last forever.

"..... . I shall discharge my duties without fear or favour and shall uphold the unity of the federal republic of Afrika, so help me God". With this oath of office, Chief Calistus Adekunle had assumed office

The Prisoner of Afrika

as chairman of the interim Government with a promise to do his best for the nation. Upon assumption of office Chief Adekunle had tried to restore everybody's confidence in the transition program, immediately Government also entered into negotiation with university lecturers.

Gen. Bello knowing the fate that was going to befall him, had in the last few months become very irresponsible. A move which had led to the non-payment of salaries of civil servants this negative development had led to a strike. The interim Government had successfully ended the strike by providing money for payment of salaries. The interim Government of National Unity had then announced the 10th of March the following year as date for fresh presidential Elections. This date did not impress anybody. The whole nation was clamouring for the actualization of the last election held on the 12th of June. Chief Adekunle's administration had spent only two month in office when following a successful negotiation with the university lecturers. The eight month old AASUU strike was finally called off and the university authorities began announcing resumption dates so that academic work could resume.

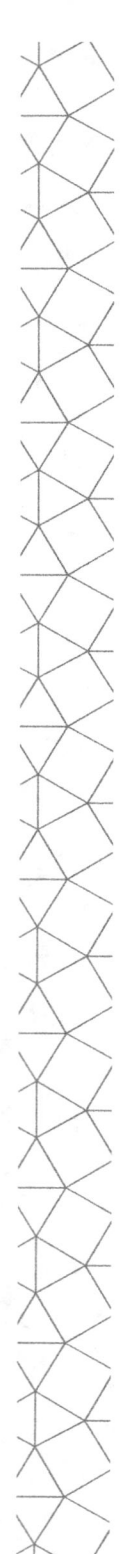

232

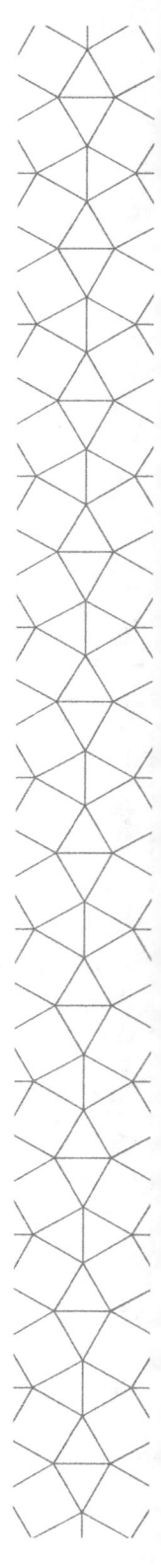

Chapter Thirteen

Chief Callistus Shobanjo Adekunle, B. Sc, LL. B M. Sc, the Asiwaju of Egba Territory Assumed office with a determination to right many wrong inflicted on the people by the previous regime. Some of his efforts were already yielding very good results. But it was not yet "uhuru" as they were still many more rivers to cross in the search for enduring democracy and unity. The Chief knew what was expected from him, and on his part he was willing to give his best. The search for a capable hand to clean the mess left behind by the outgoing president had not been easy. So daunting was the task that even the president's second-in-command Admiral Vincent Livingston had refused taking up the post. Eventually, the Knight in shining Armour had emerged in the person of Chief Adekunle and now the destiny of the nation rested in his hands. To steer a diverse nation like Afrika, the chief would need all the experience gathered in his thirty-five years sojourn with the United African Corporation where he had left as its Chief-Executive Officer (CEO) to head the interim National Government. To everybody, the

Mike Effa

Chief had led a chequered life.

"What else could one wish from life? Many were bound to ask, but the Chief also had his own enemies or critics whichever way you want to put it. Many people were angry with him for accepting the post of Chairman of ING, a move which had led to his being called "an evening lawyer", and thus not worthy to be called to bar. All the criticism fell on deaf ears, as far as Chief Adekunle was concerned the ING had a mission "and they were not going to be stampeded out of office by a bunch of crazy individuals hungry for power. . ." he had said addressing a press conference. The problems to be tackled by the new administration were many. If he were to make headway the Government would have to drop most of the ministers used in destabilising the country.

One negative thing Pres. Idi Bello Succeeded in doing before being disgraced out of office was to increase the price of petroleum products.

The Labour Unions decided to hold their peace while awaiting the inauguration of the interim Government. The New Government of unity had hardly settled down when the Labour Unions began their agitation for a downward review of prices. initially, the Government especially the Minister for

The Prisoner of Afrika

Petroleum was adamant. He had even said in a press conference, "this government is willing to shed blood to maintain the price of petroleum product".

Quite an uncomplimentary remark it had won him more enemies instead of friends. Chief Callistus Adekunle, Chairman interim Government eventually intervened and the prices were brought down to three AfriPounds from a previous price of five pound without a single drop of blood being shed. This was always the problem with his beloved nation. The government due to its insincerity was always appointing as ministers, individuals who had no regards or feeling for even the down trodden masses. It was this calibre of ministers that had to be dropped immediately because they were not working for the overall interest of the country.

Following a successful negotiation with the universities lecturers, their eight-month-old strike was called off. The University of Kalabar was one of the universities to resume on the first day of November while lectures began the following day. The students spent one more week before their first semester exams commenced. A new cabinet had just been sworn-in. it had been a minor cabinet reshuffle only two ministers those of education and information respectively were dropped. People were impressed,

Mike Effa

"I think these people are set for business". Somebody said one day in a bus,

"yes they just had to drop those two," Another passenger replied.

"why did they have to drop only these two?" Dike asked.

"It's simple, the first passenger replied, "these were the agents used to destabilize the country", he concluded.

They were all reflecting the opinion of majority of Afrikans, but then they existed a group of Afrikans with a different opinion made more vocal with the return of the SDP candidate in the cancelled Presidential elections.

This people were not too surprised at headlines of the next day especially the Concord which carried a headline "Interim government is illegal says court". Dike didn't bother to read the story because he was disgusted with most of the politicians, in fact some of them have been openly inviting the army to seize power and sack the interim government of National Unity because to them the situation was not improving and to this group the ING was just a sitting duck. It was really disheartening to hear this calls considering the fact that the country had spent close to three hundred million Afripound on a

The Prisoner of Afrika

transition program that had refuse to end, thanks to the antics of Afrika's political Maradona who in the end had been disgraced out of office. "Thank God Afrika's Maradona has been chased out of Office. At least we can now face our first semester examination. I can hardly wait to finish and become a graduate too am not a child anymore, Dike said to himself.

The first semester examination was already in top gear when the unexpected happened on that seventeenth day of November he was revising while fidgeting with the radio to get the latest on the world cup qualifiers. He was however not alarmed to hear the national anthem. Chuks his roommate was surprised.

"why are you surprised?" Dike asked.

"it's no big deal it can only mean an address by the chairman of the ING", he said, the anthem finished playing and they listened intently to hear the voice of Chief Adekunle instead they were disappointed with what followed next.

"Fellow Afrikans, I Gen. Sani Ahmed wish to intimate you of developments in our beloved country. We are all aware of the transition program which had begun some years back and had to be aborted due to certain problems. Again you all witnessed the breakdown of law and order as well as the inability of the various governments to arrest the situation. We have decided to act fast to save the situation therefore the ING is hereby dissolved to be replaced by a people's Ruling Commission. The national Assembly is hereby dissolved. All States Executive Councils are also dissolved. All State Houses of Assembly are dissolved forthwith. All Governors are advised to handover to the Brigade-Commanders in their respective states. Fellow countrymen I will like to inform you that this administration is a child of circumstances we will do our best to restore democracy, at the shortest possible time, parties will not be sponsored by Government. Individuals will be free to form and belong to any party of their choice. Ladies and Gentlemen I will like you all to go about your business without let or hindrance. Long live the Armed Forces". Long live the Federal republic of Afrika. Thank you all".

The national anthem played again.

"Transition without end" Chuka said and they all laughed.

"No. This one is Interim transition", Monday another roommate of their said. "Why?, Dike asked, "The transition program gave way to an Interim Government and both have collapsed, so this is

more of an interim transition arrangement", he said.
Afrika had once again return fully to military rule, to
those who knew Gen. Sani Ahmed very well. They will
tell you the guy was a coward and only acted when
prodded, so reasoned many Afrikans that for him to
stage this coup meant he had the backing of
certain politicians. With democratic structures
demolished the actualization of June 12 was going
to be difficult. With a new administration in the show,
traditional rulers, politicians including the SDP
aspirant at the botched presidential election, in fact
the chief will later recommend his running mate for
a ministerial position and other eminent personalities
began storming Zuma Rock City to welcome the
new Head of state and to indirectly tell him not to
forget them when the packages drop. When the
solidarity visits became too much, government
immediately placed an "embargo on further

n the third week of February, Dike
began his degree examinations, his
parents were happy for him,
"Very soon you will become a
graduate", his mother had said that day.
"Yes", he had replied very excited at the prospect.
"Remember it's either a second class upper or

nothing," his mother said.

"I shall do my best," he promised.

They finished the exams, submitted their project and vacated the campus. Normal academics continued for other students. Finishing the degree examinations was one thing and the results were another ball game as they spent the next three months at home before their results were released. It is a laid down rule that every university graduate must do a one year compulsory service, except on grounds of ill-health, married graduates could also be exempted if they applied. Since there was no age limit, Dike knew he was eligible for service to his beloved nation.

Dike kept his promise and graduated with a second class upper division, he was still waiting for the National Service call-up letter. He had made efforts through a retired Army Major to influence his posting to either Ekko City or Zuma Rock City.

"Don't worry I will get you there", the Major had assured. So Dike had no choice but to wait. The Shakkassalli family was a large one in all they were twelve in number, eight girls and four boys. Out of these seven were graduates with the remaining members either in high school or other tertiary institution. With time, they would all graduate and

The Prisoner of Afrika

their father would take a well deserved rest.

"Oh God! Let them post me to a good state-o!", Dike prayed silently. To while away time, Dike became a laundry man washing mostly for family members for a pittance or chicken change.

"Don't worry your letter to Dogawa state will soon come," his younger brother consoled. "Hey be careful, I don't want any Prophet around me, " Dike replied.

"Don't you know words are powerful. For your information, I'm not going to that state okay?"

When call-up letters and posting were released a week later, Dike was standing inside the yard when Kris arrived from school.

"Have you seen mine?"

"Dogawa state ", Kris said cutting him off.

"Dogawa State?" Dike asked with anxiety, "go to school and see for yourself", he said and went in to greet their parents leaving him to his fate.

"Dogawa of all places", he said to himself. "of course I will find out", Dike said to himself as he walked into the house. He believed Kris. The day he received the call-up letter and calmed down thereafter refusing to even consider it any further and refusing to blame anybody for his predicament. His parents and other family members advised him to take it as God's doing", and wished him a happy service, year.

II

Dike`s reasons for not wanting to serve in Dogawa was not farfetched. The state was notorious for its riots and the indigenes were always hostile to non-indigenes. The Berbers who formed seventy percent of the population were too emotional and temperamental for his liking. This was the much he knew about them, but he did not discount the fact that he will come to know their other side like the back of his hand after the one year of exploitation by blood sucking agencies and individuals called employers.

"Father it is you that knows why I should be sent to this state", Dike said, looking up to heaven. To think that this major just deceived me and I almost paid him for services never rendered.

"Well, I commit my soul to God Almighty."

A few days before Dike departed for Dogawa State, Chief Sowoolu Declared himself President of the Federal Republic of Afrika.

The Military authorities were stunned by his actions. This was a treasonable offence and everybody

The Prisoner of Afrika

including the chief knew what he was playing with. On his return from exile, he had something which amazed everybody. He had written a letter to the disgraced Afrikan dictator, "pleading that their relationship be restored and that it was Gen. Ahmed who was actually his enemy as well as traitor. Upon receiving the letter, the retired president had quickly faxed it to the head of state. To say the least Chief sowoolu`s actions amounted to the proverbial hen that had flirted with the fox. It was surprising to many people who knew the part the chief had played in the sacking of the Interim Government to suddenly declare himself President. Another funny aspect of his declaration was that his would be Vice President was the minister for foreign affairs in the new cabinet. The chief had nominated him for that position and now the chief had just declared himself president without a vice-president. The military authorities were not going to take things sitting down. Everywhere was tensed. More so with a statement the Chief had made on the day of his inauguration, "any attempt to arrest me will tear this nation apart". He had said the one thing Afrikans didn`t want . Another civil war. Afrikans were amazed at the position the Chief was adopting because initially it appeared he had been willing at the onset to forget everything, but after the inauguration of the South Africa's Black President and his subsequent meeting with the South African Leader and the United States Vice President, Chief Sowoolu had returned determined to actualize his mandate. More so when he discovered that Gen. Ahmed was indeed a liar and was bent on sidetracking him from his mandate.

The journey to Dogawa was not without its own hassles, apart from the bad roads which made driving difficult they had to contend with roadblocks manned in most cases by customs and Immigration officers. Every vehicle that plied this road was made to stop and its occupants made to answer any questions asked by immigration officers when their bus approached. They flagged them to stop which the driver did the Immigration Officer came over. Good afternoon everybody", he greeted.

Dike looked at his watch it was half past two already, "You there", he said.

He looked up.

"Me?" he asked casting sideway glances to see if he was referring to somebody else in the bus.

Yes! You!" he replied,

The Prisoner of Afrika

"Yes. What can I do for you? "Dike asked adjusting himself on his seat.

Are you a national of this country?" He asked, the question sounded funny.

"Yes I am", Dike responded still smiling.

"Which state do you come from?", he asked.

"Kalabar State", he responded replacing the smile with a frown.

"May I see your ID card please?", he requested.

"Sorry. The identity card is in my bag which cannot be reached".

Satisfied, he left Dike and walked over to where two men whom apparently were not Afrikans were being questioned about their papers. The road was cleared and the bus was allowed to proceed. Travelling from Kalabar state to any of the Northern states is not an easy task as Dike was to find out distance was a major reason why those who could afford it always went by flight. Not being in a haste to report to camp, he decided to travel to Zuma Rock city to spend some days with Ada and her three children. The bus was originally destined for Zaria State so when they reached kaffin- keffi, Dike dropped off at the junction while the bus turned right and headed for the town en route its destination. He crossed over to a small park where taxi`s were parked.

"oga wey you dey go?". the man asked,

"I dey go Zuma Rock City", he said,

"na how much una dey take?" he asked.

"From kaffin-keffi to Zuma Rock city na thirty-five Afripounds", the man replied. Without further argument, Dike took a seat. It turned out to be the only space that was left. Immediately, the taxi moved out.

Zuma Rock City is the new Capital City of Afrika. The transfer was finally effected by President Bello immediately major Ndjamena's Coup was crushed. A lot had been spent on making the city fit for Government. It was 6p.m. in the evening when they entered the park. Getting to his sister's house was a Herculean task , after two near misses he located the house situated on ministers Hill near the Head of State`s guest house.

Ada and her children were very happy to see Dike, but a bit sad because he wasn't going to stay long. Throughout his brief stay, he tried his best in ensuring that it was a memorable one; especially for the kids. On Tuesday morning, Dike was ready for the last lap of the trip to Dogawa State.

"Okay go well o, stay out of trouble", she advised. Having never been up North before and if not for the national service, Dike didn't think he would ever come this way. He found a Nissan-civilian Bus operated under the National Assisted Mass Transit Scheme (NAMTS) , paid the fare, and settled down in the front seat., The Bus was almost full when he arrived. At half past nine, they pulled out of the City Park and the journey to Dogawa was on.

The National Service scheme came into existence a few years after the civil war. It was another means the Government wanted to use in hastening the process of reconciliation. It involved university and polytechnic graduates being sent to different states to serve. It was also intended that in the Process of serving one will get to know the people and the culture of the area in which he is serving thus making it possible for "Afrikans to know and appreciate themselves" as Gen. Muazu had put it way back some twenty years ago.

The bus made a stopover in Zaria State to get some fuel, meanwhile fuel scarcity was already being experienced in some northern states. It was a funny situation because the four refineries were functioning all right, so the cause of the scarcity remained a mystery.

Shortly they moved on, passing interesting landmarks and beautiful scenes and spots. Dike couldn`t sleep like other passengers were doing, this was not strange in itself, it was to be expected given the fact that he was new in these parts so his anxiety certainly got the best part of him. Even when the driver finally stopped Dike was not sure of where they were, so he asked a man in babariga as the dressing here is known. "Please, are we in Dogawa?",

"You are new?", he asked,

"Yes", Dike responded.

Before he could say more, the man got down the bus and disappeared. Eventually, he got down from the bus, Dike accosted another man dressed in babariga too and had tribal marks a common feature among the Berbers and the Hausawa people who made up the northern part of the country.

"Please how can I get to Jarko?", Dike asked. Jarko was a county in Dogawa state and the orientation camp was holding there. It had been a Teachers training college, which was no longer in use.

"Are you a corfer? ", The man asked looking at Dike suspiciously.

"Yes I am", came his reply.

The Prisoner of Afrika

"Okay," he said and motioned him to follow him which he did. They walked on for about two minutes then stopped suddenly in front of a bus where he engaged another man in a brief conversation before turning to Dike.

"This bus will take you to Jarko the last bus stop is where you will drop", he said, and they shook hands while Dike thanked him profusely and boarded the bus.

He tried to engage one or two passenger in a conversation but in each occasion he ran into a blank wall. One thing he didn't see immediately was that not everybody up here understood English, unlike down south where you could engage anybody in a conversation.

Throughout the trip, which lasted over one hour, Dike kept wondering if he wasn't dreaming about everything. The bus reached Jarko. With the help of the bus conductor, he took an "achabbar" as the motorcyclists are known in this part.

Dike had looked at the bus conductor when he said, "oga" you go take achabbar reach de place". "What?" He had asked and the bus conductor without further delay pointed at a group of motorcyclists. Immediately, Dike knew what he meant. It sounded funny and he committed it to memory he had a lot of learning to do.

Orientation camp was a continuation of the confusion already being felt in the country. Everywhere was rowdy, but it did not stop him from exchanging pleasantries with two of his colleagues from the University of Kalabar. He knew there will be more. With time they will know themselves. He finished registration that same day, but could not get the kits till the next day. In the morning when a soldier sounded the bugle, he refuse to go out on the grounds that, "he had no kits ".

Camp life later turned out to be amusing. Soldiers drawn from the 13th Brigade in Dogawa drilled them. The camp commandant was a young, suave and dashingly handsome Captain. The male corpers could see the effect on the ladies who were falling over themselves all in an effort to please the captain in every way possible. Mostly, through the use of their "greatest asset" which had been known to melt even the strongest of hearts. Other camp officials including the state director, Mr. Francis Teju, all benefited from the kind donation by female corpers who saw it as an opportunity to influence their posting to good places. The losers were the male corpers and the female staff among the camp officials most of whom were married and even then no male corper was going to chase a woman old enough to be his mother. Dike was drafted into twelfth platoon commonly called "JJC platoon". The acronym meant Johnny Just Come. Most of them had just reported and many platoon members didn't know their left from their right. The state director was another smooth talker, while addressing the corpers he extolled the state in which they were serving.

"You are blessed to be in dogawa state", he said.

"The county chairmen are waiting for you eagerly,", he said.

The corpers were happy to hear this piece of news and everybody was itching for the following week when they will leave camp to begin their primary assignment. The three weeks spent in Jarko was a regimented one of course they were handled by soldiers. In camp, light out started by ten p. m and corpers were punished for flouting this rule.

ne morning they arrived the parade ground to find condoms scattered about.

"What a mess", somebody said.

"Only three weeks and most people cannot control themselves", another said.

Mike Effa

"We have a lot of dog amongst us ", they all burst into laughter and dispersed as the soldiers came and drove them away.

The endurance trek is one aspect of camp life. Dike enjoyed most. The endurance trek that Saturday had been challenging they had set out in the morning in twelve columns. They sang, made jokes, and progressed. Gradually they scattered and everybody had to answer his father's name. Eventually, all reach the rendezvous by half past three. The weather was fair as it had rained on the way. After about thirty minutes rest, they began the return trip to camp. Those who could not make it had to join buses on the way back. Dike was tempted to do the same but when he saw many girls walking, he decided to walk back to camp. Besides, he had always taken pride in the fact that he was tough so now was the opportunity to prove and convince himself of that assertion. He did prove himself right by walking back to camp on foot. The funny part of it is that most of the soldiers including the camp commandant couldn't return on foot. They had to commandeer a bus back to camp. It went a long way to prove that the corpers were even stronger then the soldiers and their officers. Orientation camp came to an end Monday of the

The Prisoner of Afrika

following week. After the parade, it was time to receive their letters of posting. This brief moment was tagged the Moment of Truth or Reality. Many corp members especially the girls had bribed with everything possible. Now, it was time to see if their gifts and donations would make a way for them. Right from his first day in camp, he had never considered this line of action. Besides, he didn't have the money to bribe with. Rather, he had prayed to GOD to take control and had forgotten about the issue till this very moment. He got near the window.

"what is your number?", the soldier asked.

"596", he replied.

The soldier pulled out his letter and gave it to him. Immediately, his eyes went to the space reserved for employers and boldly written was Beyoro university.

"I got it", he screamed with excitement.

"What is it?" victor his roommate in camp asked panting.

"God has answered my prayers and I've been posted to the university", he told victor still panting,

"Bravo," victor said, "but check it properly to ensure it's true". he advised. They went through the letter together there was no mistake.

On his part, victor had been redeployed to his state of origin for reason best known to him. Dike was also happy that orientation camp had ended. He'd been fed up with the parades and the way girls in his platoon looked at the guys. Throughout his stay in camp, he made it a policy not to socialize, and with the girls especially. Apart from the casual "good morning", nothing more happened.

They reported to the university and were introduced to the corper liaison officer. Some of their colleagues were rejected on the spot so it began to dawn on them that the state director had lied to them. Mr. Balarabe Bello addressed them in his capacity as the university's corper liaison officer. He intimated them of accommodation arrangement and concluded by warning the corpers not to task the students financially via handouts. This did not bother Dike as he had already made up his mind not to give anything of this sort and to finish whatever assignment he was given within the stipulated time. When he had finished addressing them, he provided transportation to the corpers lodge which was right inside the city. Lodge one was all right in terms of security. In the event of riot, one could escape but not so with lodge two. Here they were in the heart of the city completely surrounded by Berbers and Hausawas who didn't hear a word of English, and then they also had to put up with the "dreaded almajiris". These are a group of boys under school age, but are not schooling and will never see the four walls of a classroom.

Lodge two was an old, decrepit, and dirty building. Initially, the corpers resisted and were almost succeeding when one of them broke ranks and went in to take a room. Dike sighed disgustedly and went in committing his spirit to God for safe keeping throughout the one year; he was going to spend in the city. He was allocated room nine.,

While handing over the keys, Balarabe smiled, "you will be alright", he had said.

"I hope so", Dike said in reply.

"I can assure you, he continued, "the North is safer than the south", he said, entered his car and drove off.

Dike was to spend the next twelve months in terror. Everything was wrong with the lodge. Before they knew it they were polarized along ethnic lines and that was how they started having problems.

In lodge two, the most troublesome corper was Umar Rima from Rima state. If you made a remark

Umar must reply and in most cases end by saying "pucking shit".

One funny aspect with Umar was his case of mixing letters thus instead of "fucking shit" he will say "pucking shit. In the midst of these squabbles, Balarabe Bello the Liaison officer started showing his true colours.

Then the exams came. Throughout the four years, he spent in the university, Dike never saw the type of corruption as that exhibited by students here. Lecturers were bribed with different gifts and if you were the horny type, girls in your class were always willing to buy their way out with their asset. While the exams were going on, one of their colleagues went too far in the bribery business. In his case he started hunting for students who had failed. He confided in Dike one day.

"I think you are going too far," Dike warned.

"Chicken," he said. "Nothing will happen. . . "

But it did happen when he bit more than he could carry. He got involved with a female student whose guardian was a lecturer in that department. A trap was set and he caught this guy red-handed. He was, of course, reported to the National Youth Service office and rejected by the university on grounds of examination fraud. The rest of the corpers took a cue from there.

In life, you tend to meet a lot of people both good and bad. Dike met Benson while in the lodge, a fine and easy going gentleman, who later began staying with Dike and influenced his life in many ways. Lodge two had its share of characters. Victor was one of them. Victor was a "chronic smoker". Victor would smoke anything smoke-able Lodge one also had its problems. Most conspicuous of them all was a guy called Bolaji and his girl friend Folashade, all corpers. They were fond of fighting like a married couple and they were living together. Whenever they were fighting, other boys will move in to separate. Shade was a very horny lady who needed to be satisfied sexually every time. One particular day she was in need of her "usual medicine" her man was not willing to supply.

Out of frustration she grabbed him by the balls and they started fighting again. After they had been separated the boys were curious.

"old boy, what happened now?" One of the boys asked.

"Don't mind that stupid girl who is never tired of

Mike Effa

being mounted every time. " the other boys began to laugh. This even encouraged Bolaji to go on.

"I was trying to sleep when she came and was disturbing me to give it to her and when I refused; she grabbed my organs probably to take it by force."

"So you beat her", one of the boys interrupted him

"Yes, I had to get her to let go of my organ", this drew another round of laughter. "Please you shouldn't fight again –o, it's not good". One of the boys advised and with that all dispersed to their rooms.

259

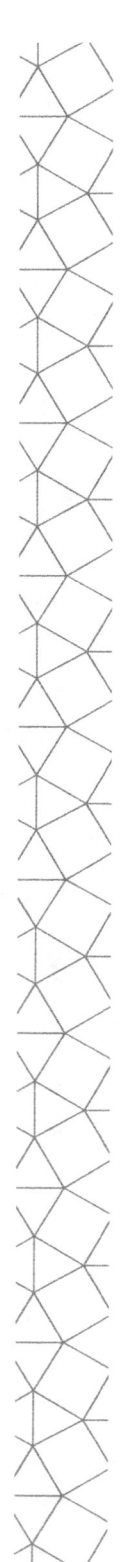

260

Chapter Fourteen

The service year moved very fast despite the political upheavals, which included the trial of chief Sowoolu and the removal of two service chiefs for holding contrary views to those of the head of state. Dike and his colleagues prayed for the day they would pass out and leave the north, then without warning university lecturers started another round of strike added to this came the problem of fuel scarcity. While one could see what led to the lecturer's strike, one could not fathom the cause of the scarcity. But then, the middlemen were there and you could not ignore them. The middlemen were powerful and influential and had friends in Government so whenever the middlemen were broke, Government will give them the chance to create artificial scarcity so as to shore up their dwindling financial base and when this is done the supply of fuel suddenly returns to normal and that was the main reason behind the fuel scarcity. Quite, a vicious cycle. . Matters were not helped when a man was beheaded for desecrating "the Holy book", and the perpetrators even had the temerity to march through the town displaying the man's head. Law had really broken down, even the State Government could not arrest anybody. Throughout January of the New Year, there was tension in Dogawa state as the non-indigenes protested the unjust killing of an innocent man. In the midst of the tension, people had to watch their tongue. Already in the lodge they were divided, the situation dragged on till March. One evening they were watching the evening news when a news item featured people carrying placards.

"What is this?" Gabe asked.

"No to coup. Down with coup plotters", Gbenga read to the hearing of everybody. "Another coup attempt," Dike asked in surprise.

"Yes another coup attempt", Mike who had just joined them answered.

"And there are many Northern military officers and plenty of southern journalist as well as two former heads of state ", Mike concluded.

They were all flabbergasted by the news.

"which heads of state are involved", Gbenga asked.

"No problem we will get the names sooner or later", Gabe said.

"who is the leader of the coup?" Dike asked.

"okay, it is this officer who was chief of army staff in

The Prisoner of Afrika

Gambia", Mike replied.

"Oh Col. Umoru and a onetime military governor of Bida state", Gbenga said.

"oh-oh the guy who had made jest of Major Ndjamena's coup now he is in soup too", Dike said and they laughed.

The coup saga dragged on for a long time appeals for clemency was sent to Government. The plotters were tried and sentences were later commuted to life imprisonment.

In April Dike, travelled down to Kalabar for his university's convocation it was a grand reunion with his colleagues most of whom they had lost touches. Dike's convocation reception was handled by his mother. it was a success.

Dike returned just in time to prepare for the final passing out parade. A lot of things had happened while he was away, a very serious misunderstanding had occurred between Jorbert who was staying in the lodge with Sani and Dauda a corper from Birnin-Gwari State According to Gabe, the timely intervention by Benson saved the situation. Dike was shocked to hear this. Meanwhile, Balarabe had come rather than settling the issue. The corper

Liaison officer decided to be partial. Not that it mattered after all in a few days they will pass out and leave the useless and unfriendly state and their people for good. A few days after the lodge war, Gabe had gone to see Balarabe so that he will be allowed to spend some months in the lodge to enable his wife put to birth before going home finally. That evening, Dike asked how it went.

"My brother people are wicked," he began" Balarabe Bello turned down my request saying I will be cheating the northern Afrika Government", he said.

Dike didn't know how to react. "this man is a moron", he said.

"What does he mean by Northern Government?" he asked. "Are we practicing confederalism?"

"So what are you going to do?" he asked

"My Head of Department says I should stay for at least two months till when the baby is strong enough to travel".

"That's good", Dike said, "the idiotic Balarabe can go to hell with his lodge" II

The final passing out parade took place on the fifth day of May, which was a Friday. On returning from the parade ground, Dike came out and sat on the balcony and watched his colleagues depart for

The Prisoner of Afrika

good, he wished he could go too but no way. His friend, Benson had just secured something in form of a job for him. The University had not paid them their May transport allowance yet, so most of the boys could not wait. Many of them had given theirs to friends, but it was not so with Victor. Not knowing what to do, he came upstairs to Dike.

"Dike", he called.

"Please, here are my documents. Help collect my transport allowance and post it to me.",

"Okay", Dike said, receiving the documents.

Later on, Tony Coke returned from a drinking spree. He was sober enough to hear what Dike had to say about his encounter with Victor as soon as he finished.

Tony laughed "do you know why I'm returning now?" he asked.

"No I don't", Dike said.

"I did this so that I will not give Victor any money. That guy does not trust anybody", Tony said.

Dike was a little bit confused, "so why did he ask me to collect his money and send it to him?" he asked.

"it's simple", Tony said, "he had no choice. He doesn't trust you, he had said so only he never knew you will hear", Tony concluded.

"Alright no problem," Dike said.

Mike Effa

Inside, he was very angry at the insult and back stabbing action of Victor and he resolved that when the money was paid Victor was never going to get his money and that is exactly what he did when the money was paid later in the week.

That night a cigarette vendor came to draw a debt of three hundred pounds owed him by Victor- but Victor had gone back to his state.

He remained in the lodge and started work, two months before passing out, three of them had been introduced to one Mazi Okeke, a resident in Dogawa. Meanwhile, Benson worked with Mark Fuzz Chartered Accountant with offices situated at Niger Road. On the other hand, Mazi Okeke was the sales and marketing manager of Asbestos Ltd. The company specialized in producing roofing sheets made from asbestos or cement. Their products were really selling and Mazi Okeke was responsible for appointing distributors. Of course, that he was making money was also very obvious. Mazi Okeke wanted to start publishing a newspaper, already an office had been rented with a sign board that read NATIONAL CONSCIENCE MEDIA LTD.

On seeing the sign board, Dike's impression of Mazi Okeke was that of a serious man. On Friday morning, two months before passing out, they had

The Prisoner of Afrika

gone to see him to finalize arrangements. They arrived Sharada Phase Five in the nick of time; they did not get down to discussing till almost twelve midday. While they were still waiting, Benson called and Mazi Okeke told him they were with him already. The life of a marketing manager is quite a hectic one. You have to deal with a lot of customers. So, this Friday was no exception. Eventually he succeeded in disposing all his customers and then got down to business. He apologized for the delay and then went on to explain his plans and why he needed them.

"I believe you are not strange to a newspaper? He asked.

"Yes" they responded.

"Mr. Dike, I learnt you are a writer"? he asked.

"Yes", he replied.

As at that time Dike was working on some stories he hoped would be published one day. Of course, this was the major reason why he was being offered this job.

"We will like to publish your stories", he said.

"It will be a pleasure", he replied.

They discussed at length and at the end of it all Dike was asked to apply for the position of staff writer with a salary of three thousand Afripounds and Kyrian

Mike Effa

who was a mass communication graduate for the position of Acting Editor. The only lady who went with them refused to take up the job on the grounds that the salary was too small. that remained the setting till in May when they passed out and commenced work.

Publishing did not commence immediately. Kyrian was mandated to scout around and come up with a suitable place with a good price where they could go with their dummy for the actual printing. Three days after, he started work. Dike was knocked down by a bout of malaria for almost five days he was groaning from malaria. Only Kyrian paid him a visit. Mike who was in the same lodge with them went about his business as though nothing was happening. His roommate Sani was later to confirm this nonchalant attitude in Mike. Benson showed concern and Dike appreciated it. National Conscience was a small media outfit. The board consisted of Mazi Okeke as Chairman and publisher, Kyrian was editor while Jobert Jafo who had joined earlier was deputy editor. The position of feature editor was given to Dike. Mazi Okeke's wife, Benson and three other businessmen completed the editorial board.

The Prisoner of Afrika

III

he following week, Monday had begun as usual. Dike was in the office when kyrian came back panting.

"What is happening?, he asked.

"Riot in Bata", he said.

Dike was speechless for some time, "is it spreading fast?" he asked.

"I think so", Kyrian replied sitting down.

"when this is over I am returning to Ekko City", he said.

Dike didn't reply, his mind already in deep thoughts. He had always dreaded the day this negative trend will occur. Now, it had. If only Jobs were not scarce, he would have packed all his bags and gone like the wind. The Military Administrator once again was slow in acting. The situation was brought under control when soldiers from the 13th brigade were brought out into the streets with orders to shoot at sight. They got to know the details when work closed and he went back to his lodge. According to Mike, "a very minor fracas had started it all and it had led to many deaths and burning down of churches.

"What about the police?" Dike asked.

"The police and the fire service had refused to respond to distress calls by the Vicar of the Anglican

Church who had watched helplessly as his church was consumed by fire". Mike said.

Later Benson returned and confirmed it all.

"This country is finished," he began, "can you imagine the Police Commissioner asking a church member why they didn't defend their church?" Benson thundered, "It's a shame nobody is saved in this damned town".

They remained in the city while the riot lasted and the only means of protection was to sleep lightly, but they secured their rooms by connecting the door to a live wire. By Saturday, there was total peace but Dike was no longer at ease living in the city. Meanwhile, Balarabe had given them two weeks to vacate the lodge. Fortunately, a good friend of Benson had given him his Boy's quarters. Despite the deadline they were dragging their feet, but it all ended when the Muslim brothers began distributing leaflets advising non-Muslims to leave the city and Dogawa State in general. A Jihad war was in the offing according to the leaflet. At this point, they didn't need to wait for Balarabe before moving. It now occurred to them that their lives were in danger. On Tuesday morning to the surprise of Sani and Mike, Benson and Dike vacated the lodge in the early hours of that day. Dike packed his belongings to the last pin in an attempt to ensure that the Almajiri's hovering around didn't find anything valuable. Whether Balarabe came didn't matter to them anymore, their new place of abode was the boys" quarters of Mr. Essen Edetson.

Their new host worked with The Afrikan National Petroleum Corporation.. He was the Assistant Depot Chief of the Dogawa depot. The boys quarters was a two-bedroom affair. One of the rooms had been already occupied by a family of five. How they managed no one knew. Mr. Edetson was happy to see them move in.

"in the least my wife will stop disturbing me about giving out the room to anybody", he said that evening.

Their neighbour they later came to know was Papa Ejima was neither black nor fair. He was in fact more of an albino and was a very proud man who had no regard for his wife and his sister-in-law. In fact, the way he related with his wife's sister had prompted gossips that he was having an affair with his wife's sister. Mama Ejima and her sister were fond of adding an "E" to Joe's name, thus whenever his name was mentioned you will hear Ejoe instead of Joe. It was very funny.

They had stayed for only two weeks when they had

their first squabble. Ejoe was fond of looking into Benson's room through the window whenever he was going out.

" look well well", Dike will shout at him. He wasn't deterred and Dike wasn't finding it funny so he complained to Uwem a brother to Mr. Edetson.

Uwem disliked them so for him this was an opportunity to embarrass the useless people. He reported the case to his senior brother who wasted no time in cautioning papa Ejima.

Later, when Uwem visited he narrated their reactions to Dike. Mama Ejima's sister decided to make an issue out of it when she threatened to deal with Dike. "I go show am say no be only him go school", watching Uwem, Dike knew he had really found everything funny. Of course, she couldn't do anything.

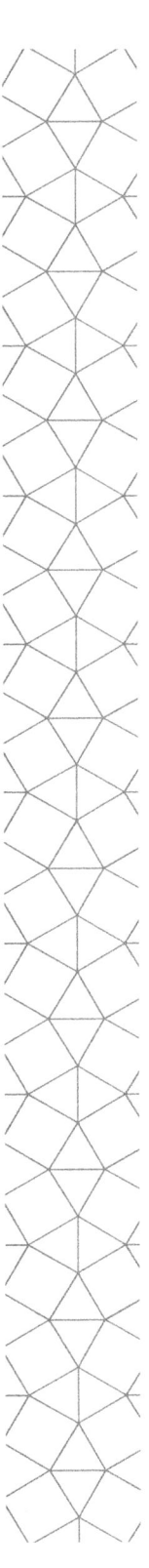

273

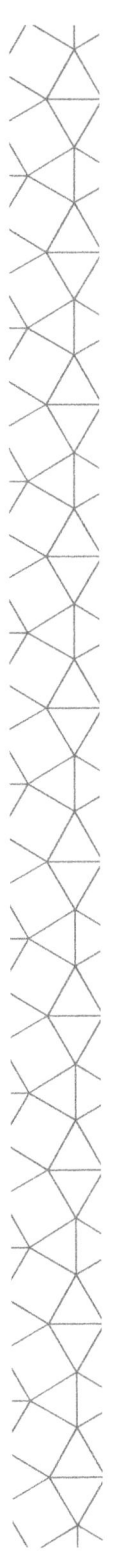

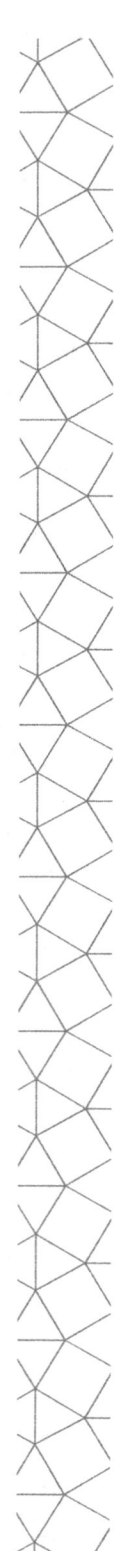

274

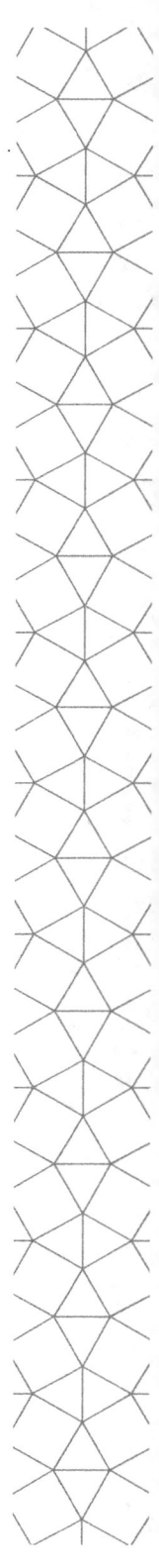

Chapter Fifteen

After one and half months of ground work, they were yet to publish. Kyrian had made a lot of proposals; all had been rejected by Mazi Okeke. Frustrated, Kyrian had quietly left at the end of June and gone back to Ekko city to continue with his soap business. Mazi Okeke was furious when he eventually discovered.

"So the editor has vanished?", he asked after one week of no appearance by Kyrian.

"I don't know Sir", Dike had replied.

Looking back at the first forty five days, the cracks were already there. It had started when their salaries were cut on grounds that they were absent for two days. Mazi didn't trust Dike and Kyrian. He preferred to trust Jobert because they graduated from the same university. As Editor, Kyrian was supposed to be in charge of the Imprest account but Mazi Okeke for reasons not stated by-passed Kyrian instead put Jobert in charge of finance. Although Mazi didn't know it, Jobert had two jobs. He was a teacher at an Army Day School, a factor that accounted for his coming late to work. Apart from these problems, Kyrian had once confided in him, "I can only stay if I am given a gun and good accommodation".

"That's fine", Dike had replied.

"Put it in writing and send it to the publisher", he advised.

"No, I won't he should know the security in this town is very poor", Kyrian had replied. However, he had taken the only way out which of course was to leave quietly. Still, things didn't improve. Dike's salary was slashed down to two thousand seven hundred Afripounds and he had completed two months without employment later. All these problems prompted one of his sisters into suggesting that he should leave Dogawa. "Going back home is no problem but what about job ? ", Dike had asked, She saw his point and encouraged him to stay on. Dike had thought Jobert was a friend. He admired him because when he was in the lodge he humbled himself so much, alas Jobert was really a brown snake in brown grass. This guy could kill. While trying to get things moving, Jobert had already started a campaign of calumny first against Kyrian and then Kyrian left. He was happy because on Benson's advice he was made editor. Quite a big mistake, as Benson was to discover later, and then he turned on Dike. Dike was only a Deputy Editor and he was no threat to Jobert, yet he was running him down. Benson was not spared either he received his own dose of the running down. Mazi Okeke was a man who believed and listened to gossips a lot. He believed Jobert and eventually his relationship with Dike deteriorated badly. Even Benson never agreed when he complained. He even reported Dike to his sister who wrote back advising him "to fight for his rights like a man."

Mazi Okeke was a very proud man who always liked having his way he didn't like advice. Initially, he had wanted to use the name NATIONAL CONSCIENCE in identifying his paper. He was advised against it because a club bearing that name was already in existence and was waging a war against the Federal Government. Mazi had been to Zuma Rock City thrice and on each occasion he was denied registration. Eventually, he agreed to an amendment. The National Conscience remained as the name of the company while the newspaper was to be known as the "Afrikan Conscience. Even then, registration remained elusive. Considering distance and the dangerous roads, they ruled out printing in Zaria State. They didn't search for too long before stumbling on Peak Precise, a printing outfit managed by two brothers. At this point, Jobert had gone very far in his campaign of calumny. He had so washed down Benson before Mazi Okeke that in the end Mazi Okeke now had no regards for Benson anymore. Benson's opinion was no longer sought, Mazi Okeke though he was paying the bills but unconsciously the newspaper belong to Jobert who was running it like a dictator.

Dike knew it was only a matter of time before he will be thrown out. It was under this state of uncertainty that they took their typed written articles to the press for the printing of the maiden edition. Benson though sidelined still showed some interest in the whole thing.

"I think this first edition should be delayed a little", he had said by way of advice. "Then call Mazi and discuss it with him", Dike suggested.

"That's your job go and see him and discuss it with him", he countered.

"Look", Dike began, "this man does not listen to advice moreover with the way Jobert is running me down. I don't stand a chance".

The issue was not discussed any more. Nobody knows if Benson did call, but on his part Dike refused to go to discuss it with his boss. Rather, he made his

The Prisoner of Afrika

position known to Kalu who was in charge of Gilt Edge a subsidiary of Alpha and Omega Group of companies which had Mazi as Chairman while his wife was General Manager. Later, in August the preview copy was printed, the quality was disgustingly poor. The vendors rejected it. One day while doing a feedback survey, Dike approached a vendor.

"Oga which paper you want?" the vendor had asked.

"You get Afrikan Conscience?", Dike asked.

"Which one be dat?" he asked again. Dike explained how their paper looked like.

"Oh that paper?" he asked.

"Yes na dat one I want", he said.

"Oga no vex that paper na real load nobody dey even look am sef" the vendor said, leaving Dike to attend to another prospective buyer. He engaged over ten other vendors at the end he discovered with dismay that they had failed woefully. Of course, it would have been a miracle for a paper that was poor in quality to sell even ten copies. Being a weekly paper, it was withdrawn at the beginning of the following week. One thousand nine hundred copies were printed and distributed. The same figure was returned as unsold. Mazi Okeke was not aware of this initially. He had become so proud to the extent that in an editorial meeting he had openly congratulated the Editor on a nice job.

Dike was hurt at this but he had no choice. He complained to Jenny his girl friend.,

"I think you should go and see him in his office", she advised.

"Really what difference will it make?" he asked. Benson was blunt in his reply.

"He did it to hurt you", he had said that evening.

Dike kept quiet but inside he was seething with rage while wishing his employer a lot of evil things.

"When is the next edition coming out?" Mazi had asked a few days before the preview copy was scheduled to be withdrawn from the streets.

There wasn't a reply. Dike had given Benson a complete run down on the situation. "What did I say here?" he asked pacing the room.

"Have you informed okeke?"

"No I have not but the so-called editor is aware of the situation" Dike replied.

Mazi Okeke had been itching for news about the preview copy already in the market and Jobert true to form capitalized on this to dent Dike's image further. Eventually, Benson broke the news to him.

That evening Dike almost died with laughter when

The Prisoner of Afrika

Benson recounted the whole thing.

"So you called him?" He asked for the third time that evening.

"I told him not even a copy was sold and he almost dropped the phone".

"He has not seen anything yet" Dike said.

"His effort is commendable at least it will earn him a spot in Stephen Pile's book of failures" Benson said.

"What an effort – that's rubbish. "

Jobert was misleading Mazi Okeke and at the same time was siphoning his money. Dike did not care anymore, he was fed up already. If the paper went under that will even be good for him at least it will afford him the opportunity of leaving without hurting anybody. A major re-organization was made. Kalu was seconded to the conscience as circulation manager. He was older and had more experience. It didn't take long before a cold war started between him and Jobert.

II

Two pretty girls Patsy and Hadiza were added to beef up the staff strength. Patsy hailed from Akwa state and was a graduate of Political Science. She was employed as Advert Executive. Her job was to source for adverts. Hadiza though a youth corper was given the position of staff writer. Hadiza was good in writing poems in the Hausawa dialect. Both girls were interesting to work with and Dike enjoyed their company throughout the period they worked together. . Dike loved and admired Patsy. She was a complete woman, every man's dream of what a woman should be. Patsy was beautiful, shapely, and always smelled nice. Amongst the six of them, Jobert was the only guy with money to throw around because of his other jobs but Jobert had one problem. The guy had a very bad body odour. It baffled everybody and they wondered why this guy could not take care of himself …

"and he has girl friends", Patsy had said that day while discussing with Jobert.

"That's the problem with most women. They will bed a skunk so far as he meets their immediate financial needs".

"It's not true", Patsy countered. And they let the issue lie as it was and changed the topic of discussion which was timely too as Jobert came in a few minutes later.

Based on Benson's advice, Dike started going to Asbestos Ltd too to see the Chairman. He started by passing Jobert just like Kalu was doing. Jobert didn't know initially then they met each other in Mazi Okeke's office the Monday that the second edition hit the streets. This edition was much more improved and its quality was good. Copies were sent to Zaria. More circulation outlets had been created but in the last minute Mazi Okeke jelled and attempts to send papers to other outlets was aborted. Meeting in Mazi's office meant Jobert could not run him down again. Since Mazi loved gossiping like village women, Dike too, made it a habit of going to his office, During one of such visits, Dike was explaining his position when Mazi cut in, "Don't mind Jobert, I will make you editor of the magazine section".

Dike didn't know how he expected him to respond but he kept calm and listened while he rambled on. The next day when Dike came to work, he discovered Jobert was not talking to him. The situation or cold war dragged for days. At a meeting the following week, Kalu reported and Mazi Okeke expressed concern.

"You mean my editor and his deputy are not talking?" he asked

"Yes", Kalu responded.

"Tell me gentlemen how can we progress. Jobert what happened?" he asked the editor. When Jobert was not forthcoming, Dike was asked to explain his position which he did. Whereupon Jobert decided to say something.

"Sorry this is not a court" Mazi Okeke said.

"but Sir –"Jobert persisted "you had your chance but you refused to take it", Mazi said cutting him off. He then spoke at length explaining so many things at the end he concluded by saying, "he who is interested in the existence of this organization should show by standing up-"

He hadn't finished when Dike stood up.

"let's work together", he said as he shook hands with Jobert who refused to stand but proudly said, "you are welcome".

The publisher then continued advising them, "Jobert as a leader learn to complement others", he smiled and continued, "it won't be out of place if you complement Mr. Dike on his wavy hair and curly moustache like that of the late editor of the Week Magazine." They all laughed. "Or give pretty Patsy a peck on the right cheek every morning", they laughed again as Mazi stood up indicating the meeting had come to an end. Truly, Jobert was excited by the idea of pecking Patsy. Once while discussing about the girls, Jobert had said this of Patsy, "she is an amiable girl" and both of them that is Jobert and Kalu had laughed. It was later coined

The Prisoner of Afrika

into a phrase "as amiable as amiantus". Amiantus is a roofing product but nobody could establish the link between amiable and amiantus.

"We went to Mazi's office today" Dike told Benson.

"Your usual meetings" Benson replied.

"At the end of the meeting Mazi told his editor that he should peck the ladies each morning on the cheek".

That evening, Benson rocked with laughter as Dike relayed everything to him.

"what a mess Jobert to peck a pretty girl like Patsy?" he asked still laughing. "He will bite off her ear and ejaculate into his trousers", Benson concluded and they both laughed. "And Patsy's boyfriend won't agree" Dike added.

In the second edition, Dike had written an article on Women's Liberation . Under the topic, he had posed a question, "are women really under bondage?" because the talk of women liberation with some styling themselves "champions for the feminist cause" called for concern. In Afrika, the women are equally represented and enjoy equal employment opportunities.

"So what could they be looking for?" he wondered.

In his opinion, he saw it as a ploy by woman to shirk their responsibilities as wives and mothers. The women in Afrika got so hyped-up with the issue that most mothers especially the new bred began neglecting certain essential duties like breastfeeding their babies. Rather, they preferred to load their babies with cow milk. The women or rather mothers forgot that depriving the babies of breast milk destroyed the chances of closeness between mother and baby. It further opened the babies to attack from different diseases.

Was the Woman at War?. War with whom?, and who had declared the war?. Apart from the articles he had written, was another article condemning the military administrator over the shoddy manner he handled the last crisis in the state. The article had raised dust but nothing came out of it. Dike was excited.

"This is journalism" he told Patsy.

"This khaki boy will see my true colours," he boasted.

Then without warning the security services struck their office that morning.

"We're asking for Dike Shakkassalli," they said. Dike appeared.

"So you wrote against the government," he asked,

following it with a slap.

Dike retaliated and hell was let loose. The other security agent using his walkie –talkie radioed their office and more men were sent. Dike was given the beating of his life .

"Let's just kill him and stop wasting our time," one of the men said.

"I don't want blood on my hands, –okay", their leader replied, "but let's beat him up some more".

So the pounding continued. Satisfied, they left him with a battered face and swollen lips.

"Next time, you won't write against the Government."

Immediately, Patsy rushed him to the hospital. Benson was angry with Dike for allowing this kind of problem come upon him. He was in the hospital when the next edition entered the market.

III

Unfortunately, sales of the next edition were very poor despite the interesting articles. One thing they were yet to learn was that a newspaper does not bulldoze its way into recognition. You have to announce its arrival, and when it does arrive you have to launch it with the vendors and then with the general public. The publisher was well known and if he had done this, the newspaper would've survived. Being a proud man with an empty head, one could pardon the ignorance initially, but after being tutored by Kyrian on these things his pride would not let him admit or follow Kyrian's instructions and so the paper suffered losses from unsold copies. Out of the one thousand nine hundred copies printed, only ten copies were sold. That Saturday evening at Peak Precise, while the paper was being printed Mazi Okeke arrived with his nephew; a guy named Williams.

"Good afternoon sir, " Dike had greeted, but he bluntly refused to answer. After ascertaining the quality of one copy that had just come off the machine, he congratulated the editor, paid for two copies and left. Dike was not surprised, he knew it was Joberts handwork. So, when sales returns was nothing to write about Mazi Okeke was mad and that afternoon he had raged "your salaries are due very soon is it from ten copies that I'll pay your salaries?" he thundered Dike just stared into space without any reply.

At this point, Benson had withdrawn completely and his name-dropped from the director's list. That evening when Dike relayed the whole episode to him, he laughed, "Mazi Okeke must have thought very soon he will buy a Mercedes Benz after two editions".

Dike smiled.

"Quite a big mistake" he said.

"You don't know how some people reason?" Benson said.

Dike smiled again, "you know after a love making session with his wife, they'll start daydreaming on how the paper will expand-". Dike could not hold it in, he started laughing cutting Benson off

"You know," he said, "that's how they do. He will say when money begins to come, we will buy more cars. "

"He must be a big dreamer".

But underneath, Dike was disturbed at the prospects of losing his job. So one Tuesday afternoon, the three of them conferred on what to do to save the paper. "Okay this is it. Dike you will write a proposal on what steps to be taken," kalu said and Jobert agreed.

Sheepishly, he agreed to write the proposal to be presented to Mazi Okeke, next Monday in his office. Before writing the proposal, Dike had complained to Mazi's wife on the way Jobert was running him down and her husband's attitude towards him.

" Dike, she had said.

Mike Effa

"Don't worry about these things. We know what we are doing," she had said by way of consolation. "We know Jobert has two jobs," she said. Dike left, whatever it was, they knew they were too slow in their reaction and he concluded that Mazi Okeke was afraid of Jobert. When kyrian was around they had meeting almost every week but as soon as Jobert took over following Kyrian's sudden exit. The meeting stopped and Mazi Okeke as the sole owner of the paper suddenly developed cold feet and Jobert was left alone to do as liked.

Dike had lodged a complaint before, but Mazi Okeke refused to act instead he told Jobert who confronted Dike immediately. Of course, he denied to keep peace. Jobert had really consolidated his position and he did not hide it.

One day while discussing he had boasted to a lady who had come in search of employment, the discussion was being conducted in his mother tongue but occasionally he changed to English. During one of such moments, he had boasted, ". . . As for our publisher I" influence him a lot and he listens to me too" He had said, Dike was not surprised neither did he doubt him. Action speaks louder than words, he had seen a lot to convince him. These childish talks by Jobert in front of a lady did not deter him in any way. On Monday they arrived to see their boss, his secretary a gentleman known as Emma knew their mission so he smiled them into Mazi's office.

"good morning sir," they greeted.

"Morning gentlemen," he replied. They sat down in the section used for holding meetings and when his visitors left they moved closer while kalu presented a report he was asked to write. Alongside the proposal, Dike had been mandated to write. Mazi disposed Kalu's report and focused his attention on the proposal. Surprisingly, he decided to read it out loud, "plan of action for salvaging the Afrikan conscience – what is this?" he asked rhetorically.

Dike hunched forward in a move to say something but instead Mazi continued reading finally looking up when he had finished reading.

"who wrote this?" he asked.

Kalu and Jobert hesitated in answering.

"We wrote it ", Dike said, damning the consequences.

"This is an attempt to secretly insult me," Mazi said handing over the proposal to Ichie Cyracus whom in the short while Dike had worked with Mazi he had discovered him to be a sort of houseboy to the big boss.

"What do you think of it?" he asked Cyracus, "this is very saucy. You people should be careful o! Ichie replied and at the same time agreeing with Mazi's position.

"Mr. Dike", Mazi Okeke called, "next time cross check facts before committing yourself!" Dike looked straight nonplussed.

"You have to do your job. Take this your plan of action out of here," he said, throwing it at Dike. "If you guys are tired then you say so and I will not hesitate in recruiting fresh hands", he concluded, turning to face Ichie Cyracus. That was a sign for them that the meeting was over and they filed out of his office. Throughout the return journey to the office, Dike refused to be drawn into any conversation by his other colleagues. He was angry at being betrayed by these two. Besides, his mind was still on the proposal that had just been rejected. Dike was disturbed so he decided to consider what he had presented not long ago. The paper had problems, everybody knew that and Mazi Okeke was a member of the Lion Club as well as two other clubs and was a member of St. George Anglican Church.

"So was it a crime if an employee suggested to his boss to use his connection in saving a project which

The Prisoner of Afrika

he had sunk a colossal sum of money?" he asked himself. Certainly it wasn't and Mazi Okeke could as well go to hell and kiss the devil's arse for all he cared. The problem with Mazi Okeke was his pride. He never saw anything good in other people he was in his own opinion the only perfect man on earth. The reason for his unjustified anger laid in the fact that in these clubs he had no clout and from the church angle he was just a bench warmer hence the expression of anger over the suggestions. That evening Dike showed Benson the proposal, after going through it, he was quiet for a while.

"You don't know people. Jobert and Kalu asked you to write this?" he asked.

"Yes", he answered feeling very stupid and angry with himself.

"You allowed those crooks to use you to gain favour?" he said.

Dike kept quiet.

"Now Mazi will go home and will show it to his wife they will discuss it and his anger will return again", Benson said pacing up and down.

"I have the letter he gave it back to me", Dike said without delay.

"Okay but you should not have written it. Nobody will give you food and then return to feed you," he

Mike Effa

advised. Dike had nothing to say. "It is your job to see that the newspaper makes headway in the market", Dike smiled as his mind went back to this same statement Mazi had made some weeks and he felt something was wrong somewhere. He rationalized how they suffered in getting the paper through the various stages only for them to take it into the market to sell as vendors. If journalism was like this then the sooner he quit being a journalist the better for him. The publisher had reacted. It was all right.

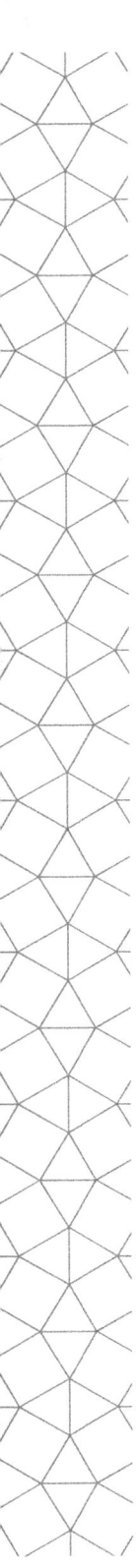

295

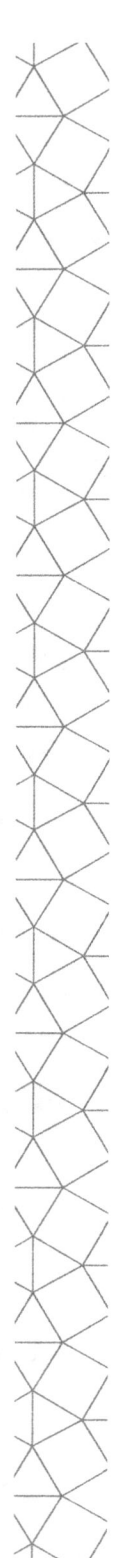

Chapter Sixteen

With the lifting of the embargo on employment Dike started making plans to travel to Ekko City to fill the Federal civil Service Form.

"I hope you're warming for your trip to Ekko city to fill the civil service form", Benson reminded him one day.

"I'm really warming up," Dike said.

"This one no be the kind job wey person go say him don arrive now", Dike said in broken English.

"Of course, is it from this pittance that you will use to marry and sustain a wife and raise kids?" Benson asked.

"Impossible!"

"Of course it's a stop gap job pending when a better and promising job will come now"

Arriving Ekko city he located, Col. Obere's house where he was to lodge. Col. Obere was his father's friend.

"How was your trip?" he asked.

"It was fine", Dike replied.

"When was the last time you heard from home?" Col Obere asked. Dike told him. The following day he

Mike Effa

went to the commission to get the form but he was in for a big surprise.

"You need a form?" He was asked.

"Yes"

"Sorry forms are finished but if you can pay two hundred pounds I will sell you this one", the man said.

Disgusted he paid collected the form and left. After filling the form he returned it before leaving Ekko City back to Dogawa. On Monday, he resumed work everybody was curious because he had overstayed.

"What happened?" Patsy asked.

"My sister was sick," he lied.

Dike knew they doubted his story, but Jobert was very sympathetic and showed it by expressing his concern. A week into November they received their October salary.

"Two days were deducted from your salary", Jobert announced

"why?" Patsy asked.

"no problem it's okay", Dike said trying to ensure that Patsy did not say anything more on the issue because somehow he felt Kalu and Jobert were still carrying tales to Mazi.

The Prisoner of Afrika

II

The second edition had been published in September. Since then for reasons best known to their publisher, no edition had followed again. But they continued to write articles and cover events which were never published. But, covering these events enabled them to get their share of the "Brown envelope" usually given to Journalists who cover events. One day, on his way home, Dike met one chap who introduced himself as Pat Jang. Pat was a correspondent with the Voice Newspapers. He had recognized Dike. He was sure they had met before.

"I don't know which paper you write for, and all journalists are to gather at No. 12 Kassim Bello way next tomorrow". he said.

"Okay I will be there. Thank you very much,", Dike said and they parted. He discussed it with Jobert and got his consent to miss work for that day. So on Thursday morning with the aid of an achabbar, he made his way to the address Pat Jang had given him. Other journalists had arrived. Dike noticed a young man who kept looking at him. He was a bit older than Dike. They greeted and introduced themselves. Jakobson like Dike was the deputy editor of the Pyramid Newspaper. The paper has its head office in Zaria State and also maintained another office in Dogawa State.

A Peugeot Wagon was later provided to convey the reporters for the trip to Minji County where the Mass Education Agency was launching a mass literacy programme; there was not sufficient space, so Dike could not join other reporters. One of the reporters spoke to one of the agency's driver who had just come in a Land Rover.

"Okay enter through the back", he said. Dike was about to climb when the driver moved at top speed he immediately let go the door of the Land Rover. He was lucky. In that split second he would have been seriously injured maybe he would have lost his thirty-one set of teeth. one having been removed years back in a navy hospital. However Dike found his way to Minji County arriving a few minutes before the military administrator of Dogawa State, then the launching started and he discovered everything was being done using the Hausawa dialect. He was unable to write and just sat "like a fish out of water". The launching was brief as it ended an hour later. With the departure of the administrator, a vehicle was provided to convey the reporters to the venue of the reception while the driver was making his way to the venue one elderly reporter was very disturbed that they will miss out in the feeding.

"We will miss everything," he said nobody answered.

"Before we get there everything will be finished", he said again yet nobody responded he kept quiet. The reporters reached the reception venue to discover indeed nothing was left except the apologies of the agency officials. That was just the beginning of their problems. Later, the bus which had brought them to the reception venue was commandeered to carry the agency officials back thus leaving them stranded. Sometimes in the midst of the wicked, there will always be one with a human heart and a human face. In the midst of their hopelessness help, succour came in the form of an agency official who apologised again on behalf of his boss.

"Certainly, it is a day of apologies", Jakobson said then the official bought roasted meat popularly known as "suya" for all the reporters then organized a pick-up van to convey them back to Dogawa.

"What a trip", One of the reporters said while they were boarding. The pick-up brought them back to the Agency's office where another round of disappointment awaited. The reporters demanded to see the director of the agency but were politely turned down with, "he is not in".

"that's a lie. The man has locked himself in the toilet," one of the reporters said "and instructed them to tell us he is out", Dike said, angry over the shabby treatment.

"We want our brown envelopes", another reporter yelled.

Sensing trouble a senior agency official addressed the reporters at the end he asked them to come back the following day.

"Rubbish", a reporter said as they left dejected.

"Tomorrow never comes" Dike said.

"You are right anybody who ventures to come here tomorrow will be chased away", Jakobson said looking out of the window of the taxi.

"It had been a waste of time", Dike said to himself.

He had made the trip so that he will get his share of the brown envelope. His finances were in a bad shape as a result of the paltry two thousand seven hundred pounds he earned which when converted amounted to only forty dollars. He had almost injured himself when that crazy driver moved the Land Rover even then he had made the trip only to be maltreated and then stranded only to return in a pick-up van like an Anti-crime police unit on afternoon patrol.,

"What a loss," he mused. However he put the whole

incident behind him.

Dike started visiting Jakobson and later on he got to meet Aisha the Editor of Pyramid Newspaper. As a result of their friendship he learnt of the existence of vacancies in their organization and he applied for the post of sports reporter. Meanwhile, their newspaper the Afrikan Conscience could best be said to have died. It had become virtually impossible to publish anymore and they knew "close down" was imminent, though worried he knew it was not the end of the world to him. Having already alerted Mr. Edetson of his plight, Mr. Edetson in turn had requested for his credentials promising to help him get a job with the ANPC.

ith everything looking bleak, one evening Benson had returned from work. A few minutes later, he called Dike.

"Yes", he answered.

"You will apply for the post of a purchasing and stores executive," he informed him.

"All right, thank you", he said.

"By the way I suppose your credentials are here?" he asked.

"no I left them with my sister the last time I travelled",

Dike replied.

"How can you do a thing like that–supposing your employer asked for the originals?"Benson queried.

Dike was speechless. They later resolved that he will apply and start work while making concerted efforts to get his documents sent to him. The next day he phoned his sister and informed her of latest developments and requested for his credentials to be sent to him.

"But I told you to take them with you", she said on the phone. Again Dike was speechless it was very obvious he had made a mistake "okay" she said, "I will send them. " Dike was worried and prayed seriously that God will not let this job pass him by. His prayers were answered; that weekend Mr. Edetson came in from Kalabar where he now worked following his promotion to co-ordinator, Liquefied Petroleum Gas Project, he was to co-ordinate the Eastern Zone. Dike approached him that morning ." good morning Sir" he greeted.

"yes my brother. How are you?" he asked in reply and they discussed briefly then he went on to make his request.

"Sir?" he answered.

"Please I want to make an unusual request", Dike told him.

The Prisoner of Afrika

"Yes go on. You're free", he said.

Dike knew he must have wondered what it could be then he told him what he wanted.

"ahh you are lucky I've not submitted your application yet," he said.

Dike laughed while Mr Edetson explained why he was holding back the application. Then he went in and brought the credentials for him, Dike expressed his gratefulness and rushed to the nearest business centre and made photocopies.

Later in the afternoon, Mr Edetson left for Ekko city with the 2. 30pm flight and Dike ensured his documents were in Mr Edetson's briefcase. Excitedly, he settled down to write his application whistling a tune as he wrote. He paused to gaze at the sheets of paper that had brought him misery and insults. All the same I thank God for everything. Dike said to himself. God has answered his prayers, it was only a matter of time and he will leave. That evening he handed over his application to Benson.

"How did you come by these documents?" he asked. "I retrieved the copies I gave to Mr Edetson."

"Okay" he said

"So on Monday, you'll come to Heritage furniture company by half past one", Benson said.

"Okay" Dike answered.

"When you get there and I've not come just wait for me," Benson added.

"Alright I shall be there", he told Benson shortly before he boarded a bus for Gadan-kaya.

III

The weather was beautiful and his spirits were high. Despite his travails with the state security services, Dike did not stop writing. In fact, on being discharged from the hospital, he had written two articles. The first article took a swipe at the government's clamp down on freedom of speech while in the second article, he blasted the government for taking sides with the Nigerian dictator over the killing of a renowned environmentalist who was fighting for payment of compensation over damage to farmlands by multinational oil companies. Mazi Okeke while looking at articles on ground had seen these two articles.

"Ah I don't want to die before my time", Mazi said.

"We won't publish them" Jobert added.

"Why not?" Dike asked angrily.

"You are not cut out to be journalists do not look for trouble again" Jobert warned.

"Yes. Jo is right don't look for trouble because I will

abandon you if it happens again", Mazi added.

"Okay I've heard you all,", Dike said. Cowards he said within him. Thank God I shall be leaving soon. It was obvious that Mazi Okeke wanted to be government's image launderer. Dike was thankful that God was using Benson to create on opening somewhere else for him.

So Mazi Okeke and Jobert could continue with their fake romance and floor cleaning journalism.

At exactly half past twelve in the afternoon, Dike left office. Fortunately, his other colleagues were out, getting to Heritage Furniture was a tricky business. But based on directions earlier given which was further made easy through his ability to identify certain landmarks he was able to get there, it was already One o" clock when he entered the premises. There was no "maiguard" at the gate. He proceeded unchallenged into the office areas. On looking to his left, he saw a sign The Managing Director, written on it and then a man who didn't look like a Managing Director was coming out.

"Good afternoon Sir",

"Hello, good afternoon", the man replied and was about going out, but Dike's next question stopped him in his tracks.

. "please sir I am looking for Mr. Benson" he said, "he has not come – just sit down and wait he will be around soon", the man replied and continued on his way out.

Dike waited for hours Benson never showed up he left at the close of work and returned home. After explaining what happened they agreed to meet on Tuesday at the same time.

Fortunately this time they all kept the appointment like gentlemen. Benson motioned and Dike followed him into the MD's office.

"Good Afternoon Sir", he greeted and sat down.

"Alhaji this is the young man I was telling you about", Benson began, "he will take over control of purchasing and stores", Benson said.

"Good, very good", Alhaji replied.

"Dike, Alhaji Ahmed is the General Manager of this company," Benson said.

"Mr. Dike you are welcome to Heritage Furniture"

"thank you Sir", he replied.

On their way out Benson stopped to greet a noisy white man whom on sighting him had come smiling.

"Lawyer", he called.

"I am very happy to see you today," he said

The Prisoner of Afrika

pointing at Dike.

Benson informed him, " this is the new purchasing, sales and stores officer".

"Oh my brozer, you are very welcome", he said. From his accent, Dike knew he was a Korra. They abound in Dogawa State like flies.

When Benson returned from work, Dike had a thousand and one questions to ask.

"So that is Heritage Furniture?" he asked.

"yes but it has a lot of problems", Benson said. Dike recalled that as a corper he had often heard Benson talk about this company.

As a matter of fact Benson was a director in the company. However, he was acting as alternate director on behalf of Mrs. Karim, wife of the late chairman and founder of the company.

"Wait o", Dike said.

"Who is that Korra?" he asked.

"Okay that's Adou Karim brother of the late founder", he replied smiling.

"He respects you a lot", Dike observed.

"Yes that is because, I put him in that office you saw him in", Benson said.

"No wonder, he respects you like that", Dike said.

"Yes and as a matter of fact, Adou is a good business man and a hard bargainer too", Benson added, Dike laughed at his description of Mr. Karim. "The G. M. will only come in the morning, after going round the factory will lock himself in the office and read newspapers. As soon as it is time for break off he goes. "

"For how long has he been general manger?" Dike asked.

"ehm let me see – Asoni, was removed in January, okay ten months", Benson said.

His first day at work was an interesting one he reported early Benson came and introduced him to the cashier who was acting as store keeper. Mr. Sunday Ikenga was an indigene of APA State.

Dike spent the whole day at the factory and didn't show up at their office in Gadan-kaya. Benson had even suggested, "do not resign till the month ends when you might've collected your salary".

Actually that was his plan. What he didn't know was, while they were scheming Mazi Okeke was scheming too. The next day he appeared and met only Patsy in the office.

"Where did you go throughout yesterday?" she asked and Dike tried to parry the question but Patsy will not let go. Patsy sometimes nagged as if she were his wife. When he could not hold on anymore, "Okay I've gotten another job", he said.

The Prisoner of Afrika

"Congratulations", she said and they shook hands.

"Please I will appreciate anything you can do to get me out of here," she appealed.

"No problem my friend even plans to employ you as outside sales agent," Dike said. "oh God", she said excitedly.

"When?" she asked.

"I don't know I will find out," he promised her. For the next two weeks Dike continued to put up a one hour presence at their newspaper office. It was clear they would fold up any moment. Before the month ended he received his employment letter, he even showed it to Benson who collected it and proceeded to read it.

"Haba some people will die of bad belle", Benson said.

Dike looked up curiously.

"Listen to this", he said and proceeded to read the letter" … with reference to your undated application for employment, I am pleased to inform you that your application has been considered. You have been employed as the purchasing, sales and stores officer, your total salary will be four thousand six hundred afripounds. We hope you will co-operate with other staff to ensure the success of the company. I wish you good luck. Signed Ahmed. . . "

They laughed.

"What a contradiction Benson said "you are pleased at somebody's employment but you could not insert date" he observed.

Dike was not surprised at the tone of the letter, Ahmed had been opposed to his employment but he could not do much because Benson was his director. Even when his salary was being fixed, Ahmed had insisted "Dike shouldn't earn more than the sales lady", he had said.

"Do you know this boy is a graduate?" Benson had thundered.

"But the sales lady has a qualification too," Ahmed said.

"okay let me see," Benson insisted, it turned out to be an Advanced Diploma.

"Moreover it was just the "To whom it may concern letter", I just threw it back at him and left", Benson said.

With the attitude put up by Ahmed, Dike knew things were not going to be rosy.

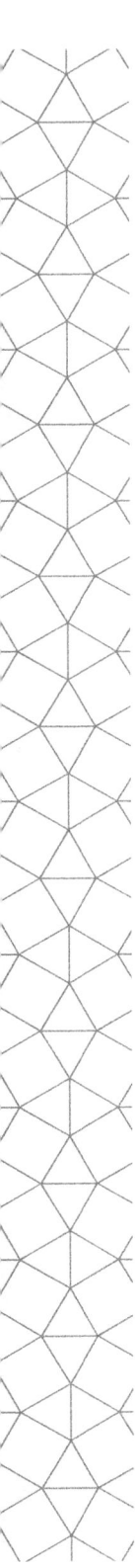

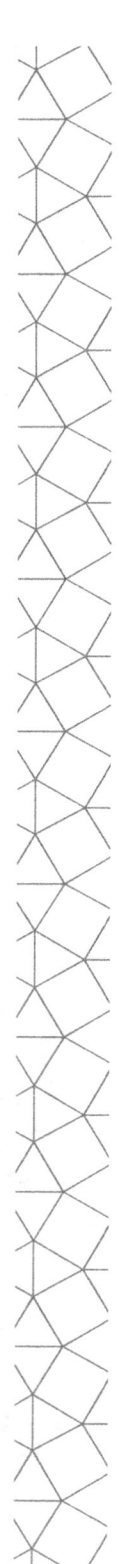

314

Chapter Seveteen

The factory workers it was clear respected Benson because he had saved them from doom when he took over complete control of the company. Ahmed in his short sightedness coupled with a lack of vision had not been able to prevent the company from going down. In the ten months, he had been there he had embezzled one million eight hundred thousand Afripounds. Whenever he was asked about the company, he would be quick in telling you.

"Things are bad–in fact we will close down this December". That was his motto. But the controls by Benson had cut him off from the company's finances and with Adou now a sales manager the company very slowly began to experience a revival. Thanks to Benson and Adou, the company shortly before Christmas executed contracts worth one million three hundred thousand Afripounds. With these salaries, end of year bonus and director's fees were paid.

Once Adou was telling Benson and Dike, "this Alhaji is useless – he come tell me company close in two weeks", he said.

"you know what I tell him?" he asked them.

"no" they replied.

"I tell him Alhaji it is your yansh that will close in December".

They all burst into laughter. Dike had not officially resigned from the conscience yet and they were approaching the end of the first week in December and their November salary was not forthcoming, luckily he was paid half salary at Heritage Furniture.

One evening he ran into Patsy at Bata.

"you didn't come today, we had a meeting with Oga" she said.

"is that so?" Dike asked. "there will be another, meeting tomorrow. Oga says he will only pay when he sees you personally so be there",

Pasty said. Dike reported for work before leaving for Mazi's office for the meeting. He reached Mazi's office to find other staff there; . Later they were shown into Mazi's office and the meeting began. He could see Mazi was crossed this morning and he spoke at length on how he had hoped they will come to be directors in the company he blamed the editor and the deputy for the problem which had killed the newspaper at the end he concluded by saying, "... my investigations reveal that the

The Prisoner of Afrika

editor is a teacher too. I don't want his services anymore. Dike will take over as editor. As for you, Dike, for refusing to discharge your responsibilities I had wanted to dismiss you but my wife prevailed so I've decided to give you another chance", he said.

But Dike laughed inwardly, "if you knew I am leaving very soon you won't be giving me a second chance".

"However, except for Jobert, the three of you will get will get your salaries for last month, " Mazi concluded.

Dike heard him clearly they were five so minus one that left four of them. He was about asking when more customers entered and they left his office. That morning while waiting to see Mazi, Jobert had been carrying the dummy of what should have been the third edition. One of Mazi's friends saw him, "wallahi editor by the time you publish this—referring to the already typeset dummy—it will be very stale", he said.

Everybody laughed Dike felt embarrassed but grateful he was not the editor. Then a couple of minutes later Jobert lost his job and without the comfort of his November salary.

"If I don't get my salary I will stop work-o", Dike told Kalu raising his eyebrows for emphasis. Kalu

Mike Effa

promised to approach Mazi to pay his salary, if he did nobody knows because Dike never got the salary. He became very irregular at the Gadan-Kaya office of the Conscience newspaper. After about two weeks, he appeared at Gadan-Kaya. He was in the office when Mazi came in, and was about leaving when Dike approached him "Sir the month has ended I have not received my salary" Dike said.

"Which month?" he asked.

"November" Dike replied.

"Didn't you hear when I said there will be no salary for two of you?" he asked. He drove off and left him standing there staring into space. He was angry. On impulse, he followed him to his office at sharada he was still adamant. They exchanged words again. Dike had wanted to really insult him but he changed his mind.

"Dike, what do you want again?" Mazi Okeke asked.

"I want my salary", he replied. Mazi Okeke had visitors when he entered thus when the argument became heated one of the visitors suggested, "I think it will be better if we went out it doesn't concern us".

"No stay and hear everything", Mazi insisted apparently very pleased with himself.

"I gave this man a job–, he refused to do it and now

The Prisoner of Afrika

he wants his salary", Mazi told his audience.

"Young man please don't joke with your livelihood. Jobs are scarce", one of them said. Dike kept quiet.

"Throughout the ten months you—-"

"It's only six months," Dike said interrupting him.

"what do you mean?" Mazi asked.

It was funny, his customers laughed and he was happy to see Mazi Okeke look foolish. Then Kalu came in.

"Kalu please take this man and find out what he wants", he instructed.

Kalu came over smiling please let's go out for a second", he suggested.

Dike went out with Kalu. Five minutes they returned Kalu knew his problem so there was no need to waste time.

"What does he want?" Mazi asked Kalu.

"Sir he wants his salary", Kalu replied smiling.

Dike kept calm and watched them ramble.

"I gave him a job, he refused to do it – instead he was fighting the editor and then he abandoned the job", Mazi said.

"Oh you wanted me to just sit and let Jobert mess me up, isn't it?", he asked.

"Why won't I abandon the job when you refused to pay me my November salary?" he asked to the hearing of everybody.

"Dike, if you think you've been unjustly treated go and report to the man who brought you and then we will talk", Mazi said.

"Nonsense," Dike said

"Thank you" he replied.

"It's a small world", Dike said again as he left Mazi's office, on that note he ended his engagement with Mazi Okeke.

Dike's arrival in Heritage Furniture did not please anybody, he had deprived the old staff of certain things and he was to check Adou too because his discount rate was too high. Trouble had started when a customer came one day Dike was not in the showroom, Sunday had come to the store to alert him so he had boldly entered Adou's office folded his hands across his chest like a thug while watching them discuss, "Please if we need you I will let you know", Adou said.

Dike left because he did not want to create a scene before the customers and went straight to the G. M to lodge a complaint. When Benson returned he informed Dike that he had been to see Adou.

"He was complaining about you", Benson said, he

The Prisoner of Afrika

now told Benson his own side of the story. Then Benson started laughing, "Adou said the customers were afraid. So he told them sorry – don't mind him he is not educated."

Dike burst into laughter he recalled how he complained to Benson.

"Lawyer", he had called him.

"This your man, how old is he?" he had asked.

"I don't know" Benson had replied.

"Guess," he prodded.

"May be thirty" Benson said.

"Oh lala you see I start working here five years before he was born", Adou had said further, "lawyer three positions for him is too much he will be too powerful".

"Don't worry he won't be". Benson had consoled Adou. Dike laughed till he began to feel pains on his sides.

II

Dike applied for casual leave, he was however told to shift it to the day after, as his attention would be needed during the annual stock-taking exercise. Two days after the stock-taking exercise, Dike knocked on his sister's door in Zuma Rock City.

Mike Effa

"Dike welcome", the children shouted happily. Then their mother came out and they greeted.

"Are you going to spend the New Year with us?" she asked. He shook his head, "no I intend travelling to Kalabar on saturday, " he told her.

Dike arrived Kalabar to a hero's welcome; his younger sisters were the first to sight him.

"Dike has come," they shouted happily, coming to embrace him.

The re- union was marvellous. He had been away from home for almost ten months, "Dike you've lost weight, " their mother observed.

"Yes true", Rhoda agreed. He was pleased to see everyone hale and hearty.

"Happy Xmas in advance", Kris said as they shook hands.

"Boy, the north is tough", Dike said. "I received your letters and I read them carefully" he said smiling.

"So how is Dogawa state?" Roda asked.

"Very dry, drab and unfriendly".

"But don't forget your living is earned there ", their mother chided.

"Big deal", Dike said.

"The moment I get an opening elsewhere like Kalabar or Ekko city if I delay in moving let my name be sung among the drunkard", Dike vowed.

The Prisoner of Afrika

"What is the meaning of that?" Rhoda queried. Dike just laughed. Christmas with majority of the family was an interesting experience.

They all had a nice time and in the evening Mr Shakkassalli had a drinking spree with his sons. Their father had just retired from civil service after forty years of meritorious service, so there was cause for celebration and coupled with the Xmas it was a double celebration. Dike returned to Zuma Rock City five days after New Year's Day.

Departure was a sad moment for him, he had to fight not to shed tears. Throughout the journey to Zuma Rock he slept all the way. Arriving Zuma Rock City, Dike spent only one night and the following morning he hit the road en route Dogawa city to continue with his job again, during the journey he reflected on the Xmas with the family and then he remembered the drama put up by their house help. Martha had been staying with them for the past one year and was very wayward. Whenever she was sent to the market, Martha will spend hours at the market. Nobody could tell what was wrong. Suddenly, Rosie Dike's younger sister and a nurse one morning observed that Martha looked pale and anaemic. Being a nurse, Rosie knew Martha was pregnant. She confronted her immediately.

"you're pregnant", Rosie said.

"You've started, let me go and tell mma", Martha said.

Rosie was adamant, "Martha I say you are pregnant".

She pretended to be angry.

"See let me tell you—I am still a virgin", she said and stormed out to go and report to Mrs. Shakkassalli. Eventually it was confirmed that she'd been pregnant by the sixth month. One morning, they woke up to find the door open. Their house help had absconded with the pregnancy. Dike shook his head, "what a life" he said just as the taxi entered Dogawa garage. Collecting his bag, he boarded a taxi bound for Hotoro GRA.

III

Different individuals owned heritage Furniture. After its establishment, it was managed solely by its founder, Mr. Abel Karim. With the enactment of a National Enterprises Promotion Decree, the Dogawa State Government had through one of its agents Doga Stock Brokers and Investment Properties sought for and eventually acquired a forty percent share in the company thus diversifying the ownership

The Prisoner of Afrika

structure. Mr. Karim during his lifetime was an acute workaholic. He worked too hard and had little time for food. He preferred black coffee without milk. It didn't take long before he developed chronic ulcer and after a protracted battle he lost out and died. Mr. Karim was a Korra who came to settle in Afrika because of the Civil War which had torn his country apart, even in death he could not go back to his country. Eventually, the family decided and he was buried in Damascus–the capital city of Syria.

With the death of its Managing Director, Mr. Asani Karim was appointed Managing Director. This was done with the consent of Mrs. Rachel Karim—wife of the late founder. She was Afrikan by nationality and had four children for her late husband. Due to the expansive nature of their business, Mrs. Karim spent most of her time in Abidjan where they had other businesses. This had necessitated her appointing a lawyer to represent her on the board. Asani had mismanaged the company and nobody had been willing to do anything about it. When no returns were forthcoming, Mrs. Karim had smelt a rat and their lawyer was removed from the board. Benson had taken over on the recommendation of his boss who had been a good friend of the late Mr Karim.

Mike Effa

Asani karim ran heritage furniture for eight years. The company was getting business but the money was being shared between the Chairman of the Board and Asani himself. When Benson took over from the lawyer, he identified the problems of the Company and concluded that sweeping changes must be made if the company was to progress. Mr. Asani Karim was removed in January. His dethronement was very dramatic. With the coming in of the New Year, the board had to decide the fate of the chairman and the M. D. Besides Asani had no Share in heritage furniture, he was the M. D. based on the goodwill of Mrs Karim. During its first meeting for the year the chairman had moved the motion and while the chairman was returned, Asani was removed. It only dawned on him later that he had lost his position as MD when he was told to vacate the office. Asani fought back and succeeded in taking the former chairman with him. Alhaji Balli Maibala was appointed the next chairman, while Alhaji Amed Maikudi was appointed acting- General Manager. Asani's brother, Adou Karim had rejoiced on day the Asani was removed. When their late brother's will had been read, the lion share of his estate had gone to his widow, while Hassan was given Karim Steelwood; Asani inherited over ten

The Prisoner of Afrika

thousand shares in the Abidjan business. Adou was not given any property.

The incident that left Adou in penury occurred after the sacking of the second Republic by the khaki boys.

Following the coup that over threw the politicians, the military government enacted a decree prohibiting everybody travelling out of the country not to carry money exceeding one thousand dollars. Adou was arrested at Ekko City International Airport with five thousand dollars and was tried by a military tribunal and jailed for five years. With the toppling of Gen. Attah, and the assumption of power by Gen. Idi Bello, Adou's senior brother used his contacts within the army in getting his brother out of prison two years after he was jailed. It cost him a lot of money. On the day Adou appeared in the factory, his brother was mad with him.

"You are a thief", he said, slapping him very hard.

"You stole my money", he shouted.

The senior staff came out and prevailed on him to take things easy. Adou was demoted and stripped of all privileges and became a common staff clerk, a position he occupied till Benson came in fully and he was elevated to sales manager again.

Adou's problem with the law was caused by his wife.

Mike Effa

Korra nationals residing in the country are very proud. They are also racists and the most corrupt set of people under the sun. Adou was a popular jovial person and he was quite generous. Whenever he flew out of the country he made the customs and immigration boys happy. The last trip which had put him in trouble was to be made with his wife. On reaching the airport one of the custom officers had made a funny remark and Karim's wife had responded by calling the officer a bastard. The officers held their peace till the moment when Adou was about to board. He was stopped and taken into a room where in the presence of his wife, he was searched. The search revealed a thousand dollars tucked in his socks and this landed Mr. Karim five years in prison without option of fine.

Alhaji Ahmed Maikudi's ten months in office was a continuation of the eight years of embezzlement by Asani. During the Asani years, substandard products was the order of the day, Asani will ensure a job is done. But as soon as the money is paid, he will refuse to pay the suppliers.

"No money," he will say, but the next day he and his family will fly out to Abidjan on holidays. Ahmed's case was worse. He embezzled the capital as well as the profit. To support his selfish aims he by-passed

The Prisoner of Afrika

the accountant and preferred to deal with the cashier Sunday Ikenga.

Once the accountant, Mr. Essienson was narrating his plight or rather ordeal in the hands of Alhaji. He told Dike how the G. M. had approached him once. "Mr. Kletus, please don't be offended that I am by-passing you in every financial issue", he had said.

"No problem", Mr. Essienson replied, "of course there was nothing he could do Ahmed was a staff of DSH and they were holding sway in the company. Ahmed was notorious for taking I.O.U's which he never paid back. Whenever he wanted money he'd call, "Ikenga?"

"Sir," the cashier would answer.

"Akwai kudi" he'd ask.

"ee akwai", the cashier would reply. "

Na wa?" .

"akwai pounds dubu biyar," Sunday would say, "To bani dubu uku".

This translated as "do you have money?"

"yes I have".

"How much do you have?"

"five thousand pounds"

"Okay bring me three thousand pounds".

Ahmed was running the company like a boys scout jamboree. Following his lackadaisical attitude the company lost all its customers, with no business coming the workers would arrive and proceed to sleep till one p. m. When they would go out for break or half time then return by two p. m and sleep again till four p. m. Thus, completing the second half . The factory workers were just like pregnant women. At the end of each month, Alhaji Ahmed will either sell a major asset or go to the banks for an overdraft in order to enable him pay workers salaries. This was the sorry state of Heritage Furniture when Benson took over

Knowing it was impossible to get working capital from any bank, the only solution had been to sell some of the company's assets. A generator was immediately disposed, but Ahmed in connivance with Adou embezzled the money More so, Benson was not around the day it was sold.

More assets were disposed later and all amounted to ninety–eight thousand Afripounds. This money was used to procure raw materials; Benson had gone to the market with Adou to buy all these things.

The next time he suggested they go together Adou got angry but became sober when reminded where he had started. Adou too is a proud and ungrateful person when Dike was introduced as the new purchasing officer. He had asked a question they didn't find funny.

"Lawyer", he had called Benson.

"You mean I go bring millions and give Dike to go to market?" He had asked.

"You cannot do everything", Benson had told him.

"But me karim", Adou countered. Adou was so proud of their name, to him it was the most important name on earth. He had once boasted to a director, "you know the karim name very big and important –

"yes, very true", the director responded quite amused.

To Adou, being a member of the Karim family entitled him to do everything in Heritage Furniture but his brothers had not reasoned this way when they dumped him in the showroom as a mere sales clerk while out of frustration had consumed cigarettes at a frightening rate. Matters were not helped when Ahmed took over as Acting General Manager at the end of the month Adou will not get his salary, on enquiring Ahmed will tell him funny stories like, "you see the company is in trouble so the Board said all management staff should not be paid. " Meanwhile Ahmed has taken his own salary behind

Mike Effa

As Sales manager, Mr. Karim had opposed Dike's employment too but there was nothing he could do. He tried many times to harass him but Dike told him off. He later resorted to calling him "store keeper". A title which Dike found very insulting considering his level of education. Since Adou wanted trouble, he resolved to make life difficult for him too. It was clear already that the man was becoming scared of him; it was as a result of an incident in January. Adou was already preventing him from doing his job, Dike complained but Benson calmed him. So one day he supplied materials without invoices Dike received them with an instruction to show the cheque he dropped with the cashier so that Benson will sign. But, he purposely refused to carry out his instruction. He was in the cashier's office when Mr. Karim came in.

"Lawyer he come?" he asked without even saying hello.

"Yes he came ", Dike replied.

He knew where Adou was going but he wasn't going to pre-empt him.

"You show him the cheque?" he asked again.

Of course, he did not show Benson the cheque so he mumbled what looked like a reply. Adou left and went to his office, a few minutes later he came back to the cashier's office Dike was still there, he sat down too.

"You show Lawyer the cheque?" he asked for the second time.

"No", Dike said clearly damning the consequences suddenly he grabbed him by the thigh.

"out,". he yelled.

"to where", Dike replied standing up.

Immediately he stood up too, maybe out of fear that Dike might slap him. Knowing he wasn't going to win this particular battle he soberly sat down.

"me I give you instruction why you never carry my order?" he asked. The Accountant decided to intervene and succeeded in explaining the situation to Adou. Adou was a tactician, since he was buying and supplying to the company on credit as the stores officer Dike only had to refuse receiving the items and Adou will lose his money. Therefore to him, it was important that he was in Dike's good-books. Later in April that year, Alhaji Ahmed Maikudi the company killer was finally asked to proceed on three months leave to facilitate an investigation of his ten months in office.

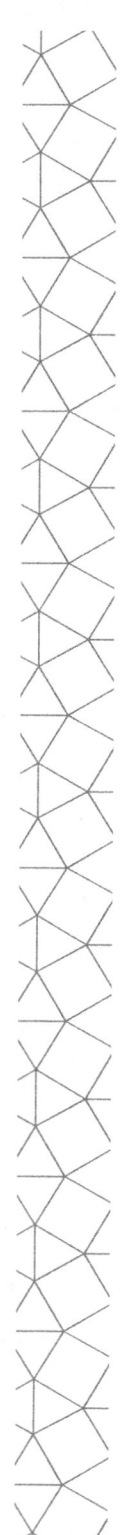

334

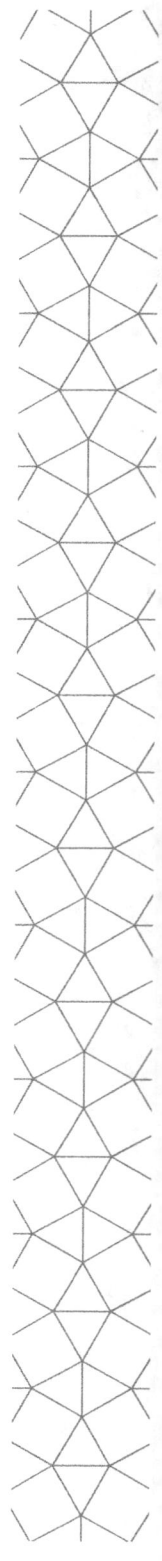

Chapter Eighteen

A poor man has no brother, the saying goes.

Throughout the six months, Benson and Dike spent in Mr. Edetson's boys" quarters and nobody ever cared to pay them a visit. But as soon as they took over the main house, the first person to take advantage of this opportunity for his selfish aims was Augustus. Dike got to know Augustus when he came to see Benson one morning in December. Benson was planning to travel so they were out trying to put things together, so he had to stay with the Edetson's till they returned. Augustus had come to report to Benson how Beatrice his girlfriend had gone ahead to report him to their pastor. Both of them were members of Life Saving Ministries.

"What! She did that?" Benson asked surprised.

"I was in their house with her when we heard a knock, on opening her sister entered with the church maiguard.

"Beatrice what is happening?" he had asked,

"This is terrible so what did she say in reply?" Benson asked,

"Nothing. Instead, the maiguard told me I was

wanted by the Pastor and he had a dagger with him".

"Of course he wouldn't dare use it now, so what happened then?" Benson asked

"I followed them to the pastor's home, the pastor warned me to stay off Beatrice and be faithful to my wife", he replied.

Benson was silent for almost three minutes. "When I return, I will go and talk to her", he said.

"Oh no. What about the stigma on me?" Augustus asked sorrowfully almost shedding tears. Augustus was so upset that he refused the tea that was served him. On their way out of the yard, they met Mr. Edetson and his family getting set for their final trip to Kalabar.

Augustus became curious.

"Who takes over the main house?" he asked when they were out of ear-shot.

"We are taking over", Benson informed him.

"That's great – it means I will do all my rough play here", he said.

They all laughed. They reached the airport and waited till the aircraft took off before leaving. Dike had thought Augustus was joking till one evening when he came back to meet Augustus and Beatrice chatting happily with Benson.

The Prisoner of Afrika

"Is this not the lady who reported him?" Dike asked after they had gone.

"My brother am surprised when I got to the office last week he had quietly told me not to bother going to her anymore that they had reconciled. This was the first thing he told me before even wishing me happy New Year".

Dike was speechless,

"Have you ever seen this girl before?" Benson asked.

"No, I've not. Dike replied.

"Then how did you know that was her?" Benson asked. He smiled.

"you know-when you hear a particular story like this an image of the other person forms in your mind— and secondly Augustus looked too excited clearly betraying his emotions", Dike replied.

Benson was quiet.

"I think you're right", Augustus" excitement clearly betrayed him.

"Even if you were meeting her for the first time. it won't take long to know what's happening" Benson said.

After the first visit, it became clear to Dike that Augustus was serious about using their house for "rough play".

"But, in the least, it will not be in my room", Dike had

said, consoling himself.

Two weeks later Augustus accompanied by Beatrice knocked on their door. They came loaded with oranges and ice cream. Benson knew why they had come.

"Ah! You brought oranges?" he asked.

"They want to entertain us in our home," Dike said from the kitchen and they all laughed heartily. He continued with his chores then he heard the front door open and then close. He knew Benson was going out so as make way. Shortly before they left for Benson's room, he heard Beatrice stretch herself and in the process said "Jesus is Lord".

When Dike came out to change the cassette, except for a sweater on the floor and polythene bag with ice-cream the parlour was empty. Suddenly he changed his mind and went back to the kitchen. When he came out again the polythene bag containing the ice-cream had disappeared probably after the first three rounds they had decided to refresh themselves with the ice cream before going back to continue with the show. When they finally came out after what seemed like eternity, Beatrice's hair was ruffled and even to an untrained eye like Dike's he could see Beatrice was exhausted and she confirmed it all

The Prisoner of Afrika

when she collapsed on the chair and said, "thank you Jesus".

Dike had a hard time controlling himself from laughing. Efforts to see them off was turned down with a "don't worry we will be okay" answer. He locked the door and laughed for a long time. While discussing one day, Dike brought up the issue, Benson laughed.

"Is she thanking God for the adultery she committed?" he asked. They laughed again.

Unfortunately, Augustus lost out and couldn't use their house for "rough play" anymore. Dike was happy to see his back. Apart from the rough play one other time he had come with another girl. While they were in the room, Dike smelt a foul odour for a long time, he was at a loss in his attempt to place the odour,

"Could it be this guy's semen that smells like this?" he had asked himself. He switched off the air conditioner and opened the windows. However Dike was able to find out when Augustus visited with another woman. They had a weigh scale in their parlour, suddenly Augustus stood up and removed his shoes. Immediately the odour filled the whole parlour. "My God, it is his shoes that is giving this foul odour", Dike said within himself. He must have noticed the expression because he said.

"Oh it is my shoes?" he asked and went on to check his weight.

"Anne", he called.

"Let's see how much you weigh", he said and Anne mounted the scales.

"You weigh eighty pounds", Augustus announced. Benson was in the room when the weighing was done, Dike pretended as if he was unaware of what was happening.

"Why does he allow his shoes to give such a foul odour?" he asked Benson on their way back after seeing them off.

"You know that is the problem with most people. Instead of buying readymade shoes he opted to construct this "smelling caterpillar" he puts on. Benson said.

"Ah, sorry but what really … happened?" Dike probed further.

"You know as an auditor, the leather he used in building his shoe was given to him at the Tannery he audited-"

"oho. I see", Dike said, "they might have given him leather that was not properly treated".

The Prisoner of Afrika

They were finally spared the agony of Augustus, his rough play and his smelling shoes when he started a campaign of calumny against them. Augustus was envious of the fact that Benson had just bought a fridge. He reported them to anybody who cared to listen on how they were embezzling funds at the furniture company. He informed his audience that Dike and Benson were doing a lot of over invoicing. Dike was mad at hearing this, Augustus whenever he visited them he ate as if the world will end tomorrow. Augustus had benefited immensely from his association with Benson. When the cholera epidemic hit Dogawa and its environs, Benson had given him yet another opportunity to make money by authorizing his wife who was a nurse to come and inoculate the factory staff and workers. Dike had refused to take that inoculation. After all, as he told other staff, "it is a matter of hygiene".

His refusal to be inoculated turned out to work to his advantage. The next day the whole workers and staff reported sick. They had to close early to enable them rest properly. Augustus and his wife made money out of this. It bothered Dike a lot that Augustus could repay them in this manner. There was nothing they could do other than to cut off every link to prevent being poisoned.

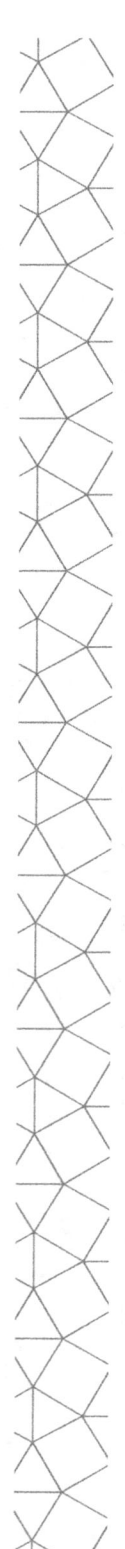

342

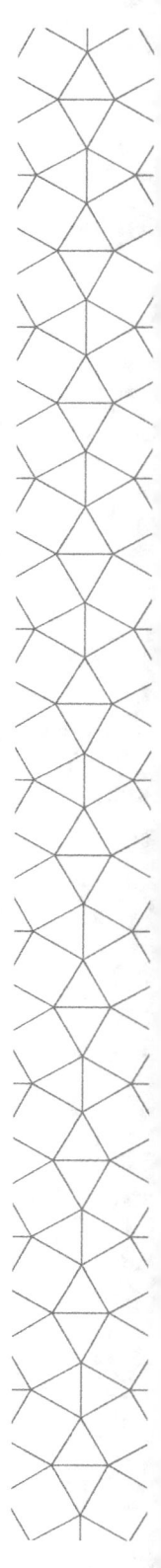

Chapter Nineteen

The peace of mind he thought he would have when he disengaged from the Afrikan conscience remained elusive, he had stepped on very big and sore toes and they were determined to crush him but he would fight back too. The most vocal of his opponents was the sales lady, she had raged on discovering Dike was earning more than herself.

"Dis one wey dem dey employ executive dis or executive dat with dis kind salary dis company go survive so?" she had remarked one day to the factory engineer.

Dike had received a good deal of antagonism from the sales lady and the cashier. But ,he carried on as if nothing was happening. Rumours were circulating that he was stealing fabrics from the store and this rumours had reached the chairman though he didn't know initially. Then one Saturday morning Alhaji Balli MaiBala, the company's Chairman Board of Directors, appeared and demanded he wanted to inspect the stores. Dike took him to the stores to see things for himself.

"But it's empty", he observed. Dike kept quiet, that

was another problem Dike and Benson were also facing – the DSIP angle. Maibala was a staff of DSIP so was Ahmed Maikudi, when their man ran the company without vision or foresight they didn't complain neither did they come to inspect the stores.

While one could understand DSIP's intrigue it was difficult to fathom the sales lady and the cashier's positions. Academically, both of them did not have the ordinary Level certificate, it surprised. Dike how the sales lady came to be in possession of an advanced diploma in political science. The cashier had once reported him to Benson that he connived with Adou and allowed Adou to take a gas cylinder from the stores. Dike was mad when Benson confronted him at that moment if he had seen Sunday Ikenga he would have squeezed his neck. The next day he confronted him on the issue of the cylinder and other stories he had carried about him wearing expensive clothes. Sunday was shocked.

"No, no, Dike I didn't say you connived with Adou, I said he deceived you into giving him the cylinder", he bad replied.

"Then why are you carrying stories about my dresses?" Dike asked.

"Me-ee, you've been misinformed I didn't say that",

he denied vehemently.

Mr. Essienson had to intervene and appealed to him to let it be. Then three weeks later, Benson showed Dike a petition alleging that they had embezzled forty thousand Afripounds.

"These people are finished," Benson said.

"Whoever wrote it is stupid. The forty thousand was given to Adou to buy fabrics so what else do they want?" Dike asked.

"You know", Benson began smiling.

"Chairman asked, Mr. Benson who is Otis Musa?. I told him we don't have anybody like that then he allowed the petition to go round and now it's in my possession".

They laughed.

"You know the chairman thought I will be ruffled and was watching me closely".

"It's Sunday who wrote that petition", Dike said

"yes it's him" Benson concurred.

The news spread like wild fire. His relationship with Sunday deteriorated and he started watching out for any slip by Sunday which could be used in firing him. Then on, Friday afternoon, Benson summoned Sunday to a meeting. Dike was present so was the accountant and the factory engineer. When they were all seated Benson spoke briefly on his status in the company.

"if you people don't know I have the power to hire and fire," Benson said speaking for a couple of minutes then he paused.

"Sunday, who is Otis Musa?" he asked.

Sunday didn't know what to say, then Benson showed him the petition.

"Who wrote this?" Benson asked.

It was too much for Sunday. He stood up.

"Sit down", Benson commanded.

"Oga, abeg make I stand-up" Sunday pleaded and it was granted. Benson was now addressing them when Sunday interrupted, "why don't you let him finish",

Dike said to Sunday. Benson continued with his speech. While the exchange lasted, the factory engineer Dike observed was busy nodding his head apparently pleased with everything then Sunday said.

"Oga before I die I will kill somebody-o".

"If you kill anybody, we hand you over to the police" Benson replied and they all laughed.

Sunday knowing what would befall him had to do everything possible to free himself. "Who is Augustine?" he asked.

Immediately, Augustine's face took a very deep

frown.

"Who is Augustine?" Sunday asked again "will you shut-up", Augustine commanded. "Oga, Dike, this Augustine you are seeing is a green snake in a green grass", Sunday said. Augustine suddenly went pale.

"What about you? Are you not the one who has been leaking secrets to the ladies?" Augustine accused apparently making a last minute effort to save face.

"Don't divert the issue". Benson warned.

"I will give you people only two weeks to own-up, but if you allow me to investigate then whoever it is will be sorry" he said.

They took this as a sign that the meeting was over and filed out. Dike returned to his office, he had just sat down when Sunday appeared.

"Dike you hate me," he accused.

"No you are wrong I don't hate anybody", he replied.

Be careful with that engineer, when you travelled did you not give him the key?" he asked. It dawned on him fast that Sunday had just made a point, but he kept quiet and continued staring into space.

"Augustine had accused you of stopping his overtime claiming that you were responsible for him not getting an increase in salary and promised to deal with you," Sunday said. Whatever doubts Dike had immediately disappeared. He remembered, when he travelled he left the key to the store with the engineer and the duplicate of all purchases made were kept in one of the desk. That is how Augustine got his information and without finding out properly went ahead to write one of the most foolish petitions in history. While analyzing the whole situation, Benson said, "I am convinced it's Augustine who wrote that petition"

"Yes". Dike said cutting in.

"Didn't you see how he reacted and decided to divert the issue so as to save face" he pointed out.

What annoyed Benson most was the area in which Benson was described as Dike's godfather.

"Godfather? I am more of a godfather to him than you. After all, you were employed by Ahmed but I had to fight for him and he decided to thank me with a petition instead".

Dike merely nodded his head too shocked to speak. He remembered the part he had played among the workers to get them accept Augustine and his best friend had stabbed him in the back. Right from that time he resolved within him to keep his secrets to himself and keep Augustine at arm's length.

The Prisoner of Afrika

II

The office staff consists of four men and two ladies. Dike was a university graduate while Augustine had the National Certificate of education (NCE) but earned the same salary as Dike. The accountant was an experienced man with a sound A levels so Mr. Benson concluded that these three officers could not be classified as clerical staff so the cashier was instructed to start preparing a separate voucher for the "Senior Staff" as they were now being called.

Ordinarily, there is no big deal in this. But trust women and their childish ways of doing things. Of course, the cashier leaked the whole thing. The women suddenly nicknamed them senior staff. While Augustine and Mr. Essienson laughed it off having been part of the system, Dike being a man without any sense of humour, didn't find it funny. A face off with the women began. Then the petition saga blew open. Augustine had written the petition using a fictitious name "Musa Otis". The women knew it, even the accountant and the cashier knew only Dike didn't know about it. The women decided again to add another nickname to the already existing name. Augustine was "Ottis Musa", Mr.

Essienson was "executive otis" while Dike was nicknamed "junior Otis". While this negative development raged Augustine continued with his chameleonic role of changing colours to suit the side he found himself at each moment.

At the federal level Gen. Sani Ahmed, Grand Commander of the Order of Afrika finally announced a transition programme that would terminate at the end of the decade. While this was a good sign, the fundamental question remained unanswered. Matters were not helped when Chief SowoOlu's eldest wife was shot dead one hot afternoon in Ekko City. The assassination was taken by many as a dastardly act and condemned by every decent human being.

"The police have been mandated to bring the killers to book," the inspector general of police had told reporters. Nobody was convinced by this move. Mrs. Sowoolu as far as everybody knew was killed by the Junta's hit squad because of her position on the annulled presidential election. Three months before her death she had definitely said in an interview, "if I am given a mandate I will ensure that nothing gets in the way, in fact I will do everything possible even

The Prisoner of Afrika

losing my life to protect that sacred trust".

Now she was dead while her husband was being held incommunicado. The investigations continued.

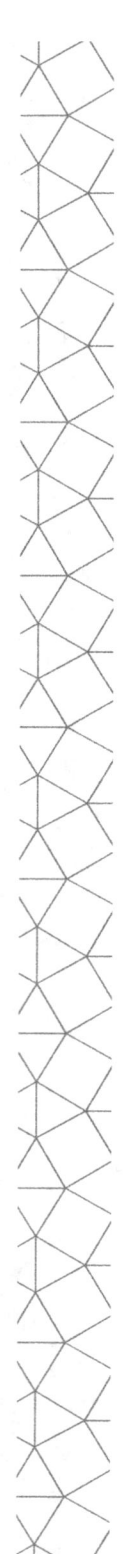

352

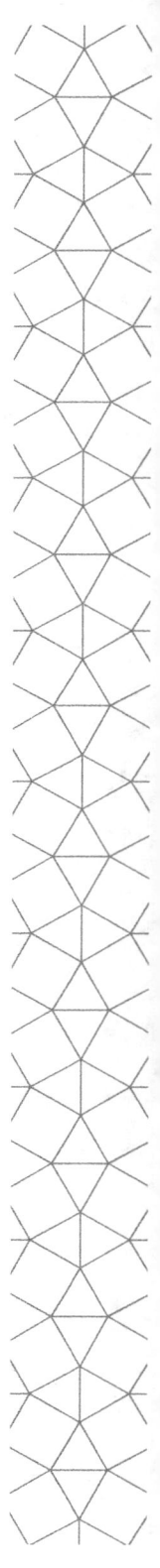

Chapter Twenty

Three weeks later, on Saturday precisely Dike had returned from work and was in the kitchen when Benson returned from their office accompanied by Clement a colleague. After the food, Clement pushed back his chair, "hmmm Dike, did your girlfriend come to prepare this?" he asked. They laughed.

"No", Dike said.

"I hope you will be able to marry because bachelors who cook very well seldom marry", Clement said. They laughed again over the joke.

"You'll be going to Ekko City tomorrow", Benson said suddenly.

"What for?" he asked curiously.

"Mrs. Karim phoned and was requesting if I could send somebody very close to me, to go and bring her children's passports for one Lebanese who is a visa merchant", he explained.

"Where are there going?" Dike asked.

"Okay, they are schooling in the United Kingdom and are scheduled to return in September", he said.

"But why me," He asked rather incredulously.

Mike Effa

"Because you are available-and she had instructed that it should be somebody who can trace her house so I told her you are a graduate and you work in the factory", Benson explained. Clement smiled and Dike joined in smiling too. His stomach began to knot this was due to the tension in him as he looked forward to flying and also his meeting with Mrs Karim whom he was going to meet for the first time. There was a blackout due to power failure so Dike decided to go to bed early. He had just lied down on the bed when he heard what sounded like somebody crying. It was night already he became disturbed praying that it didn't turn out to be somebody weeping over a dead relative. He approached the parlour.

Clement and Benson were tackling certain issues, "did you hear that crying?" he asked and went on to open the window and it was clear. The voice was Mama Ejima's "Una come-o, Una come-o, ee don kill mee-o" she was crying repeatedly.

Dike rushed to the boy's quarters. It had rained that afternoon so they couldn't be fighting outside as he was coming he heard papa Ejima say "you no go leave me, I go kill you."

Dike arrived. Benson followed shortly,

"what is it:" he asked tiredly.

The Prisoner of Afrika

"this bastard! This bastard with no place to stay, he carry my face press for pillow, a pregnant woman faa?" she asked no one in particular.

"My brother you fit give me twenty Afripounds make I go bring my brothers wey dey for Mobile Police make dem come teach dis bastard lesson".

Dike gave her the money and left immediately before some crazy fellow attacked him. Her husband was ashamed and remained inside.

"I have seen things", he said as soon he entered their house.

"you've seen things" Clement said smiling. On their way out, Dike and Benson saw two men entering the yard.

"you know say na husband and wife palaver be dis so make we take am gently", one of the men was saying to his friend whom it appeared was in a haste and was itching too to beat somebody that night.

Clement boarded a bus and as the bus zoomed off they returned to the house, due to the power failure they opted to spend some time outside before turning in for the night.

Mike Effa

II

Dike left for the airport at about ten O'clock on Sunday morning. Throughout the ride to the airport his mind was focused on the encounter he was going to have with Mrs. Karim and her children.

"Mrs. Karim is a very snobbish and authoritative lady", Benson had warned. He'd nodded his head not having anything to say. "And when you get there don't tell her anything negative about Adou let her know the problems of the company", he instructed further. Dike had heard a lot about the Karim's being rich they always had the tendency of assessing strangers. This information influenced his choice of dressing. He arrived Dogawa International Airport at half past ten, almost every ticket counter showed signs of any activity.

"Good morning sir," he greeted as he approached the counter.

"Good morning", the man replied, "can I help you?"

"Yes please is there any flight to Ekko City today?" Dike asked.

"yes, there is" he replied. He paid for a flight ticket which was about three thousand one hundred and fifty Afripounds. The SCOBE aircraft arrived a few minutes later and they boarded. Even though he

The Prisoner of Afrika

was boarding an aircraft for the first time Dike didn't have any problem locating his seat neither did he request the assistance of anybody in fastening his seat belt. A few minutes later, the aircraft left the tarmac and began taxing for the runway preparatory to take-off while this was happening on board an air hostess demonstrated how to fasten the seat belt and pointed out to passengers the various exit routes in case of an emergency. The lights went off and the airhostess took her seat as the Boeing 727 gathered speed and thundered on the run-way and took off. He had read a lot about planes and now was experiencing flying. It was funny in a sort of way and he almost laughed when the aircraft flew into clouds and they experienced bumps in the air. They cruised at an altitude of twenty-nine thousand feet above sea level. An hour later, they entered Ekko City airspace, "Ladies and gentlemen in a short while, Insha Allah, we shall be landing please fasten your seats belt", the pilot warned. There was a flurry of activities inside the aircraft and at ten minutes past the hour they touched down at Ekko City Airport. From his calculation, the flight had taken one hour ten minutes and it had been fun while it lasted. Being a stranger to most parts of Ekko City, Dike had to take airport taxi to get to Mrs. Karim's house in Victoria Island. He reached the house, paid the four hundred Afripounds demanded by the driver and went into the yard. On reaching the compound, he sent in the letter Benson had given for her through one of the security guards. She responded by sending her steward who informed Dike thus, "Madam say make you wait outside till her stranger go".

"okay", he said and continued waiting. He never saw any stranger leave throughout the period, he spent waiting outside. Anyway he knew within him that she was trying to make him know he is dealing with his employer so he must move when asked to do so and vice versa. Feeling a bit nervous, he was asked to come in later.

Mrs. Karim appeared exactly as Benson had described her, tall, beautiful and flashing a smile capable of making a monk weak at the knees.

"Good afternoon Madam,", Dike greeted standing up.

"You are welcome, Mr. Dike,", she said stopping a few yards from him and stretching her hand.

"I believe you had a nice flight?" she asked.

"yes I did, " Dike answered

"Madam say wetin you go drink?" a steward came

to inquire.

"oh nothing—thank you."

Shortly before the steward left for the market, Mrs. Karim came to inquire personally "Mr. Dike probably you had a light breakfast at the airport—are you sure you don't want toast and tea?" she asked.

"No Madam," Dike said at the same time thanking her for her concern.

Actually, he was not really hungry, though during the flight he had a very light meal. He was determined to stay with that till later in the evening when dinner will be served. Besides the impression one makes matters and as a disciplined man Dike was not in the habit of guzzling down food like a war refugee. He spent the rest of the day watching T. V. , Dike was to be shown to his room when the steward returned from the market but as afternoon gave way to evening so did the steward delay in coming back from the market. Mrs. Karim and the young lady whom he discovered was her daughter were worried and they showed it. After looking out through the window for the third time.

"Won't you drink something?" Mira Karim asked. Her mother was standing by the window, of course she heard everything.,

"thank you—but I don't feel like drinking anything",

he replied. It got dark and the steward didn't show up.

"Dike sorry for the inconveniencies, your room is not made up yet but I can't leave you in the parlour. Come I will show you to your room when David comes back he will come and lay the bed," Mrs. Karim said. It was clear Mrs. Karim was at her wits end.

"No problem ma," he said. And he followed her to the room she indicated. The room it turned out was her eldest daughter's room, so he was to spend the night there. Dike surveyed his room for the night and was amazed. There was a compact Disc on one side and on the dressing table was an array of assorted perfumes and creams. "Phew", he whistled, "it's good to be rich", he said.

Looking at the bottles of perfumes and jars of cream, Dike was sure if all these were sold the money realized would be enough to pay his salary for one year. He decided to lie down a little, but the day's exertion began to take its toll and he slept off without even undressing. His slumber must have lasted about an hour or thereabouts for he suddenly woke up as a result of shouting from the parlour. He listened it was David, the steward explaining why he'd kept so long "...Madam as I dey inside bus, one man wan enter he come march me so we begin fight, Police come arrest us go station", David said.

"So you are coming from the Police station?" Mrs. Karim asked sounding very angry from the tone of her voice. David later came into the room and laid the bed while Dike had dinner.

Dike had thought that the documents he was supposed to convey back to Dogowa were ready and he will return with the first flight, he was disappointed, instead Mrs. Karim sent him to the British High Commission to get a visa form, she had called Dike that morning, while dishing instructions.

"...Are you educated?" she asked. "Yes I am", he had replied. On their way to Marina, he reflected why the Karim family was like this. Adou had told some customers, "he is not educated". And now, he had just been asked if he was educated. The taxi reached marina while Dike went into the British high commission collected the form and came back.

III

ike left for the Airport around two O'clock in the afternoon. Buying a flight ticket in other parts of the country is easier. At the domestic wing of the Ekko

city Airport it's a different ball game entirely and if you are a first timer you are bound to fall into the hands of touts. And that, is exactly what happened to him. He had just alighted from the taxi when a man in black trouser and white shirt approached him.

"Sir are you going to Dogawa?" the man asked.

Due to fear that he might not return that day because of his late arrival at the airport and with no knowledge of flight schedules he succumbed to the antics of the man in black and white.

"Yes. Please is there any flight?" Dike asked "yes but it is booked already. However, if you are with an identity card it will be easier getting you a seat on that particular aircraft", he told Dike who couldn't help believing him.

The black trouser and white shirt his newly found assistant was wearing turned out to be the uniform worn by SCOBE airways staff right from the pilot to the ticket clerks. The fare back was the same with the fare in Dogawa. So, he counted out three thousand one hundred and fifty Afripounds and gave it to him and helplessly watched him go with his ID card and money. Dike prayed fervently that he didn't end up a victim of fraudsters. Fortunately he came back, "it's not possible he said, "but if you

The Prisoner of Afrika

can bring seven hundred and fifty Afripounds.

"I might be able to get you a seat,", he said. Without delay, he handed over the money to him. He had to get back to Dogawa that evening therefore if it meant spending the whole four thousand pounds on getting a ticket he would so far, he got to Dogawa that day.

His assistant returned with a fight ticket, Dike smiled happily.

"You are lucky I have secured you a seat in the first class section he said. He thanked him profusely and even gave him a hand-some tip. Shortly the aircraft arrived. Dike was seated in the ninth row, he sighed angrily on realizing he had sat on the eighth row on the trip to Ekko City. There was nothing he could do at this stage so he gave it up as the price to pay for his inexperience. Throughout the flight, his mind was on the loss he had suffered at the hands of a callous airline staff. Before flight 614 touched down at Dogawa Airport the hostess, a pretty dark lady ensured that they had their money's worth and the pilot, Captain Usman, thanked his passengers for patronizing SCOBE airlines and wished them a happy stay in Dogawa state. SCOBE is one among the indigenous airlines licensed to operate in Afrika.

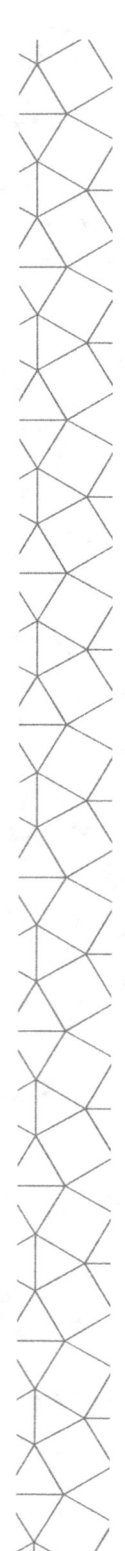

364

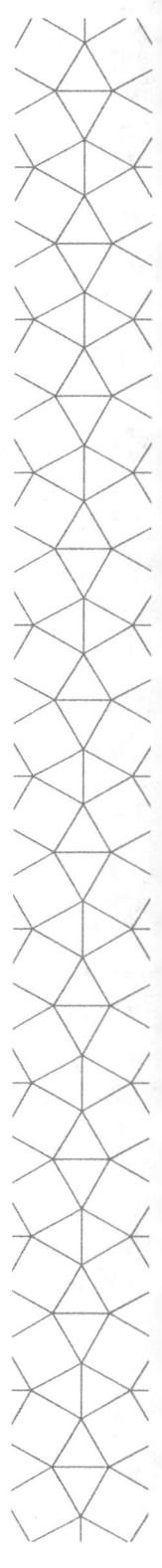

Chapter Twenty One

Benson was out of the office when he came in, but arrived a few minutes later only to find him at their reception, "ah you are back," he said.

"Yea," Dike answered.

They went into his office, and he immediately telephoned Mrs. Karim to inform her of Dike's safe arrival with every document intact. The rest of the conversation was conducted in their dialect. Benson and Mrs. Karim are indigenes of Brass State. At the close of work, they went straight to Mr. Kamal a visa Merchant. A Korra by nationality, Mr. Kamal managed a travel agency and also procured visas for a fee and he dealt mostly with the British and American consulates in Zaria state. His office was closed.

"Let's check his house", Benson suggested. He was not in.

"We will check back in the evening", Benson said, "let me drop a note then we will go home".

Later in the evening, on their way to see Mr. Kamal, Benson decided to fill him in on what he had discussed with Mrs. Karim.

"You know as soon as she picked the receiver and I told her you had come straight to my office on arriving with all the documents intact, she was very happy.

"Oh Dike is very competent she said," and they both laughed it was nice to receive such a warm compliment. It made him feel good.

"But she said you are too shy, and you don't talk hence her decision to put you in her daughter's room so that the boys will not disturb you-"

"oh is that so? Dike asked rather rhetorically.

They came back again. Fortunately this time, they were lucky to meet Mr. Kamal because his Mercedes was parked outside. Benson knocked and allowed some seconds to elapse, they were about to repeat the process when the door opened and Mr. Kamal appeared clad in pyjamas.

"Good evening Sir", they greeted.

"yes please come in" he said it appeared he was getting ready to go to bed when they knocked. Benson gave him the letter.

"Are you Mrs. Karim's children?" he asked looking at them as if they had just returned from space.

"No we are not, I work with Mark FUZZ firm of Chartered Accountants, and my partner works with Heritage Furniture Company", Benson said.

The Prisoner of Afrika

When he was through with the letter, he looked at the visa forms and other related documents.

"Does she have the money?" he asked.

Immediately, they showed him Mrs. Karim's statement of account.

"Okay I am convinced on the financial aspect, but the documents are not current. All I need is just a letter with one or two lines and the consul will issue the visas," he said. Benson called Mrs. Karim that night and they discussed at length then they took their leave. Before Dike departed for Dogawa. Mrs. Karim had instructed that Benson should write down in a report any information he might have on the company. He remembered this on Tuesday evening and informed Benson as instructed.

"You went to extremes", he was saying.

"Mrs. Karim expressed her disappointment that she couldn't find out anything from you—you see it is because of your withdrawal that made her ask if you are educated and she will also see it as inferiority complex-".

"That's her problem. I sat in the parlour alone, even when she came out she only spent some minutes before going in. No questions were asked. Was she expecting me to start talking like a tape recorder?" He asked angrily. Benson saw his point and when he spoke again he picked his words carefully.

"I did ask her why she didn't ask on the things she wanted to know that's not how I do my things she had said I don't have to force information out of somebody's mouth". Dike was angry at both of them, he had flown to Ekko City at short notice to help her sort out a few things, but instead of thanking him he was being given bullshit instead. If Mrs. Karim wanted information on her company, it wasn't going to come from him. At least, she was represented on the Board and she had to know Dike didn't fly all the way to come and discuss a company that had been mismanaged for six years through no fault of his. There and then he resolved not to come back and made his position known.

"That is not the point", Benson countered, "I have never told you this before it's bad for a man to be shy. Moreover one should not over do things either".

Mr. Kamal finally got in touch with Benson on Saturday afternoon. The visas were not given.

"The consul requested for a personal appearance", he had told Benson. To back his claim, he showed where the consul had minuted "P. A" meaning "personal Appearance" he saw with

The Prisoner of Afrika

him. Later Benson made a call to Ekko City, Mrs. Karim had travelled her daughter informed him. Benson then informed her on Mr. Kamal's inability to secure the visas. Therefore, Dike should be expected either on Sunday or Monday which was a public holiday too. Dike got his stuff ready to travel on any of these days even though he had vowed not to go back. He discovered he had no choice since he had started the job he had to finish it. Dike arrived Mrs. Karim's house quietly, she was in and was surprised to see him probably her daughter didn't tell her he was coming hence the surprise.

"I received Benson's message, I travelled and just returned on Sunday—we will apply for the visas here in Ekko City", she said.

"Yes ma" Dike replied.

After dinner, Dike bade them goodnight and went to bed, this time not in her daughter's room but with David her steward. Dike felt even freer with David because they were all employees.

II

n Tuesday he left for the Immigration office to cancel Mrs. Karim son's previous passport and buy a passport form. He was very much at home for

the last part of the task, He was however at a loss why a passport valid till the end of the decade should be cancelled without any cogent reasons. Matters were also complicated when Dike couldn't see Mrs. Karim's friend.

he approached a young immigration Officer who briefed him on the lady's whereabouts

"So how I can get this passport cancelled?" he asked. The officer collected the passport and flipped through, "but it's still valid for the next five years and even then we cannot cancel it without a very strong reason", he concluded.

Without further delay, Dike reported back to Mrs. Karim.

"Ah thank God you're back I was getting worried—I can see from the form in your hand that you saw my friend?" She asked.

"No Ma," Dike replied "I didn't see the lady I bought the form. With regards to the passport the argument here is the passport is still valid and they cannot cancel it except we give them a very strong reason".

It was then Mrs. Karim told him the truth, "the passport had been lost so we made a new passport, only to find the missing passport two weeks later.

The Prisoner of Afrika

"Armed with a sworn affidavit he went back to his young immigration officer friend. The passport was stamped cancelled at a cost of five hundred Afripounds. He rushed back to the house, collected the passports and other supporting documents and left for the British High Commission.

As the taxi sped on towards Marina, he prayed that there will be no hold up so that he could finish early and return to his base. Fortunately, he arrived early and everything was proceeding like clockwork when disaster struck and hopelessly Dike saw his plans crumble. The visa section was situated on the ninth floor it was here that a high commission official turned him back on grounds of incomplete information.

Angrily he rushed back to inform Mrs. Karim. Mira opened the door, "how was it?" she asked.

"The information is incomplete, " he told her bluntly.

While trying to rectify the situation, her mother came out, "what's the problem?" she asked while also complaining on having been disturbed from her sleep. Her daughter told her what had just transpired.

"That's a stupid mistake," she said. Her daughter showed clearly the effect of that statement on her. Mira, as far as Dike could see was not used to harsh words, they must have been pampered a lot and why not? After all they are a very rich family. It was half past one when he returned to the High Commission, the guards refused to let him in despite his explanation. Defeated, he left sad and dejected at the fact he wasn't going to return to Dogawa that day. Besides, he was not equipped to stay that long. Mrs. Karim was in the parlour having a salad meal when he came in.

"Any success?" she asked.

"No Ma", they have closed for the day", he told her.

She sighed, "God knows best—my daughter is inside her room praying. As soon as you left she went in to cry", she said.

Dike smiled. I love women who cry he said within himself. On hearing Dike's voice, Mira came out seconds after he had finished making his report. "Oh mum I'm sorry—"

"No don't be... being sorry over a small issue of this nature makes me sad. So please don't be sorry at all. Dike is here, he will finish everything tomorrow by the Grace of God," she said.

"Very good. Why feel sorry?" Dike wondered, after all Dike the son of a poor man is very much around to do your dirty work, he said within himself displeased at his situation. If this is what it means to have

The Prisoner of Afrika

money, then I must work hard to make money so that my children too will have the many good things of life. Dike vowed. On Wednesday morning, he continued from where he had stopped the previous day. Armed with the necessary information he left for the high commission where came face to face with one of the officials. He went through the passports then he looked at Dike "where are they?" he asked.

"At home", he answered.

"Sorry they will have to put up a personal appearance so we can ask them a couple of questions. it won't take long. Till then, have a good day", he said returning the passports to him. Dike rushed out of the High Commission building immediately.

"Taxi", Dike flagged the driver who slowed down.

"where to?" the driver asked,.

"Elephant way, Victoria Island", he responded.

"One hundred and fifty pounds", the driver said, without arguing he jumped into the front seat and they sped off. Mrs Karim was in the parlour when Dike entered, "they are requesting a personal appearance Ma", he said. The children were still in bed when he came in. They were roused from sleep and told to prepare.

"I'm sure they want to issue the visas today", Mrs. Karim said hopefully. "I hope so", Dike said gently. Mrs. Karim's second child decided to watch TV and eat toast instead of getting ready to go with the other children. An appeal from his mother to get prepared was in vain. At a point, he even told her mother, "please leave me alone I'm old enough to take care of myself".

Dike stared at the young man in total disbelief and shook his head. Mothers of those days will not tolerate this kind of rubbish. But then, it all depended on how you trained your child. For the Bible says train up a child the way he should go and he grows up he will not depart from it. Indeed, it was a sad development to hear a child asking his mother to leave him alone.

"Okay suit yourself," his mother said quietly. Dike returned to the High Commission with two of Mrs. Karim's children. Mrs. Karim had four children only, the eldest being Mira who was a Law student. At the visa office, he was denied entry by the officials on the ground that he had no business being there and besides the owners of the passports were around. His pleas to be allowed to go with them because they were under-aged fell on deaf ears. He persisted, the guard remained adamant. Of course

The Prisoner of Afrika

he had to let them proceed and he stepped out of the queue to avoid being rough handled. When the guard was less tensed, Dike approached him and his colleague who had just come down from the ninth floor. He explained his position again and his second colleague authorized him to proceed to the ninth floor ignoring the protests from his partner. The two children were quite capable of conducting themselves. They later came out looking very disturbed.

"Any success," Dike asked Mohammed.

"They are not willing to give us the visa", he replied, brushing past him. It appeared he was not in a mood to talk so they rode the lift in silence. On their way out, Dike brought out two hundred pounds and advanced one hundred to the guard who had blocked him initially. The greedy man in him urged him to take the whole money but Dike held back the other hundred and gave it to another colleague of his. He missed the guard who had assisted him earlier on. They arrived home to meet an expectant Mrs. Karim and her daughter looking a bit disturbed.

"Did you get the visas?" she asked the children, while her countenance changed too. Both kids suddenly started talking at the same time "take it easy, one after the other", she chided.

Mike Effa

Mohammed then took over and narrated how they were harassed, abused and bullied by a light skinned mulatress in the visa section.

"I don't know why that lady is always there, she is not even a Briton but she's very bitchy", Mira said apparently disgusted with the visa officials.

"Yes, she was employed to do their dirty job of harassing Afrikans seeking visa to enter Britain", their mother said. At least, they got an interview date. The kids would travel with me and then I will come back to handle their appointment".

"You've done well Dike thank you", she said. Dike nodded his head in response to her show of gratefulness.

"Did you see John?" She asked. John was their second steward from Cotonou. The man is very heady and has been giving her employer problems. Not sure of the visa fees Dike had requested for extra money. But the money they had with them had been sufficient and they had finished and left before John arrived with the additional money.

"No, Ma'am we didn't see him", he replied.

"They didn't see John", she told her daughter.

"We had gone to the bank together. The queue was much. Fortunately, my friend Bimbo was the one paying—so I called her Bimbo please can I have

The Prisoner of Afrika

ten thousand Afripounds and she threw it to me despite the protest from other customers. And without counting, I gave the money to John who left immediately with the car hire while I returned to my position on the queue", she said demonstrating every action. Dike marvelled again at the respect money can bring to any individual. But one problem with the rich is their unhealthy desires to keep stockpiling while refusing to allow the wealth circulate. The rich in the society prefer and love to gather but are always afraid to lose. Mrs. Karim was afraid of losing ten thousand pounds.

"Well, that's his business if he has decided to abscond with the money", she said obviously. It was clear that she was worried.

"Benson had said you worked in the company?" she said.

Dike affirmed the positive.

"When were you employed?"

"November last year", he said.

"And my representative didn't inform me. If it were not for these visas I wouldn't have known. Not that I am complaining but at least he should have informed me. what is your position and how much are you paid? I want the truth because I will find out", she said.

Mike Effa

Calmly and without haste Dike told her his position in the company as well as his salary

Before turning in for the night, Mrs. Karim had briefed Dike on the next day's assignment and if he heard her correctly no mention of taking her eldest son who was over twenty to the High commission was made. He was therefore surprised when he came in the morning only to be confronted with a new game plan. Meanwhile Dike was still hopeful of leaving for Dogawa on this Thursday.

"Dike you will accompany my children to Marina if you are not allowed to go in then come back with the driver,", she instructed. On their way to enter the car, Ahmed had wanted to seat in front but Mira spoke rapidly in Lebanese and Ahmed sat behind with her. Dike didn't understand Lebanese but actions sometimes speak louder than words. Of course, he was an employee and so he could not rub shoulders with his employers. On reaching Marina, of course Dike had no passport. He couldn't go in, so he instructed them on what to do. With this task partly accomplished, he left for the main assignment,

The Prisoner of Afrika

"Please endeavour to check on us in an hour's time okay?" Mira instructed.

"Okay", Dike answered. The immigration lady he had come to see was nowhere to be found, all her colleagues could say was "she had not come yet". However another lady officer informed Dike the lady he was looking for was on maternity leave. From the immigration office, he rushed down to Marina partly behind schedule. He looked around, but there was no sign of the children so he approached a guard.

"please did you see a white boy and girl around here?" Dike asked still looking around.

"I think so", the guard said. He then left and went to wait for one more hour before going home to find out. Just then he saw John, there was no way he would have recognized Dike from behind because when he left the house in the morning John was yet to report for duty and then he didn't know the type of dress Dike was putting on. "John" he called quickly, he turned.

"Oh thank God – they have returned a long time ago, they sent me to come and see if you will be here", John said.

"How nice of them," he thought.

"Okay, let's go". And they boarded a taxi. The driver had not covered up to two hundred meters when

he ran into a police checkpoint. The driver stopped.
"Come out", the sergeant ordered.

"We are going to search you," he announced.

Quickly, Dike put up his hands into the air as a sign that the search could go on, everybody knew the police very well. Another name for them was "accidental discharge" and Dike didn't want to be their next victim. Moreover, with violent crimes on the rise the police were empowered to shoot at disobedient vehicles that refused to stop.

After the search, the sergeant asked Dike, "Are you a citizen of this country?"

"Yes" he answered.

"Then can I see your ID card?" he requested. Dike realized he had made a mistake. His identity card was not with him.

"Sorry I don't have it here", he said with both hands still up.

"Put down your hands, you are not a prisoner of war and this is not a war front", the sergeant said and they laughed. They warned them and then asked them to go.

"This country will kill me-o", Dike said still laughing.

"John did you show him your ID card—by the way what differentiates us from the Beninese, Ghanaians, Togolese or Nigerians?" Dike asked.

The Prisoner of Afrika

"My brother I've never seen this before", the driver replied without taking his eyes off the road.

"You found him?" Mira asked as if Dike had been reported missing.

"The go-slow is terrible – that's why I couldn't come on time to the High Commission as agreed", he told them. Dike had stayed longer than planned. He had exhausted the few shirts he brought with him even his underwear were in bad shape. At about half past two, Mira's mother and their aunty returned from the market. It was obvious Dike looked a bit tired, it occurred to her he had not had breakfast, David had prepared breakfast at about half past eight in the morning but he declined eating because he wasn't used to eating early in the morning.

"John", she called and the steward appeared.

"Please prepare some food for Dike", she instructed.

"Madam, David prepare food for morning, he refuse to eat", John complained. Mrs. Karim's reaction was very funny,

"Okay, okay", she said clapping her hands,

"Please get a cane and come and flog him for refusing to eat in the morning". John left while Mrs. Karim explained the situation to her sister. John's action baffled everybody.

This was the same person whom a few hours back they had joked over the police search and Dike recalled how on Tuesday afternoon while having breakfast and lunch combined he was eating slowly so John thought he was afraid. When he came to drop the water he said,

"Chop chop no fear". But now he was seeing a different John. Mrs. Karim was annoyed,

"Sometimes I feel like boxing his face", she said to her sister. The food was served a few minutes later. Mrs. Karim was billed to fly out of the country, later that night she had booked in advance with Air Africana. The flight was scheduled to depart by eight O'clock in the night, check-in of luggage was billed to start from half past five. Knowing the time was at hand Mrs. Karim motioned Dike to come closer and she handed over her passport and the tickets and then briefed him on airport procedures then concluded it this way "… the few days you've spent with us had shown you are capable and trustworthy, please keep on being good".

"Thank you Ma'am, Dike said.

David came in to announce the taxi had arrived they loaded the suitcases and left for the airport.

"Thank God demdey go today—dem too worry",

The Prisoner of Afrika

David said in pidgin English,

"Alright that is how you complain about your employer I will report you to her", Dike said jokingly. David laughed. Of course he knew Dike would never do that. This particular trip to the airport from the hold-ups they were encountering was going to be difficult. They had just cleared the second hold-up when they ran into another. The third in a row.

"Oh my God", he exclaimed. "If this goes on we will never reach the airport in time", Dike said.

III

It was hectic at the Air Africana counter, Dike argued seriously before the luggage tags and boarding passes were issued. This was done on the condition that Mrs. Karim and her children will arrive before the aircraft landed. He was not perturbed with the condition. "One down, one to go" he said to himself happily. He then pushed the boxes to the customs officers.

"Where is the owner?" one of them asked.

"Oh—, she will be here soon" Dike said casually.

"What is inside?"

"Clothes"

"Can we search it?" they asked.

"oh why not—feel free".

"What are you to her?" they asked,

"I am an employee in her company".

"Are you her public Relations Officer?"

"No". "Are you her brother?"

"No I am an employee in her company", Dike repeated himself to another officer who had just joined them.

At the end of it all, he tipped the customs officers with three hundred Afripounds and they passed the luggage. Dike tried convincing the airline staff to convey the luggage with others to the tarmac,.

"They will be nobody to identify the luggage and it will delay the aircraft", the official said.

"The aircraft is scheduled to land at half past seven in the night and take off again at half past eight. If the luggage does not get there by eight then forget it", another official said.

Dike began looking at his watch and praying that the aircraft be delayed wherever it was. Half past seven the aircraft had not landed, but Mrs. Karim and the children were yet to come. He knew it was the hold-up that was messing things up. To ensure a smooth transition he stationed David outside to watch out for a blue Peugeot 505 car. From his position, inside he had a clear view of David outside

The Prisoner of Afrika

so that the moment David sighted them and moved he will know and come out to hand over her flight documents to her. From the control tower, they announced the arrival of the aircraft. It was already seven-forty five p.m. At exactly eight O'clock, the counter was closed and the tags removed. Dike had lost three hundred pounds for nothing. The first call to board came at fifteen minutes past eight. He had succeeded in calming himself but when the call came he was frantic and was pacing up and down. He was worried because if Mrs. Karim missed this flight then he could as well say goodbye to his own plans to return to Dogawa.

Suddenly, Dike saw David move and then he saw the blue Peugeot car. He rushed out to meet her as she was entering the departure hall.

"Ma, they are boarding", he said gesturing with his hands to indicate the urgency of the situation. If Mrs. Karim was perturbed by what he had just said she decided not to react, she strode in looking cool like a cucumber and moving with the grace and poise of a wife of a Head of state. Dike explained the situation to her. How they refused to check in the luggage on the grounds that the owner of the luggage might miss the flight. Just then, the second and final call to board was made. Mrs. Karim and two of her children who were going with her had to rush so as not to miss the flight,

"What about the luggage?" he asked quickly.

"We will try to board take the luggage back to the house", she instructed. Air Africana flight 530 was on a three leg journey that will touch Lome then to Abidjan, and will finally end in Johannesburg, South Africa. A few minutes later flight 530 took-off while Dike loaded the luggage into the boot of the car and returned to Mrs. Karim's residence at Elephant Crescent. Mira was sad, as he explained what had transpired at the airport and later left for the stewards room to sleep.

On Friday afternoon, Dike prepared to take his leave.

"You are about to leave?" She asked. Dike nodded his head in response. She handed over his airfare to him,

"Thank you very much for running around for us. Goodbye", she said.

"Goodbye too and my regards to everybody please tell them we regret the inconveniences they may have suffered as a result of their luggage being left behind", Dike said,.

"No problem—it's not your fault the Air Africana

The Prisoner of Afrika

people did it," she said. Dike came out of the house, stopped a taxi, and left for the airport.

At the airport, the aircraft did not arrive till almost half past five. He was shocked over proceedings at the airport, getting the ticket had been a tug-of-war and now it seemed boarding the aircraft was going to be a Herculean task he watched helplessly as some rich people were allowed to jump the queue and board before others that was the problem with Afrika corruption was high. The airport touts hovered around the aircraft like vultures. Dike even caught a glimpse of one Unikal student among the touts,

"What is this one doing here?" he wondered. Well he couldn't blame him. If it hadn't been for striking university lecturers, this guy will not be here he'd observed sadly. After what seemed like eternity, he boarded the aircraft and lowered himself into the seat tiredly and fastened his seatbelt. Going-up towards the cockpit, the flight steward noticed the passenger seating next to Dike and occupying the seat near the aisle had not fastened his belt.

"Your belt" the steward pointed out.

"What about your own?—leave me alone it is God that saves."

"Okay, but I'm going to fasten my own", the steward replied.

Mike Effa

With the flight instructions given, the lights were switched off while SCOBE flight 650 gathered speed and took off for Dogawa State. It was already dark when they took off. They had been in the air for about fifteen minutes when the passenger occupying the seat by the aisle spoke, "are these people not going to serve us some food?" he asked,

"I don't know", Dike said. This passenger was a very funny man. They were discussing the Olympics.

Suddenly, he went quiet. When Dike looked towards the cockpit, he saw why he was quiet. The air hostess was pushing a trolley loaded with assorted dishes towards them having served those in front. He opted for potato and chicken, while Dike went for spaghetti and chicken. On opening, he compared both dishes and immediately pointed it out to the hostess, "see this man's own is more than my own. "

"Yes, both of you requested separate dishes", the hostess replied. The man was not going to give up and in order to avoid a scene a plate of "spaghetti and chicken" was handed to him and peace was restored.

Dike was eating gently whereas his friend was attacking the chicken with anger and stuffing his mouth at the same time. Looking at him from the

The Prisoner of Afrika

corner of his eyes, he saw his jaws working very hard like those of a crocodile and in a jiffy both plates were empty. He belched noisily and went on to extract meat particles from his teeth using his hands. At ten minutes pass eight o'clock, flight 650 landed at Dogawa International Airport.

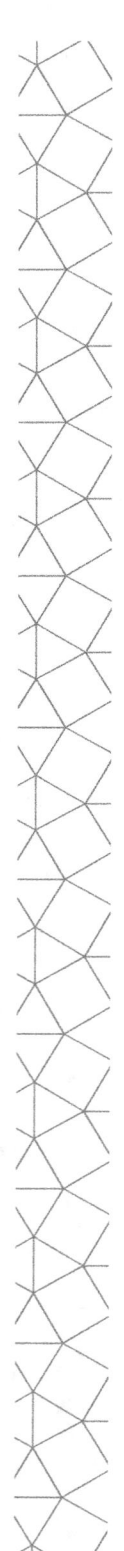

390

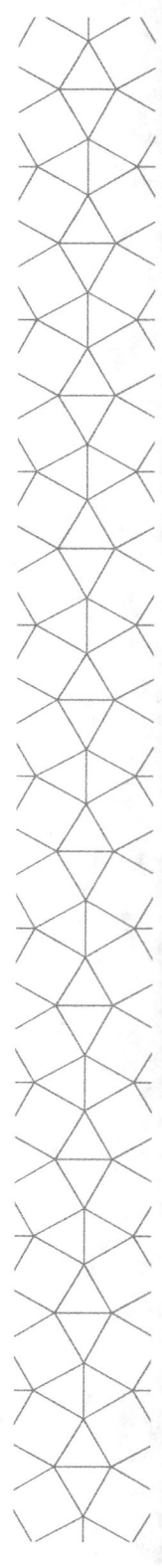

Chapter Twenty Two

Dike took an achabbar from the airport straight to their residence at Hotoro.

"Ah! You are back! Welcome", he said.

"Thank you", Dike replied.

"What about Mrs. Karim did she give you anything?" he asked.

Dike laughed bitterly, "Rich people are terrible. They are ruthless. Mrs. Karim didn't give me anything else besides my airfare,", he answered.

"My God that's serious", Benson said.

He then went on to narrate how he ran around right from Monday he arrived to Friday afternoon when he left.

"Mrs. Karim had travelled back to Lome on Thursday I checked in her luggage –"

"And yet she left you like that?" Benson asked interrupting him.

"Yes, she said I should go on being good". Benson hissed disgustedly.

"na good we go chop?" he asked in pidgin English.

On getting to work the following day, he learnt they had been a protest following a two day delay in the payment of July salary. Thanks to Adou's greed he couldn't get his salary till after about nine days into the month of August.

D ike ran into Ali Dogo one afternoon. Ali Dogo was once a security agent at Heritage Furniture. But, he lost his job when he was caught with items stolen from the upholstery section. Adou had reported to the Police and Ali was arrested and charged to court. Being a minor offence, the presiding magistrate had sentenced him to three months with an option to pay a fine of one thousand Afripounds. His brothers had paid the fine and thus saved him from going to jail.

"You're looking good, how are you?" Dike asked.

"Fine", he answered.

"Have you been able to get another job yet?" Dike inquired.

"No but somebody promised me a job at a textile factory. Did you know Adou sent his wife to meet me at the Police station?"

"For what" Dike asked,

"To implicate you now. The wife told me my husband say he will give you two thousand Afripounds, get you a new job, and release you

The Prisoner of Afrika

from cell if you agree to tell the Police that Dike gave you those items," Dogo said.

Dike was shocked and stared at him terribly upset.

"So I refused and we started arguing and a police constable came to find out what was wrong I told him see this woman's husband wants me to implicate my brothers for nothing. Adou's wife left in shame", he concluded. Dike was too shocked to move. He regained his composure thanked Dogo profusely and they parted ways. While reflecting on the whole issue, the pieces began to fall in place. He recalled how annoyed Adou was on hearing Dogo was jailed for only three months.

Never trust a Korra. The only true Korra you find is a dead one. Dike had always been a stumbling block or rather a thorn in Adou's flesh, so he had thought this was an opportunity to get rid of him by forcing Dogo to implicate him in the theft case. He informed the Accountant who was shocked at the callousness of Adou. On getting home from work, Dike reported it to Benson who on the contrary dazed him further by blaming him for doing business with Adou. Dike was angry and resolved to confront Adou immediately. It was clear to anyone who could see that if he was cooperating with Adou, he wouldn't have done this to him. Instead of taking the issue up, Benson told Dike to go and offer a thanksgiving in church.

Really, he was grateful to God who made Dogo refused to give in to Adou's antics. If he had mentioned his name, in his position as store keeper, it would have been hard for anybody to believe he didn't give those items to Dogo. The next day, Dike confronted Adou in the presence of the accountant.

"I swear I never do such terrible thing!"

Dike knew before even confronting him that he will deny, "I'm not surprised by your denial but God will judge.

However, he had also learnt never to trust anybody in Heritage Furniture especially the engineer whom he had given a wide berth because he talks like a market woman and is a very good tale bearer. With his elevation to position of sales manager, Adou was now in charge indeed and all the Directors of Heritage Furniture it seems had been placed under a spell or maybe they were just afraid of Adou or else how could Adou who had the key to the factory and who was actually stealing items ranging from furniture to machineries. Go and tell Maibala the evening lawyer and Musau his houseboy as well as Alh Babura that it was the store officers that were stealing, and these men with their shallow brains believed Adou.

"Why won't they?" Dike wondered, after all at the end of Board meetings their sitting allowances were paid by Adou and straight from his pocket. Matters were not helped either by Benson who it appeared had been bought over by Adou too. Hence, his utterances one day at the conclusion of one of their numerous board meetings, made the chairman and the other directors came out of the conference room.

"Accountant", the chairman bellowed impatiently.

"Sir", Mr. Essienson answered.

"Where's our sitting allowance?" he asked angrily.

"How much is it?" Adou asked, immediately saving the accountant from further bullying.

"Three thousand five hundred Afripounds", he said.

Adou dipped his hand into his pocket, brought out the money and paid the chairman and his directors like small boys and they departed smiling. In the process of bringing out the money, a wad of dollars had shown itself and the directors craned their necks to see it properly.

"Hey, I will like my own allowance to be paid in dollars,", Musau said. They all laughed while Adou hit him playfully on the chest with the wad of dollars.

So, under the circumstances, they were bound to believe everything Adou told them. But then, even Dike knew that nemesis would catch up with Adou quickly.

Two months after attempting to get the mai-guard implicate him, Adou's second son with four other boys were arrested for defrauding one businessman of over half a million Afripounds. Adou spent a lot of money to get his son off the hook, and that was not the end of it. About three months later ,this same boy was arrested for stealing a mobile phone belonging to a Lebanese person. The boy was beaten and detained. Adou spent money again to get him out of police detention. For days, the boy stayed in doors and when asked Adou would say, "he's not well—he get accident". While sympathetic with Adou over his plight and despite what he tried doing to him, Dike could not help using Adou's affliction as a case point in warning those who were trying to damage his reputation to desist from their evil acts because most of them had children. So, whatever you plan for somebody else's child be sure that it will follow your children or nieces or nephew as in the case of the sales lady who at thirty -seven was yet to marry but had nephews and nieces.

The Prisoner of Afrika

II

Then one day the engineer disappeared without any trace and Dike was left to confront his detractors who included the sales lady with a fleshy face sufficient to cover five other people; also included was the cashier, Sunday Ikenga. Sunday was more dangerous than a snake. You would often hear workers say "person wey no fear Sunday no go fear God". Sunday was notorious for cutting factory workers salary illegally. Bringing up the rear was the machinist, a fellow known as Sylvester. He had a potbelly and stained set of teeth. These were the people who now embarked on a campaign of calumny against Dike unknown to him. Their aim was to damage his reputation and get him into trouble ,also as a way of spiting Benson who stripped them of their extra jobs. while the sales lady had doubled as purchasing officer. Sunday doubled as store-keeper. Everybody in the factory could recall the atrocities Sunday committed while in the store. On Sundays, Sunday will not go to church he will pack his dirty clothes in a travelling bag and come to the company to wash. After washing, Sunday will line his bag with screw nails then put his clothes on top and off he went. The following day Sunday would try to dispose his loot in the market. Complaints were lodged against Sunday yet no action was taken against him and the sales lady who remained untouchable till Benson arrived and bulldozed the three of them off.

Replacing them with Dike, this development had not gone down well at all with the three musketeers and it was obvious they were not going to give up without a fight. They had replied in form of the petition which was written by August in but it failed still they didn't give up. They continued framing stories and taking them to the chairman. It got to a point the chairman Board of Directors secretly mandated the sales lady to watch Dike the Accountant and the sales Manager.

Alh Mai Bala's tenure in office remains the funniest tenure in the history of Heritage Furniture. While he lacked vision and directions, but he is very good in calling Board meetings without an agenda. It was on record that as company chairman Alhaji Mai Bala held thirty-six board meetings in one year at an average of three meetings per month. Funny enough, these meetings served as an avenue for witch-hunting staff that were non-indigenes of Dogawa State. It was also an avenue for some of the directors who were civil servants like Mai Bala and Musau to make extra money in form of sitting allowances.

Of course, it's obvious that Alhaji Mai Bala is so overwhelmed with the position of company chairman

III

Shortly before the Sallah holidays, the company was closed down for one week. All the factory workers were asked to stay at home. Within the office, Sunday and Dike whose reputation had been severely battered were also asked to stay at home. Before the holidays, Dike observed there were ten mattresses, mirrors, a puff and a centre table. On resuming a week later he discovered two of the items had disappeared. On investigating ,it was discovered Rifkata Rita and Adou had connived and stolen these items. This was a big opportunity for him to turn the tables and he grabbed it with both hands. This is the chance I've been waiting for he said. Immediately, he reported to Benson but unfortunately Benson refused to take up the case. Naturally people might be tempted to ask why he didn't go to the chairman. The answer is simple. The chairman is emotionally unbalanced and very biased. In fact he can best be described as a tribalist. So that was why Dike didn't go to him. Secondly, those who were running him down went to these directors because they are of the same stock and they had access to them. He had access to Benson so he reported to him. Unfortunately, no action was taken. Despite the fact that it was obvious they had stolen, Rifkata did not give up on her attempts to frame-up Dike. The complaints continued even though those reporting are the very people who were really stealing. Of course a man will not steal and then go and report to the police that he has stolen. The problem with the women especially was this: while Rita was just being petty and bitchy despite the fact that she was old enough to be his mother and that soon she will become a grandmother. Rifkata was ugly men merely used her as a sex object coupled with the fact that she was not educated so her frustration could be understood. But then, she was making some money from the side and from other shady deals with Adou. So what else did she want? Dike wondered. As a result of the complaints against him, the board ordered that an inventory of all items in the company be taken.

The inventory taking was carried out on a Saturday

morning. On reaching the engineer's office, it was discovered the welding machine that was kept there had disappeared. There was confusion.

"What's the meaning of this rubbish? "Dike asked perplexed.

"Relax we'll find it", Mr Essienson replied.

"Be calm nobody will get you into trouble"

while Dike was worried because he had the key to the engineer's office. Sunday was very happy that at last he was in serious trouble.

"Somebody go sleep for cell o", he'd said. Initially, it was resolved that it should be kept secret but Sunday took it upon himself to spread the news right up to the chairman.

Another board meeting was called; the issue of the machine came up. Fortunately, Benson was mandated to invite the police to re-arrest those workers linked with the loss of the first machine. While Dike was busy having sleepless nights and praying like he'd never done before, he failed to see that he could not be arrested because he did not have the keys to the entrances. If anybody was to be arrested, it would be the sales manager and Sunday who had the keys to the factory. Sunday was too blind to realize these facts. The machine issue stayed that way till December when majority of the factory workers including Dike were asked to stay at home for two weeks. On resumption, he discovered certain items had been stolen again from the showroom. Of course, by those who stayed back.

"Yahoo! This is my chance to pay them back in their own coin", Dike said to himself. Getting home he told Benson. Benson having been informed by Dike smiled, "you see. God is wonderful. If they're arresting, it won't be only you," he had said.

"You just be cool I've got a surprise for all of them and I shall spring it soon and when I do it things will change for the better".

"Well I hope so" Dike said. Benson decided to wait till the next board meeting.

Meanwhile, the sales lady was making noise mostly on the missing machine she did not know that everybody was aware of the mattresses she and the typist had stolen. The factory workers loyalty began to shift because they now saw Rifkata in her true colour. The next board meeting was held in May and the machine was discussed under matters arising. Benson explained how his attempts to bring in the police failed. The sales manager concurred, "Yes, lawyer is right I destroyed the first case because the sales lady was spitting fire that one of

The Prisoner of Afrika

the factory workers who was arrested was innocent,". Benson informed the other directors, "the machine was in the factory and not in the store. In fact the only machine left is inside the store even as we speak".

Further attempts by a director from Dogawa State properties was politely turned down by Alh. Babura who had told him, "nobody is responsible for the machines inside the factory, everybody right from the mai guard is a thief so let by gone be by gone, we should rather check future occurrences, " he had concluded.

A resolution was passed and while the meeting lasted, the machinist, a fellow named Sylvester and the sales lady patrolled the meeting area with the hope that they would be invited to say something on the missing machine but they were disappointed. According to Benson throughout the meeting, he had put the chairman under pressure by confronting him with certain statements he'd made to Sylvester and the sales lady. So while they were busy patrolling, they did not know that plans were being fine tuned on how to pay them off.

"This people are so foolish", Benson told Dike.

"I'm in charge here and nothing happens without my knowing and do you know that the directors had

Mike Effa

actually wanted to invite the sales lady and warn her to respect herself?"

"Is that so". Three days later, it was rumoured Dike was leaving, without clarifying issues, the "reporters" as usual rushed to the chairman to inform him that the "suspect" was leaving.

The chairman smiled, "listen the person you're suspecting can sue you or the company for defamation of character—the case has been resolved if the first machine had been recovered then he would have been made to pay for the second machine. So, go back to your jobs and leave board decisions for directors".

This bit was relayed to Dike by Mr. Essienson who had accompanied them mostly out of curiosity.

"Dike", he called smiling, "for the first time the chairman spoke like a man" he said.

"I told you remember? Nobody will put you in trouble"

"Anyway I really thank God."

It was obvious that Mr. Essienson was right because Dike could see disappointment clearly written on Rifkata's puffy, pimple infected face.

Later that night he relayed all that happened to Benson.

"Ooh that's a real verdict of the decade", Benson

said.

"At least, Alh Maibala has spoken like a man", Dike added.

"They are so foolish", Benson said.

"So you know I had informed the chairman about the mattresses?"

"You did?" Dike asked.

"Of course, and Maibala just sighed. Benson had said if it was so then we would've linked the loss of the machines to her and the typist then dismiss them."

"But it's not too late to dismiss them", Dike insisted.

"Well don't worry let's leave it like that," Benson advised.

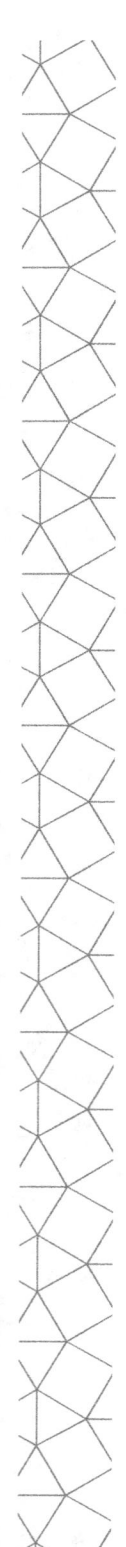

406

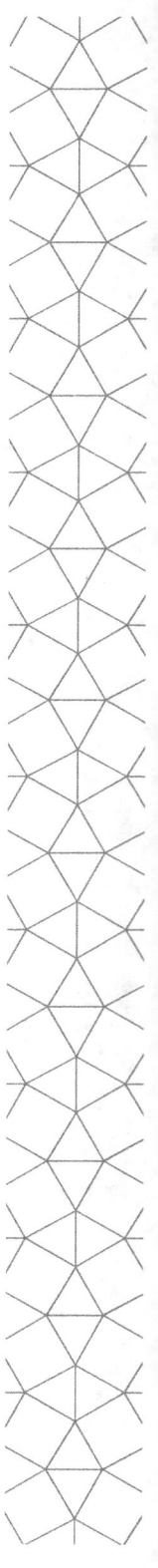

Chapter Twenty Three

Shortly after events at Heritage Furniture Company were resolved in his favour, Dike received a call from home.

"A job offer," he said to himself after dropping the phone thank you Lord for remembering me. Throughout that day, he behaved differently and time moved very fast. Immediately, he went home arriving their flat by 4. 30pm he didn't wait too long before Benson entered too.

"How was the factory today?" Benson asked after they had greeted.

"Nothing fantastic except for one man who came with a request for furniture worth three hundred thousand afripounds"

"Well for a company like heritage furniture it's a lifeline." Benson said.

"Yes it is," Dike agreed.

"Anyway I've been offered a job by a family friend back home".

There was silence for a while as Benson drifted off in thoughts.

"What kind of job is it and how much is the salary?"

he asked.

Dike gave him all the details "it's good," Benson began, "at least this will show those people in the factory that you've not reached your last bus-stop. "

"I thank God o for this opening," he added.

For Dike, living in Dogawa state had been hell. There were a thousand and one reasons to dislike the state and it ranged from the heat, volatile nature of the state. and the biased nature of the people. All these factors combined would make anybody quit speedily. Dike had stayed after youth service just because of the job that was offered him by Mazi Okeke through Benson's influence. But a job offer in Kalabar meant two things, first he would be with his family members and second, Kalabar was a cool and quiet city with enough rainfall to take care of the issue of high temperatures as experienced in Dogawa. On Monday of the new week, Dike arrived Heritage furniture looking like somebody back from America.

"Dike you're looking radiant –what's the secret?" Mr Essienson asked. He broke into singing-

"This is my turn to shine, and I will arise and shine"…

While he sang, Mr Essienson watched very amused.

"Oya, Dike tell me the good news", he urged. Without further delay he brought out his letter of resignation.

"what is this?" Mr Essienson asked, taking a look at the paper," It's like this"; as from today, I cease to be a staff of Heritage Furniture-".

"It's a lie, you don't say, " Mr Essienson interrupted.

"You want to be jobless", he pointed out,

"Not at all, it's taken care of". Dike replied. They both lapsed into silence for a while.

"Okay", Mr Essienson began.

"So you're leaving, remember me –o". he laughed.

"Of course, I will remember you. As a matter of fact, I shall be writing to all of you," Dike promised.

Dike's letter of resignation was presented to the G. M that morning and before closing was paid his outstanding claims for the month. With all his belongings neatly packed, Dike bade Benson farewell and on Wednesday morning, he left Dogawa state for Zuma Rock City en route to Kalabar to take up his new job.

Meanwhile Afrikans did not experience any positive change in their lifestyle. Rather the dictator who was calling the shots in Zuma Rock City continued his reign of terror. Extra–judicial killings continued to be the latest trend. Due to the fact that Gen Ahmed the Afrikan head of state loved praise singing and flattery so much, overnight, praise singers took over the scene. In fact, Sycophancy became the order of the day.

It was common sight to see politicians who had participated in the last transition program falling over each other, carrying tales, blackmailing one another just to curry the favour of the dictator. In any case it was not for nothing since their sycophancy secured them contracts from which they earned a living. It was a clear case of using what you have to get what you need. Gen. Ahmed was also working hard though the fraudulent transition, he had begun to transmute into a civilian dictator the following year but only time would tell if the dictator will continue to hold sway in the helm of affairs of the Republic of Afrika.

II

The New Year met Dike in his seventh month as a staff of Fintan and Gen Associates. that he was happy and contented was an understatement. It was in his fourth month that Dike realized he had made a mistake coming to work here.

Fintan had been given a very big contract and

The Prisoner of Afrika

there was plenty of money to go with it, but Fintan was a very greedy man of course this was the disadvantage of being poor for too long. In heritage furniture despite its poor finances, staff were still paid Christmas bonus but that was not the case with his new job.

"What have I gotten myself into?" he moaned that chilly December evening.

"what's the problem?" his mother asked.

" I left Dogawa for this job thinking it had prospects but seven months after Fintan is yet to treat me well- to worsen matters he refused to pay us Xmas bonus despite the fact that we posted profits of over two million afripounds".

"Kwa! Say no more," his mother interrupted. "Your boss is a selfish man"

"What do you mean?" Magy asked.

"you're not related in anyway always remember that and I think you should continue the search for another job. " She advised.

Things did not improve at Fintan & associates in fact following the sudden death of the Afrikan dictator after eating apples with prostitutes from Togo, their contract was terminated by the state government. Since they had not planned for the future and their boss had been living a reckless life financially, salaries could no longer be paid regularly. The staff became disenchanted and started looking for jobs elsewhere. Fintan wasn't bothered, as soon as he caught any staff writing application he would sack the staff on the spot.

In that manner Fintan sacked all his employees including Dike who had also been caught applying for a job at the EPZ complex. So Dike finally made his exit.

He was the first person to be employed at fintan & associates but he was the last to be sacked you can never be too careful in life, he said to himself.

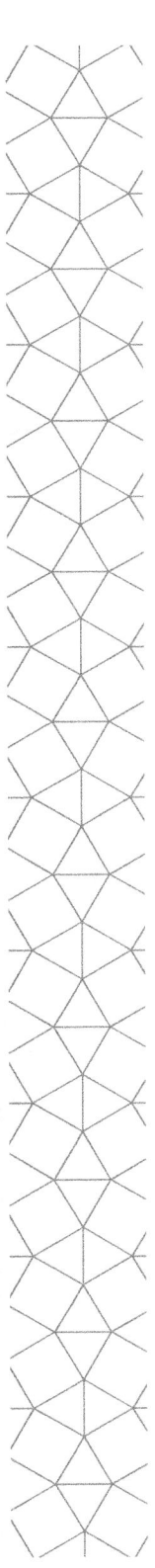

413

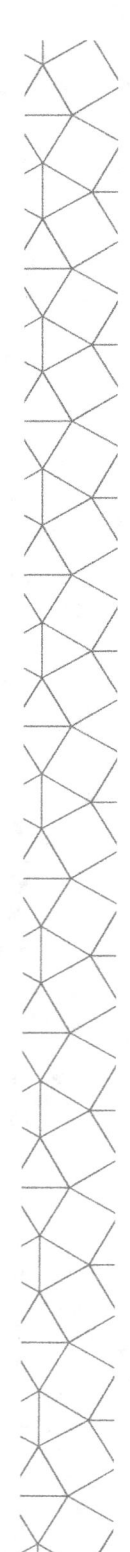

414

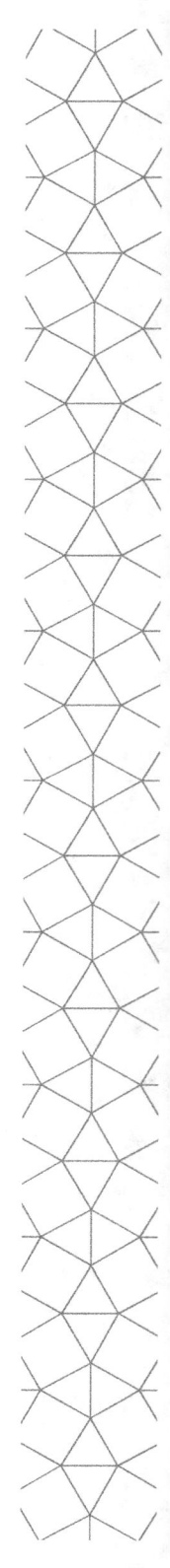

Chapter Twenty Four

Two months later after taking over as Head of state following the death of Gen Ahmed-the Afrikan dictator, Gen Boko announced a genuine transition program. Actually the transition program had commenced after series of meetings with different ethnic groups across the country. Gen Boko followed up by granting presidential pardon to all Afrikans imprisoned for one offence or the other during the dark days of the military junta headed by the late dictator. Apart from the change in headship other negative trends like corruption and embezzlement continued unabated. It was not new in Afrika to hear that civil servants in a given state were being owed arrears of salary while the military administrator of that state would be busy travelling around the world. Among those released from prison was former head of state, Gen Olu Hakot , The former commander in chief had been arrested on trumped up charges of plotting to overthrow the late dictator . But everybody knew that the former head of state's problem started when he canvassed at the U. N for sanctions to be imposed on Afrika because of Gen Ahmed's refusal to restore democracy .

The transition program of Gen Boko ended eleven months later, with the swearing in of the civilian president for the fourth republic. In the person of Gen Olu Hakot who at this point had dropped his military title to adapt to his new position as president in a democratic setting. There was so much euphoria over the fact that the military was quitting politics for good. Nobody cared about the fact that a military man in mufti was being left behind to govern the nation. Afrikans in their euphoria overlooked the fact that the president was once convicted and sentenced for plotting against the state. However, many saw it as a good sign. They reasoned that the new president having had a firsthand experience of life in prison would adopt a soft approach in leading his people. But Afrikans were in for a rude shock.

Two years later after assuming office, Afrikans were still to be taken to the Promised Land standard of living took a nose dive as inflation rose while the government compounded the situation by increasing the pump price of petroleum products

The Prisoner of Afrika

from twenty- two Afripounds to thirty Afripounds as part of government's desire to commence total deregulation of the downstream sector. This increase was condemned nationwide and labour groups responded by calling a nationwide strike which lasted two days . The strike was suspended after negotiations pegged the price of petrol at twenty- six pounds per litre.

Within this two and half years in which there was no improvement in the lot of the common man, Afrikans began to take a second look at those who were at the helm of affairs. The president was too busy globetrotting with his vice to care about the plight of his subjects" unemployment. Crime and corruption were the order of the day.

President Olu Hakot, it appeared was deaf to the cry of the masses. Known as the "travelling salesman", the President was called upon by his subjects to reduce his foreign trips. Instead the President followed this up with a request to the National Assembly for approval to buy a new Presidential jet costing over five billion Afripounds. The national assembly rejected the request out of a guilty conscience over their inability to improve the lot of their people. Afrikans had not seen the last of their president and his corrupt party.

Mike Effa

II

Three weeks after losing his job with Fintan Associates, Dike was at home trying to get over the anger and frustration of his experience with their so-called family friend. After going over the whole episode in his mind for hours on end, he dozed off, still sitting in the parlour. "Dike, Dike", Kris called.

"Yes, what's up?" he replied sitting up.

"Did you go out today?" He knew what his brother was talking about.

"Look, the job situation is terrible, " Dike said.

"I walked the streets of Kalabar and the only story that came my way was sorry no vacancy", Dike said.

"Meanwhile the government is doing nothing", Kris said. "Anyway I think you should apply to this place".

"Oh", Dike exclaimed. "Where did you get it?"

"They did not advertise in the papers, a friend of mine who works with the bank gave it to me – but I'm not interested. "

"Why now?" Dike asked. "Let's apply together"

"No don't worry just go ahead and apply", Kris urged.

Without further delay, Dike wrote his application attached the supporting documents and went to

The Prisoner of Afrika

submit at the Neon Development Bank branch office in Kalabar. It took three weeks before he was contacted.

"I've been invited for the aptitude test", he told his parents. "That's nice", his father said.

"I hope you've prepared well"

"I have and I know, success will come my way".

The aptitude test was written in the bank's head office in Uyo town. They were tested in four subjects namely English, Mathematics, General Paper and Logic. During the test he noticed a lot of malpractices going on. Hmm..when shall we rise above things like these?, he wondered. Refocusing on his answer sheet, Dike quickly tidied up just as the coordinator asked them to turn in their scripts. Since he did not know anybody, Dike returned to Kalabar immediately. Kris was the first person he met.

"You're back! How was the test?" he asked.

"Fine, I've done my best – the rest I leave to God".

Nothing was heard of the test again till four months later when Dike who was on the brink of giving–up received a slip inviting him for interview. Again, he revised intensively and on that Saturday morning he left for the interview.

They were many, so the panel adopted a strategy to make it faster. Five candidates were called in each time. Soon it was his turn, together with four other candidates they went in.

"Sit down and be relaxed", one of the panellist said. After going through the preamble, the panel began asking them questions.

Dike was asked two questions bothering on the functions of the Central Bank and the Afrikan Disposition Insurance Company. He answered these questions well.

"What did you score in the aptitude test to qualify you for this interview?" One of the men asked.

"Fifty-three percent", Dike replied.

The next candidate scored twenty-eight percent, the third and fourth candidates scored thirty and twenty–nine percent respectively while the fifth candidate in their group scored fifteen percent. And you were all invited for the interview, Dike had said within him.

"Do you know anybody on the board?"

"No I don't know anybody", Dike replied.

"Who is sponsoring you?" One of the panellists asked.

"Nobody sir", Dike replied. But, it was not so with the other four candidates whose sponsors ranged from senior military officers to big time politicians.

"All right, thank you ladies and gentlemen you shall

be hearing from us soon".

Of course, that is the norm Dike said quietly. So many people failed the test yet they came for the interview due to their connections, Dike pondered, Well in thee oh Lord do I put my trust.

On reaching home, he narrated all that transpired to his family members.

"It's terrible o", his mother said. "No wonder we're listed among the corrupt nations of the world".

"How can we develop when we encourage mediocrity and despise intelligence and hard work," Rhoda said.

"Well whatever will be, will be", Kris concluded. A month elapsed since the interview, no employment letter was forthcoming. It was Kris who put him out of his agony one evening. "My friend told me today that letters of employment have been sent out and there's no Shakkassalli among them".

"It's okay", Dike said. "That's life, getting jobs this days is not based on what you know but who you know.".

"In any case, the search for a job continues", Kris said. "Don't be discouraged – "

"Why should I be? My God knows that when one door closes another is opening somewhere for me."

"That's the spirit keep it up", Kris said patting him on the shoulder.

Mike Effa

For the first time since he graduated from the University, Dike found himself deep in the labour market.

"So this is what it looks like to be jobless", he observed. I can't stay like this for too long, I must do something and fast, he vowed. His experience with the bank did not help matters either. The entire family shared in his challenge,

"It's not forever now", Basi consoled. "In fact, I think this is the beginning of great things for you. "

"I hope so too", Dike said agreeing with his younger brother, "but you can apply to become a teacher in one of the secondary schools", his mother said.

"Mma, we must not all be teachers", he pointed out.

"Yes he's right", Kris supported. "look at me, you", he said referring to their mother, "and even Basi—we're all teachers. The slightest delay in our salaries means starvation."

"Teachers reward is in heaven", Dike said and they all laughed.

"But what about the teachers – that won't go to heaven——what happens to their rewards?" Basi asked. "Of course they will forfeit it", Dike replied him.

"You people are not serious", their mother said.

His position could be understood, teachers in Afrika

The Prisoner of Afrika

were treated like second class citizens in their own country. Afrika was one country that paid lip service to the improvement of education. Three days later another opening appeared. If Dike had accepted he would have ended up a police officer. After a lengthy discussion with his sister Roda, Dike buried the issue when he declared to his sister. "My frustration has not reached the level of me joining the police."

The Afrikan Police force was a sight to behold and they were a corrupt bunch. The Afrikan police was ill equipped and very good in extorting the standard twenty Afripounds from drivers. With Dike turning down the second opportunity, he was left alone for awhile but the family did not give up on their attempts to help him get a job.

Four months after he lost his job, Dike found himself being called upon to render some sort of assistance. It all started when his sister. Ada called from Zuma Rock City and asked him to come and assist them in taking care of their son who was about to undergo a medical procedure.

Without delay Dike got his bag ready. "This is a good break for me", he told his mother. "I'm sure after this they will get you a Federal civil service job".

"Well maybe", Dike replied, "but I'm going for humanity's sake and not because of the job".

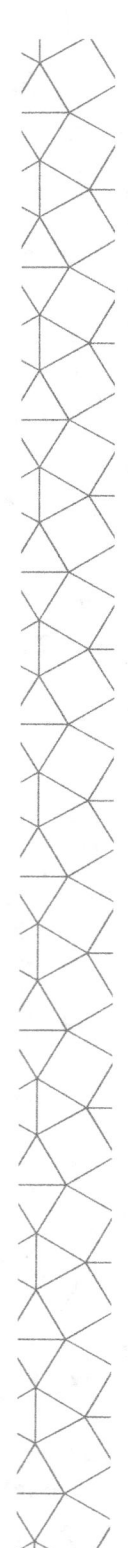

424

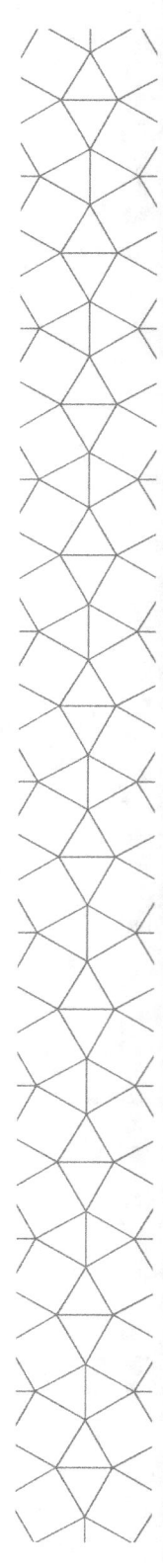

Chapter Twenty Five

Three weeks after returning from the hospital and followed up by weekly visits to the hospital for post surgery check-ups, his nephew was given a clean bill of health, Dike prepared to depart for his new job as a government worker or civil servant. On the eve of his departure, his in-law called him to the parlour, "Dike I must thank you for all you have done for us" he began.

"We thank God for everything", Dike said.

"...So for the time that you spent here, I`ve put together something by way of a job for you..." he was saying.

"Thank you sir", Dike replied. "Furthermore, you`ll need this letter" he said.

Receiving the letter and flipping it over he saw that it was addressed to a certain Professor Makinde Akkiliz in Ekko city.

"The professor is the director general of that agency and he is going to employ you", his in-law said.

"Dike be a good staff and do your job diligently", Ada advised.

"No problem I shall put in my best," he promised

On arriving Ekko city, Dike made enquiries on how to get to No 10 Obalende Street in Anthony village. The first person he talked to merely said he didn't know the second person was more helpful, "you're going to Obalende Street?" the man asked.

"Yes and in Anthony village all you've just to do is to take a bike and it will drop you there ".

"Thank you," Dike said. The bike man charged him twenty pounds to his destination. He paid without bothering to negotiate.

" Oga we don reach no 10 obalende street ", the bike man said.

"Thank you" he responded and got off the bike.

Just as he was about opening the gate, it was Dr Emoh, "welcome sir" Dr Emoh said jokingly.

"thank you doctor", Dike responded, "so how are you now and how's life in the big city?" he asked.

"Let's go in first," doctor said.

"Ekko city is interesting with plenty of challenges you've got to be alert and very smart" doctor warned.

"very interesting" Dike responded.

"To survive here you must be ahead of your rival".

"Eko city is the home of all kinds of people, you would see pick pockets, fraudsters known as 419 in

The Prisoner of Afrika

Nigeria and then you will see babes with plenty of cash in search of men who can satisfy them sexually. These are the movers and shakers of Ekko city. "

"A very interesting orientation indeed," Dike said.

 After a good night's rest the following morning he was ready to move out. Going by doctor Emoh's direction, he trekked the short distance to the bus stop. He could still hear the voice of his host ringing in his ear, ". . . . . . . It's very easy now to get to Victoria Island"," he was saying with a smile Dike would later get used to.

"Just walk straight and you will reach the bus stop. From there, you'd hear Obalende. Enter one of the buses. Just ask questions. You've got to know how to find your way. "

He went away with his trade mark smile. Dike also went his way reaching the bus stop, he entered a massive bus popularly known as "Molue". The drive was smooth because there were few vehicles on the road.

From obalende, Dike took the next bus heading for Adeola Odeku street and at half past eight he was standing at the gate of the agency that he would soon join.

Mike Effa

"Oga good morning," Dike greeted the gateman,
"my brother good morning na who you wan see?"
the gateman asked in pidgin.

"ehmm," Dike said as he dug into his folder and
came out with the letter.

"Ookay, Prof Akkiliz?" The gateman asked.

"Yes" he responded.

"Just go to the office, then ask dem go show you
oga office".

"Thank you very much, " he said and went in. After
one enquiry, Dike found himself in the office of
professor Akkiliz" secretary.

"Yes what can I do for you?" the secretary asked,
"please I want to see the Prof," Dike replied.

"I know that," the secretary said.

"It's not yet visiting time so you can leave a
message and come back later", Dike was taken
aback by what the secretary had just said.

"Madam please! I have nowhere else to go. I've
come all the way from Zuma Rock city and...

Just then, the door opened and a lady came out of
the professor's office. "

"Shade, what's going on?" she asked

"Nothing serious except for this visitor who wants to
see Oga before visiting time, " Shade replied.

"Well, just help him", the lady said, still she stopped

at the door and came back. "Why do you want to see oga?" She asked.

"I was asked to give him this letter," Dike said, showing her the letter.

"Come ", she said taking him by the hand they entered Professor Akiliz " Office.

"Oga, this man has a letter for you ", she said.

"Good morning Sir ", Dike greeted.

"Yes, how're you ?" he replied before he started reading the letter.

"Okay", he said taking off his glasses.

"How is your brother -in-law ", Prof Akkiliz enquired.

"He's fine Sir. "

"Listen, young man, here we work very hard and do not encourage laziness. I employed you because I owe your in-law a favour, so do not disappoint him. Okay?".

"I won't sir ", Dike replied.

"Alright, take him to Mrs Abuh" he said "you may go with her".

"Thank you sir," he said shutting the door behind him.

Mrs Abuh's office was five rooms from that of Professor Akkiliz . They were both on the same floor. Mrs Akodo knocked once and both of them went in.

"Madam well done o", Mrs Akodo greeted.

"Good Morning madam", Dike greeted.

"This is a new staff ", Mrs Akodo said

"Oga said I should bring him to you".

"Ohh! That's alright, young man you're welcome to the Agency", Mrs Abuh said.

"Thank you ma", Dike replied. What a nice and warm lady he said within him. Mrs Akodo excused herself and left.

"So what is your name?"Mrs Abuh asked.

"Dike Shakkassalli", he replied.

"you'll write an application letter for employment attach photocopies of your credentials and bring them tomorrow with you okay?"

"Yes madam!" Dike replied.

"Okay you can go", Mrs Abuh said dismissing him.

Dike was confused, perplexed.

"What is this?" he asked himself, is this how civil service is disorganised, casual and without form? Any way we shall see, he consoled himself. he was served his letter of employment as "administrative officer grade ii", and thus became a staff of Afrikan Science and Medicine Agency. The Agency was a parastatal under the Ministry of Technology and Developmental Science. While professor Mankinde Akkiliz was the Director General and Chief Executive Officer, Mrs Abuh, as Dike found out was the principal Administrative Officer. Mrs Abuh was a staff of the ministry only seconded to the Agency. There were many others like her. On the other hand, there were other staffs like Dike because they were employed directly by the Agency. They were tagged "Agency Staff" while Mrs Abuh and her colleagues described themselves as "Ministry staff". Hand in hand, they teamed up with professor Akkiliz to unleash hell on the so called Agency Staff! First, they were kept for three months without salaries and when confronted Mrs Abuh coldly told them it is government policy. "

"Na wa o," Dike said on their way to their various offices.

"It is an attempt to frustrate us, " Kate said. Kate Wilson was a scientific Officer in the Research department and had reported on the same day with Dike.

"First that same Mrs Abuh said we are not entitled to twenty-eight days in lieu of hotel accommodation- but they paid themselves", he said angrily.

"This is wickedness and Mrs Abuh as you can see is going to be a mean human being", Kate observed. "Well I don't have anybody so I leave my case to God. "

"Ah nawa o with the civil service. No wonder they're

always looking haggard because of their wickedness".

"But the scripture is clear on that," he pointed out.

"All these people will reap what they have sown".

"But that will take a long time, " Kate lamented.

Dike merely smiled. "listen", he began, "no matter how long it takes, when it comes to the moment will be very painful. "

They parted while Kate went to her office Dike went to the gate to get sachet water popularly known as "pure water".

The Afrikan Science and Medicine Agency was formed before Dike's arrival and Prof Akkiliz was the brain behind its formation hence his appointment as its chief Executive Officer and indeed it was obvious that the Prof was reaping and well too. Three months after his employment, Dike received a rude shock one morning. He had reported for work as usual and was seated on his seat waiting for any assignment that might come his way. Suddenly, Prof Akkiliz appeared on his door step.

"Good morning sir, " he greeted.

"What've you been doing since you were employed?" Akkiliz asked.

Dike was taken aback initially. What kind of stupid question is this he wondered?

The Prisoner of Afrika

"Well sir, I've not been given any task to perform, " Dike replied.

Immediately, Mrs. Abuh was summoned, "your staff is complaining that you've not given them something to do, "Prof Akkiliz said.

"Oga no problem we shall do something about that," Mrs. Abuh said.

While the DG proceeded with his office rounds, Mrs. Abuh stayed back.

"Don't mind him," she said to Dike, "he's always disturbing the staff with irrelevant questions."

Dike was at a loss over the scene he had just witnessed.

"Is this what civil service is all about?" he wondered. Meanwhile those at the top are busy siphoning government money through projects that are never executed. Only God will save this country from corruption, he said to himself. Well I can do nothing but develop myself in any way possible. I cannot beat them but I'll rather not join them.

Gradually, he settled down to the routine of coming to the office. Instead of roaming about till closing time he invested his time reading books. Then he noticed another trait and that was late coming. Staff will arrive very late but in the time book they would sign that they came in early. Little wonder the gateman had remarked when Dike resumed on the first day.

"oh, Oga, you come early o. Anyway when you settle you too go begin come like them".

Eventually, the puzzle fell into place and Dike began to appreciate what the man had said but he continued coming to work early. Mrs. Abuh was a chronic latecomer. Prof Akkiliz, it appeared, was afraid of the ministry staff and was only powerful when it concerned the so-called agency staff. Dike was appalled with everything about the agency. I don't know this kind of job with nothing to do and people come to work on selected days . Now, it's true what they say about government's business being nobody's business. The private sector remains the place for serious minded and result oriented individuals, he thought to himself.

II

In November of that year, the agency conducted a staff interview with the aim of ratifying the employment of the agency and Prof Akkiliz also used that opportunity to employ all his kith and kin. After the interview a lot of funny stories emerged. one of such was that Prof Akkiliz asked the permanent secretary

The Prisoner of Afrika

in charge of the interview panel to let him dismiss some staff; their excellent performance notwithstanding. On the other hand, he begged for the retention of his kinsmen who had failed woefully at the interview. The permanent secretary was at a loss over this display of double identity by the DG. In order to save his kinsmen from being thrown into the labour market he backed off his desire to lay off those staff whose faces he did not like. But Prof Akkilz was not done yet. Early in December, he directed Mrs. Abuh to issue all the staff that were interviewed letters of termination of appointment. This was contrary to the permanent-secretary's recommendation And though Dike and his colleagues went home without the comfort of their December salaries, Prof Akkiliz retired the money into his account using some of it to send his children back to the United States of America.

The New Year began with everyone going about with great expectation. Professor Akkiliz no doubt hoped to consolidate his position of CEO in this New Year and why not? After all, he had been having a good run so far. The overhead of the agency amounting to half a million afripounds each month was his for the taking. As far as the agency was concerned, he was in charge and nobody would take that from him. But things began to change when in January a petition was written and sent to the ministry overseeing the agency. The petitioner a female staff of the agency was protesting the non-payment of her December salary by professor Akkiliz and his cohorts. Unfortunately, the petition didn't go far as Prof Akkiliz bribed his way through the director of personnel management services. The seed, however, had been sown. The man was walking on a tight rope but to him he thought with the petition buried he was okay. Although nothing came out of the petition, it did not mean the ministry was silent on Prof Akkiliz conduct. Unknown to him and the DPMS, the minister was conducting a secret investigation on him. Dike was privileged to know through his sister who also swore him to secrecy.

"You must keep it to yourself o!" his sister warned him.

"No problem. You can trust me, "he had assured her.

Life continued as usual for Dike and his colleagues, while those in the CEOs good books were getting one favour or the other. The rest of the staff had to wait for their salaries. This trend led to an increase in eye service and tale bearing. , Makinde Akkiliz loved women and gossiped a lot. He believed that he

The Prisoner of Afrika

was a good looking man thus the female staffs were at his beck and call. Though some female staff did share his bed with him others did not and they paid dearly for it as Prof. Akkiliz began harassing them and threatening to sack them. The trap that caught Prof. Akkiliz finally sprung in September. It all started when twenty million Afripounds was released to the agency as capital votes. The money was meant to improve the agency and staff welfare but Prof. Akkiliz had different plans and it did not cover any of the above. But, he didn't envisage any problem from the accountant whom before now had always allowed him to have his way. Events took a new dimension when Prof. Akkiliz reported the accountant to the ministry and the accountant was immediately transferred. But, Akin Bello was not going to give up without a fight. Dike could imagine the accountant saying, I will show you too that I know the way to Zuma Rock city. So gathering his facts, the accountant left for Zuma Rock and two days later Prof. Makinde Akkiliz was redeployed to the ministry as director of Records and Establishment. Not only was he given Forty-eight hours to handover and report to the minister. It was jubilation galore among the "agency staff" especially.

"How're the mighty fallen," Dike said.

"Not only that, they fell empty handed, " Charity added.

"But we must pray that God will give us a good chief executive because this man was more like a thief executive," Kate said.

"It's true, but right now I'm in a mood to celebrate, " Dike said.

"Really this is a miracle, " Charity chipped in.

"I never believed this man will fall, " Kate said.

"He made passes at me even told me why I'm I wasting my time with a poor boy like you."

"Did he have to go that far" Dike asked interrupting Kate.

"Wait let me finish, " Kate said.

"Do you know what else he said?" "No!" Dike replied.

"He said you don't have money and clothes.

"This was too much for Charity and she burst into laughter.

"This man is sick, in fact he's mad, " Dike said very annoyed. "Imagine the cheap lying scoundrel blackmailing his son's mate just because he wants a female staff. "

"Let him come and eat the money now," Kate said.

"Is it so easy?" Charity asked.

"The stupid man—my December salary will pursue

him and his family wherever they go. "

"And there shall be no peace for the wicked," Charity added.

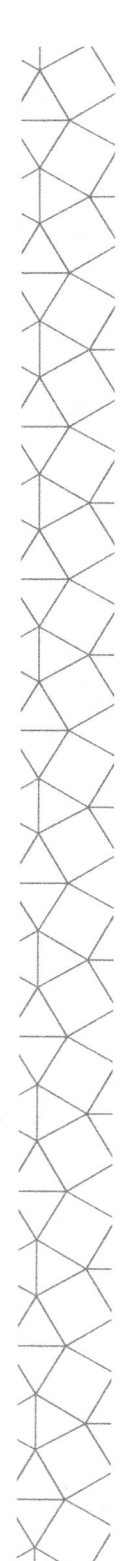

440

Chapter Twenty Six

Two days before taking his exit, Prof. Akkkiliz gathered the staff for his last address to them.

"Am sure many of you are happy with what has happened to me," he began. Bastard you got what you deserve. Dike said inside him while keeping a blank face.

"Well am leaving you all I plead that you cooperate with the in-coming CEO, " he said and rushed out of the hall because he was on the verge of shedding tears. A couple of days later Prof. Akkiliz was gone and Mrs. Abul began holding forth as acting chief executive officer.

"Oh boy you need to see Oga as he was handing over, " Henry said.

"tell me what happened?" Dike asked.

"Ahh Oga wept like a baby, " Henry said.

"Of course, Akkiliz has to weep for his sins, " Dike said sarcastically.

"By the way who will not weep over twenty million Afripounds—I'm sure the man would've added more grey hair on his head. "

"You are not serious Dike, " Henry said, and they

both laughed.

"That's life, " he added. "Man proposes but it is God who disposes of our plans. "

Mrs. Abuh's reign though not a long one was marred with wickedness.

In her first two months, she did not hide her excitement and as the statement goes "Power corrupts while absolute power corrupts absolutely.

"Under her regime the capital vote was disbursed and instead of buying brand new items, refurbished or second hand items were bought. Meanwhile the invoices claimed cost$ for brand new items. Mrs. Abuh's regime introduced a new dimension into corrupt practices. That Mrs. Abuh was greedy was not strange. Staff did not fare any better. Moreover, Mrs. Abuh being junior in rank to the director of personal management meant the D. P.M would always have his way without any opposition. Thus, the agency became a dumping ground as more staff were brought in but no effort were made to change the allocation on personnel coming from ministry of finance. While staffs were frustrated and dejected, Mrs. Abuh helped herself with agency funds and fed. Fat. Mrs. Abuh was shy of holding meeting with anybody.

When approached one day for a meeting, Mrs.

The Prisoner of Afrika

Abuh dismissed them, "abeg you people should not let us waste time reaching decisions that won't be implemented".

She continued to dodge meetings and rather began to show her bitchy side by hounding female staff for wearing trousers to office. Mrs. Abuh really cherished her current position and the perks of office that went with it. Thus, in her bid to consolidate Mrs. Abuh who paraded herself as a believer in God stooped very low and followed one of her friends to a spiritual home. The assignment of the spiritualist was to give her a portion or do some spiritual gymnastic that will keep Mrs. Abuh as chief Executive officer for two years a period that would have seen her amassing a lot of wealth through stealing funds meant for staff welfare. However, the bubble burst earlier than planned and the news leaked out to the whole staff of the agency.

"My God, you mean this woman who calls herself a born again Christian can stoop to go to a juju man?" Mr. Hallas asked.

"Ah Oga, what won't people do in their lust for power, Dike replied.

"Dike, I'm really disappointed in this woman," Mr. Hallas said.

"You see her so gentle, harmless".

"Deception of the last order," Dike said.

"Mrs Abuh is an epitome of evil and corruption. Don't be deceived when you see her moving sluggishly like rat rescued from a drum of palm oil—the woman is a thief."

"Oga mi, how did the gist come out?" Dike asked.

"The woman is a user," Mr. Hallas began "after getting what she needed from Mrs. Okeodo, she has been trying to get rid of her from the agency".

"By how?" Dike asked.

"She included her name for promotion and you know in the service once you're promoted you'll be transferred".

"Ah na wa o for juju mistress Abuh you can't eat your cake and have it," Dike said, "Mrs. Abuh is a chronic hypocrite. "

"You are right", Mr. Hallas said.

"I wonder what our future in this agency will look like and to think that I left a scheduled organization for this place because I believed it had prospects and now see what is happening".

Dike shook his head, "maybe the new Chief Executive that will take over will make the difference", he said.

"I agree with you, if we get a Chief Exec. that's focused we shall all retire from here", Mr. Hallas said.

"Why do you say so?" Dike asked.

"Ah, there will be work to do and less time to gossip".
With the news out that the Acting Chief Executive
was guest to a juju priest, Mrs. Abuh became very
vicious and mean to staff. She was operating under
the consciousness that the staff was making jest of
her and this really brought out the ugly and bitter
side of her. The Staff continued to groan under the
yoke of Mrs. Abuh.

Meanwhile, Professor Akkiliz was involved in some
subtle move to make trouble in the agency using
some of his stooges but his move was uncovered.
Mrs. Abuh wasted no time in reporting to the DPM
who in turn reported to the minister.

Immediately, Professor Akkiliz was queried and
banned from the premises of the agency. This news
drew laughter from the staff.

"When will this man stop making a fool of himself",
Charity asked.

"Twice beaten twice shy", Kate added.

The situation did not change, two months later Mrs.
Abuh framed the accountant, Mr. Akin and reported
him to the DPM who immediately transferred the
accountant out of the agency.

Mr. Abacha Okorah took over as Head of Accounts
department.

Immediately, Mr. Okorah started to manifest certain traits, which bothered on arrogance and impatience.

"When will these setbacks come to an end?" Dike groaned.

"I don't know, " Bayor said, "but we must have hope".

Academically, Abacha Okorah was a standard six holder. He had joined the civil service after the war at age twenty and had risen from the ranks to the officer cadre. So far, he had made a fortune from the service through fraudulent means because the salaries of civil servants in Afrika were nothing to write home about. He had been too preoccupied with making money to bother improving himself academically. It was obvious that the issue of inferiority complex would set in, but for the moment he was head of the accounts.

II

While Dike and his colleagues moved from one challenge to another, the government of the day did not help matters either. For the third time in his first four years as president, Chief Olu Hakot announced another round of price hikes in the price of petroleum products as part of the deregulation process. Of course, the Labour union took it up with the government over their so-called reforms. It was followed by a sit-at-home strike. Initially, the government was not willing to budge. The president had said openly, "People will return to their jobs when hunger begins to bite..." but when one week later, the strike was still on amid a lot of losses to the nation's economy. Government reluctantly agreed to Labour's demands that saw a cut in the pump price of petroleum products. The strike was called off. But, Afrika was in trouble because Crude oil that was supposed to be a blessing had become more like a nightmare. Instead of reviving the agricultural sector, the government would rather pay it lip service. The Labour Union under the leadership of Comrade Adams Awale was prepared too in its bid to keep government on track.

"We're ready to lay down our lives for our country men and women to live", Comrade Awale had declared. Records also had it that President Olu Hakot in his hey days as head of state was the first leader to increase the price of Petroleum products. So, as it appeared, he had come back to finish what he started as a military dictator. It was obvious he wasn't going to have his way this time because the Labour Union was there to curtail his excesses. Meanwhile as the run-up to another general election began to gather momentum things took a dangerous dimension as Afrikans woke-up to hear of political assassinations in various parts of the country. Afrika was under siege again. Nobody could trust the other. The Police could not come up with answers to the killings. It was obvious that this challenge was beyond the police who were yet to curb petty crime and armed robbery in the country. The government too had no answer to the misfortune that had befallen the country and put the citizens under bondage.

"God dey", the average Afrikan man would say. Indeed it was only the Almighty God that could turn around the situation in Afrika.

rs. Abu's reign of wickedness was terminated eight months later with the resumption of the much expected and talked about Chief Executive Officer.

"Na wa! This kin juju wey last only eight months", Bayor said mockingly.

"My brother, I never see this kin juju before o", Dike added.

"Wetin you want see again?", Charity chipped in.

The Prisoner of Afrika

However, they were not the only staffs that were talking. The coming of the new Chief Executive only eight months after diabolical steps were taken to prevent it was bound to influence a lot of side talk from staff. Unfortunately, too there was little or nothing that Mrs. Abuh could do to stop the talking after all she had brought it upon herself due to her greediness and lust for power.

"Dike o. Things'll change for good", Mr. Hallas said that same day in his office.

"Yes I agree with you", Dike added.

"Now we shall be focused and begin to enjoy the job for the first time".

But Mr. Hallas said something fundamental, "if the new CEO will be sincere and honest then the fortunes of the agency will change indeed".

"Why do you say so?" Dike asked.

"Some agency staff were openly voicing out the hope that ministry staff will be sent away", Mr. Hallas said.

"It's too early for that," he protested.

"Yes it is, but the Ministry workers are saying there is no point to hope for that because the CEO too is a Ministry staff and they all know themselves. "

"Therefore she won't take an unfavourable decision against them", he concluded.

Mike Effa

The following day the entire staffs of the agency were summoned into the hall for a meeting with the new chief executive officer of the Afrikan medicine agency. By nine O'clock the entire staff of the agency were seated and awaiting the presentation of the new Chief Executive. The new boss of the Afrikan Medicine agency entered the hall at quarter past nine followed by Mrs. Abuh who would return to her position as Principal Administrative Officer.

"Thank God! At least the era of gossips was over, " Dike whispered to one of his colleagues, "The future looks bright. "

"Good morning ladies and gentlemen", she greeted.

"Good morning Madam", the staff replied.

"My name is Dr. Tamoga korimugu Dogarri and as you all know I'm the new Chief Executive of this agency.", this was followed with a round of applause by staff also interrupting the Chief Executive.

"...together we shall move the agency forward", Dr. Dogarri said. Dike and the other members of staff listened with rapt attention as their boss spoke on.

"I am very easy to work with, I know things are a bit rough in Ekko City especially the traffic situation but that should not be an excuse to be absent from work", Dr. Mugu again cautioned.

"This is an interactive session so you're free to make comments and ask questions," she said taking her seat. The floor was open, a couple of hands went up and one after the other they were recognized and each staff spoke based on area of interest. With no further questions or comments coming from the staff, Dr. Dogarri took time to respond to the queries from her staff.

"Thank you all for speaking your minds, I'll do my best to address these issues", she promised.

"Have you received the salary for the month?" Dr. Dogarri asked.

"No Madam", the staff replied.

"Why – Accountant what is wrong? She asked.

"Nothing Madam the salaries just arrived, we shall pay soon", Mr. Okoroh replied.

"One more thing have you been paid your leave grant?"

"No, money is still being expected and we shall pay as soon as we get the money", Mr. Okoroh added.

"That's fine – because I'm a welfarist, I believe strongly in the welfare of my staff". Dr Dogarri said. This statement drew another round of applause from the staff.

"My dear staff let's work together and promote our

agency and we shall all be happy – thank you", The meeting was over as Dr. Dogarri left the hall. The staff followed en suite.

"Dike, we're in for good times", Mr. Hallas said inside his office.

"Yes o, it is the dawn of a new era", he added excitedly.

"With what I'm anticipating to happen, you don't need to bother looking for another job" Mr. Hallas said.

"Oga na true", Dike replied. Mr. Hallas was the head of the Training Unit and Dike was in his unit.

Mr Hallas was friendly, kind, efficient and hardworking while Dike was obedient and hardworking too. They had a good working relationship thus they got on well like friends.

"I'm sure all the departments will be overhauled for efficiency, productivity and results" Mr. Hallas said.

"It's about time we woke up from the slumber that Mrs. Abuh pushed us into because of her lack of focus", Dike said.

"Don't mind her. It's only juju she knows how to do", Mr. Hallas added. "Juju Mistress", Dike said hissing as he left his Head of Department's office for his own office.

Dr. Mugu Dogarri began to settle in gradually. There

were many challenges. In the eight months since Mrs. Abuh had it her way, a lot had gone wrong; from poorly-made furniture, faulty and fraudulent purchases, to outright mismanagement of funds. The twenty million pounds that had consumed Prof Akkiliz, the former accountant, had of course been spent and it was obvious that more heads will roll. Then, the bubbles burst and the secret deals were now open deals. On how the twenty million was spent, Mrs. Abuh could not account for four million pounds. That was the problem with the leaders and those lucky to find themselves in positions of influence always ended up enriching themselves while those beneath them wallow in deprivation and want.

Mrs. Abuh took time to feed fat on funds meant for the agency's development while the staff went empty handed except for their salaries. However, Mrs. Abuh was not alone she had godfathers" in Zuma Rock city so investigation into the funds in question would be difficult. The only answer Mrs. Abuh gave to any question asked was "…I don't know o".

Frustrated, Dr. Dogarri issued her a query and she in turn contacted her godfathers in Zuma Rock City. Dr. Dogarri was prevailed upon and the matter died down. Before resuming as Chief Executive of the agency, information reaching the staff had it that Dr. Dogarri had been a director without portfolio in the Ministry. She had before now been serving as Director-General in the women's Affair commission from where she was removed owing to an attempt to embezzle a large sum of money running into millions of Afripounds; that she was not committed to prison was due to the magnanimity of the minister who showed understanding as an accomplice and rather buried the case. But Dr. Dogarri did not go unscathed she was sent on compulsory leave and was never called back. At the Ministry of science where she was before being posted she was very cantankerous, so the Minister while thinking of how to get rid of her was informed that the Afrikan Science and Medicine Agency had not been given another Chief Executive Officer since losing the first one.

Immediately, he had her posted to the agency to fill in the vacuum.

III

Dr. Dogarri came to the agency like a pregnant and ravenous shark. Having been out of power and money for almost three years, she was very hungry and eager to return to the big life again. On noticing the hunger in their boss, the accountant and the auditor immediately and subtly began to manipulate her to their own selfish ends. At the beginning of the year, the agency was given zero under capital allocation while the overhead was put at Four hundred and seventy five thousand Afripounds. Initially, Dr. Dogarri was frustrated and close to tears. Rumours even had it that she was having a rethink until the two evil geniuses got to her. Overnight, the Chief Executive changed dramatically and became very unfriendly. Her unfriendliness was displayed when staff from the research department decided to pay her a courtesy visit as well as press for the payment of certain allowances not being paid. Dr. Dogarri after hearing them out was very blunt in her reply.

"I want to thank you all for your so-called courtesy visit", she began.

"I'd like you all to know this I've come with two mandates. One is to develop the agency and that's only if you cooperate with me and my second mandate is to close down your agency if you're heady and troublesome..." she paused for awhile looking around the faces of the staff from the research department.

". I'm sure none of you wants to be out of job. You all know how terrible the job situation is. "

With nothing else to say the research staff filed out of Dr. Dogarri's office. Dike was numb with shock when Bayor recounted all that the Chief Executive had told them.

"And you know while she was dishing out her threats the accountant, the auditor and Mrs Abuh were nodding their heads like lizards", Bayor said.

"Ah, these people have succeeded in penetrating her", Dike said. "We must get to face her in all forms. "

What kind of agency is this? Dike asked himself first it was Makinde Akkiliz and his reign of oppression, frustration and intimidation. Next came Mrs. Abuh, the worm, and with her, a period of wickedness and witch hunting. Just when the staffs were hoping for a breather, Dr Dogarri arrived with signs of possible rebirth but that has given way fast to fear, threats, and sycophancy. It seems this woman wants to start the reign of terror. Presently, Dike left his office and went to seat with his boss again.

"You're back. Hope no problem?" Mr. Hallas asked.

"Not really", he began.

"Except that I'm just worried about the utterances of this terrorist they sent to us for a Chief Executive".

The Prisoner of Afrika

"Dike", Mr. Hallas called, "this woman is the anti-Christ and those two men have gotten to her by destroying the image of the staff just for what they will get."

"No problem they will get their reward and we shall be here to see it", Dike said. The cash crunch did not improve immediately and Dr. Dogarri had told the research staff that the allowances that were even being paid to them would be reviewed. Dike recalled this bit from his discussion earlier with Bayor. "What can this woman be planning against us?" he wondered.

It did not take long find out at the end of that month precisely the entire staff were given the crudest and unkindest shock of their lives. Dr. Dogarri and her two new friends had arrived at a new formula to tackle the crunch and it was to deduct the allowances that staff had received for the last six months. The staffs were confused as this exercise went on for three months with most staff going home with as little as one thousand afripounds while the big three fed fat. At this time, Mrs. Abuh was out of the picture and was really doing everything possible including fighting the staff just to get into Dr. Dogarri's good books.

The three months passed, despite the promises she

made the allowances were not restored. The agency being a small one it was not difficult to get hard facts. The staff soon discovered all that was going on.

"This is what I call dogarritisation," Dike said.

"What is that?" Mr Hallas asked.

"Oh it's a new concept in economics. Dogarritisation is simply the art of deducting staff salaries under the protest that they're not entitled to it and then turning around to embezzle the money".

"You're funny", "We've been robbed again. And this anti-Christ, God will punish her and all those assisting her to cheat helpless staff. God will judge everybody."

The reign of terror continued, staffs were no longer getting their correct salaries Dike was baffled to discover that on paper he was earning Fifty thousand Afripounds but the amount that he took home each month was twenty-eight thousand Afripounds while the balance when put together would be shared between Dr. Dogarri and her cohorts. Dr. Dogarri's reign of terror left staff totally impoverished. With hunger on the increase, sycophancy took a new turn. Staff began implicating staff. This negative trend was more prevalent within the accounts department. The

The Prisoner of Afrika

head of accounts was not comfortable with certain senior staff who were holding key positions in the department so the best way out was to implicate them. The staff did not know anything was amiss till that fateful morning when they were informed. Dr. Dogarri would address staff by ten o'clock in the morning. Dike did not find the announcement funny. What else does this thief want to say? He'd wondered.

For the two years that Dr. Dogarri had held way as Thief Executive, she had succeeded in impoverishing the staff. Only staffs who were carrying tales from one point to another were allowed the crumbs from the table. Dr. Dogarri was only concerned with improving her lot and catching up on all that she had lost when she was disgraced out of women's affairs.

"No problem. Keep stealing, nemesis will catch up with you all sooner or later," Dike said within him.

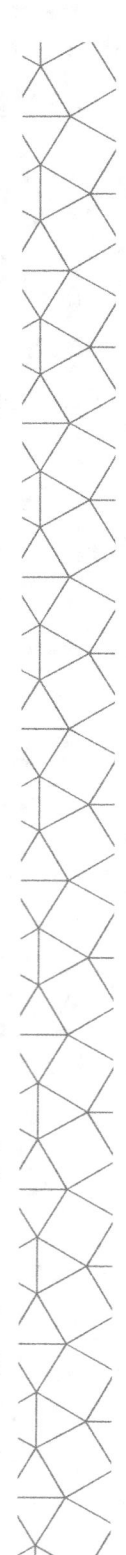

460

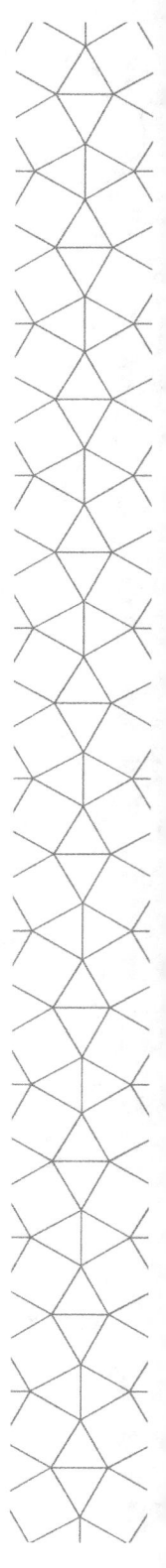

Chapter Twenty Seven

The insecurity to life continued as the elections drew closer. Prominent citizens were being wasted on daily basis, and the government had no answer to the big question. Election in Afrika was more like selection and the politicians would tell you, "Whether you vote for us or not we shall win."

The elections came and went with President Olu Hakot winning another four year term. In his first broadcast to the nation, he introduced the vexed issue of fuel price hike. For the fifth time in five years prices of petroleum products went up again and as usual the Labour Union which was now the only hope of the masses replied the bully in a language he understood best. Another strike was called again and as usual a period of negotiation ensued with Labour getting a price concession.

But, one funny and sometimes annoying thing with the marketers was their ability to reflect a new pump price seconds after an order is given. The moment labour strikes and a reduction in price is ordered, it will take a longer time for the filling stations to reflect the agreed price, with some claiming that they

461

need engineers from one part of the country to come and effect a given price. Thus, and pending the arrival of these pseudo-engineers, those filling stations would continue with business as usual. It was a sad situation for the nation called Afrika.

In other countries blessed with crude oil, one discovers that they have peace and are enjoying this blessing in absolute tranquillity. The case of Afrika was different and why was it so? There was too much injustice, oppression and fraud, so much blood from the minorities had been spilt to maintain a grip on the crude oil by other ethnic groups. Rather than be a blessing, it was a curse; a fish bone that neither goes up nor down. The marketers too in their mad drive for huge profits continued to compound the situation for the government.

Indeed, it was a clear case of things having fallen apart with the centre too feeble to hold. Apart from the crude oil wahala, electricity was another nightmare in Afrika. Citizens were harassed to pay their bills monthly, yet could hardly enjoy light for seven hours in a stretch.

The electricity corporation was nicknamed "Never Expect Power Always", but smaller countries within the continent were enjoying constant power supply with some even celebrating ten years of

The Prisoner of Afrika

uninterrupted power supply. Dike and other citizens couldn't help but wonder when things will turn around again for their beloved country. Afrikans really needed a reorientation because corruption had eroded away what was left of the moral value of the people. Money and wealth was now the god of most Afrikans, and it did not matter how one got the money as far as he could be counted among the rich and oppressors in the society.

One aspect people could not understand with the president was his sudden boldness. As military head of state, Gen Olu Hakot was the most timid and cowardly officer in uniform especially in the moments of uncertainty that followed the death of Gen Bako in the botched coup attempt. But, suddenly, the general turned president had become a village tyrant inflicting hardship on the citizens without feelings while making a show of fighting corruption.

It is quite sad to note that Africa remains the only continent that has produced more idiots as leaders. From the republic of Afrika to Nigeria to Democratic republic of Congo one hears of morons like Mobutu, Idi Amin, Samuel Doe, Bokossa, Abacha, Charles Taylor the war criminal turned refugee. Here again was another minus for the Government of President

Obasanjo. If he could grant asylum to a murderer like Taylor who was responsible for the killing of Nigerians in Liberia, then it meant if Satan came calling for the life of Nigerians, the president would hand over Nigerians to the devil.

II

By ten o" clock, the staff of the agency were already seated and waiting for the address from the chief executive of the agency. Dike sat close to his Oga. Mr Hallas to his left while his office colleague and friend Ike sat to his right. Ike was a nice guy from a good home. His parents were comfortable so Ike could afford to come to his office each day in a Honda Civic car. Ike was an accountant and a chartered too. It was only a matter of time, and Ike thanks to his qualifications will move to greener pastures. The three of them were talking when Dr Dogarri was sighted.

"The terrorist is coming" Dike said.

Ike laughed. "Old boy, I bow for your guts o", Ike said.

"See how she is walking", Mr Hallas commented, "honestly, this woman is a real anti-Christ".

They could not talk more as Dr. Dogarri entered the

hall. Staffs were bitter due to due to the impoverishment visited on them by Dr. Dogarri but like the ravenous and vicious shark that she was, Dr. Dogarri did not care.

"Good morning Madam", some staff greeted standing while other staff just stood but did not greet.

"Please be seated", she said.

"Let me tell you all today…" she began.

"Ehn there is fire on the mountain" Dike said to Ike.

"Some of you think you are highly connected. If there is anybody that has connection in this agency it's me. I have connection as far as the presidency so those of you who think you can misbehave because of the people that brought you here should be careful or I will recommend that you be shown the way out and your so-called godfathers will not do anything about it."

The entire staff listened as their chief executive droned on. What could be the reason for this sermon in the hall? Dike wondered.

"…It has come to my knowledge that Mr Adeleke, Okoro and Ebitimi of the accounts department were photocopying payment vouchers. Whatever you want to do with them, I don`t know. You want to petition? Be my guest", she said with a degree of hysteria in her voice. Dr Dogarri was scared, frightened and she showed it.

". . When I started working many of you here were not born. Listen! Nobody is marginalized in this agency. All of you must learn to wait for your turn", she warned

Turning to the three accused staff, "For your information and in your own interest return those vouchers," she said and then sat down. The floor was now open for other people to speak. A couple of senior and junior staff spoke. All praising Dr. Dogarri for her achievements these people are sick, Dike reflected. Shortly before leaving the hall, Dr Dogarri spoke again praising herself for having paid the salaries of the new staff to date and the meeting ended.

"Dike let me see you in my office", Mr. Hallas said on their way out of the hall.

"Did you see what happened today?" Mr Hallas asked.

"Yes I did this is the crowning of terrorism and intimidation", Dike replied. Just then Ike joined them, he was laughing.

"My oga has finally gotten the license he needs to remove Ebitimi from the position of cashier".

"Okay, he had refused to conform so they had to

get rid of him fast", Dike added.

"This woman is a shameless thief. Hear her talk of connections. A real bitch that's just what she is," Mr Hallas fumed.

"Imagine descending so low to trade accusation with staff".

All the while Ike was just laughing.

"This is a miniature of the country and you must learn to wait for your turn".

They all laughed.

Of course, it was obvious that staff would react in many ways, two years as chief executive Dr. Dogarri only succeeded in employing her kinsmen and the money used to pay their salaries turned out to be arrears of the old staff. When the old staff heard of this injustice they continued to heap curses on her, and hoping that something will happen that will take her away.

Back in her office, she held a quick meeting with Mr Okoroh—the accountant and Mr Egbeyemi, the auditor, and they reached certain resolutions which were implemented immediately. Firstly, Ebitimi was removed from his office popularly known as "CPO". Then, the three of them were each given fifty thousand afripounds to appease them. It leaked out two days later actually it was a plot to smear their image.

"So these guys were later given money to back off?"Mr Hallas asked.

"Yes that's shut-up money ", Dike added.

"They don't know it but they can never open their mouths to talk again. "

"At least their turn came. "

As the year began to draw to an end, staff got to hear from the auditor that their chief executive on arrival at the agency had told them that so far she had served government with nothing to show for it and had told them this was her chance to steal money and build a house before retiring. So, they had assisted her as Dike concluded. To achieve this devilish desire they had come up with the plan that had deprived staff of their academic allowances. Every month after paying salaries, eight hundred thousand Afripounds was left in the personnel account, being staff allowances which were no longer being paid. At about October, which made it ten months, the total money saved was eight million Afripounds. This was shared between the big three, and Korimugu Dogarri succeeded in raising money to build a house.

The Prisoner of Afrika

On the day the money was shared, Dike and some of his colleagues watched in total amazement as the Chief Accountant stashed his loot into the boot of his car before their very presence. It was just like he dared them to do their worst. Korimugu Dogarri sustained her impoverishment of the staff of the agency through blackmail with termination and threatened the entire staff with closure of the agency. More so, since the agency was not scheduled. In the promotion interview that took place in November, the union leader, Mr. Kuako was not promoted. To worsen matter, Mr Kuako was called in and warned by the roguish DPM to back off the issue of academic allowances or lose his job. The year ended with no sign of the monies stolen by Dr. Mugu Dogarri being returned. Three days to the New Year Dr. Dogarri was transferred to Zuma Rock City. She had been made Director General in the Ministry of Labour and Productivity. The staff of the agency did not know whether to laugh or cry while some thanked God for taking the thief away. Other staff hoped that labour union would break her head soon. Yet, another group of staff were sad because their benefactor was gone and the future looked bleak for them. Mrs. Abuh was also swept away by the transfer, she wept bitterly. This time, there was no delay in appointing a successor. Mr. Okadar Jabez was appointed successor to the outgoing chief executive. Mr Jabez was not new to the system. He was serving as deputy director before the transfer. The striking thing here was this; the Minister, Dr. Dogarri and Mr. Jabez all hailed from Brass. So, they were perpetuating an agenda with government funds.

After the exit of korimugu Dogarri, Dike one day did a calculation of the remaining balance of his salary that was embezzled by the antichrist and her cohorts. Out of the fifty thousand afripounds that he was supposed to earn as salary no thanks to Dogarri Dike had been paid only twenty-eight thousand afripounds. At the end of twenty-four months, Dike discovered that he had lost five hundred and twenty -eight thousand afripounds to the ravenous shark they had for a Chief Executive Officer. No wonder people most time refer to them as the Thief Executive Officers. It was a huge loss, capable of making somebody develop malaria by force. With such money, Dike would have been able to get a decent apartment, settle down and maybe even buy a car. But, Dogarri the thief had impoverished them to a standstill. "Only God will reward this woman for what she has done to us. "

The Prisoner of Afrika

The New Year rolled in with the promises of a better future. But, in the agency staff began to see the real Mr. Jabez. Matters were not helped either, as the agency's Chief Research Officer brutishly edged everybody out of the way and in the process adopted the portfolio of personal assistant to Mr. Jabez as well as being Chief Research Officer. Things deteriorated as Mr. Mtume Akuve brought in the divide and rule strategy and selected some staff to work with him. Actually, these were his bootlickers who were always going to his office to pay homage. It was obvious that the CRO was very hungry and would not brook any opposition in his quest to be relevant in the sharing of all monies that came to the agency. Together, they pushed the accountant and auditor into the dust bin stripping them of whatever powers they had enjoyed during the reign of terror. On realizing that Mr. Jabez was chopping alone, the accountant and the auditor tried to get into his good books without success. Out of frustration, they suddenly realigned with the Union they had fought in the past to agitate for payment of allowances. Indeed, levels had changed and a pharaoh had come that didn't know Joseph. Staff soon discovered Mr. Jabez's true colours. He was a politician who would promise and would not deliver.

It was obvious too that Jabez just like Dogarri, the thief, was out to enrich himself. Supported by the savage and primitive chief research officer, it was certain the staff of the agency were in for another rough ride.

Later, in March, a promotion interview was conducted for senior staff from the three departments namely administration, accounts and research.

Mr Jabez as agency's CEO and Akuve were also members of the panel, the promotion examination was simple as some of the staff said. But, when the results were released many staff failed. Of course, a lot was wrong with the entire process. First, the team from the Ministry of Science and Technology led by the Director for Personnel Management Services were mostly concerned with the duty tour allowances. Thus the Chief Research officer handled the marking of the examination. An unofficial investigation revealed that all those who failed were not in Mr Jabez and Akuve's good books since they were not in the habit of going to pay homage. Darkness had indeed enveloped the agency like a blanket.

Staff situation deteriorated as staff arrears and welfare were by-passed for mundane things and the staff continued to groan from hardship and injustice. Only those who were serving the CEO in different capacities depending on your gender enjoyed things like attending workshops within the country and abroad. But, Dike refused to be moved because the bible says that "the evil man has been reserved for the evil day".

The politician just like the terrorist will go one day after all Akkiliz had left also. Just when the staff of the agency thought they had heard the last of Prof Akkiliz, he surfaced again. But, not as the chief executive of the agency . Having lost out in his bid to corruptly enrich himself through stealing government funds, Prof Akkiliz had become a church planter. A situation which suddenly saw him become General overseer of about three churches, and as at that moment his third church was marking its first anniversary. The Prof had found another way of making money out of gullible people looking for signs and wonders. He had also dropped his "professor" title and was now being addressed as "Prophet,(Dr) ". All these information was gleaned from the envelopes his nephew brought to the office to beg for money from staff like Dike and others who had been at the receiving end of Prof Akkiliz's dubiousness.

Mike Effa

Meanwhile, working in the Afrikan Science and medicines Agency remains a nightmare as the agency is facing a lot of challenges. Just like other thief executives, staff of the agency have not fared any better while Mr Jabez fed fat from the agency's capital and overhead allocations, giving contracts to family members and girl friends. Jabez just like the president has been busy using government funds for personal gains trips to China, Brazil, USA, Kenya, South-Africa, London, Spain, Japan, and the Netherlands were all undertaken on the average of three trips per month. If Satan was to organize a workshop in hell, Mr Jabez would certainly be amongst those that will attend. Mr Jabez like those before him relished the blackmail, intimidation, threatening methods of ruling. He was very good in nicknaming staff. He once described a staff as small elephant but the staff could not do much but conform like prisoners, more so in a country where government was keener in sacking workers than creating jobs.

The retrenchment exercise that Dike feared finally caught up with him. And though he did not lose his job, the experience was harrowing as the chief executive of their agency and his assistant did everything possible to taint the image of staff so as to get them sacked. It was more of a witch-hunting exercise, more so for staff like Dike who was not liked. Some of the staff were reported for travelling out of the country to attend international workshops and conferences. While other staff were accused of coming late to work. In Ekko City, with its chaotic traffic situation only a mad man like the chief executive, the kangaroo panel overseeing the so-called right-sizing exercise would say a staff that enters the office at half past eight o'clock in the morning is late. Instead, of the consultants originally scheduled the team turned out to consist of a retired director of personnel management services in the ministry. His successor and two friends of Mr Jabez who were also Directors General of Parastatals. All these men were out for one thing, the duty tour allowance that is usually paid for outstation trips. Mr Jabez had been parading himself as an epitome of excellence, but Dike later discovered that his so-called DG was nothing but a liar. His claim of being a former Bank Director was a fat lie and the man had been jobless before he was brought to the agency to be recycled. His last job had been with a multi-national Aid agency where he had been fired for incompetence and gross inefficiency. Mr Jabez could best be described as a village tyrant and a vagabond in power to borrow a bit from the music legend "FELA". Dike preferred to describe him as an unrighteous vagabond. He also has to put up with the antics of the chief research officer and some of his greedy colleagues in the accounts and admin departments- where there is so much betrayal and back stabbing.

Dike has no choice, or if at all he had it, is limited fear of the unknown had caused him to cling to his job like a drowning man. The jobs are scarce the economy is ravaged by inflation and government is planning to cut jobs by retrenching civil servants while spending huge sums of money to come back to power. Afrikans have been so battered even when during the year, president's Hakot's junketing yielded fruits by way of debt relief the masses could only watch like zombies.

The Paris Club had granted debt relief to Afrika, Nigeria and twelve other poor countries within the continent. This gesture saw Afrika getting a relief from its debt burdens in which $20bn was written off from Afrika's $35bn debt.

There had been rejoicing and back slapping by government officials. However, this development could only be applauded when the lot of the common man changes. The question again

The Prisoner of Afrika

remains Afrika had been granted debt relief, what next? Moreover when Pres. Hakot leaves office will the incoming administration toe the line of financial stinginess in order to keep the foreign reserves growing while Afrikans died from starvation and also keep the nation from incurring foreign debts or will they unleash their own round of corruption and squandermania and thus finally paralyse an already crippled economy? Only time would tell.

Despite the noise on corruption and the debt relief government officials were still looting the coffers of the nation., the Inspector- General of Police had stolen almost eighteen billion pounds meant for police welfare. So while the roguish IG and his family fed fat on police funds, his men were dying from hunger. At the states level governors were having a field day looting funds from the coffers of their states and taking them abroad to be stashed away. In the process, a governor was arrested and arraigned for money laundering but while awaiting trial he escaped disguised as a woman. Afrika indeed had sunk to serious levels of decadence, high level of internet fraud was now very common among the youths who were all very eager to make money at tender ages. One could not blame them so much as they spent much of their time at home instead of being at school. And no thanks to Government's insensitivity as well as desire to fight university lecturers. Infrastructures had finally collapsed. Power failure was a way of life. The skies were not safe either- Afrikans now preferred to travel by road due to unsafe skies. Security too remained a grave source of concern for the citizens, as a crazy terrorist group went about bombing churches and government offices for reasons best known to them. Meanwhile the federal government was finding it hard coming to grips with the terrorists, leaving Afrikans with no other option than to turn to the almighty for protection.

Again, it was shameful that a country like Afrika well endowed with resources which if properly harnessed and managed would have made her strong and rich enough to even colonise Britain. Alas! It was not so as bad leadership and corruption had turned the supposed giant of the African continent into a beggar nation going about cap in hand begging for loans and when granted later on begins to beg for debt relief. It is a disgusting thing and subsequent governments should ensure this ugly trend did not happen again.

Hence, there is need for Afrikans to be more concerned with their choice of leaders in

The Prisoner of Afrika

subsequent elections. Men of integrity are what Afrika needed to move forward; not thieves, nor sit tight dictators looking for tenure elongation or clinging to power even when they are not fit to rule. It was also time for the Afrikan People's Democratic Party to pack their bags and quit, because in their last twelve years in power they had not improved the lot of Afrikans. But only the citizens can bring this to pass by voting them out in the next general elections.

As for Dike he discovers that to face the unknown. One needs a fearless heart. He is confused and scared of falling in love again. Patricia his last girlfriend had left him for a younger man lucky enough to be working in a bank. The girls too in Afrika are more conscious of material things than love. And who wants a starter anyway? With these challenges, it becomes difficult for him to love again his prospects of settling down as a family man fades too like the evening sun and he is not getting younger either.

"What a life," Dike said while reflecting on his pitiable position one day.

At forty, I'm yet to settle down and life they say begins at forty. "So when will my own life begin?"

Dike asked loudly.

In fact, first I will drop this nickname—the Afrikan boy. It has not favoured me at all. It has rather turned me to "the prisoner of Afrika". Nobody will call me the Afrikan boy anymore, Dike had vowed strongly.

Sadly, he discovers that as the Afrikan boy he had shared a similar fate like his country. It is disheartening that after thirty- eight years of political independence his beloved country is yet to mature democratically and economically. Matters are not helped either by the military and their cabal of retired generals who are holding the nation to ransom by reason of their bad policies and corrupt ways of life. The ex-khaki boys ought to know that they are not technocrats, they have no business in politics; talk less of ruling a whole nation like Afrika. Corruption remains the bane of development for the giant of the African continent, with government officials, lawmakers and civil servants looting the nation's treasury as if it was a jamboree. And its government remains ineffective in the battle against corruption.

Fortunately while individuals die, nations remain. Things will change one day Dike hopes, but his prayer is that his beloved country for the sake of future generations will mature politically and economically.

God forbid his beloved country becomes another Alan Paton's *Cry The Beloved Country*.

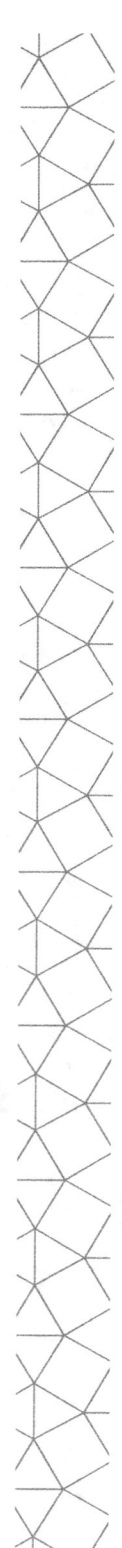

482

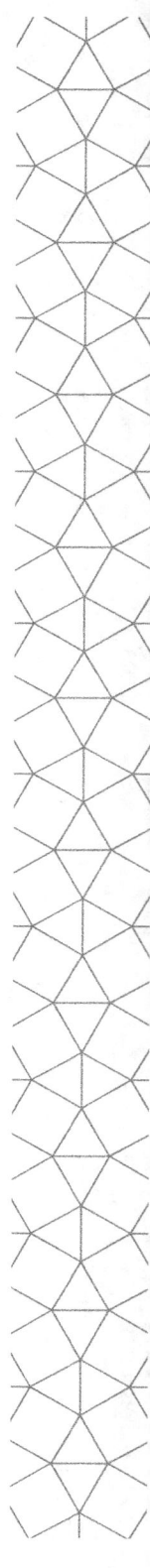

Epilogue

Surprisingly for Dike and his colleagues, things dramatically changed in the agency. It all began when a letter came from the ministry asking Mr. Akuve to justify his rise to the post of deputy director considering the fact that he lacked the requisite qualifications. While they were still battling with the query, a Save Our Souls letter was quietly written and sent to the ministry. Still trying to come to terms with the letter from the agency, a petition was received by the minister with a copy being sent to the anti-graft agency. The petition titled, "save us from the pharaoh of the 21st century" and signed by a concerned staff. This warranted action being taken and the anti-graft agency moved in to investigate the allegations of corruption levelled against the director general and his second in command.

A system review was carried out on the agency covering the human and financial resources of the agency. Through the review, a lot of corrupt practices were uncovered- Mr. Jabez and his second in command had been awarding contracts to themselves through the use of proxies, In a couple of case's forgery of staff signatures was also discovered. Administratively there was no head of Admin, The director general had polarized the department to enable him have his way.

The repercussion was obvious, for contravening the law—the DG and his deputy were relieved of their jobs by the minister while the anti-graft agency arrested the evil and nonidentical twins who were prosecuted and jailed for fraud, embezzlement and forgery. The internal auditor was also indicted, but not arrested he was however recalled by the office of the accountant general. Staff of the agency danced for joy including those staff that had pretended to be loyal to the former DG and his deputy. A new chief executive with the requisite qualifications was appointed without much delay. Directors were also sent to the agency to provide checks and balances and ensure that the new chief executive did not run the agency like Saddam Hussein, the former dictator of Iraq or Gen Abacha of Nigeria. Dike was ecstatic; suddenly things were looking bright again.

"ehen, now the agency is back to life I hope that one day things will change for Afrika like it has changed for the Afrikan Medicines agency," Dike prayed silently.

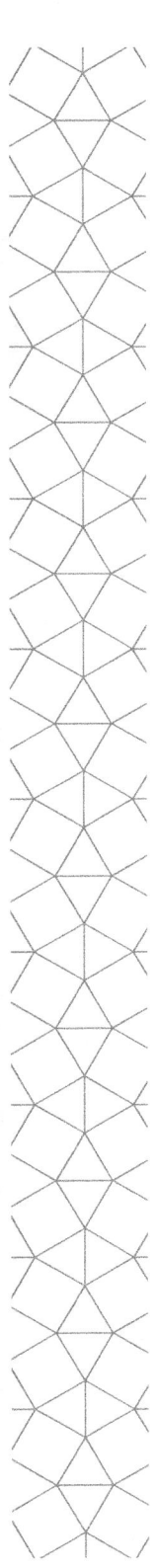

485

About the Author

Phantom House Books proudly presents Mike Effa's political fiction title, The Prisoner of Afrika.

Mike holds a joint grad degree in Political Science and Adult Education from the University of Calabar, and a Masters degree in Educational Administration and Planning from the National Open University of Nigeria. His first book, The Man Without a Backbone, was published by Read Lead Books, Pennsylvania, under the author pseudonym Pita Hakeem.

Mike hails from Cross-River State, is a proud family man living with his wife and son, Asher Effa, in Lagos, enjoys football, and works as the Principal Admin Officer with the Nigeria Natural Medicine Development Agency.

For more books by Phantom House Books, NGR, visit our website or request our titles at your nearest retail bookstore.

www.ingramcontent.com/pod-product-compliance
Lightning Source LLC
Chambersburg PA
CBHW051429260626
47162CB00001B/10